Resounding praise for the novels of
KAREN TRAVISS

"Satisfyingly complex. . . . [Traviss] at times evokes
the earlier moral fables of Le Guin . . . at other times
the revisionist critique of expanding human
empires . . . and at times the union of romance with
SF that we see in the work of Catherine Asaro or
Lois McMaster Bujold. . . . The fact that Traviss
manages to keep these sometimes conflicting modes
in balance, mostly through her strong sense of character, suggests that she's a writer worth watching."

Locus

"A fascinating cast of characters involved in a richly
complex situation. . . . Her people are convincingly
real. . . . Traviss has created a vivid assortment of
alien races, each with distinctive characteristics and
agendas. . . . She brings a rare combination of insight
and experience that will greatly contribute to our
field."

James Alan Gardner, author of *Expendable*

"Stellar."

Jack McDevitt, author of *Deepsix*

"Traviss takes what could have been a rote collection
of characters (marines, cops, religious extremists)
and slowly adds depth, complexity, and color."

BookPage

"In Shan Frankland, Karen Traviss has created a
tough, interesting, believable character."

Gregory Frost, author of *Fitcher's Brides*

Books of The Wess'har Wars by
Karen Traviss

MATRIARCH
THE WORLD BEFORE
CROSSING THE LINE
CITY OF PEARL

MATRIARCH

KAREN TRAVISS

An Imprint of HarperCollinsPublishers

This is a work of fiction. Names, characters, places, and incidents are the products of the author's imagination or are used fictitiously and are not to be construed as real. Any resemblance to actual events, locales, organizations, or persons, living or dead, is entirely coincidental.

EOS
An Imprint of HarperCollins*Publishers*
10 East 53rd Street
New York, New York 10022-5299

Copyright © 2006 by Karen Traviss
ISBN-13: 978-0-06-088231-0
ISBN-10: 0-06-088231-X
www.eosbooks.com

First Eos paperback printing: October 2006

HarperCollins® and Eos® are trademarks of HarperCollins Publishers Inc.

Printed in the U. S. A.

10 9 8 7 6 5 4 3 2 1

*For Lyn Graham, Martin Welsford, and all those who
put truth before convenience*

Acknowledgments

My grateful thanks go to Charlie Allery, Bryan Boult, Debbie Button, Suzanne Byrne, Karen Miller, Dawn Woodring, Dr. Ian Tregillis, and Chris "TK" Evans, for critical reading; to my editor, Diana Gill, and my agent, Russ Galen, for keeping me in line; and to Greg Bridges, for dazzling visual inspiration.

MATRIARCH

Prologue

F'nar, Wess'ej: November 2376

Recycling won't save the Earth, and neither will prayer.

The Eqbas are coming. It might be a few decades away, but they're still coming, and I know them. They're very hospitable, they love their kids, and they can kill millions without losing a second's sleep.

You can reach shock overload pretty quickly. After the first headlines and the protests and the panic, human beings tend to settle into apathy if it's not their life that's on the line. News is about *now* and *here* and *me*.

When we wandered into a war zone in the Cavanagh's Star system, *that* was news. When we got greedy and nuked a neutral world out here, that got plenty of attention too; and so did the fact that the wess'har blew our warship—*Actaeon*—out of the sky.

But we're twenty-five light-years away from Earth, and domestic crises edge alien wars well down the running order now. When there's fighting and suffering on your own doorstep, do you care that we've pretty well exterminated an entire alien race ourselves? Do you care if a woman spaced herself rather than hand over the parasite she was carrying— and *survived?* Does it matter that the local wess'har are so pissed off with humans that they've called in the big guns to visit Earth and teach us a lesson?

If you don't, you probably will in thirty years' time. Because that's roughly when the Eqbas Vorhi fleet will reach Earth, and they're not visiting to say they come in peace or any uplifting shit like that. They're coming to punish us for genocide. And while they're at it, they want to restore Earth to a state of environmental balance. In brief: a lot of humans are fucked. Most of us, probably.

They don't see us as special, you see. That's just our view of the universe. It's not widely shared.

The Eqbas Vorhi fleet is on its way, and there's nothing we can do about it. My news desk is losing interest by the day.

It all feels so far in the future.

But I know it's not.

Private journal of Eddie Michallat, BBChan correspondent on Wess'ej, Cavanagh's Star system: the only independent observer, 150 trillion miles from home.

1

You detonated cobalt bombs on Ouzhari in your greed to keep c'naatat to yourself. The bezeri who died were collateral damage—that is your phrase, is it not? Now Earth will learn what collateral damage really means.

CURAS TI,
senior Matriarch of the Eqbas Vorhi,
in a response to the Foreign Secretary of
the Federal European Union

Bezer'ej, Cavanagh's Star system: continental shelf off Ouzhari island, December 2376

Mohan Rayat gave up the reflex struggle to stop his lungs filling with water, drowned—which was nowhere near as painless as they claimed—and plummeted into the crushing black depths where the light of Cavanagh's Star never penetrated.

You bitch, Frankland.

And he wasn't dead.

You sanctimonious bitch.

He was shaking uncontrollably and convulsing, but he wasn't *dead*.

Rayat was aware of the kaleidoscopes of colored light rippling above him in the mantles of the last surviving bezeri. He was a living corpse, a man imprisoned with his victims, a man who couldn't die.

Hold on to that. Whatever the parasite does to you, you're still a man.

He had no air supply and no suit. He could taste blood in his mouth: or maybe it was just something in the silt billowing around him. He sank down on the seabed, facing upwards, crushed by pressure and a searing agony in his head beyond any pain he'd ever experienced. For a moment he wondered if his survival was the result of a primal diving reflex, and not the intervention of an alien parasite.

He'd never told anyone how scared he was of water. Now he never had to fear it again.

Somehow he could still see: green, violet, blue. Coils and fractal patterns of ludicrous fairy-lights danced overhead, the chatter of the bezeri—the few who had survived the irradiation from bombs he had detonated.

I never meant to kill you. You just happened to be in the way.

But the bezeri couldn't hear him. He couldn't even hear himself. The silence was overwhelming, but although he could still reason, and he knew his eardrums were ruptured, he still expected to sense the sounds of his own body. It was surprising how much you noticed the absence of your own heartbeat.

His heart had stopped. He had no idea how he could still be conscious.

So Frankland must have gone through this when she stepped out the airlock: dead and not dead, aware that her whole body had ceased to function and existed solely by the grace of a microscopic parasite called *c'naatat* that was worth destroying worlds to capture.

You bitch, I beat you. I got your precious parasite in the end. Suck on that, bitch.

No sunlight: he could have been at least a thousand meters down, then, below the depth where light penetrated. When silent screaming panic overtook him—screams he couldn't force out of his airless lungs—he concentrated on numbers to stay sane.

I should be dead. A thousand meters . . . maybe one hundred atmospheres . . . ten thousand kilospascals . . .

But his mouth opened in a panting reflex anyway, because he couldn't take in what *c'naatat* was doing to keep him alive at this depth. The cold burned him. He should have looked around for Lindsay Neville but all he could think of right then was Frankland, drifting in the vacuum of space without a suit. She'd spaced herself to stop him getting hold of the *c'naatat* she carried. And—bitch, bitch, *bitch*— it had all been for *nothing,* because no matter how bad things were now, he'd got what he'd come for, and a small sane part of him rejoiced.

I beat you, you bitch. And your precious bloody Ade and your pet wess'har helped me do it. I hope you find out, oh shit yes I pray you do, you bitch.

It was amazing what you could hang on to when you needed to pass beyond death. God, numbers, vengeance: whatever it took. He seized them all.

Shan Frankland had survived. And so would he—somehow. And he could wait.

2

We've had our environment screwed for centuries by the Americas and Europe and the Sinostates. They shat out their crap and we paid the price. Now it's our turn to fuck them. We can invite anyone we please into our territory. And that includes aliens who can bomb them back into dodo country.

The Right Honorable JAMES MATSOUKIS MAP,
Pacific Rim States lead delegate to the United Nations,
in private conversation with the Canadian and
Indigenous Peoples delegates

F'nar, Wess'ej: December 2376

"She's going to fucking well skin us when she finds out," said Ade Bennett.

The soldier kept pace with Aras all the way up the steeply carved steps to the top of the terraces, no mean feat for a short human male. Aras wondered if he would have managed it before his physiology was altered by *c'naatat,* and suspected that he would. He was a Royal Marine: he prided himself on his fitness.

"We'll find a way to tell her," said Aras. "And she may not understand our reasons at first, and she'll swear at us like she always does, but in time she'll calm down and life will go on."

It will go on, yes. That's the one thing a c'naatat *host can be sure of. But not as before.*

As soon as he said it, Aras knew things wouldn't be that simple. How did you tell your *isan,* your wife, your matriarch, that you'd thrown away her sacrifice? Shan Frankland had spaced herself rather than let Mohan Rayat get a sample of *c'naatat.* And now Aras—or Ade, whoever felt bravest— had to tell her that they had *willingly* infected the man with it.

And Commander Lindsay Neville.

That would probably infuriate her most of all. The woman she called Lin had tried to be a pale imitation of her and succeeded only in disappointing her. Aras knew Shan well enough to guess that: if you survived unimaginable pain and terror, drifting for months in space, unable to die, you didn't easily forget that kind of ordeal or forgive its necessity.

Ade paused at the top of the steps to catch his breath, hands on hips. Stretching nearly two hundred meters directly beneath them, the city of F'nar covered the slopes of the caldera, an amphitheater of pearl-coated terraces carved into the rock.

"I'm the one who did it." Ade wiped his nose with the back of his hand. "So I'll explain it to her."

"No. I'm—"

"Yeah. You're her old man and I'm not."

"You'll be her *old man* too, as you put it."

Ade shook his head and began walking along the terrace to the far end of the caldera where the home they shared was cut into the stone.

"If I don't tell her and then I sleep with her, she'll pick it up from my memories. And *then* she'll kill me." He speeded up a little to the pace he described as a *yomp*. Aras had never worked out what that meant. "And if I tell her first, she'll kick me out anyway. So either way—I've lost her. I might as well face it like a man."

Aras had lived with *c'naatat* for centuries by human reckoning, and its ability to manipulate genetic material and keep its host alive still surprised him. It seemed able to do very nearly anything; it tinkered, it borrowed, it scavenged, it rearranged, it remodeled, and it defended. One set of genes that had taken its fancy was genetic memory—a legacy from his isenj captors when he was a prisoner of war. And, as *c'naatat* crossed membranes from host to host, in blood or in the act of copulation, memories surfaced in other minds.

Sometimes the memories it picked up were terrible. Sometimes it simply showed you how other people truly saw you. And sometimes they were both the same thing.

"Ade, it's not the memory transfer that you fear."

Ade didn't look round. He was a compact, muscular human with a distinctively upright posture. His rifle bounced a little, slung across his back. "No, it's trying to hide it from her, mate. I can't do that."

Aras had always been sure of his duty until the *gethes*, the carrion eaters, the secular humans, had come to Cavanagh's Star in pursuit of a lost colony and commercial gain. Shan had changed his life out of all recognition. He wondered if he now resented her for that, but no—he had *infected* her. Without *c'naatat*, she could have gone home again; and Ade could have gone with her. Aras found himself back in the circular argument, wondering if he should have gone to live among the bezeri remnant to help them rebuild instead of letting Lindsay Neville and Rayat take his place.

He had never had such cyclical, dithering thoughts before. A wess'har accepted reality and dealt with it, never glancing back. Humans fantasized about alternate realities to avoid the only one they could actually influence. He realized he was becoming too human.

"We'll tell her *together*," said Aras. *Ade is my housebrother. We share genes now. We're committed.* "The bezeri wanted them alive. We'll explain that to her, and face the consequences."

"You talk a good game." The *clop-clop-clop* of Ade's boots echoed off the flagstone terrace. "And I'll be right there when she hands you your balls on a skewer."

"I have no balls," said Aras.

Ade snorted. It sounded like bitter amusement. "Neither will I after today."

The marine was right. Shan would be more than furious; she would feel *betrayed*. Loyalty and honesty seemed to matter more to her than love.

But if they had no other choice but her, then she was confined to her own infected kind as well. If she rejected them, she had nobody.

Aras felt shame—real *human* shame—at thinking so manipulatively. A female was a precious and scarce gift, one a *c'naatat* carrier could never have expected. He could never be allowed to father offspring and pass on his condition; but he could at least have an *isan* to love and look after. Unlike him, though, Shan Frankland didn't fear being alone. She dreaded doing what was *wrong*. Loneliness alone would not bind her to him—or Ade.

Ade paused at the pearl-coated door, slipped his rifle onto his shoulder, and listened as if he was about to storm the house.

"She's not back yet." He put his hand on the latch and pushed it open. There was no need for locks among wess'har. "Got time to rehearse our excuses."

They could hide nothing in the end. Shan had developed a wess'har *isan*'s olfactory system, and she could smell the pheromones of agitation, anger, fear. She would certainly smell something was wrong.

At least I'll still have a brother.

"Perhaps she'll see why we did it."

Ade laid his rifle on the shelf next to the door and hung up his jacket. "I don't think so somehow."

"She forgave you for shooting her. She forgave me for infecting her with *c'naatat*."

"Let's hope she works in threes, then."

They stared at each other for a moment, knowing the answer. Shan cared about consequences. She cared about how things fitted into the bigger picture, and what she feared most—what the wess'har feared most—was that *c'naatat* would get into the wider human population somehow, with all its attendant disasters.

Perhaps Shan would see the contagion as Rayat's punishment. Aras considered the irony: Rayat had been sent to seize it for the FEU. Whether he really was a Treasury agent or military intelligence didn't matter now. He had it. But he wasn't going anywhere, because there was no way off Bezer'ej, not without wess'har or Eqbas assistance. It was the ultimate punishment—a cold dark eternity trapped with your prize and no way of using it, confined with the bitter remnant of the species you helped kill.

Aras wished he had Eddie's gift for presenting unpalat-
able information with selective grace. He was sure he could
make it seem like a triumph.

"Your turn to cook dinner," said Ade.

They stood side by side at the table, slicing *evem* and the
last peppers that had ripened on the windowsill. Ade always
seemed to seek refuge in dull routine, as if he could refash-
ion and erase the brutal and chaotic world that had made
him by mimicking the uneventful lives of lesser men. He
was very precise about the thickness of the slices.

"Bugger," he said quietly. He examined his fingertip,
crowned with a welling blob of dark red blood. "Cut myself."

C'naatat still seemed to be a novelty to him. He licked
the blood away and watched the cut as it closed and faded,
then resumed his task.

Half an hour later, Aras heard the distinctive thud of
Shan's footsteps approaching the door. He wished that he
could suppress his scent the way she did. Ade looked at him
and shrugged.

"Here we go," he said.

The door creaked slightly before it swung open and
brought in a gust of cool, damp air.

"Hey, you two," said Shan. She forced a smile, and that
wasn't like her at all. "I'm home."

F'nar plain, Wess'ej: Eqbas Vorhi camp

They were leaving.

Eddie Michallat gasped to a halt in the center of the
Eqbas camp. The bronze bubble habitats clustered on the
plain were rolling together and coalescing like mercury,
metamorphosing from little globe-like tents into a huge tapered cylinder of a warship, a belt of brilliant red and blue
chevron lights pulsing along its length.

For a moment Eddie forgot his straining lungs and stared
at the technology that made him feel like a particularly re-
tarded amoeba fresh out of the primordial slime.

The warship had almost completely assembled itself. He looked around for the small survey vessel that had been the vanguard, Da Shapakti's ship, and noticed it wasn't there any longer. Maybe the destroyer had swallowed and absorbed it too. How did they route the services and the controls? How did they keep it vacuum-tight in space? He found he had a thousand questions whose answers would almost certainly be something along the lines of *forget it, chimp*.

Esganikan Gai strode towards him. He could always ask her; it was her ship. She was the boss-woman.

The visiting Eqbas wess'har might have looked different to their native Wess'ej cousins, but the females still had that same ability to make you crap yourself. No wonder Shan fitted in with them so well. Esganikan's brilliant copper-red plume of hair bobbed as she stared down at him and cocked her head to get a better focus, four-lobed pupils snapping from open flower to tight cross-wires and back again in an instant, just like all the wess'har. Looking any of them in the eye was still hard. There was no single point to focus upon—just the uneasy sense of being the center of their aim.

And Esganikan was *tall*. Eddie felt like a little kid lost in a towering forest of adult legs again.

"What do you want?" She lacked charm but, unlike Shan, she was incapable of even feigning it. "We leave soon for Bezer'ej and Umeh."

"I know." *You owe me one.* He'd lent her his database to learn English. He wasn't sure yet of the Eqbas approach to repaying favors, but if it was the average wess'har one, it was unpredictable. "Can you take me to Jejeno?"

"We have a presence to maintain."

"So can I get a ride with you?"

The Eqbas matriarch—flat-faced compared to the elegant, long-muzzled wess'har he'd grown used to—glanced over her shoulder at the embarkation going on behind her. "Why?"

Eddie found himself detaching from a recent, raw memory. "Now that Minister Ual's dead, I need to make contacts within the government again."

"So do we."

"Yes, but *can I come too?*" You had to be direct with them; they had no concept of being abrupt. Eddie wondered if his natural diplomatic touch was being corrupted by close contact with species who were as outspoken as five-year-olds. "Please?"

She cocked her head again. "Be here tomorrow when we leave."

"Thank you."

"At your own risk."

It always was. "I get it."

Esganikan turned and swept back to the ship. Eddie watched her go, still feeling sweaty and uncomfortable from running, and reminded himself what she was—an *alien*, the commander of an alien warship, a warship that was stunning in its size and technology and was just a small part of a much, much bigger fleet.

Earth had nearly thirty years left to prepare for the invasion. The fact that the Australian government had invited the Eqbas guaranteed no happy endings. Eqbas wess'har were the guests who never knew when it was time to go.

Eddie made his way back to F'nar at a sedate pace this time. He was used to the higher gravity, but it was still a long walk across the rolling plain of rock and tufts of sage green vegetation to the point where the terrain became lava buttes and the city was suddenly visible. Homes and terraces were carved into the cliff walls of a long-dead volcano. Whatever the weather, whatever the light, it was always beautiful, coated in a shimmering layer of nacre. It was, as the human Christian colonists called it, the City of Pearl.

The pearl happened to be insect shit deposited by billions of *tem* flies, but Eddie didn't let the reality spoil his sense of wonder one bit.

Nor did he let the equally accurate word *invasion* sully his irregular news reports. Twenty-five light-years away on Earth, his BBChan colleagues had abandoned diplomatic euphemism and used it with B-movie relish; but now the panic had died down, and humans were fighting each other again.

Okay, deep down, we all want to run the headline ALIENS
INVADE EARTH. *Admit it, you tourist.*

So Eddie admitted it. It was a journalist's fantasy story,
along with IMMORTALITY DISCOVERED and EARTH NUKES
ALIENS. And he'd done those for real, too. But it wasn't so
mindlessly thrilling when you were part of the cause of it,
and he still blamed himself. If he hadn't started digging
when Shan had survived a fatal head-wound, *c'naatat's* extraordinary restorative powers would still have been a secret. And a lot of people would still be alive—

No.

I didn't bring Actaeon *here. That started the shooting.
I didn't make anyone nuke that bloody island to destroy*
c'naatat. *All I did was . . .*

He could rationalize all he liked, but he knew he *had*
played a hand in helping Minister Ual defy his own government. And, however accidental the shot that killed Ual, the
isenj politician was still dead.

*Like Shan always said: dead's dead. Doesn't matter how
or why in the end.*

Eddie was so lost in thought that he tripped and looked
around instinctively out of embarrassment. But there was
only a lone *v'guy* flapping slowly overhead and the occasional pop as one of the many creatures that lived in bubbles
on the rocks ventured out to grab something smaller to
eat. Wess'ej was a carefully preserved wilderness and the
wess'har trod so lightly on it that they were nearly invisible.

*They're not native to this planet. They're invaders of a
kind, too. Maybe this is how the Eqbas will behave on Earth.*

He could keep wishing, anyway.

He walked on, feeling conspicuous, keeping his eyes on
the uneven terrain beneath his feet. At the pillars of pearl-
coated basalt plugs that formed a natural gateway to F'nar, a
little alien seahorse waited for him.

"Eddie!" Giyadas had that wess'har double-voice like a
khoomei singer's. She provided her own faint chorus even
when speaking English. "You're going to Umeh."

"Yes, sweetheart." He ruffled the stiff mane that ran from

front to back across the top of her head and she walked with
him. "With Ual gone, I need to get to know other people in
the government."

"You called them *people*."

"They are. Even if they're isenj."

"I meant that *gethes* usually only call *themselves* people,
so you must be learning to be civilized."

Gethes: carrion eaters. Wess'har were strictly vegan. Eddie didn't mind being lectured in moral evolution by an alien
child. Sometimes he preferred the company of cockroaches
when he saw what humans could do. "Yeah, I hope so."

"I want to come too."

"Ask your mother."

"I have to learn an *isan*'s duties."

"Not my call."

Giyadas was the equivalent of a six-year-old, maybe.
And it was too bloody dangerous for a little kid in the
middle of—of what? Another invasion? Umeh was the dry
run for Earth. What happened to the isenj homeworld now
would happen to *his* home before too long.

"The Eqbas containment field will protect us," she said.

"I've covered wars, sweetie. Lots of them. You're never
safe anywhere in a war zone."

"But you're still alive."

Her logic was gnawing and inexorable. Like a human
child, she was persistent; but she was also subtle and frequently two steps ahead of Eddie.

He wasn't used to that—not even from adults. "And Ual's
dead."

"That's not your fault."

"I'm still getting the hang of the wess'har concept of
responsibility."

"You helped him to what he wanted to do. He chose
badly—for himself, anyway. For his planet, he chose well."

Her incongruously adult tone always unsettled him.
"That's true. But what if you know someone is doing something stupid, and you don't stop them?"

Giyadas cocked her head this way and that but didn't look up at him. "He only harmed himself in the end. He has the right to choose to do that."

"Outcomes, eh? Always outcomes." Wess'har didn't care about motive. What was *done* mattered; what was *thought* was irrelevant. "You're probably right."

Giyadas lapsed into silence. She spoke when she had something to say or ask, and beyond that she was content to observe. She spoke English with Eddie's accent. And she would be the next leader of F'nar if and when she grew more dominant than her mother Nevyan.

It was inevitable. They didn't vote. It just happened, and there were never any wars about it. Eddie had a moment of wondering whether invasion by a species like that was such a bad idea after all.

He reached the center of the city—one of a number of little self-governing states scattered discreetly across the planet—and began the punishing walk up the network of terraces that lined the caldera. Giyadas kept pace as if she was keeping an eye on an idiot.

"Lindsay Neville is dead," she said suddenly.

Eddie's calf muscles were coping better with the climb these days. But he almost missed his footing.

"Okay," he said.

"And Mohan Rayat. I saw Aras and Ade return."

So they'd handed them over to the bezeri, or at least the few that were left. Eddie wondered how smart squid executed prisoners; he also wondered whether to change the subject, but wess'har didn't deal in euphemism even to spare their children. Giyadas could take it. "I expect it was quick."

"Did you say goodbye to her?"

That kid never misses the jugular. "No, I'm afraid I didn't."

"Do you wish you had?"

Yes. She was a friend. "What would I have said to her anyway? Serves you right? Trust in God? What do you say to someone who's killed thousands of innocents?"

"I thought you might know," said Giyadas forlornly. "I

know how the isenj treated Aras when they captured him after he had killed so many. Perhaps you might have told her to be brave."

She was suddenly both a child again and a wess'har, genuinely wanting to *know* things. It wasn't rhetoric. Eddie was never certain if it was naïve candor or insight so profound that he didn't quite grasp it. He suspected it was a blend of both. At the top of the steep steps that ran up the terrace, Giyadas slipped ahead of him and they walked in silence on pearl flagstones. Males followed, females led. The kid was falling into adult wess'har habits. So was he.

Eddie's view of wess'har went in cycles, unfathomable miracles one month and then almost family the next. Right then he felt like Uncle Eddie, and the thought crossed his mind that a trip to Umeh Station would mean human companionship again, humans in numbers, and human *women*. There were two female Royal Marines based on Wess'ej: incongruously pretty, slight Ismat Qureshi, who could probably take his head off without breaking a sweat, and Susan Webster, built more on the armored vehicle scale of things but pleasant enough company for a trained killer.

And then there were the colonists, biding their time on Mar'an'cas Island, a long way north of pretty, temperate F'nar. Eddie didn't fancy his chances of romance with the devout Christians there, not even with Sabine Mesevy.

If he went back to Earth with them, it might not be home any longer. It probably wasn't; nearly eighty years had elapsed.

Giyadas pushed open the door of her family's home and a wave of cooking smells and warbling voices spilled out. At the table in the big communal room, Dijuas—the youngest of Nevyan's four recently acquired husbands—sat suckling his infant son. Two of her three other males, Lisik and Livaor, were preparing *evem* for lunch, their long multijointed fingers stained yellow from the sap.

Nothing fazed Eddie now. *Seahorses. Yeah, think seahorses.* They had gold eyes, from citrine to topaz to amber, with four-lobed pupils that snapped shut into crosses. He sat

down next to Dijuas and reached to stroke his fingertip across
the child's head, eliciting an approving rumble from the father. The baby looked less like a stick insect now: he was
recognizably a little wess'har male, a bald one, and three
times as big as the palm-sized creature that had spent most
of its time in Dijuas's gestational pouch.

"Fulaor," Dijuas said carefully in his double voice, tone
on tone. "*Fu—la—or.*"

Eddie pursed his lips and made a continuous humming
sound before trying to add the second enunciated note. He'd
practiced overtone singing for hours until his skull vibrated.
He still couldn't quite manage it. The wess'har larynx, or
whatever passed for it, could shape sounds like human lips
and tongues before it even reached the mouth to pile on more
phonics. Wess'u was more of a complex song than a language.

Eddie tried again. "*Oooooooofffffffffff . . .*"

Dijuas trilled loudly and the chorus of amusement was
taken up by Lisik and Livaor. They found it hilarious. Eddie
dissolved into giggles too. There was something touchingly
childlike about the wess'har zest for life, and it was easy to
forget that they also switched instantly to a much uglier
mode and waged total, destructive war without prisoners.
Chilled or punching, as Shan Frankland described them;
there was no middle ground.

Nevyan appeared in the doorway.

She was considered short for an *isan*—a matriarch—but
she was as tall as Shan, a six-footer, and equally fearsome in
her way. Her gold tufted mane bobbed, giving her the air of a
Spartan soldier, and Giyadas watched her intently as if studying her style. *This* was how to be a seahorse warrior queen.

"You mustn't mock Eddie," Nevyan said in English.
She gave her males a quick glance and—Eddie knew, even
if didn't affect him—a quick burst of her dominance
pheromone. *I'm the boss. Shut up.* "He tries hard."

"We're just having a laugh," said Eddie.

God knew there were few of those around to be had lately.
Every time he found something funny, or enjoyed food, or

just realized that life was richly fascinating, he thought of dead bezeri on the irradiated shores of Ouzhari, and Par Paral Ual, killed by his own nervous troops.

And dead Lindsay Neville. Unlike Shan, she wouldn't return from the apparent dead and resume her strange life 150 trillion light years from home.

"I want to visit Umeh after Esganikan has completed her talks with the isenj," said Nevyan.

"I think it'll be a dangerous place."

"I'm the senior matriarch of F'nar, and I intend to meet the isenj government, dangerous or not." Nevyan was still very young, but she had all the seasoned steel of her mother, Mestin. "They're my neighbor and my enemy. Esganikan is just passing through this system. That makes the situation more critical for us, and we might well have different agendas."

Eddie was aware of Giyadas staring up at him in expectation. She could always smell a tense debate and it fascinated her.

"I thought you two trusted each other," said Eddie. "She's one of your own."

"We both originate from the same species, but you might have noted that Eqbas Vorhi doesn't conduct its affairs as Wess'ej does."

Yeah, I know, you're the hippy dropouts and they're the militaristic right-wingers. But you *still took out an Earth warship without blinking, doll.*

The Wess'ej wess'har just wanted the humans punished and put back in their box, confined to quarters on the speck of rock at the galaxy's edge, and no more: the Eqbas wess'har wanted to sort out Earth's environmental excesses as well.

"That means I can go to Jejeno," said Giyadas, evidently satisfied. "I want to see it for myself."

"I made a right little reporter of you, didn't I, doll?"

"Knowing is very important." Giyadas was more speculatively curious than any other wess'har Eddie had met. "And finding out for yourself is more important still. You taught me that I could only trust my own eyes."

Eddie worried what else he'd taught her without realizing it. He also worried how he had shaped her view of humans, because she would be a matriarch herself before too long, one with access to armies.

"Sometimes you can't even rely on that," said Eddie.

Humankind had kicked over an anthill far from home, and found that the ants were smarter, bigger and far more technologically advanced than they could ever imagine.

And, like disturbed ants, the wess'har were pissed off at the brutal intrusion. They would head for the source of the irritation and deal with it: and the source was Earth.

3

"Look, forget the bloody aliens. That's thirty years away. I'm more worried about this government surviving the next thirty months. Australia and the rest of the Rim States aren't going to pose any kind of threat unless they suck in the Africans by playing the Moslem card. Canada—well, I don't know which way they'll jump. Depends on what the Americas do. So leave the Foreign Office to deal with Eqbas Vorhi."

MARGIT HUBER,
newly appointed Secretary of State for Defense,
Federal European Union

Bezer'ej: the Ouzhari shelf, depth unknown

Mohan Rayat fought to stop trying to breathe. He thought of space for a long time, and concentrated on all the advantages of being at crush depth for humans instead of floating in hard vacuum in zero-g.

He was far better off than Frankland had been.

I'm oriented. I've got gravity. I can move.

And I'm not alone.

C'naatat had invaded his cells, and if he had any thoughts of suicide then he had no idea how to carry it out. He'd lost any sense of how long he had been submerged, but it couldn't have been long. A few minutes; a few hours. Not days, not weeks, not years.

Look around. Focus on something.

What? There was no light except the bioluminescence of his captors, apparently waiting overhead. He concentrated hard on his arms as they rested on the satin-cold mud, spreading his fingers and raising one hand a few centimeters, then letting it fall back. The silt billowed up in slow clouds—he could taste it—and it dimmed the bezeri's rainbow light-talk for a while.

But . . . he had *moved*. He was oriented and he wasn't actually in pain. He wasn't dying: he was *changing*.

He could feel it. The searing cold had now been replaced by real heat, a fever burning within him, and all his reflexes to breathe and struggle for his life had faded. They had been replaced by a desire to open his mouth and . . . almost *swallow*. He raised his head a little.

And now he could *see*.

But he could see in ways that he hadn't thought possible. As he got to his knees, he found he was aware of tall funnel structures spaced around a clear area of seabed, extending up the slope of a submerged cliff, almost a sonar map in his field of vision. Whatever he was seeing was beyond light. He felt buzzing in his sinuses—had they repaired themselves, or had they metamorphosed?—and an inexplicable urge to press his tongue to the roof of his mouth.

And he could *hear*. The sound flooded back in as if someone had turned up the volume.

His hearing had returned, new and alien, and the chatter of the ocean's life rose from a vague murmur to a cacophony of disorienting, directionless noise. Panic washed over him again and he fought for calm, scrambling onto all fours and disturbing the seabed again.

Concentrate on the next thirty seconds. Nothing more. Count. One, two, three, four, five, six . . .

Something caught against his collar as he turned his head. He sat back on his heels and put his hands to his throat; it felt like soft strips of sponge had stuck to his skin. Something was growing in his neck. His fingers probed instinctively, urgently.

They slipped into huge gaping slits.

Gills.

Oh my holy fuck gills no no no—

He patted frantically down his chest and felt inside his shirt to find that the slits went down into his chest and aligned with his ribs. For some reason he wanted to sob. He should have been glad to be alive, but he suddenly wasn't, oh God *no* he wasn't. He got to his feet, churning the mud into clouds, and the bezeri moved in. He could pick out their bright-lit mantles, three or four meters long with their tentacles, the last of a population that he had decimated with cobalt-salted neutron bombs.

And now he could distinguish a human shape, but he could hardly call it seeing in this permanent night.

Lindsay Neville was a sonar scan, iron filings bristling on a magnetic field, a brass-rubbing outline of the woman she had been in the visual spectrum. She crawled across the seabed on all fours and then stood up, unsteady, arms spread as if expecting a fall.

Surrendering to the bezeri had been her idea.

She parted her lips and he heard a long groan of what sounded like expelled air, but her lungs should have been flooded by now. They were both alive in a nightmare that should have ended in a quick death.

"Rayat . . ."

The sound fizzed with a bubbling note. *Cavitation. Shrimp make sounds by cavitation. Hang on to the facts, stay sane, stay in your forebrain . . .*

He pursed his lips, more out of instinct than conscious thought. It was harder to make sound than he imagined. Whatever rapid *c'naatat* adaptation had given Lindsay the ability to manipulate microscopic air bubbles would emerge in him too. He was counting on it. He had things to say.

"Lamp," he mouthed. Could she see him? Could she lip-read? He could.

She held it up. The large round signal lamp that the wess'har had built to talk to the bezeri in their language of colored light had survived the dive. That was something. At least they could communicate with the creatures.

It was going to be hard to find something appropriate to say to them. But the more Rayat watched and felt the changes the *c'naatat* parasite was making to him, the more he felt he'd been right to do whatever it took to keep the organism out of the wrong hands.

Sterilizing Ouzhari island hadn't destroyed the source of *c'naatat*. Even if that had made the deaths of the bezeri sadly unnecessary, it had also shown him how very high the stakes were. The parasite was even more remarkable and exploitable than he'd imagined.

This is for my government. This thing can't be trusted to commerce, either.

He could see Lindsay Neville clearly now. He could even see the detail of the shoulder tabs on her shirt. She'd taken off the commander's rank insignia long ago.

And gills.

They were slightly everted, like lips down each side of her neck. He was glad he couldn't see himself. Changes like that had to be accepted gradually, not appear shockingly in the mirror one morning.

"We killed them, you bastard," Lindsay mouthed. Her wide-open eyes were like a statue's in his altered vision, a grayscale image devoid of pupil and color. "We *killed* them. Now we pay for that. *Forever.*"

Rayat thought that forever was much longer than he had in mind.

Upper terraces, F'nar

Shan Frankland let the stream of water from the shower spigot play on her head and stared at the sliver of hard soap cupped in her hands.

It was the last of the bars made by the colonists of Constantine before they were evicted from Bezer'ej. The scant lather smelled faintly of lavender and lemon oil; but there were no lemon trees left now. The biobarrier that had kept the colony enclosed in a cocoon of terrestrial conditions had gone, and the alien wilderness of Bezer'ej had reclaimed the island.

It didn't matter. She knew how to make more soap. But it was another symbol of how Earth was slipping further away.

Nearly eighty years adrift from home, everyone she knew and served with now dead, and her own body so fundamentally changed at the cellular level that she could survive in space without a suit, how much further *could* it slip?

She'd almost stopped noticing the play of bioluminescence in her hands. Violet light shimmered in her fingertips and vanished again, a legacy of one brief foray into the world of the bezeri. Aras had never picked up the photophore genes, even after so many years of contact; she couldn't work out why she had.

You slipped. You slipped right across the line. You're on the wess'har side now. Or maybe the Eqbas. Not human, anyway.

There was more than just 10,000 years of rapid evolutionary separation between the two kinds of wess'har. They didn't even think the same way sometimes. But wess'har identity was defined by what you did, not what you thought.

"Breakfast!" Ade called.

"Okay," she said. "Give me a minute."

She soaped herself. Apart from the lights and a lack of body hair and a little more muscle—and she had always been fit—her body looked much the same as it had been when she was a regular human. She made a point of checking daily. The claws had come and gone, and nothing truly and visibly alien had emerged. *C'naatat* had carried out minimal tinkering: it hadn't radically reshaped her appearance as it had Aras's. What went on beneath the skin, though, was another matter, and that still disturbed her at times because she saw the color spectrum of a wess'har, and the images of heat in darkness, and sensed the world in ways that reminded her she was no longer fully human.

She'd survived in conditions that only bacteria and lichens seemed to be able to tolerate. *Deep space.* What would happen at the end of time? The bloody thing kept you alive for centuries, maybe millennia.

How am I going to die?

She'd never worried much about that as a normal, fragile human being, even in a job where she risked being shot each time she went out on the streets.

But you got the gene bank. You did it. Even if bloody Perault conned you, even if that was just a ruse to get you out here, you did it. Go dance on her grave sometime.

But she wouldn't be going back to Earth to do any dancing. *C'naatat* had to stay here.

Above the steady rain of water, she could hear Aras and Ade outside in the main room, talking in subdued voices punctuated by the occasional *chink* of glass bowls. They weren't happy. She didn't need to hear that: she could *smell* it.

Go and deal with it.

Shan wrung the water from her hair, toweled herself dry, and pulled on the remnant of her uniform. The brown riggers' boots didn't go with the black pants or jacket, but that was all she had now, and nobody out here cared if she was wearing the wrong uniform order.

Maybe Ade did. He still wore his Royal Marines' rig, minus the badges of rank. He gave her a nervous smile and indicated the plate set out for her.

"Beans," he said. "Did my best with the sauce."

There was a limit to what you could achieve with soy beans, tomato pulp and the local food crops, but Ade had pushed the envelope. He was a resourceful if eccentric cook. The Corps had taught him how to live off the land, so making do with a limited larder was no great challenge.

"Great." Shan uncovered something black and glistening with her twin-tined glass fork, an oily, dark disc with vanes on one side. "Is this a mushroom?"

"Correct."

The novelty distracted her briefly from the unspoken question. *How did Lin die in the end?* "Want to tell me how you managed to get hold of mushrooms?"

"Shapakti," said Ade.

"You didn't beat it out of him, did you?"

"No, Boss." The Eqbas biologist was wary of Ade's aggressively protective streak. "I just said that if he was going to start reviving species from the gene bank, he might find edible fungi really interesting. He did. It was a surprise for you."

Shan broke off a chunk of mushroom with her fork. It smelled wonderful, and the taste surpassed the aroma. It was amazing how uplifting familiar food could be a long, long way from home.

"Fantastic. I mean it, that's *fantastic*." The praise didn't prompt Ade's usual reaction of an embarrassed grin. He just shrugged, still agitated. She sawed another chunk from the mushroom with the edge of the fork and placed it in Aras's bowl. "You tried this yet? Nothing like fried mushrooms to start the day."

Aras jerked back his head as if scalded. "Fungi."

"You'll like it."

"It's *fungi*. Isenj smell of it."

She'd forgotten that, but Aras hadn't forgotten being a prisoner of the isenj, and she'd absorbed the memories of what they'd done to him. Smells were very evocative. It was enough to make him freeze in that wess'har alarm reaction.

"Okay, sweetheart." She retrieved the chunk of mushroom and gave it to Ade, wondering why the smell hadn't triggered her memory too. *Shit*. "I'm sorry."

Breakfast fell silent except for the occasional scrape of glass on glass. How long she could she *not* ask what had happened? She didn't have a good track record on tact. Ade stared into his bowl of beans, wearing his don't-hit-me expression. Aras—long dark braid draped over one shoulder, still that elegant blend of heraldic beast and man—simply looked her straight in the eye, unblinking as only a wess'har could be. But he said nothing.

"I thought I'd germinate these tomato seeds," said Shan, and rattled the container in her pocket in the hope of getting some conversation going. "See how they do out here."

Ade and Aras sat eating in grim awkward silence, wafting a citrus tang of agitation. She suppressed her own scent—a habit now—and pushed the small box across the table towards them.

She'd expected them to be subdued. They weren't like her: they didn't get triumphant satisfaction out of seeing the guilty punished. But they were upset. There was no other word for it.

I should have done it myself.

She'd never let anyone do her dirty work before and this reminded her why. They made her feel *guilty.*

Aras picked up the container and turned it over in his hands. The unpatented, illegal seeds that Shan had carried with her for years and light-years—more out of defiance and hope than certainty of settling long enough to plant them—tumbled inside.

"It's winter," said Ade, voice strained by tight throat muscles. "Funny time of year to sow them."

Shan tried to find a focus in the patterns of sauce that nestled in the bottom of her bowl. "I know people back home who keep theirs growing all year."

Home just slipped out, but she was sure she felt no pain in saying it now. It was just a location, nothing more. There was no way of removing *c'naatat* from Aras's cells, so he had to stay here, and so she'd stay too, and so would Ade. It was the way things were. They were a team, a family.

Sod it.

Maybe the prisoner handover was too distressing even for Aras to discuss, and wess'har weren't squeamish. Neither was she. Ade—well, Ade had seen terrible things in combat and coped with it, but his violent father had left him struggling when it came to hurting women. Lindsay had been his commanding officer. It must have been hard to watch the bezeri take her, even if she'd helped Rayat detonate the bombs.

Shan took the container out of Aras's hand and tipped the seeds into her palm.

"Okay," she said, patience expired. "What the fuck really happened?"

Aras and Ade both flinched at the same time.

"We delivered them—" said Ade.

Aras interrupted. "This is *my* responsibility, not Ade's. The bezeri were *always* my responsibility."

It was another of his wess'har non sequiturs. They had their own logic, switching topics instantly. Shan wondered if he was establishing a pecking order as senior male in the household and putting Ade in his place.

"Look, I'm sorry if it was traumatic. I just want to know so that I'm not treading on eggs the whole time." She patted his arm and felt him lock his muscles in that alarm reflex. "I'll find out anyway, won't I? All your other bad memories surface in me sooner or later." She glanced at Ade. "And so will yours."

Sooner or later. Yeah, I have to do something about that. Ade's your old man too, remember that.

She could lean on Ade, she knew it. She could scratch away at his guilt about shooting her, about abandoning his mother, about the bezeri, about his dead comrades, about always feeling that he let people down; but she was determined not to fall prey to expedience, because none of it was true. She couldn't do it to him.

"They're not dead," he said suddenly.

Oh God. A switch threw somewhere and she defaulted to Superintendent Frankland, the unshockable copper, the persona that could cope with this. "But you handed them over. Didn't you?"

"Yes."

"Well, between the anti-human pathogen that's been spread around Bezer'ej, and the bloody ocean, I'm having trouble with the *not dead* bit."

Oh God. Tell me you didn't chicken out.

Ade held up a warning finger as Aras opened his mouth to interrupt. "The bezeri wanted someone to help them rebuild so we—I gave them Neville and Rayat."

"I'm missing something here." *No, you're not. You just don't want to think that they did something so bloody stupid.* "How?"

"It was my idea," said Ade.

You might be wrong. Calm down. "What was?"

"Infecting them with *c'naatat*."

Shan was inured to shock after a lifetime in the police force, but disappointment in the few people she trusted still had the power to make her stomach churn. Her skin felt as if it was tightening and freezing across her body from her scalp to her hands.

Oh shit. No, no, no.

Ade was silent, eyes wide, teetering on that edge of admission that she'd seen far too often in interrogations.

"You deliberately *gave* them a dose?"

"Yes. I did."

"You gave *Rayat* the fucking thing?"

She tried to take it in. She'd sacrificed *everything* to keep it away from the likes of that bastard. She'd committed suicide—or she'd stepped out the airlock, anyway. *C'naatat* had had other ideas. That should have given Ade a clue about how she'd react if they just *handed the frigging thing over—*

"Yes," said Ade. "Both of them, Boss. I'm sorry."

"*Sorry?* I fucking *spaced* myself rather let Rayat get a chunk of me. He's a spook, for Chrissakes. Have you any idea what a bastard like that can do with this stuff?"

"Boss, I—"

Her pulse pounded in her ears. "*Have* you?"

"The bezeri wanted someone down there with them. He isn't going anywhere. Neither is she."

Steady. Think, think, think. "Who else knows about this?"

"Nobody. Just us."

"Tell me exactly what happened. Where did you leave them?"

"We took them out above the continental shelf. It's well over five hundred meters deep. I saw them go into the water and the bezeri came up to meet them. They've got them down there."

"'Course, with *c'naatat,* they could just *walk* back to shore." It was no good: she had to alert the Eqbas now stationed on Bezer'ej, and she had no idea how they'd react. The wess'har matriarchs had once been on the brink of executing Aras for infecting her. "I'd better warn Esganikan. What the fuck were you *thinking?*"

Aras cut in. "*Isan,* this was my idea and if Ade had not prevented me, I would be with the bezeri now. They wanted me and I was ready to join them."

It was a slap in the face. Shan leaned back a little and

fought to separate the reality of yielding *c'naatat* to Rayat
and Lindsay from her hurt feelings.

You're my jurej. *Wess'har males are supposed to be loyal.
You aren't supposed to put the bezeri's needs above mine.*

The selfish, petty thought caught her unawares. She folded
her arms.

"Terrific. It's always good to know I can rely on you." She
knew he understood sarcasm, even if most wess'har—literal,
eye-wateringly honest—didn't grasp it. "Thanks. Thanks a
lot."

"Da Shapakti could remove your *c'naatat* and you could
return to Earth with Ade if I weren't here."

"Do you ever listen to a word I say? I told you I would
never abandon you."

"You did that when you spaced yourself."

"Yeah, and I didn't want to." A voice in her head reminded her she was a hypocrite, because she hadn't put
Aras's needs before her duty. Keeping *c'naatat* from Rayat
overrode everything. "But you knew why I had to do it."

"And I felt I had to act for the bezeri. But both Ade and I
are here now, and the bezeri are as satisfied as they ever can
be. That's all that matters. Intentions are irrelevant."

That was the wess'har way; action counted and motive
didn't. Apologies were worthless to them, because events
were a reality that couldn't be erased by mitigating circumstances or genuine regret. *Dead's dead.* She said it herself
most days, and long before she'd even heard of Cavanagh's
Star.

"Well, actually, *matey,* that's *not* all that matters." She
found her attention fixed on Aras's charcoal eyes; they were
all iris and almost no sclera, just like an animal's, not a gold
wess'har cross-hair gaze at all. Her face burned and the
pressure in her ears felt close to explosion. Ade's restless
movement caught her peripheral vision. "What *matters* is
that we don't have this bloody parasite under our control
any longer. A *government agent* has it. You know what he'll
do with it?"

"He's not—"

"Supersoldiers. Then they flog it off to the pharmacorps, because no government can resist money in the end. Or it gets out into the wider population by accident. *Pandemic.* You can spread it by sex, by body fluids, by wounds. You can do the maths, Aras. Wasn't that why you quarantined Bezer'ej to start with? Because you saw what happened in the isenj colony there?"

"This is *one man,* trapped on Bezer'ej."

"No, this is a *spook,* a very competent spook, and Lindsay Neville too, and even that idiot bitch can be trouble."

"How can they leave? How can they pass it on? The bezeri never caught it from me, and I moved among them for nearly five hundred years."

"There's no such thing as *can't* in this universe, Aras. Even the bloody dead come back to life." Shan could feel her own voice becoming thin and compressed in her own skull. "And Rayat *will* find a way, trust me. I would if I were him."

You lost the will to live when you thought I was dead. But you were ready to run away and live with the bezeri.

She tried to shake that thought out of her head. It was a selfish thought, a woman's reaction without consideration of anything beyond her own hurt feelings. It wasn't professional. She tried to slap it down.

Ade moved. She saw him reach out cautiously, slowly. He laid his hand on her forearm and she concentrated on not jerking it away. His expression was the utter dejection of a beaten child.

"There's another way of looking at it, Boss."

"Really?" She was fond of Ade to the brink of falling in love, but right then she wanted to punch the shit out of him. The impulse appalled her. He usually brought out the vestige of her protective urge, but she'd vented her anger on him before. "Forgive me if I haven't spotted it."

"The little shit's stuck on the seabed with a bunch of aliens who hate him. *Forever.* So's she. That probably even beats hanging them."

If Shan had been looking for vengeance for the near extinction of the bezeri, then Ade had a point: it was extreme punishment, as extreme as it got. Shan wondered what changes *c'naatat* would make to the two of them to keep them alive in the deep ocean and knew that whatever it was, it might be a lot more traumatic than the largely invisible tinkering that the parasite had carried out on her.

And I know what it's like to drown. And to drift in space. Oh yes, that's *fucking bad. Living with the squid might be too good for Rayat.*

"You'd better be right," she said. "Because I'm going to have to spend the rest of my life making sure they don't pass it on. Or hunt the fuckers down and fragment them."

A well-placed detonation was the only way to disrupt *c'naatat*'s lightning defenses of its host organism. It was the way the wess'har *c'naatat* troops—accidental hosts, thinking their malleable genome had picked up just a handy adaptation for fast healing—had ended their lives when not aging or dying became too much to bear.

Ade managed to look her in the eye. "I've let you down, haven't I?"

"Bloody right you have." Shan stood up and walked over to the deeply hollowed stone set under the water spigot, the nearest that wess'har had to a sink. She couldn't stop herself raging. "How could you do such a frigging stupid thing? After all that's happened?"

"I had to make a decision there and then. We never planned to let them live."

"Jesus, am I the only one here who can think beyond the next five minutes? I pretty well *died* to stop anyone getting hold of this, but you two just hand it over, good as gold. I suppose Rayat made a really good case, did he? Talked you into it?"

"No, Lindsay did," said Aras. "This satisfied the bezeri, and stopped either of us taking their place. Because somebody had to help the few still left. Or at least give them some semblance of justice."

Shan recalled the last time the bezeri had called for justice; a scientist had been executed over the death of one of their young. And Aras had carried it out, whatever she'd told the *Thetis* camp. Even then, Shan felt it was her responsibility. She'd been in command for far too long and it was an inextricable part of her. She hated standing on the sidelines.

"Either?" she asked. "What do you mean by *either* of you?"

Ade closed his eyes for a moment and it disturbed her. She found no satisfaction in making a brave man cower. "Yeah, well . . . it was a case of both of us trying to do the decent thing. We . . . persuaded each other out of it." He paused and adopted that I-wish-I-hadn't-said-that expression. She realized that she didn't know him as well as she thought, and that meant she didn't have control of the situation. Control mattered. "I wanted you to be *happy.*"

"Ade, for fuck's sake, having you two end up as squidmen isn't going to make me *happy.*" This was why she didn't trust relationships. They weakened you. She hated herself for feeling wounded because for the first time in her life she had become used to being the center of a man's world—two men's worlds, in fact. She wouldn't make that mistake again. "Did it occur to you that I have to tell Esganikan? This is a major biohazard, in case you've forgotten."

She took her jacket from the hook on the wall and fastened it, trying hard not to descend further into diatribe and profanity, But Aras had broken the taboo of centuries to save her life with the bloody thing in the first place. Maybe the crazy god-bothering colonists were right; maybe it really was the ultimate temptation of the devil, to be eradicated once and for all.

"Where are you going?" asked Aras.

"To catch Esganikan before she leaves for Umeh. She needs to hear this from me. I don't want either of you telling anyone about this. Okay?"

It wasn't true: she could have sent a message to Esganikan. Eqbas didn't stand on ceremony and a call would have done the job. But she needed to walk away, because the Superintendent Frankland part of her was welling up and demanding to be let out to give her underlings a thorough, foul-mouthed bollocking and maybe a thump in the ear for failing her.

But that wasn't really what the Shan at the core of her felt.

That Shan was *hurt*. She'd believed them when they both said they were devoted to her. They'd put something else before her—and that was what she'd always done herself to anyone who might have been close enough to love.

Hypocrite, hypocrite, hypocrite.

It was hard to look your own failings in the face. Shan closed the door behind her and set off to look at Esganikan's alien disapproval instead.

Eqbas camp, F'nar plain

Esganikan Gai understood only too well that she would not be returning home to Eqbas Vorhi for at least fifty-five years by Earth reckoning.

She'd diverted her ship to Wess'ej to carry out a reconnaissance mission on the way back to Eqbas Vorhi. Earth hadn't been part of the plan.

The bulkhead of her cabin was set to transparency so that she could look out on the plain of F'nar even if others couldn't see in. She knelt on the deck, thinking about the time that would separate her from her own culture and took comfort in the knowledge that a society used to spacefaring made allowances for those in temporary exile. Humans, apparently, did not. Their world moved on and forgot those on deployment, and found it hard to adjust to their time-frozen ways on their return.

But there were few of them, and nobody cared.

Esganikan envied Shan Frankland, who appeared to have dealt with permanent exile by immersing in the culture in which she found herself. How did she cope with the Targassati philosophy here, the doctrine of non-intervention in the problems of others? Shan acted decisively. She did *not* withdraw.

Aitassi, the ussissi aide who accompanied Esganikan, sat back on her haunches and waited patiently for instructions. All her pack—males, juveniles, sisters—were part of this mission. She had left nobody behind in suspension to await her return to Eqbas Vorhi in the way a few of Esganikan's male crew had.

I've had enough of this task. I must make Earth my last mission. I want to have my own clan.

"Connect me to the *gethes*," Esganikan said quietly.

"It's time they allowed us direct access to the minister," said Aitassi. "I dislike this rationing of contact."

"At the moment we have no choice." Ussissi were impatient creatures. Esganikan was never sure how they found the forbearance for deep space missions. "We go the long route."

"You need an interpreter."

"I speak English well enough now, if I concentrate."

There was a dubious pause. "Very well."

Part of the bulkhead became opaque and formed an image of the blue United Nations portal that used the communications link the *gethes* called an ITX. A human male appeared on the screen. Esganikan concentrated on his face, trying to read the eye and brow movements that she interpreted as anxiety. He had dark skin, even darker than her own, and she could see no blood vessels as she could in the pale-skinned variety of human. Blue veins were visible in Shan Frankland's wrists. The blood could be seen pulsing through them; sometimes she seemed as transparent as a bezeri.

"I want to speak to the Pacific Rim lead delegate," said Esganikan, seeing no need to identify herself.

There was the usual five-second delay caused by the light-speed relay between the ITX node and Earth. She was used these imperfect communications. "I'll see if Mr. Matsoukis is available."

"Why can I not have a direct link to the Australian government? They are our hosts."

"Ma'am, this isn't something I can—"

"*Gethes*, we are coming. The more we discuss matters between now and then, the easier our task will be."

The man gazed out of the screen in baffled silence for a moment. "I'll get my supervisor."

Humans didn't appear to be able to take decisions on their own. The image defaulted to the blue holding screen and Esganikan waited. The humans' need to be told what to do and follow orders might work in their favor: they might be more cooperative in due course.

She glanced to one side of the screen. Outside the ship, a steady drizzle was falling. A fine haze of tiny, fast-growing plants tinted the usually arid gold plain with dark red and purple. They appeared to have sprung up overnight.

"Captain," said a male voice. Esganikan jerked her attention back to the screen where a thickset *gethes* with glossy, almost black hair—like Barencoin, one of the human soldiers—sat fidgeting, clasping and unclasping his hands. "I'm sorry to keep you. We live in a universe of bureaucrats."

We don't. And the rank confused her. She had only recently learned what a captain was. "Why can we not talk when we wish, Matsoukis?"

Jim Matsoukis was not the man she wanted to talk to. She wanted direct access to the Australian government in the form of Canh Pho, the head of state who had invited the Eqbas Vorhi mission to his territory.

"The United Nations is insistent on keeping the ITX link available to all nations, ma'am."

The *gethes* were mesmerized by instantaneous communications; it had lured them into their alliance with the isenj. They loved communicating. But they never seemed to *listen* to responses, and they often communicated useless and untrue information. She decided they had no real need of ITX. They simply wasted it.

"Communication appears to be a significant aspect of power for humans."

"It certainly is. You're aware that military and diplomatic pressure was used to stop the Europeans monopolizing the ITX?"

"Yes, but I fail to understand it. Suppressing information will not change what happens."

"I think we treat information very differently here."

Matsoukis licked his lips; agitation, she assumed. "I'll certainly take the matter up again."

"Give me the latest environmental data you can provide."

"Have you got access to the United Nations databank?"

"No. What is that?"

Matsoukis frowned. "Out of date. I'll ensure you get ours. The information is disputed in some quarters."

Ah. Humans can never agree on facts. Everything is filtered by their needs and expectations. "Can you predict what your environmental pressures will be in thirty years? I need to ensure we bring the appropriate countermeasures."

Matsoukis looked as if he didn't understand. *Isn't my English clear enough?* She knew that look now. She'd seen it on the face of Eddie Michallat, a creasing of the brow and a slight head movement, both quickly suppressed. "If you can receive data, I'll get you the latest real-time information from our satellites. The ones *we* control. Topography, climate, land use, bathymetry. Then you can judge for yourself."

Esganikan was pleasantly surprised by his transparency. With the information she had from the matriarchs here and from Umeh Station, she could build her own projection of Earth's environmental changes.

"Your biggest problem is still rising sea levels and temperatures." She called up a map of Asia and the planet's southern hemisphere and reminded herself that Australasia was three major land masses—Australia, New Zealand, and Antarctic Territory—and the Pacific Rim States seemed to mean those plus a scattering of islands stretching almost to the Sinostates coast. She decided she was dealing almost entirely with the individual and dominant state of Australia. "Or I should say that your diminishing landmass requires a reduced population."

"Yes, flood and storm defenses are now taking eight percent of our GNP." Matsoukis seemed to miss the point, perhaps deliberately. "That's our national income. I realize you don't have our kind of economy. It's a mechanism to allocate scarce resources among competing users—"

"Your economy is . . . an ecology of resources controlled by the exchange of tokens. It must remain in balance or some benefit at the expense of others. Yes, I think I understand economies. Life itself is an economy."

Matsoukis flashed white teeth, a ussissi's threat. Aitassi didn't react; she was almost used to human gestures now. "We're under considerable pressure to withdraw our offer to allow you to land in Australian territory."

"What form is this pressure taking?"

"The threat of military action. We're fairly immune to trade sanctions because we're self-supporting in terms of food and raw materials."

Esganikan looked at the chart again. "You are an isolated group of islands. Can your enemies launch an attack at that range?"

"Yes, but we have allies. Canada and Greater Norway. You understand the strategic significance of that?"

Esganikan looked at the map again and rotated it to look at Earth from its northern pole. Canada stretched halfway down the North American landmass, almost level with a place called Washington. Norway and its territories faced it across a stretch of sea. The allies were in easy striking distance of the Sinostates and the FEU.

"If your enemies attack you, that will not stop us landing," said Esganikan. *I've carried out opposed landings before. You'll be nothing compared to Garav.* "Tell them that. Or I will."

"They want us to withdraw the offer."

"You cannot."

"I know. We never give in to pressure."

"I mean that now you have invited us, we will come even if you do withdraw the offer. The need is established."

Matsoukis paused. His mouth was slightly open but no sound came out. Esganikan smelled someone enter the ship, someone who projected strong *jask,* a very dominant *isan.* She concentrated on her English skills and put the distraction out of her mind.

"I'll—I'll get my office to transmit the data now, Captain Gai."

That's not my name. No matter. "I await it."

"Good day, ma'am."

The screen deactivated and the blue opaque panel floated on the gold and red plain beyond the bulkhead. Esganikan inhaled and Aitassi turned her head slowly.

"Now there's a man who's shitting himself," said Shan Frankland. She walked across to the bulkhead, put her hand against it, and made that quick compression of her lips that said her mind was not on the subject she was discussing. There were violet and gold lights in her fingertips and palms; Esganikan was still fascinated by that. "Do you understand how he reacted?"

"Probably," said Esganikan. *Shitting.* She searched her memory. "I alarmed him."

"I don't think he'd worked out that he can't *un*invite you. That's a bit of a shock for a human."

"Have you come to offer your assistance?"

Shan thrust her hands in the pockets of her knee-length black coat and shrugged. She seemed at ease with her bizarre parasite, utterly human except for the bioluminescence in her hands. "Do you need it?"

"I would never refuse it. Your grasp of English is superior and you know your own people."

"That's reassuring. But you really want Eddie Michallat for that. He's a journalist, so he's no more normal than I am, but he's a lot better at dealing with subtlety."

"Is that a refusal?"

Shan paused. There was no hint of her scent now. Her *jask*—her matriarchal dominance pheromone—had obviously been a warning and now she had suppressed it. Esganikan no longer took it as deliberate deception, but it still unnerved her.

"No," said Shan. "Just a suggestion. But that's not what I've come here for. I have to tell you something."

"Tell me, then."

"I've got two more human *c'naatat* cases on Bezer'ej." Still no scent, or facial expression; but the muscles in Shan's jaw had tightened and her shoulders were set as if she had tensed her muscles ready to attack. Her pale gray eyes blinked occasionally. Esganikan found the single black pupils unnerving. "The bezeri wanted someone to help them rebuild and they got Commander Neville and Dr. Rayat."

"They are . . . submerged?"

"That's why they needed *c'naatat*. Hard to do the job without it."

"Are you angry?"

"I'm certainly not happy about it. Look, I'll make sure they don't spread the thing, even if that means terminating them. The bezeri never contracted it from contact with Aras, though, so they don't appear to be easy to infect."

Esganikan thought of the bioluminescence in Shan's hands, genes she had somehow picked up from the bezeri. Humans did seem susceptible. "Who did this?"

"Irrelevant."

This isn't a problem. It's controllable. This is simply . . . interesting. "One of your *jurej've?* Not you. Not after the steps you took to keep it away from the *gethes.*"

Shan's *jask* wafted through the cabin, not strong enough to kick Esganikan's system into ceding to her, but emphatic enough to make her point. "You leave Aras and Ade out of this. I said I'd *deal* with it."

"If I thought any of you were an environmental risk, you would not be here now."

Shan stopped blinking completely and her pale skin turned slightly yellow.

"Ask Chayyas how I respond to threats," she said quietly.

Esganikan was baffled. She'd made a statement of reassurance, nothing more. She heard Aitassi click her teeth.

"That was not a threat. You know we do not make threats." *Perhaps my English isn't as good as I think.* "I will warn the recovery team on Bezer'ej to maintain contamination precautions."

Shan seemed placated, or at least the *jask* scent vanished

and her shoulders dropped a little. But her expression—or total lack of it—left Esganikan floundering for cues.

"You might be able to remove *c'naatat* from humans, if you have to," said Shan. "Shapakti ran the tests."

"But not from wess'har. He said so. And that is why you stay here, because one of your *jurej've* cannot be restored to his normal condition."

Shan tilted her head very slowly, just a fraction. For a moment Esganikan wondered if she was developing wess'har pupils and needed to incline her head to focus better. But it seemed to be only a mannerism.

"I'd never abandon him," said Shan. She made a move towards the exit and paused at the hatchway. "He's been through enough."

"Commendable. Will you come to Umeh tomorrow?"

"Do you need me to?"

"You want to see what might take place on your former homeworld. You may bring your *jurej've*."

Shan remained impassive, unreadable. "How long?"

"As long as you wish."

"Okay. A few days. I'll front up tomorrow morning. I assume you're still going to have access here."

This was delicate politics. The F'nar matriarchs didn't want a long-term Eqbas base on Wess'ej. Esganikan was withdrawing to Bezer'ej, where Shapakti's team had begun decontamination procedures of the irradiated area.

"We will maintain contact with the colony on Mar'an'cas, and we will visit F'nar," said Esganikan. "Eddie is coming to Umeh."

"I bet he's in a feeding frenzy," said Shan, making no sense. "See you tomorrow."

Aitassi watched her leave, head tracking like a cannon turret. Esganikan waited for the data to transmit from the Earthside ITX node. She would examine it later with Shapakti and the rest of the environmental interventionist team.

"Do you have plans for Shan Frankland, Commander?"

"I need a neutral human to accompany us," said Esganikan. "The Constantine colonists have their own agenda on return to Earth. Shan Frankland sees matters more from the universal perspective."

"She's unwilling."

"Everything I know of her tells me she was an *isan* long before she acquired wess'har genes. She'll do a matriarch's duty when the time comes."

"She won't leave her males."

"She can bring them with her."

"But she fears *c'naatat* entering Earth's population."

"I doubt that she understands the level of our biohazard precautions." Esganikan decided she could utilize Eddie Michallat if it came to it, but she far preferred Shan Frankland. She had the measure of her commitment: she didn't put her own species above all others. And she was a sister matriarch. "Perhaps she doesn't want to return to Earth anyway."

"Perhaps she has had her fill of responsibility," said Aitassi.

Esganikan doubted it. If there was one thing she understood about Shan, it was that she couldn't get enough of it. She would tire of not being the decision maker. She seemed to think the universe was her personal responsibility.

If all humans thought that way, the task ahead would be far easier. Only those who did could be allowed to survive.

4

Preach the gospel at all times . . . and when necessary, use words.

SAINT FRANCIS OF ASSISI

The Exchange of Surplus Things, F'nar

"You hiding from Frankland?" asked Mart Barencoin.

Ade glanced up from the fan of playing cards in his hand, conscious of the stares of the rest of his Royal Marine detachment. The five men and women had embarked with him in *Thetis* what seemed like a lifetime ago, when he was still a regular human being; they'd been as good as family.

There was Jon Becken, a blond kid in his twenties, and the two engineer-trained commandos Sue Webster and Bulwant Singh Chahal. Martin Barencoin was a good bloke for all his mouth, and Ismat Qureshi, who had to cheat a bit to make the minimum height and weight to pass selection, could drop a man twice her size. They were a solid team. It felt as if they'd been here forever and not just two years.

"No," Ade lied, thinking of the here and now again. "I just want to play cards with my oppos. Got a problem with that?"

Barencoin shrugged and went back to studying his hand. They might have been kicked out of the Corps but they still behaved like marines, and he was still their bloody sergeant. He could shut Barencoin up.

The air was cool and scented with wet green scents of vegetables that didn't grow on Earth. Wess'har went about their business around them, depositing produce and other items they didn't need and selecting items left by others; they were totally communal and greed didn't seem to cross their minds. They took no notice of the six human soldiers

who had set up an informal mess deck in the nearest thing
F'nar had to a formal public building.

Yes, they were *alien*. And Ade had their genes inside him
now. He checked every day for changes to his body but so
far all he had developed was an absence of body hair and
bioluminescence around his tattoos. It made taking a piss a
truly surreal experience.

"You going to tell us about it, Sarge?" Qureshi kept her
eyes fixed on her cards. "How did Commander Neville take
it in the end?"

Oh shit. It. Death; or *not* death in this case. At least he
could tell some kind of truth, but he had no idea how he
would ever tell them exactly what he had done.

"Calmly," he said.

"And Rayat?"

"Same."

Ade thought they looked disappointed. None of them had
liked Rayat from day one, and when he turned out to be a
spook their mood of told-you-so was overwhelming. There
was an unspoken assumption that he wouldn't die well. Ade
wondered if he should have told them otherwise; but that
was shabby. The bastard could take it. Like Shan, he could
face *worse* than death.

*You were ready to take that dive, weren't you? And now
you're bloody relieved Rayat and Neville did it for you.
You're a coward, like Dad always said.*

Ade closed his eyes as firmly as he could, pressing down
his lids for a moment to shut out the shame and his father's
voice. Qureshi laid her cards on the makeshift table of an
upturned crate, starting with the ace of spades. She seemed
to have taken his expression as a sign he had a crap hand.

"Twenty-one," she said. "Anyone stupid enough to play
me again? Sue? You up for it?"

"Yeah," said Webster, and passed her hand to Chahal for
shuffling. "What are we going to play for this time?"

"I'm out of chili sauce."

"Awww, *shit.*"

"It lasted *three years.*"

"Izzy, you can eat *anything* as long as you've got chili sauce. How long before we can harvest the habañeros?"

"Four months. Even with Shapakti's lighting."

They'd sneaked a few chili plants into the experimental rainforest habitat that the Eqbas biologist had created to test the resurrection process of the gene bank. He had two blue and gold macaws in there, real ones. They could even speak eqbas'u now. Shapakti didn't mind the marines sticking a few pots of seedlings in the habitat because he knew they missed home comforts just like he did. The make-believe forest was a nice place to retreat to—underground, sealed, and oddly full of the smells and sounds and textures of Earth.

But I don't belong on Earth any more.

"What we going to do, then?" Becken scratched the scar on his nose. "We're not much use here, apart from gardening."

"Got to eat," said Qureshi. The terrestrial crops took time and effort, even within the biobarrier that Aras had created for them. It was sobering when you had to grow everything you ate. "Got to get more chili sauce on line."

"Anyone fancy asking the colonists if they want us helping out on Mar'an'cas?" Webster, engineer-trained, like Chahal, was still set on getting running water and heat exchangers set up in the refugee camp. "We can try again."

"The ungrateful fuckers told us to piss off, remember?" said Barencoin. "You know, when we arrested their mate. They're touchy like that."

"They might have calmed down now they've got a date for going home," said Qureshi. "And there's this Christian forgiveness thing, right?"

"Izzy, we handed what's-his-face over to Esganikan for execution."

"Jonathan," said Webster.

"Yeah, Jonathan. I think that's all we've done in three sodding years, isn't it? Arrested some bastard or other for someone else to deal with. Frankland, Jonathan, Neville, Rayat. Oh, but Ade managed to slot Dr. Galvin all on his own. That's something."

"Silly cow shouldn't have got in the crossfire," said Qureshi sourly. "Ade and I slotted some isenj too. So you can shut it."

Ade had never lost sleep over Galvin. That surprised him. But she'd ignored the curfew and every safety warning; somehow, she didn't fall into the category of women he should have protected, and he wasn't sure why.

"It's not home," Ade said. "Earth isn't their home. They've been here for generations."

"Bezer'ej," said Chahal. "Not here. Not Wess'ej."

"Okay, *Bezer'ej*, then." If Ade looked outside now, he might have seen the cloud-marbled crescent of Wess'ej's twin planet. "They always planned to go back one day. It was their mission. But if we're going to feel like spare pricks at a wedding back home, how are *they* going to cope?"

"I didn't think you were going back," said Qureshi.

"No, I'm not."

"Then what's this *we*?"

Whatever the court martial back on Earth had decided in their absence, they clung to their routine and discipline— and identity. That was something no government could take away from them. And Ade found it very hard not to think of himself as *we*.

"Shan says she's going to see if she can get the court martial finding quashed," he said. "A pardon. Back inside."

"Well, hoo-fucking-ray." Barencoin leaned a little to the left so a wess'har could get past him with a large crate. He didn't glance up from close inspection of the hand he had been dealt. "The Defense Ministry listens to her, do they?"

"Watch your mouth. She's the only person who gives a fuck what happens to us." Ade bristled. That was *Shan* he was talking about, his missus, the love of his life, the Boss: he wouldn't tolerate disrespect from *anyone*. "And when you get back home, it'll be the Eqbas who'll be looking out for you, not the frigging FEU."

They could handle anything; they were all Extreme Environment Warfare Cadre. They'd skydived from orbit, camped out on ice floes, and fought in jungle and city. But being dismissed the service along with Lindsay Neville for the Bezer'ej bombing was the one thing that upended them.

"It was a lawful order," said Barencoin. "At least transporting the stuff was, so don't go all bloody guilty again. The fireworks were all Commander Neville's doing. She never even gave us any orders about that—and she did it herself, so there was at least one scrap of decency in the bitch."

"Yeah, you argued, Mart."

"So did you."

"Should have done more than argue."

"And then what does that make you? We've got rules. That's *why* we've got rules, so that we don't decide to do stuff we've not been asked to do by the elected government, and turn into some fucking uniformed mob like some banana republic's army storming the Parliament building."

"Okay."

"No, *not* okay. The way it is. Thinking for yourself is one thing, having an opt-out army is another. It might look principled to you, but it's asking for fucking chaos."

"Loads of people have made a stand in the past."

"For Chrissakes, Ade, there was no stand to make. How would you have stopped Neville, and why? Slotted her? Really? Is that lawful? Once you sign on the line, the overall objective isn't your call."

Shan thought the same as Barencoin, but Ade couldn't hide behind . . . well, *sophistry.* That was what Shan called bullshit excuses. If the marines hadn't helped land the devices on Bezer'ej, Lindsay Neville wouldn't have been able to do it on her own. Nor would Rayat.

It was the kind of call you could only make in hindsight. He still felt he should have made it.

The wess'har didn't, though. They had weird ideas about guilt and responsibility. They'd blown up *Actaeon* and wiped out entire isenj colonies on Bezer'ej in retribution, but as far as they were concerned the marines were innocent and Lindsay Neville and Mohan Rayat were guilty. Wess'har didn't think like humans.

"You want the court martial finding overturned too?" said Chahal. "If they quash it, you've got to go back, haven't you?"

"I'll settle for resigning. I can't go anywhere." There was no point telling them the technicalities of removing *c'naatat* and why—*c'naatat* or not—he had to stay with Shan and Aras. He took his fighting knife from his belt and drew the blade down the inside of his forearm, letting blood well from the cut. It hurt like hell. He *needed* to do this, to show them what it did until they really thought it through just the way he had night after night. "Take a good look at this and ask if you want a dose getting loose on Earth. 'Cos I don't think you do."

Sometimes even *he* needed to see it for himself to believe what had happened to him. The marines simply stared, and he was aware they were looking at his face rather than the rapidly healing wound on his arm.

"Yeah, you're not going anywhere, are you?" said Barencoin. "Just as well you've got Frankland to keep you warm."

I wish. I've blown it now, I reckon. She'll never let me touch her now. She's fucking furious.

"Yeah," said Ade.

Webster turned away and fanned out her cards in her hand, looking unimpressed. "We've got a few years to sit out before we can head home. I'd rather concentrate on getting through that first. It's not a given."

"We could go back to Umeh," said Chahal.

"They're kicking off a civil war by all accounts."

"That's what we do best." Chahal inspected his cards. "War and stuff."

Qureshi looked more in need of a square meal than ever. She was getting too thin. "Whose side? It's not our war. And what use are we going to be to them? The Eqbas have kit that makes the ESF670 look like a water pistol."

So that was what was gnawing at them now; they weren't the top of the military food chain any longer. Ade considered that. It hadn't struck him before. He still clung to his professional pride because it made him who he was, but getting kicked out didn't dent that half as much as realizing you weren't the best any longer.

Morale needed boosting. He was still the bloody sergeant.

"Buck up, you buggers," he said. "Pound for pound, a Royal can still show them how it's done."

Qureshi managed a grin. Even Barencoin, the miserable bastard, seemed placated. *When did Mart get so sour?* Ade laid down his cards and stood up.

"I'm going for my run."

"Suit yourself," said Barencoin, all disbelief.

Ade wasn't lying. He really *did* run each day, through the center of the city and the alleys that threaded through the bottom of the caldera and out onto the plain itself. He ran every day because routine mattered. Routine gave you discipline and structure, two lifelines he clung to.

The wess'har were used to him now; they knew he ran for no purpose other than to stay fit even though *c'naatat* didn't need to worry about that. But today he was running to catch Shan as she returned from visiting Esganikan's camp.

He stopped at the pearl-coated pillars of basalt at the city boundary, running his fingertips over the polished surfaces. The fine drizzle was still falling. For F'nar, this was a cold winter, and there had even been snow for a few days. Sometimes the place felt like home as long as he didn't look at the alien vegetation and wildlife, and even then he found some echoes of familiarity in them. Maybe that was the legacy of Aras's memories, carried on the blood that Shan had mingled with his when she head-butted him.

You shot her. You helped capture her for Lindsay and Rayat. Jesus, if she can forgive you for that, maybe she can forget you infected them.

Eventually Shan appeared in the distance, striding in that piss-off way that defied anyone to stand in her path. Ade decided she must have been a fearsome presence in uniform when she patrolled Reading Metro. She was still bloody scary now.

Shit, he loved her. He loved her *because* she was scary and always knew what to do when things went pear-shaped. She had a nice arse, too.

He wondered how angry she could get with him; she'd

kicked the shit out of Rayat, but it wasn't physical pain he dreaded, just rejection. Whatever it took to get back in her good books, he'd do it.

Shan didn't meet his eyes as she walked. She drew level with him, hands thrust in her pockets, and then stopped to stare at his hair.

"Needs cutting," she said. "I never realized you had curly hair."

Ade ran his hand self-consciously across his head, wiping away beads of water. He needed to take the clippers to it. "Sorry. You told Esganikan about Bezer'ej?"

"Yes. She doesn't seem to give a toss. Funny, isn't it? I expected her to go barmy."

"Oh." Shan was doing her slow burn. He preferred it when she just blew up and got it over with. He always thought he knew what her flash-to-bang time was. "*You* give a shit, though, Boss."

"Oh yeah."

"What are you going to do?"

"Do what I used to do in EnHaz, I suppose—assess the risk and contain it. Something tells me I ought to go and finish the job, but I'm not sure how to carry out a detonation under water."

"I meant about me and Aras."

"Ah. That." Shan looked carefully blank. "Continue feeling pissed off and let down, and work out why." She started walking and he followed her. It was worse than a punch in the face, and he'd had a few of those. She had her detached copper's voice on now, the one that he knew she used when dealing with those who meant nothing to her. "See, Ade, I don't know if I'm pissed off because you did something I spaced myself to *avoid* doing, or because you and Aras competed to see who could run out on me the fastest, or because you created a major environmental hazard. When I work that out, *then* I'll decide how fucking angry I'll be."

Ade wanted to make things simple for her. He wanted to stop her feeling obliged to take him on just because she'd infected him by accident. He wanted her to have a happy life at last with Aras, whether that included him or not.

"I thought I was in the way, Boss."

"I'll *tell* you when you're in the way. Okay?"

They walked on through the damp gleaming alleys and up the narrow steps cut into the rock. He couldn't bear the cold silence and tried to force a conversation.

"Boss, whatever you decide to do, I'll help you sort it."

"I don't *know* what to do. That happens sometimes. I don't have all the answers."

"What would you have done differently?"

She didn't even pause for breath. "Dumped those two bastards in the water and let them drown."

"Even if the bezeri asked for someone to stay with them?" *If either of us sleep with her,* c'naatat *will transfer our memories. She'll find out about Aras anyway. I might as well get that over with, too.* "They asked Aras to stay with them weeks ago. He was in a right state about it."

"Oh, and he never thought to mention it to me? Fucking *great.*"

"There were things you didn't tell him, remember? Like being the DNA donor for the bioweapon?"

"Yeah. There's nothing wrong with my recall."

"And . . ." Ade wasn't arguing with her, he was sure of that. She'd let the wess'har use her DNA to create the pathogen that would kill any human who set foot on Bezer'ej. She'd left Aras to grieve. He just wanted her to see how decisions got made, and that she made them the same way. "You ran out on *him,* in a way."

"I did." Her voice dropped. "But I still didn't hand over *c'naatat.*"

"Yeah, but you still infected me, accidentally or not."

"I nutted you after you emptied a frigging clip into me."

"But motive doesn't matter, does it? That's the wess'har way."

"Yeah. I sucked vacuum for months thanks to you, but I'm all better now, so no harm done, eh?"

Oh shit. "Boss—"

"Just piss off or shut up. You choose."

Shan's coat flapped as she climbed ahead of him in silence. The caldera echoed with the thud of boots and the occasional double warbling note of wess'har females making that territorial call that unnerved him. Even Nevyan did it. It was very *animal.* Ade felt suddenly crushed and alone.

I've fucked this up completely. How do I get her to even like me again?

He followed her into the house. Aras was grinding soybeans to extract the milk and a smell like wet cardboard filled the room. He looked up and then carried on with his task using one of the hand-mills that had once been used in Constantine.

"I'm going to Umeh tomorrow for a few days," Shan said. "But I'm not sure if I want to leave you two buggers on your own. I can't trust you."

"Take Ade," said Aras.

"You got a reason for staying here?"

Aras held up the bowl of beans. "A great deal of soy to process. And Black is unwell."

Black and White were two of the lab rats that Aras had seized from Rayat back on Bezer'ej, in the days when he just seemed to be an irritating scientist in need of a good hiding to make him understand what *no* meant. That was two years ago: Black and White were now old and frail. Aras was fond of them. All animals were people to him.

Shan cast a glance at the cage on the storage cabinet. "I want your word on that."

Aras tipped the pulverized beans into a sieve and let the milky liquid run through into a bowl. "I'll still be here when you get back."

"If you're not," she said, "don't expect me to come running after you."

She disappeared into the room she shared with Aras and didn't close the door. Ade could hear the snap of fabric and the ripping sound of her grip being opened. She was packing.

He glanced at Aras with the solidarity of a brother. "At least she hasn't kicked us out. That's a start."

Aras shrugged just like a human. It was almost possible to forget that he'd started life as a wess'har. "If you accompany her to Umeh, it gives you some private time to copulate with her. She may well take a less hostile view when she's bonded with you."

Ade winced. There was *crude,* and then there was *cold.* Aras was still wess'har at heart, and they were now in the odd world of wess'har genetic transfer, where females and males passed DNA across membranes and changed each other at the cellular level. *C'naatat* was almost made for wess'har. But Ade didn't see sex like that at all. He just wanted Shan, and the idea that she would be bonded to him simply because they swapped genes felt grim and soulless. He wanted her to choose him. He wanted her to *love* him.

"I'll let you know if I come back with my nuts intact," said Ade. "That's probably the best I can hope for."

"I expect *c'naatat* could grow them again," Aras said, and Ade was—as ever—unsure if he was joking or being scrupulously wess'har-literal.

Ade didn't have Eddie's gift of the gab, and Shan was immune to flattery anyway. He had to deal with her like a bloke. No crap. Just the facts. She'd eat him alive if he tried to cajole her.

The bedroom door opened. Shan stood with her fists on her hips and for a moment Ade braced for a broadside. She'd heard them. Coppers had some uncanny natural radar. Her lips parted.

"There's one thing I want to say to you two," she said. Her face was drained of blood, made even whiter by the contrast with her black hair, and she'd obviously been chewing over the earlier conversations. "*Loyalty.* You can do what the fuck you like, but there's one thing I demand from you two and that's *loyalty.* You do *not* go behind my back. You do *not* decide what's best for me. Is that clear?"

Ade nodded, silent. "Yes, *isan,*" said Aras.

She didn't have to say she was the Guv'nor. Ade was glad

she was, and he knew Aras liked it that way too. Wess'har matriarchs ran the show. A female who could punch her own weight and then some was normal here; but it was still both sobering and arousing to stand within striking distance of that kind of dominance.

Shan stared at them for a few moments as if she was going to say something else, then turned and went back into the bedroom, where she packed audibly. Given how little she carried with her, she took a long time doing it.

"'Ras, show me how to do that soybean thing," said Ade, looking for diversion. A Royal Marine could do anything. He'd make soy milk and tofu and even bloody cakes if he had to. "Might as well be useful."

It was a silent and awkward day, and an uncommunicative evening.

That night, Shan slept on the sofa.

Bezer'ej: continental shelf, Ouzhari

Lindsay Neville fumbled with the signal lamp, kneeling in the cold mud, now able to detect everything around her for some distance.

She couldn't call it seeing. She could detect light and she could see a lot better than she should have been able to in these black depths, but she could also visualize contours and densities and movement. She had no idea how; she had an urge to open her mouth wide, and somehow images were forming in her mind. At first they had reminded her of grainy reproductions of carved reliefs, but now they were much sharper. She could detect fine detail.

She could see Mohan Rayat, sitting on the seabed and groping around him as if he wasn't sure where he was.

Oh my god oh my god oh my god I've changed into something else and I'm not me anymore and—

Rayat put his hand to his neck.

He had *gills*.

Lindsay had to know. She knew before she touched her

throat but it was still a shock when her fingertips—cold, but
not numb—felt soft unfamiliar spaces under her jaw.

She felt her lips part in a reflex that would have been a
yelp of shock but it never emerged. She let her arm drop to
her side and found she was still clutching the signal lamp.
Would she always need it to talk to the bezeri? Might she
develop the bioluminescence, and then the language?

I won't be human then. What am I now, anyway?

She put eternity out of her mind. Even planets died in the
end, and their oceans with them.

Great billowing shapes with tentacles trailing moved
towards her in pulsing movements, propelling themselves
with jets of water. They settled in a semicircle, translucent
and yet a complex sac of dense tissue filled with voids of
varying sizes, rippling pinpoints of colors through their
mantles in dazzling patterns.

Lindsay activated the signal lamp and held it up.

At first she heard random chatter booming from the device as it picked up and translated the light patterns from
the bezeri. Then she moved it so that it was facing straight
at one of the creatures.

You never thought what your bombs would do to us.

Lindsay's brain merged the multilayered image of light
and density and faint electrical impulses. *Is this how Shan
sees things?* She chose her words carefully.

"I didn't know they contained cobalt. I'm truly sorry."

The lamp flared a sequence of colors. There was no way
of knowing how well it translated.

We may not survive even now. There are too few of us.

Lindsay was aware of movement behind her. Rayat was
picking his way through the mud, trying to balance in unfamiliar terrain and currents.

"We'll help you," she said. The lamp projected her words.
"Give us a chance."

"Give me the lamp," said Rayat.

"Sod off. I'll do the talking." She focused on the bezeri
again. Concentrating kept her panic under control. It stopped
her thinking about what was happening to her and what would

happen for an unimaginable time to come. "What do I call you?"

You will retrieve our archives and help us preserve them. They are all we have left. If we die out, then at least we leave some existence behind us.

Perhaps they hadn't understood. "Do you use names? I'm Lindsay Neville."

Eeeenz.

It took Lindsay a few moments to grasp what the bezeri was saying. It was trying to pronounce her name.

"Lindsay," she repeated.

Leeenz.

"Yes. *Leenz.*"

Saib.

"Saib." Lindsay repeated it. "Saib."

I am a patriarch. My children are dead.

"My child is dead, too," said Lindsay. David, premature David, who would have survived if Shan had given him a little of her altered blood. "I can understand that much."

How will you eat?

Rayat cut in. "*C'naatat* will enable us to digest anything, I'm sure of that."

The lamp didn't translate; Rayat was beyond the range of the mike. Lindsay hadn't even thought about the daily routine of life, and the fact she had overlooked that appalled her. She had to get a grip.

Could you starve to death if you carried *c'naatat?* Shan survived months drifting in space without a suit; Lindsay didn't want to test what *c'naatat* could force her to survive at this depth. And as soon as she thought of that, she remembered something that she was sure she'd never experienced.

A gorilla reached out with its leather glove of a hand, staring her in the eye, and withdrew. Then it rubbed its palm in a circular motion over its chest followed by a fist-on-palm gesture, over and over again. Lindsay felt shame and regret so overwhelming that it made her shut her eyes involuntarily, but it wasn't *her* memory.

It was Shan's. Eddie had told her about it: the gorilla was asking for help, but Shan hadn't understood until years later. It haunted her.

I don't want your memories but you're welcome to mine. That's what Ade had said when he transferred the parasite to her, making sure her blood didn't contaminate his. Genetic memory; another little add-on that *c'naatat* had picked up along the way. Lindsay had no idea what alien memories would surface in her, and that was an extra layer of the nightmare she had to deal with.

But it was a fitting punishment for bringing a species almost to extinction. And, unlike those who had wiped out the dodo and the tiger and the orangutan, she was now at the mercy of her victims.

Shan would have told her that it served her bloody well right.

Saib seemed impatient. *We have many records to gather. They are scattered all over this region.* He shimmered with pulsing violet rings of light and began to move away. Three others moved with him, one a constant, unchanging deep blue, the other a slowly changing palette of scarlet and green that lost its red hues as it moved further away. *We have to hurry.*

Lindsay didn't ask why. She began walking behind Saib and his companions as if she was trudging through deep snow, still trying to walk when she should have been swimming. "Come on, Rayat. Do as you're bloody told."

"It's going to be something like raw shrimp and jelly-fish," he said.

She swayed a little and then found herself striking out, lifting her legs, *swimming.*

"What is?"

"Lunch."

Lindsay wondered how she was going to spend eternity trapped with Rayat. Concentrating on familiar loathing stopped her thinking about what she was becoming, and how she would get through the next hour without going insane.

Jejeno city, Ebj region, Umeh: Eqbas Vorhi ship 886-001-005-6, Ebj airspace

"Shit," said Shan.

It was the first time she'd seen Umeh and it was every nightmare she'd ever had in Environmental Hazard Enforcement. The Eqbas ship hung about 1,000 meters above the surface of the city. Then its forward bulkhead and part of the deck became suddenly transparent.

She put her hand out instinctively to steady herself. She felt like she was falling; she'd done this before. She'd stared down through the viewplate of an automated shuttle as it plummeted towards the surface of Bezer'ej for the first time and the sensation made her nearly throw up.

For a second, she was close to doing that again.

Tight-packed buildings spread below her. There was nothing else but buildings upon buildings upon buildings, without the relief of greenery or open spaces or bodies of water. She'd seen Eddie's footage of Jejeno but it didn't come close to capturing the sheer scale of the urbanization.

Home, said an uninvited feeling in her chest. *Home.*

She tagged it as the scrap of isenj in her that went with the genetic memory. The movement she could see was packed bodies, a black and brown carpet of isenj moving through the impossibly crowded streets of the capital. *That* was inside her, somewhere.

"Shit," she said again. Crowded cities meant high casualties in any disaster; unthinkably crowded ones like Jejeno set off all her copper's emergency responses. She braced herself not to attempt to *organize* things. "Remind me not to apply for a posting here. How the hell do they manage an environment like that?"

At least the deck was mostly opaque. Where it was wholly transparent, an Eqbas crew member gazed down apparently unconcerned. Shan decided that she could manage that too, and steeled herself to step into the transparent section to look down, overriding all her brain's hardwired insistence that she would fall.

Eddie joined her in contemplating the city beneath their feet, as casual as the Eqbas. His bee cam—the size of a small orange—settled a little above the deck, recording silently. Shan wondered if Eddie was putting on a show of bravado when he was actually shitting himself. Looking down on the city, she felt like a tourist in Hell.

"I can remember when this was all fields," Eddie said cheerfully.

Ade chuckled. He hadn't said a word since they embarked. Shan wondered how she could call a truce with him now and waited for Eddie's reaction.

"Who do you actually know in the isenj government now, Eddie?" *You got Ual killed, you tosser. That's what happens when you play at politics.* "Any favors to call in?"

He shrugged. If he felt any responsibility for his part in Ual's death, he was doing a good job of hiding it. She suspected he was. "Ralassi. Ual's aide."

"Well, at least we'll get a cup of coffee, then."

"I'm good at making contacts. Trust my charm."

Shan could see Serrimissani and Aitassi talking to Esganikan in her peripheral vision. Ussissi were scrupulously neutral; they might have evolved alongside the wess'har on Eqbas Vorhi, but they also moved across the galaxy with them, and they saw no conflict of interests in working for the isenj on Umeh. Neither did the wess'har. Ussissi didn't take sides and wess'har were completely comfortable with that. It was a political and social concept that defeated most humans, and Shan wasn't sure she grasped it herself.

And yet they were *loyal*. She thought of Vijissi, who wouldn't leave her side even when she spaced herself, and wondered if they had found his body yet.

I demand loyalty. But when I get it, it just makes me feel guilty.

The ship—which had no name, just a pennant code of ten digits—moved slowly towards the dome of Umeh Station and she caught sight of a gaping black crater fringed with shattered stumps of masonry. As her eye moved out along the blast radius, the buildings became more complete and identifiable; but the shimmering river of movement made from living isenj was missing. She tried to estimate the size of the devastated area.

"Jejeno's antiaircraft battery, as was," Eddie said helpfully. "Right in the center of the city. It made the mistake of opening fire on Esganikan when she came in to land last time."

"And they're letting us come back?"

"You wait till you see the Eqbas countermeasures in action."

Ade knelt down on the transparent section of deck and braced his elbows on it to get a better look. Shan squatted down beside him. It was surprising how fast you could get used to the disorientation, especially when you didn't want to lose face.

"I don't see anything in the way of ground defenses," he said. "But then the wess'har don't invade, do they?"

The matriarchs of Wess'ej didn't: but the Eqbas wess'har did. Shan thought of the number of casualties and the chaos that an explosion of that size would have caused. It had been a long time since she'd done that kind of police work—cordoning streets, evacuating people, searching for body parts, bagging and tagging them—and in a way she missed it. Decisions had been simple and immediate. But her choices now were increasingly complex.

"Are they too scared to fire on us?" *Will Earth be?* "What's happening?"

"You'll see," said Eddie.

Umeh Station was now almost immediately beneath them. The faceted sections of its dome gave it the appearance of a glittering, wind-whipped lake in the hazy sunlight, and then two bronze blobs like molten metal began falling slowly away from the hull towards it.

The ship was disassembling itself; it was splitting off sections and landing them. *Shuttles.* Shan had seen the liquid technology of the Eqbas, but watching a vessel dissolve *beneath* you was on the bowel-loosening side of fascinating. She thought of the metal hull of Aras's craft that had crumbled to harmless dust after crashing. It wasn't reassuring.

"I thought they'd make us rapid-rope down there," she

said, finally offering Ade an olive branch. She couldn't stand his quiet misery. Shit, she loved the bastard. She was actually *in* love, which was new for her and not at all like the more gradual love she'd developed for Aras. Ade was one of the few wholly decent people she'd ever known, and an appealing mix of genuine modesty and solid, textbook masculinity. She found she had no defenses left even if she couldn't say the words. "Sod that."

"If we cut our altitude." He smiled, all eager gratitude. "I could train you, you know."

"It's not like I can do myself any permanent damage, is it?"

"Easy. Piece of piss, Boss. Honest."

The deck became instantly opaque. Esganikan strode across to them and pointed downwards. "The biodome is crowded. You might prefer to return to the ship's accommodation to sleep."

She ushered the three of them towards the forward bulkhead, Serrimissani and Aitassi following. Shan wasn't wholly prepared for what happened next. The deck sagged beneath her boots. Her instinct was that she was falling, that something was going horribly wrong, but the logical part of her brain gave the alarmed monkey within a steadying slap that said *it's just the ship reforming, stupid.*

And it did. It deformed and flowed into a well and then engulfed them in a capsule, like tropical fish in a plastic bag, safe but trapped. Ade caught her elbow to steady her.

Eddie looked slightly shaken but said nothing. Shan imagined he'd had his fair share of close calls.

"You realize you're probably going to run into the *Thetis* payload," he said.

"Then it'll be like old times," said Shan.

The last three scientists from her original mission were in Umeh Station now. Surendra Parekh had been executed, and Louise Galvin killed in crossfire with isenj; Sabine Mesevy had found god among the Constantine colonists, and Rayat was with the bezeri. That left Vani Paretti, Olivier Champciaux and the mission's doctor, Kris Hugel.

They were the harmless ones, except maybe for Hugel. If

Hugel came after her again about bloody *c'naatat*, she'd slot the bitch this time. Shan slid her hand into the back of her belt and felt the comforting shape of her 9mm handgun. Antique tech worked just fine.

The bronze globule of shiplet peeled away and ascended back to the main hull, leaving them standing in front of the dome in the shadow cast by the massive ship. A wide access road—a rare open space in Jejeno—ringed the building. For the first time Shan wondered what reception she might get, or if anyone would even know who she was. *Too bad.* She didn't give a fuck. She was well used to being the last person anyone wanted to see walk through the door.

Eddie nudged her in the back. "Look."

Above her, the piece of Eqbas ship coalesced with the main vessel. Shan noticed the faint shimmer like a heat haze distorting the cityscape. So that was the defensive barrier. It reminded her of the biobarrier that separated the Constantine colony from the Wess'ej environment.

"It's like being under an upturned glass," said Eddie. "But at least you don't need a breather mask inside the perimeter. I'm not sure if it makes me feel safe or trapped."

"Safe," said Ade, adjusting his rifle on its sling. "Take it from me."

The airlock opened and Shan walked through first, even ahead of Esganikan. It never occurred to her to hang back, even though she wasn't sure where she was going. Umeh Station was hot and crowded, like an upmarket mall full of people in naval uniforms or coveralls. Vines covered the interior and there was a fountain with incongruously attractive foliage plants in the main plaza area, including a dwarf banana tree with hands of fruit forming on it. Ade seemed very interested in the bananas.

Umeh Station had been designed for two hundred but now housed three hundred stranded humans, all that were left of the *Actaeon* mission. Everyone who was *not* here—everyone who had chosen to stay on board the FEU warship—was dead, killed because the wess'har had destroyed the ship in retaliation for the bombing of Ouzhari and the deaths of Vijissi . . . and *herself.*

Jesus Christ. I'm walking in here alive. And they're dead.

It topped the list of bizarre moments in her career. Maybe *Actaeon*'s crew would find it equally weird. And if she'd doubted they'd know who she was, she was wrong.

Who else could she have been?

"Here we go," said Eddie. He tossed the bee cam a few inches in the air as if he was flipping a coin and it floated obediently beside him. Shan was aware of Esganikan watching with faint curiosity. "Don't bite anyone's head off, will you?"

The silence started a few meters from her and spread, the hum of voices fading in concentric rings like a shockwave traveling out from a detonation. She could almost see it. For a copper, it wasn't an unusual reception.

But she was a dead woman. They'd been sure of it. So had she.

Site contractors and crew stared. Shan stared back as only she could, hands on hips, feet apart, something she'd honed to perfection over the years. Then they suddenly appeared to have something more pressing to do and walked away. The hum of conversation filled the dome again. Ade nudged her. It was only then that she realized he was standing behind her with his rifle in his hands, finger outside the trigger guard but leaving no doubt about his ability to fire.

"And I thought it was my friendly face," she said.

"Might have been, Boss." He slung the rifle again. "You can look like a bulldog chewing a wasp when you put your mind to it."

Shan waited for Esganikan to make a move. "This doesn't strike me as an ideal place for your headquarters."

"It is not," said Esganikan. "But it is a neutral point for the isenj, and convenient to contain for the time being. Ual's replacement is meeting us here for discussions about the environmental readjustment of Umeh."

Eddie and Ade glanced at each other and Shan knew exactly what they were thinking. For a species that had never had a need for diplomacy, Eqbas had a curious collection of terms that sounded like euphemisms in translation, a habit they certainly didn't have. They *adjusted* planets. They culled and they rolled back ecosystems and they *restored,* whether the dominant species on that planet wanted it or not—*especially* if they didn't want it.

Ual had invited them to solve Umeh's environmental problems knowing what he would unleash. This was the Northern Assembly's territory. The rest of Umeh hadn't been consulted.

This was a dry run for Earth's likely fate. Shan decided to take careful notes.

"So who replaced Ual?" asked Eddie. "Can't be Par Shomen Eit. He's too senior."

"I was surprised by their choice," said Esganikan. "But in the end, it is, as you say, *academic*. She does not speak English or eqbas'u. Aitassi will interpret."

"Bugger," said Eddie. "I'd rather got used to Ual's command of language. Poor bastard."

Shan was starting to feel conspicuous. She was aware of a few people stopping to look, and one of them was very familiar. It was Olivier Champciaux, the geologist from the *Thetis* mission; he stopped dead and gave her a strange little-boy wave. She found herself half waving back.

"Wherever we're meeting the isenj, let's go and sit down," said Shan. "I hate standing around."

She followed Esganikan's bobbing red plume across the dome, with the two ussissi skittering across the smooth composite floor behind the Eqbas commands. They dropped onto their rear four legs to keep up with her. Every time Shan slipped into thinking of ussissi as oversized meerkats, they reminded her that they had three pairs of limbs, and the fragile sense of home and normality she'd built crumbled a little.

Esganikan had commandeered a site office, a sterile cube of composite walls with a rickety trestle table; it hardly seemed the place for a meeting that would decide the fate of billions of isenj. Ade unfolded a few chairs and set them around the table.

"Isenj can't sit on those, mate," said Eddie. "Let's find a small crate or something."

"Surreal," said Shan. "Couldn't we manage a meeting room?"

"I think they converted all the larger units to accommodation. Don't worry. Isenj aren't as touchy as humans about protocol."

"What is *discussed* is important," said Esganikan, but she didn't sit down. Shan felt as if the matriarch filled the room, and she wasn't used to a physical presence that rivaled her own. "And it will not be a long discussion."

"Can I record it?" asked Eddie.

"If you wish."

Shan wondered what he would do with the footage. If it turned out the way she imagined, it would hardly make comfortable viewing. Esganikan probably knew that.

"She's coming," said Aitassi.

Shan had never quite worked out if ussissi had exceptional hearing or smell, or both, but they seemed to have an almost osmotic degree of communication. She looked towards the door and an isenj was walking towards them like an unsteady trolley, tottering on multiple legs. She'd seen isenj before; but that had been seconds before a firefight. She'd never sat down at a table to talk to one in a civilized fashion.

For a moment, she recalled the smell of wet leaves and fungal forest floor and agonizing pain—Aras's pain at the hands of his isenj captors. It was as vivid as if it had happened to her. She tried to shake herself out of it, and then Ade caught her eye and she wondered if he was recalling it too. The memories had spread between them like flu and they shared one another's nightmares. It was too bad that the joyful memories hadn't surfaced in the same way. There had to be some.

A ussissi trotted through the door, a small male with a bandoleer of green beaded belts rattling across his shoulders. "Eddie Michallat," he said in his high-pitched childlike voice.

"You're back."

"Hi, Ralassi. Who do you work for now?"

Well, this is cordial. Shan watched as the isenj trundled through the opening and stood before them. There were no identifiable eyes to focus on and it was covered in dark quills, each tipped with a bead of brilliant blue transparent stone. It rattled like a chandelier and it smelled of forest floor. Shan dug her nails into her palms and noticed Ade swallow hard, eyes fixed on the creature; yes, he had the nightmare memories too.

But Shan had her own personal recollections. This was the closest she had ever been to a live isenj: the last encounter with them had ended with a round shattering her skull. *Spider. Piranha. Porcupine.* Her human brain struggled for a comparison, but the small part of her that remembered what it was to be wess'har and isenj and bezeri and God only knew what else via her *c'naatat* somehow saw *enemy* and *comrade* and *stranger.* It was unsettling to say the least.

Eddie looked uneasy.

"I introduce you to Minister Rit," said Ralassi. "She has been anxious to meet you—especially you, Eddie Michallat. Her mate was Par Paral Ual."

5

The Eqbas Vorhi have invaded my world, to rescue us from our environmental problems. My husband invited them. The rest of Umeh's states did not. We are now close to war with our neighbors. I know nothing about the humans stranded here, except that they call us spiders, and little more about the Eqbas—but I know Wess'ej. And I know I have to finish the process my husband started, or his death is meaningless. So I claim my ancient legal right to his office, to his ministerial role, and I will do what he would have wanted.

RIT PAR PARAL,
widow of former Minister Ual, isenj Minister of State,
in a message to the Northern Assembly

It took a lot to reduce Eddie to speechless silence but Ual's widow had managed it. The word forming on his lips was *sorry*.

But she spoke no English.

"I admired your husband very much," said Eddie. He had almost learned to look isenj in the nearest place they had to eyes. "And I'm very, very sorry that he was killed."

Ralassi paused before exchanging a high-pitched stream of sound with Minister Rit.

"She says he was fond of you and that she thanks you for helping him to open negotiations with the wess'har."

Shit. Don't make me the fucking hero here. If I hadn't helped him, he might be alive now. "Do you mind if I record this meeting?"

"She has no objection."

They'd be speaking eqbas'u and isenj. No matter: he could get Serrimissani to translate the soundtrack if he decided to transmit the footage. Eddie had reached the stage where he recorded things anyway whether he planned to send them down the ITX to BBChan or not. *History. Yeah, evidence. Whatever.* He'd walked a fine line between observing and involvement for years, crossing it first accidentally and then knowingly, and he was now convinced that nobody could observe events without influencing them.

Quantum journalism. Quite an excuse.

Shan sat down next to Ade and simply watched. She still had that way of scanning everyone for a fraction of a second too long for comfort, still every inch the detective. He never forgot she'd been a frontline copper. That was what he saw when he looked at her; not some armed drain-sniffer from Environmental Hazard Enforcement, but a woman who'd tackled everything from riots to fraud to terrorism, and who didn't give a shit what the rules said about suspects' rights. She'd crossed a few professional lines herself. Eddie found that more reassuring than reprehensible these days.

"Your first step has to be to reduce your population," said Esganikan, in *English.*

Well, that was something. Eddie wondered if it was in deference to him or because she wanted him to be able to show the meeting to the governments back home. She tilted her head on one side for better focus and it gave her the appearance of looking gently concerned, something that he suspected was far from her actual state of mind.

"Reduce your birthrate, your population and your consumption. Then we can move towards recreating a diverse ecology that can sustain itself."

Ralassi's matte-black predatory eyes flicked to Rit and back to Esganikan, showing a flash of yellow sclera. Eddie wondered what Serrimissani thought of the other ussissi. It was hard to tell: the females always seemed pissed off with everything and everybody.

"Minister Rit asks how that can be done, because previous attempts to curb the birthrate have failed."

"I discussed this with Ual," said Esganikan. "We have tissue samples of various isenj genotypes and we can develop a . . ." She seemed at a loss for words. Wess'har had no concept of unplanned births. "A mass contraceptive. Delivered via the water supply, so that all are affected equally."

A rattling pause followed the matriarch's comment. "Minister Rit asks what you mean by *all*."

"Your highly organized water distribution makes it easy to administer and impossible to avoid."

"But does that not render *everyone* infertile?"

"It can." Esganikan betrayed no caution or diplomacy. "We can restrict where we distribute it, of course. We can target it geographically, or perhaps by genetic markers."

"What kind of genetic markers?"

"Your land masses have effectively created four distinct islands with some genetic variations between populations. We could attempt to target that way."

Eddie took in the meaning and fought to keep his reflex reaction under control. This was a fundamental taboo where he came from, one step away from ethnic cleansing. He had to remind himself that this wasn't his world and he had no right to judge isenj or Eqbas morality. It still made him flinch.

Shan didn't seem as hesitant. "But how do you decide who gets it?"

"I would prefer to exempt those individuals who would be most likely *not* to repeat the excesses of the past," said Esganikan. "But I suspect there is no easily identifiable genetic marker for that."

Eddie had to listen very carefully to the way Esganikan used language. She was precise. All wess'har—including Eqbas wess'har—said *exactly* what they meant, and they appeared to be shaping their use of English the same way. She should have said *least likely*. But *least likely* was not what she meant; she was seeking *not likely*. She intended to root out ecological profligacy by any means, including selective breeding.

Now he saw the gulf between the Wess'ej wess'har and their Eqbas origins. Eqbas intervention was dispassionate. They culled, like herdsmen, like fish farmers, like conservationists—like *humans*.

They're just like us. Oh shit. They're exactly *like us.*

It was the most fundamentally terrifying thought that Eddie had ever had.

Ralassi chattered with Rit. Eddie's gut churned.

"Minister Rit says that the Northern Assembly may agree to limiting its population using your measures if you help prevent the territory being overrun by other nations."

What was Rit playing at? Creating breathing space for her own state? It was odd to concede that quickly. Maybe she thought Eqbas were like wess'har and didn't negotiate anyway; she might have been placating them to avert total annihilation. That was probably a smart move.

Esganikan tilted her head the other way and her copper-red plume shimmered in the overhead light. "As the Northern Assembly has invited us to find a solution for them, let us begin with the assumption that your region is willing and able to embrace new approaches to ecological balance."

"So what is your strategy?"

"To identify which states and individuals will cooperate, and which will not. To aid those who do. To reduce the population in those states that obstruct the process. And to then enable the remaining population to manage and sustain the restored environment. This is a long project."

"Will you maintain a presence here?"

"If the situation requires it and as long as we are able. We expect free access."

As long as we are able. It was an oddly human disclaimer.

The bee cam hovered. Shan, arms folded across her chest, looked as if she was waiting for a suspect to confess after a long interrogation. Ade stared ahead of him with a completely impassive expression that had probably been honed by long periods standing to attention. Eddie wished he could smell moods and emotion like wess'har could.

Ralassi consulted Rit. "The Northern Assembly may face sanctions for allowing your intervention."

"How will you respond?" asked Esganikan.

Chatter. "If there is a military response, with force. It would be an opportunity for them to acquire more territory and gain access to our water supply. We have the mountainous regions, and so the meltwater and rivers. If there are less direct sanctions—we will respond by limiting water supplies."

Eddie had seen enough wars and their aftermath to work out how many deaths would result in an attack on a city so crowded that pedestrian traffic had its own rules of speed and flow. *I know what a single cannon round from the Eqbas can do.* And there were no plains or open country in which to fight battles. It would be city-to-city war: destructive and inevitably indiscriminate. Isenj knew that, and avoided it.

Esganikan must have known that too. She was a seasoned commander. "Let me speak to the other heads of state."

"Minister Rit asks you to come to her office tomorrow and she will arrange contact with the other states."

Esganikan stood up immediately to leave. Eddie pocketed the bee cam and made a move to intercept Rit, a straight hardwired journalist reflex that didn't consult his brain.

But he found he wanted to talk to her, and not for a quote. This was his friend's widow.

He missed Ual.

Ralassi watched him warily and the minister, a dark quilled ovoid just like her husband and every other isenj Eddie had ever seen, shimmered and tinkled like sapphire wind chimes.

"Do you have children?" Eddie asked.

"The minister says she has two sons."

"Tell her I'm sorry they lost their father and I know they must miss him."

Ralassi interpreted. "She says they have his genetic memories, and hers, and so he will always be with them."

For some reason that hit Eddie very hard and he felt tears prick at his eyes. He wasn't sure if it was because Ual's sacrifice moved him, or whether it reminded him how alone he was. Rit tottered out the door, followed by Ralassi, and Eddie glanced at Shan.

"So what are you going to do with *that* footage?" Shan asked. Ade, standing right behind her, put his hand flat on her back between her shoulder blades as if he was steering her out of the door. "That'll loosen a few sphincters back home."

"I hope so," said Eddie. "Does *anything* scare you? I suppose not."

"We're all scared of something, Eddie."

Ade pushed her gently. "Come on, Boss."

Umeh Station was hardly a diverting place to spend a day, but Ade clearly had ideas. As the two of them walked away, Ade slid his hand down Shan's back and hooked his thumb into the back of her belt. They looked at one another for a brief moment as if they'd suddenly seen each other for the first time and were startled by the moment of revelation.

Aww. Cute. Whatever they saw in each other, it wasn't what the outside world perceived.

Eddie realized he had only Serrimissani for company, waiting beside him like a patient but ill-tempered sheepdog. She'd looked after him during some unpleasant moments; a minder like that meant the difference between life and death when you were reporting in a war zone.

And he'd felt her needle teeth in his flesh, too. Ussissi were *not* cute.

"Weird shit, doll," said Eddie, indicating Ade and Shan. "I know the wess'har are relaxed about all that polyandry stuff, but it still feels weird to me."

"What solitary, possessive creatures you are," said Serrimissani. "Your species' permanent aggression has a root cause, it seems."

Eddie wanted to explain to her that he didn't actually want to be alone, and that humans were gregarious. But looking at the polyandrous and communal species around him, he realized he had far more in common with the isenj than with the people closest to him—his wess'har neighbors, and Shan's bizarre family.

And his homeworld now had more in common with Umeh. Earth was next in line for Eqbas environmental adjustment.

Umeh Station: plant and maintenance level

Umeh Station was like every military base Ade had ever seen except for the lush greenery. It didn't strike him as uncomfortable at all, but then a marine could make a warm bed on pack ice. It was just a matter of the right attitude.

It was almost luxurious here. They still had some dry rations, and Ade could be highly persuasive at procurement when he put his mind to it. It was amazing what people would trade to copy a few movies from his handheld once communication links were restricted.

Beneath the dome, a huge network of underground chambers housed recycling and hydroponics chambers. It was quiet and the passages were softly lit, the silence punctuated only by the faint hum of pumps and drives and the gurgling and clicking of pipes processing waste. He was waiting for Shan. She'd decided to visit the "crushers"— *Actaeon*'s regulating branch personnel—and find out how they maintained order in an overcrowded and sealed society. She needed to be kept busy. An idle Shan was trouble.

"Is that you, Boss?" He could hear her coming; he knew her walk now. He could also smell her, a blend of cedarlike wood and human female musk. *C'naatat* had given him new layers of senses. "I realize this isn't five-star. But it beats trying to find accommodation up top."

He leaned against one of the soil pipes that shunted shit from the lavatories into the separation tanks and filters that turned it into nutrients for vegetables.

"Fine by me." Shan inspected a machinery space with a door and threw her bedroll down on the floor. "Private enough."

"They say people are put off by the thought of the shit moving around down here."

"What, even the naval personnel? I mean, ships' plumbing . . ."

"Civvies, I expect."

"Squeamish buggers." She seemed to have thawed a little. "I used to do obbo duty with a detective sergeant who peed in his coffee flask to avoid getting out of the car."

"Did he finish the coffee first?"

"You could never tell with Baz. Or his coffee."

"Yeah, I got stuck on surveillance a few times. Had to piss where I was, flat on the ground."

"Don't they bag you?"

"Do you really want to know?"

That was what he liked about Shan. It wasn't just that he wanted her; he felt *easy* with her. She was blunt and uncomplicated, and he never had to guess what she was thinking. She had that same unflinching vulgarity as his mates.

So he could say what was on his mind. He was sure of it. *Almost.*

"I really am sorry about Rayat, Boss."

"I know."

"You feel you have to do something about it."

"If you were me, wouldn't you want to be sure that having two more *c'naatat* carriers on the loose isn't going to make this situation any worse?"

"Yeah."

"And you're pissed off because I'm going to second-guess you when I said I never would?"

"No."

"Look, I know you had to make the call there and then. God knows I hate armchair critics and hindsight myself." She unfastened her hair from the band that held it in a ponytail and raked it with her fingers before tying it back again. "I don't want to be at war with you, Ade. You, me and Aras. That's all there is. All there's ever *going* to be for a bloody long, long time. We need to make this work."

"Is that a pardon, then?"

"One thing I've learned from the wess'har is that there's

no point fretting about the past when you could be sorting out the future. Outcomes. Not motive."

"Meaning?"

"I'll go and find the bezeri and see what's happening. If it isn't working out the way you and Aras planned, I'll do what I have to do to remove the hazard."

"Are you going to tell Eddie?"

"That's one complication I don't need at the moment."

Ade knew Shan would dispose of Rayat and Lindsay without a second thought. He began working out how he could make a fragmentation device that would work under water. It was the kind of thing that Izzy and Sue were good at; it might keep them occupied for a while.

"I'll help you if you want," he said.

"Thanks."

"I know it's a mess, and I know motives don't matter, but I did it because I love you."

Shan nodded. "You're right. I *did* run out on Aras, whatever my reason."

It was as if she hadn't taken in what he'd said, or decided she would ignore it. He felt stupid. He'd inherited brief flashes of the most vivid of her memories—the awful ones with the gorilla and the riot shield and the boiling cold vacuum of space—and he knew that if he slept with her, he would eventually absorb others, and maybe even taste what she really thought of him.

What if she's just sorry for me? Or that she thinks I'm useless and she's just being kind?

He wondered if she had any sense of how extraordinary she was. All he'd picked up from her memory was that she thought she was smarter than everyone else and wished they'd stop pissing her off by being stupid. He wondered if he'd ever fallen into that category. There was no sign of it, but he'd looked.

"Sorry, Ade. I ought to be grateful." Shan sounded genuinely regretful. "If it's any comfort, I treated Aras like shit too. I'm just not good at receiving affection."

"We're all under a lot of stress, Boss. Even if you won't

admit it." He caught her hand and held it, not sure if she actually understood how much he loved her. He couldn't think of a word for what he felt other than *love;* but it was one-dimensional, inadequate, a word worn thin on ordinary women. He wanted a word you could present to a goddess. He needed a word that would make her understand that he now couldn't bear to let her out of his sight and that the intensity of the emotion pressed so heavily on his chest that sometimes he couldn't even swallow. "This bloody situation is almost too much to think about sometimes. That's why I just concentrate on what's in front of me."

"Yeah. Interplanetary war, genocide, immortality and Earth's next. When you put it like that, the pucker factor is off the scale." Shan's gaze was fixed on his hands, clasped around hers. Then she looked up and smiled at him. The world-weary copper had disappeared for a few moments: he was looking into a trusting, open face that had never seen pain or depravity, or looked upon her own acts of almost indescribable violence. "And the food's bloody awful. That takes my mind off the rest sometimes."

"Yes it's amazing what you can put up with if the scran's okay." Her expression defaulted to her detective mode, that intense unblinking stare. He had to let go of her hand to fumble in his shirt pocket. "Look what I blagged off the supply officer. Fresh garlic."

He rattled a little pouch of four heads of pink-skinned corms. Shan looked at it as if it was evidence and held out her hand. He placed it in her palm.

"We plant them the minute we get back," she said.

"I thought I'd cook something with them."

"When we can grow our own supply from these? I can't ask the colonists for any of theirs, not now."

"Okay. You never were one for instant gratification." The phrase felt unfamiliar in his mouth and he wondered if he was now absorbing her speech patterns. "But I'll keep one in reserve for cooking."

"What did you trade for this?"

"Movie files."

She put on her copper's face again, instantly wary and questioning. "I didn't know you had a stash of porn."

"I don't. It's all comedy."

"Sorry. I should have guessed."

"I'm a good boy, Boss."

Ade teetered on the cliff edge again. She'd said *yes* ages ago. She said she'd sleep with him. There was nobody else a man with *c'naatat* could have; the parasite spread like a dose of clap. But that step from the agreement in principle to making the first move seemed as daunting as ever.

Come on. She's seen you throw up and crap yourself in a tight spot and she's even seen you starkers, tattoos and all. You even shot *her, for Chrissakes. And now you're worried she'll laugh at you?*

"If it's any comfort, Ade, I'm scared too."

I can make my life normal. I can do all the things regular people do. It'll rewrite my past. "Coppers are telepaths, aren't they?"

"Trade secret. It's a combination of knowing who you're dealing with and watching the tells. You know. The body language. The little facial movements."

She thrust her hands in her pockets. No, she wasn't good at this. No better than he was, in fact.

Shit.

He reached into his belt pouch. Everything he owned now added up to his fighting knife, his mother's wedding ring and his medals. An unromantic fuck in the miserable bowels of an offworld base surrounded by a sewage processing plant wasn't exactly how he'd planned to seduce the love of his life, but there was never going to be anywhere more glamorous. And it beat doing it back home with Aras in the next room. Maybe wess'har thought that kind of thing was normal, but Ade felt it would take a *long* time for him to see it that way.

He grabbed her hand, took the ring and slid it onto her finger. It was loose. She stared at it.

"Jesus, Ade, is that your mum's ring?"

"Yeah." *Oh God.* That was just so wrong. *I wanted it to be meaningful.* "Sorry. It's the best I can do."

"I'm touched." She didn't meet his eyes. "Really. I am. I don't know what to say."

"I know this is pretty grim."

"So I'll do it for a pair of boots, a bit of garlic and a ring, right?"

"Boss, I never—"

"Just a joke," she said. "Honestly. Just a joke"

She laughed. She wasn't the giggly sort and Ade knew that kind of laughter from a hundred near-misses when the firing stopped. This should have been a nice dinner in a smart restaurant and a comfortable bed: but the waste macerator started up behind him with an eloquent shudder of drives, and he almost burst out laughing too. His eyes stung with suppressed tears.

"In case you're worried, I was sterilized ages ago."

"I'm missing a few essential parts too." Shan blinked a few times. "Get on with it, then. I'm not going to be any better looking tomorrow."

Oh God. How would things have turned out if I'd done this when I first had the chance, before c'naatat *was ever an issue?*

"Romance isn't dead," said Ade. "But it's not feeling very well at the moment."

"It's not doing too bad," said Shan. "All things considered."

F'nar, Wess'ej

Rats didn't live long. Shan had warned Aras about that, but he still felt sorrow at Black's decline.

He held the animal on his lap, cushioned on a pad of hemp fabric salvaged from Constantine. Black had never attempted to bite him but Aras took the precaution of wearing gloves to avoid passing on *c'naatat* if Black did decide to nip him. The rat's flanks heaved; his ribs were visible under black fur now rusty with age, and his tiny nostrils were rimmed with red stains. He had respiratory failure.

Aras had seen generations of humans die in the Constantine colony. He had outlived them just as he had outlived every one of his wess'har kin, and he had even outlived comrades he'd infected with *c'naatat* before anyone realized exactly what it did. He was the only wess'har host who hadn't been fragmented in battle or finally taken his own life out of desperate isolation.

I outlive everyone. My first isan, *my human friends, my wess'har neighbors. And these rats.*

It never got any easier.

He glanced up at the divided cage that housed the rat colony. Several small whiskered faces were staring at him. One rat had its paw flat on the softglass side of the cage, and it looked so much like a human hand that Aras expected the animal to gesture to him.

Black would recover if I gave him a little of my blood.

But it was wrong, and unnatural, and fraught with consequences; not 'least for Black, living forever while his comrades died, deprived of mate and offspring. It was a lonely life sentence. Aras had succumbed once and taken that step to save Shan's life. Would he have done it again so that the bezeri could have their penance from Lindsay and Rayat? He came close. Ade had made the choice in the end. It was a decision you could take in a second and regret—or not—forever.

As soon as he could, he'd return to Bezer'ej and find the remnant of the bezeri. He *had* to know what was happening there. After five hundred years, the world was still part of him.

Black stirred and Aras ran his fingers over the rat's head. Eventually, Black's flanks stopped heaving and he gave a little twitch, eyes still half open. Aras could feel a fluttering heartbeat and then nothing, and for a while he pondered the line between life and death and found it harder to define than ever. When he looked up, White—Black's constant companion—had thrust his muzzle through the grid of plastic that formed the cage door.

The rat knew what had happened to his friend. Aras had no idea how to communicate with a rat, but he assumed they grieved, grieving being part of the instinct of any communal animal. All creatures responded to the death of their offspring or the comrades on whom they depended; it was a necessary reaction, the organism's way of ensuring that essential bonds were maintained. Why humans thought it was a spiritual act peculiar to them, Aras had never understood. They had no idea about the nature of emotions and brain chemistry at all.

I miss Shan.

She had been away less than a day. But she was coming back, and he reminded himself how it had felt to think she was dead. The longing eased a little. He wondered if he was not so much missing her as regretting the loss of his exclusive relationship with her. But that was *human*. It was . . . jealousy.

You wanted a housebrother badly. You wanted a normal wess'har life again— isan, *housebrothers, children. You can't have children, but you have everything else. Be grateful.*

Aras took Black's corpse in his hands and laid it on the table. The he pulled on his tunic and took his *tilgir* from the hook on the wall.

The bluff outside the city was a hard climb or a long walk, and Aras opted for the walk because it was easier with tools in his belt and a dead rat in his pocket. At the top of the lava cliff, the cairn of pearl-coated rocks that Ade had built as a memorial for Shan still stood intact. Shan didn't seem to mind seeing it there, although it must have been strange to gaze upon your own headstone. Aras surveyed the winter landscape for a few minutes, noting the fine haze of low-growing foliage that had sprung up after the rain, and then made his way up the long steep incline that wound its way up to the top.

He hadn't expected to run into Nevyan at the summit.

The young matriarch knelt on her heels, hands clasped in her lap as she contemplated the view.

"I didn't know you came here," said Aras.

Nevyan looked up at him. "I followed Ade Bennett here once. The view is soothing. Why have you come?"

"I have to bury someone." Aras took Black's body from his pocket and cupped it in his hands. The little animal felt heavier than he had been in life. "One of the rats has died."

"Are the others upset?"

"I think so."

"Can you comfort them?"

"I don't know how."

Nevyan held out her hands to take Black while Aras drew his *tilgir* to hack a shallow grave in the thin layer of soil. A *srebil* might scavenge the rat's body, alien though its biochemistry was. Few humans liked the idea of disposal by predation, but it was the wess'har way. Did *srebil've* know how to dig? Aras knew they had long, hard proboscises and single sharp claws, so they would find a way.

Do I tell Nevyan about Lindsay and Rayat?

Aras decided to stay silent. He wasn't deceiving her or even concealing the fact. It was simply irrelevant; she could do nothing, and it was no threat to her. The problem was one for Esganikan to consider and deal with.

"Shan surprises me," said Nevyan.

"How?" Aras judged the depth of the tiny grave, even smaller than the one he had dug on Bezer'ej for Lindsay Neville's baby son. "You seem anxious."

"I didn't expect her to share the Eqbas view of interference."

"Shan believes she has to act. Targassat does say that those having choices must make them."

Nevyan turned her head slowly. She was very much Mestin's daughter, but he could see the echo of her father in her too, even though she had the genes of all of Mestin's husbands. "I expected her to be like us because she's my friend. Perhaps that was naive."

"You mean that you like what's like yourself."

"I thought she chose us because she agreed with us."

Did she have that choice? I infected her. She thought she had to stay, and so did I. "It's hard to tell with humans. They tend to comply with their social group. That isn't quite the same as consensus."

"But she believes in ecological balance. Every decision she's ever made has been based on that. She put it before her own life."

Aras laid Black in the grave. The body was cool and growing rigid now. Aras wanted to know what a rat thought and how it saw the world and those who persecuted its kind, but he didn't know how he might discover that. He covered the body with soil and pebbles as carefully as he could and stood back to consider the nature of death again.

"Shan believes that walking away is not the way to deal with problems," he said. "She intervenes."

"But as wess'har we confront threats to ourselves and others. We do *not* walk away."

"But we do as Targassat advised. We don't seek out wrongs to put them right, we just respond to pleas. Our forebears left Eqbas Vorhi because they disliked interventionist policies, but we didn't actually improve the universe a great deal by doing that. We just salved our consciences."

Nevyan now smelled deeply, acidly unhappy. The warm powdery scent of contentment that she normally exuded these days had vanished. Unlike Shan, she wasn't able to suppress her scent signals. It wasn't surprising she was under stress; she was very young, the dominant matriarch due to an accidental burst of dominance hormone—of *jask*—when she heard Shan was dead. She had inadvertently displaced her mother in the pecking order of *isan've,* but the fact that Shan had survived couldn't alter what had happened. Nevyan, as Ade put it, had the ball. And she had summoned the Eqbas to help deal with the human threat.

And now she was regretting it, Aras suspected. Events were overtaking her. It was a feeling he found all too familiar.

"Do you resent Shan?" he asked.

"No."

"But you're concerned that she seems to be friendly with Esganikan Gai."

"I fear losing my friend again, but she will be more than dead this time. She'll be an instrument of enforced ideology."

"And you want her to adopt the ideology of Targassat. Of nonintervention." Aras enjoyed these logic loops. He'd spent five hundred years in exile, more than three hundred of them entirely on his own except for the occasional encounter with bezeri. He'd had plenty of time to think himself in circles. "Your *own* enforcement of ideology, in fact."

"I can't fault your argument."

"You're afraid of the Eqbas and you're worried that Shan will return to Earth with them."

"Yes."

"Shan won't leave me. I know that now. And she feels responsibility for the fate of her homeworld much as I still feel for Bezer'ej. Neither of us is good at walking away."

"Preventing Earth being a threat is one thing. Adjusting its environment is another entirely."

"But they requested it. Even Targassat would have agreed that the planet is in need of adjustment."

Nevyan got to her feet and dusted down her opalescent white *dhren,* the traditional *isan*'s robe that Shan declined to wear. "I suspect I feel afraid because Giyadas is interested in Shan's ideas. We've maintained our position for ten thousand years and change is alarming."

"F'nar is just one city. And we can handle new ideas."

"Tell me, Aras. Have I made a serious mistake?"

The rest of Wess'ej took no part in relations with aliens, although their military backing was there if Nevyan called for it. They were a small population—too small to handle peacekeeping across the system indefinitely and deal with humans once and for all.

"I don't think you had any other choice," said Aras.

They set off down the slope. Life had changed out of all recognition for both of them since he had been the custodian of the bezeri and Nevyan's mother Mestin had been garrison commander of Bezer'ej.

But neither Matriarch would be around when the consequences of the Eqbas expansion into new systems were felt. That would be many, many years in the future.

He'd still be here, though. And so would Nevyan's descendants.

Umeh Station: plant and machinery level

The thrum of the generator was hypnotic.

Shan drifted in a pleasant drowsy haze and wondered how a piece of machinery could produce such a soothing white noise effect. Somehow it erased all her worries, and there were a lot of them jostling for attention lately.

But maybe it was Ade's influence, the simple normality of a male of her own species. She rested her chin on the top of his head, enjoying the brushlike sensation of short hair and the scent of male skin and lemon soap. She couldn't get up because he'd wrapped himself around her, and she didn't really want to move anyway.

"Don't fall asleep," she said. "I need to go to the toilet."

"Not falling asleep . . ."

"Are."

"I'm comfortable, 's' all . . ."

"Yeah." He was playing with the ring on her finger, turning it slowly around her knuckle. *That's how he copes. He focuses on normal things. If he can't find any, he creates them.* "It is, isn't it?"

Ade reminded her that she was human. However strongly she was bonded to Aras, however enjoyable she found his body, Ade was exactly what she had evolved to want; a human male. Everything in her that was still human said *yes, this is right, this is what you should be doing.* She found him comfortable in every sense of the word. He stopped fidgeting with the ring and she put her hand on his biceps. Human skin felt hotter than a wess'har's, warm satin rather than cool delicate suede. She hoped she wouldn't see Aras any differently now.

"Look at your hands," Ade whispered.

"Uh?"

"Hands."

She opened her eyes and focused. Violet and blue lights rippled in her skin and made her fingers appear backlit. It was only when she moved her hand that she realized light was also coming from the tattoo on his upper arm. The lines of pigment seemed to float in a violet glow. She'd seen the effect before; Ade had tattoos in some intriguing places.

He twisted his arm to peer at it. "Why does it do that?"

"No idea. Communicating, maybe." She thought of the illuminated bulkhead display in Esganikan's ship, and how her hands had flared into light when she touched it as if somehow answering it. "Funny how it gravitates towards your tattoos and not your hands."

"What's it saying?"

"Possibly nothing. Might just be a reflex."

"See, I asked Nevyan if *c'naatat* could think. And she didn't seem to want to know if it did. *I* do."

Shan tried to think of her parasite as bacteria. If she started ascribing sentience to it, then it said things like *tapeworm* and *fetus* to her. She didn't like the idea of either. That was invasion, violation, possession.

"One way or the other, it makes optimal choices. And some bloody weird ones."

Ade settled his head back on her chest. "Does it scare you wondering what it's going to do next?"

"It used to. Sometimes it tries something out and then removes it. Aras said he had vestigial wings once."

"No shit?"

"Seriously."

"Jesus. A glow-in-the-dark dick doesn't seem too bad by comparison."

"It even seems to give you what you want, sometimes."

"I never wanted landing lights."

"It totally redesigned Aras. Maybe he felt more at home being human."

"He was stuck with a bunch of humans. He likes to belong."

"He was stuck with the bezeri, but he never turned into a squid."

Ade appeared to ponder that for a while. She could see him frowning slightly. *C'naatat* had given her wess'har vision; she saw in very low light and there were blues in her spectrum that she had never seen before as a human, as well as ultraviolet. Sometimes she could see infrared. And she wasn't aware of switching between modes. It just . . . happened. She didn't like her body doing things without her consent. She'd have to work out how to control it.

"How do we make this work?" Ade asked.

"What?"

"When we go home. Me and Aras. You."

Yes, she'd thought about it. Her brain said *rota* and that appalled her. "How do you *want* it to work?"

"Sundays off?"

"Ha bloody ha. I'm sure we'll think of something."

"And you don't have to suppress your scent."

"Is this a list?"

"Sort of. You don't need to hide what you feel. Not with me and Aras, anyway. We can work it out for ourselves."

"Go on."

"And don't feel you owe me anything, Boss."

She knew she ought to be angry with him. Something kept tapping her on the shoulder and reminding her that he'd handed over *c'naatat* and that she had to fret about it. Another part of her brain said *so what—you'll deal with it.*

Of *course* she owed him something. If she hadn't headbutted him, he wouldn't have caught the bloody thing. And he made her feel as good about herself as she ever had. She owed him a *lot.*

"Do you *have* to call me Boss?"

"Guv'nor?"

"I don't want to be Superintendent Frankland when I'm on my back, to be honest."

"Okay, Mrs. Bennett." He raised his head and gave her a noisily enthusiastic kiss. "And I bet you don't like that name, either."

"Fine by me," she said. Yes, it was. "No problem at all."

Ade made a satisfied rumble in his throat and rolled over,

pulling her into his side. Something itched at the back of her mind. It felt almost like the Suppressed Briefing she'd been given three years ago, anamnesis chemically locked out of reach of her conscious mind until triggered by events. Now others' headline memories sometimes intruded on her own recollections: Aras's time as a prisoner of the isenj, Ade's brutal father, his comrade Dave getting shot beside him and the warm splash of greasy brain tissue on his face as if it were her own skin. It was impossible to know anyone better than that. Maybe that was what was making her more tolerant of Ade and Aras right now; she lived out the worst parts of their lives.

Would I have been a more sympathetic copper if I'd lived criminals' lives? Whoa, forget that. Crime, not motivation. Think of the victims. Dead's dead, raped is raped, and if your assailant puts you in a coma, his apology won't revive you. Outcomes, like the wess'har say. Only outcomes.

So it didn't matter what Ade or Aras had done if *c'naatat* was confined to Bezer'ej, and the bezeri had what they wanted.

Why can't I actually remember being an isenj or any of the other hosts this bloody thing has been through?

Ade's breathing settled into the slow rhythm of sleep, and the generator's murmur washed away the day. Shan wondered what Eddie was up to and what Esganikan was going to do when the rest of the isenj balked at the idea of reducing their population, as they surely would.

Bloody lights. She stared at her glowing hand in increasing defocus. The wreathed globe tattoo on Ade's arm flickered a response to it.

Could be worse.

Could be . . . worse.

Umeh Station vanished. She found herself having a conversation with Baz-the-Bastard, dead for decades, an old colleague. He watched her bite the end off the soya-dog.

"Shan, you got to do it *gently*," he said. "This is why you never get lucky. No *technique*."

"Piss off," she murmured. For some reason it was daytime Reading Metro outside the unmarked squad car but the interior was in semi-darkness. They were on obbo on observation duty, waiting for signs of activity in the house opposite, which she knew was there but still couldn't see.

"Why didn't you listen to me when I told you not to drive drunk?" Yes, she knew he was long dead; but it was the unreadable readout on the dashboard display that told her she was dreaming and it was too late to talk sense into Baz. "Daft fucker. You should know better."

"You're okay," he said, ignoring her scolding. "You'll do fine."

Then the windscreen dissolved into black, open, star-speckled space and the absolute cold and vacuum swallowed her and silenced her scream. A weight pressed on her shoulder. She thought it was Baz and wondered how he'd managed to follow her into the void, just like Vijissi did.

A distant explosion in her head jerked her awake and she found she was sitting upright, wide awake.

"Shit," said Ade.

He was sitting bolt upright too. Without conversation they scrambled to their feet at the same time and began dressing. They both knew what an explosion sounded like. It wasn't in her dream; it had *happened*.

"Better go and check that out," said Ade. He fastened his boots and grabbed his rifle. "Even if Esganikan has it covered."

He sprinted down the narrow passage between the banks of pipework and up the stairs, Shan right behind him for a change. She had her 9mm in her hand and didn't even remember drawing it; she couldn't imagine what use it might be in whatever situation she was about to face, but the muscle memory born of long practice took over. When they reached the ground level, still dimly illuminated with the nighttime safety lighting, a crowd had already gathered and was looking up into the transparent bowl of the dome itself.

It took Shan a few seconds to realize what they were watching. The next flare of brilliant white light and a muffled crack almost like lightning gave her a clue.

There was no sign of any Eqbas crew members.

Oh shit, she's shelling Jejeno. Esganikan's started already.

It was Shan's immediate thought. Through a gap in the vine that covered most of the interior roof supports, the Eqbas ship was briefly picked out in a white-hot halo, smoothly bronze with pulsing chevrons of red and blue light in a line around its hull.

"That's missiles," said Ade. He made for the main doors and Shan followed. "Christ, what's Eddie doing?"

Eddie stood at the doors, face pressed against the transparent sheet as if to get a better view. Shan looked for his bee cam: there was no sign of it.

"I need to go outside and have a look," he said. "You coming too?"

"Eddie, stay put," said Shan.

"Okay, then take my bee cam, will you?" Shan was aware of something plummeting towards her from overhead and she ducked instinctively. The bee cam streaked past her and came to a sudden and unnatural halt by Eddie's head. He didn't even flinch; he was used to the bloody thing, but she knew that one day she'd fire at it in pure reflex. "It can't get a decent shot through the top of the canopy. Needs to be an exterior."

"Okay." Ade hit the airlock controls and the inner doors parted. "Just stay where you are."

"It's probably safe outside." Eddie looked more exasperated than alarmed. Shan now filed him in that select group of people who ran towards trouble rather than away from it. He was one of her own. "None of that is going to get through the barrier. Seen it before."

It was only when Shan got a few meters outside and had a clear look at the night sky that she realized what he meant. The Eqbas ship was taking hits and the detonations seemed to be dispersing around it.

"That's not triple-A," said Ade. "It's air platform. Fighters. Look."

Shan let Eddie's bee cam fly free and shoved her gun in the back of her belt. Now she could pick out streaks of light in the sky, and what had sounded like an explosion was the sound of an aircraft's weapon discharging. The Eqbas ship was on station at a much higher altitude than she'd thought, perhaps two thousand meters. A narrow shape picked out in faint red light shot towards it and ejected a stream of white plasma that hit an invisible barrier and sprayed in all directions like a starburst firework. There was a second of absolute silence. Then a rumble on the lower threshold of her hearing rose in pitch until it sounded like a distant whining turbine.

Five small bolts of yellow light spread from one end of the Eqbas ship and there were five scattered detonations. She thought she saw lights streak up from the ground too, but they were swallowed in the peppering of explosions. Where there had been vague black-on-black outlines of fighter craft, there was now flaming, spiraling debris falling towards her.

She ducked instinctively as Ade cannoned into her and the first chunk struck. His arm was pressed hard across her back, holding her down.

It was oddly quiet now: just a faint drumming and pinging, far away, like hail on tiles.

She looked at Ade for a moment, waiting for impact and then realized there wasn't going to be one. The Eqbas shield—almost invisible, totally impervious—sent the debris skidding and ricocheting across the city.

Nothing landed on the concrete around them. Flame and glowing fragments rained down on Jejeno, just a hundred meters away, and the smaller chunks that hit the shield simply vaporized and the larger ones bounced.

Shan knelt back on her heels and watched, flinching despite herself. Hardwired animal fear of fire was hard to shake.

"Riot shield," said Ade.

"What?"

"Yours. Petrol bombs hitting your riot shield. I'm remembering it too. Jesus what a—"

He was interrupted by a muffled explosion and a column of flame rising in the city beyond. That was what happened when fighters were shot down over a crowded city. Shan's training said *emergency, casualties, go and sort it, call it in,* but she checked herself.

"So much for the bloody minister's assurances." She straightened her jacket. All the blissful postcoital haze had vanished, leaving her edgy and pumping adrenaline. "Stupid bastards. There won't be much of Jejeno left in the morning."

"It wasn't them," said Ade. He looked her over as if searching for injury. "Didn't you see the triple-A go up? That wasn't aimed at the ship. It was targeting the fighters."

"So who started it? What if that's the Northern Assembly army staging a coup?"

The Eqbas ship now looked like a rather pretty bronze barrage balloon. The pulsing belt of chevrons had slowed and was almost static. Then a large, sharply defined plume of yellow light—more of an ovoid—emerged from the forward section of the hull and seemed to gather speed as it moved away and then disappeared. Shan didn't hear it strike anything.

"I dread to think what *that* is," said Shan.

"Long-range missile," said Ade.

"What makes you say that?"

"Just guessing. It's what we might do if someone launched an air strike from a neighboring territory."

"Jesus. Civil war."

"Maybe. I don't know where their borders are. Do you know anything about isenj geopolitics?"

"No, but I think a crash course is long overdue."

There's a war starting. Oh my god, here we go.

Shan marveled at how easy it was to stand under a defense shield that was as far beyond her technical comprehension as magic and not panic when parts of the city outside were burning. Ironically, a well-placed explosion could do what drowning, spacing and a bullet through the head couldn't: it could actually kill her. She wondered if it had now totally distorted her assessment of danger.

"What's happening?" Eddie called. He was pacing at the open airlock, clearly in two minds about disobeying her instruction to stay inside.

"How do I know, for Chrissakes?"

"Can I go off camp?"

"Yeah, get your head blown off, Eddie. Go ahead, mate."

"Look." Ade stood staring up at the sky, hands on hips. "They're shuttling down. Must be all clear."

Eddie strode out the doors and his bee cam dropped from the upper level of the shield to hover by his head. Two bronze sections of ship descended and settled on the service road.

When Esganikan stepped out she smelled faintly of *jask*. Shan bristled at the unconscious challenge, a matriarchal reaction to the pheromone. But it wasn't directed at her.

"What was all that about?" asked Shan.

Esganikan rocked her head from side to side, a slight movement that always put Shan in mind of a oriental dancer. She had seen Nevyan do it; wess'har annoyance. Esganikan was pissed off.

"The attack came from the Maritime Fringe. They are prepared to invade Northern Assembly airspace, it seems. That changed my plans."

"How?" said Eddie, who seemed to think every conversation was an interview.

"If the government here is unable to deal with them," said Esganikan, "we will pacify the Maritime Fringe ourselves."

"Pacify," Shan said carefully. "So you really *have* launched missiles, then?"

"The Fringe has a military base at Buyg, about a hundred kilometers from here." Esganikan watched Eddie's bee cam, and Ade watched her. She glanced up at her ship as if calculating. "In a few minutes, much of Buyg will no longer exist."

F'nar, Wess'ej

Aras slept more deeply in his sporadic naps these days but the hammering at the door woke him instantly.

He'd barred it. Even Shan didn't attempt to lock the door

now. Sometimes he did things at the bidding of a memory that wasn't his. When he opened the door, a female ussissi stood staring up at him.

"What are you afraid of?" she demanded.

"*Shan Chail* prefers doors secured." Aras held the door wide open but the ussissi remained at the threshold. His mind raced: had something happened to Shan? Why had they sent a ussissi to tell him? "Why are you here?"

"We found him. We found Vijissi."

Mestin's dead ussissi aide had been located. They'd been searching for his body for months. He'd done exactly as the matriarch had told him: he'd stayed at Shan's side, looking after her on Mestin's behalf until the bitter end. He'd followed her through the airlock to terrible death.

"I'll let Shan know," said Aras. And that wouldn't be easy. She felt responsible for his death and said he was a *silly little sod* for trying to protect her, which was her way of saying that his death had upset her greatly. "She'll be relieved." A thought crossed his mind. "And he's dead, yes?"

"No, he is alive," said the ussissi. "Why else would I run all this way to tell you?"

Aras was surprised: not that Vijissi had survived spacing just as Shan had done, and that the aide was clearly infected with *c'naatat*, but that the news had not stunned him. It had merely depressed him, because now there was one more *c'naatat* carrier, and the parasite had spread to a third species.

It only took one impossible return from the dead to inure him to miracles.

6

*When do you say, "This is how things should be"? At what
point in its history do you consider a world to be balanced,
to be as it should be? Life evolves, and becomes extinct
through meteor strike, through natural disasters, through all
manner of events that have nothing to do with the misbe-
havior of the dominant species. Where do you draw the line
between the imbalance caused by one species and the natural course of events? I ask again: How do you decide what
should be restored? All we can be sure of is that as long as
we exist, we should be aware of those life-forms with fewer
choices than ourselves, and tread as lightly and as thought-
fully as we are able. All else is artificial intervention, one
opinion set above another. There is no single point of perfect balance.*

Wess'har philosopher Targassat,
on the policies of Eqbas Vorhi

Bezer'ej: south of the Mountains to the Dry Above, formerly known as the Ouzhari chain of islands

The sea around Rayat was growing lighter and greener.
Sunlight was penetrating the water: they were nearing the
surface. Decompression wasn't a problem for a *c'naatat*-
infected human.

He could sense Lindsay ahead of him, keeping pace with
the pumping, flashing mantles of the three male bezeri leading them, and she still had the damn signal lamp. If he was
going to talk with the creatures then he either had to negotiate with her, take it from her, or hope to God that he developed the same bioluminescence that Frankland had—and
that he could learn to use it to communicate.

So what are you going to say to them, exactly?

There had to be a way off Bezer'ej, and the one advantage he had now was that time didn't count for him. He could wait. No other government or corporation could lay hands on *c'naatat*. He could hold on to it now until they came for him—once he could get word out—or until he found an escape route.

His fear had started to ebb. There was nothing quite like obsessive focus to keep you going, and he cherished his.

Lindsay trod water to bring herself to a halt and turned to face him, the signal lamp hooked over her belt. Rayat was suddenly aware that he was now looking at her in the visual spectrum. The density and contour images had faded.

"Come on," she said. "Keep up."

And he heard her, really *heard* her. He was more certain of how he was sensing the world now. He concentrated, trying to work out how he had changed in the time he had been submerged. How long had they been down here? He had no watch. He was hungry, but not ravenous—so it wasn't days, unless *c'naatat* overrode hunger too.

So where did I get the ability to sense beyond the visual spectrum? How does this all work?

"I'm right here," he said. "What are they doing?"

"They're taking us to see something."

He'd hoped it was lunch. He resigned himself to watching what they ate and doing the same.

Am I using sonar? Detecting magnetic fields? Sensing chemicals in the water?

He'd had no direct contact with the bezeri. The contaminated blood had come from Adrian Bennett, and he must have contracted it from Frankland, and Frankland had the bezeri lights. Aras didn't seem to have them. Neither did the marine as far as he knew. So how did *c'naatat* choose which genes to express?

As long as he concentrated on the science, he could stay calm.

The sunlight punched shafts through the drifting red weed above them, creating clouds of garnet and ruby, and the bezeri stopped to hang in the water. The largest of them, the patriarch Saib, rippled with scattered pinpoints of light. The lamp spoke in a disembodied genderless voice.

This is as far as we can go. We want you to retrieve our maps.

Lindsay aimed the lamp back. "Why can't you go any further?"

This is a contaminated area. The poison levels may be too high for us, but not for you.

Rayat wondered how they worked out the radiation levels. They didn't seem to have any technology except the podships that Aras mentioned. Maybe they just counted the bodies and drew their own conclusions.

"There's a contamination clean-up team from Eqbas there," said Lindsay.

Saib rippled. *And they are on the largest of the Mountains to the Dry Above. But still the area is too dangerous for us. Do as I ask.*

"Okay," said Lindsay. "Where will we find the maps?"

You will see an entrance. There are chambers within. Carry out as many maps as you can and bring them back here.

Rayat interrupted. "Where are we? We must be somewhere near Christopher Island."

"At least call it Ouzhari, you bastard," said Lindsay.

That is not our name for it.

"What is it, then?"

The Smallest Mountain to the Dry Above.

"Thank you," said Rayat. "Very descriptive."

Saib and his companions hung back while Lindsay made her way through the submerged reef. Rayat followed her. *Are there predators down here?* He knew he wouldn't wander into a cave in a terrestrial sea without checking on the size and appetite of the local wildlife. What happened if the niche equivalent of a shark here contracted *c'naatat?* Risks occurred to him now that had never crossed his mind before, and the parasite began to look rather different.

You'll just have to be bloody careful, won't you?

The entrance was as obvious as the bezeri had said. It was

ten meters high, and instead of being a natural cave as Rayat had expected it was an excavated opening flanked by carved stone inlaid with colored material. Had the bezeri made this? They were capable of impressive construction, then. He followed Lindsay inside and as his eyes adjusted to the gloom he saw shelves lining the walls, most of them stacked with small flat sheets of what looked like glass.

And he could taste something unpleasant. It was like inhaling a bad smell, except that it was passing through his mouth and he had an urge to spit it out.

"There must be thousands," said Lindsay. She edged forward and then stopped in her tracks. "Oh God . . ."

"What?"

"Oh God, *bodies*." She looked down. She must have trodden on them. He could only see vague outlines; so that was the source of the foul taste. "Oh no . . ."

"Hey, get a grip. Steady."

"Do me a favor and shut up, will you? Don't you feel *any* sense of remorse for this?"

"I do, actually. But I don't regard your ritual wailing as a productive use of energy."

"You know, I think Shan had the right idea when she kicked the crap out of you. Shame she didn't finish the job."

"But she didn't. And now you're stuck with me."

Lindsay turned back to the shelves and drifted along them, picking out plates of what appeared to be resin. They were about thirty centimeters across with beveled edges.

"They're glass," she said. "They're *sand*."

Rayat didn't understand her at first but when he took one of the objects from the nearest shelf he found that she was right; they felt like lightweight glass with a layer of colored sand sandwiched between them. The sand was arranged in intricate designs, some of which looked like charts and others which seemed to be abstract symbols. Rayat took as many as he could carry and made his way back to Saib.

"Extraordinary," said Rayat.

Saib simply hung there. Without the signal lamp, there

was no possibility of conversation. Rayat laid the maps on
the seabed in front of the bezeri patriarch.

"What are they?"

Saib's mantle rippled with swirls of blue and gold light
like a wheel rotating. Rayat watched. Damn, didn't *c'naatat*
have anything that would help him understand this creature? He looked at his own hands and longed to see some
glimmer of light in them just like that bitch Frankland had.
If the genes were in her, then they would be in him now. He
wanted those lights. He wanted them *badly.*

"Try this," said Lindsay, laying a stack of maps on the
mud. She held the signal lamp in range but she didn't relin-
quish her hold on it. She had to put it down sooner or later.
And what powered it? It was going to run out eventually.

But Rayat could wait. He tried again.

"What are these?"

Maps and histories, said Saib.

"How do you make glass?"

*These are layers of azin shell. They are ancient, the old-
est of our records. Clans and territories, all their names
and deeds.*

"You commemorate them."

*Without these records, there is nothing to show we have
ever existed. They may yet be all that remains of us.*

"We do the same thing." Rayat thought of all the memorials on Earth, the painstaking records of genocide and ceno-
taphs and gravestones. Yes, names mattered. "I understand."

*Now you will answer my questions. What is this conta-
gion? Why was it worth more than our lives?*

"Because it's dangerous. It would end up destroying whole
worlds."

Our world is *destroyed. And the contagion still exists. We
died for nothing.*

Rayat wanted to say that the end had been achieved, that
Bezer'ej was now quarantined, and that *c'naatat* was now
effectively safe in the hands of the FEU; but it wouldn't
have made sense to a bezeri. He wasn't sure right then that
it made sense to him.

He picked up one of the azin shells and wondered how they managed to make the seal watertight and place the colored sand so accurately. The shades were graduated so finely that they appeared almost like a painting; the maps clear and crisp, with vividly colored symbols and lines. The next one he examined was a very accurate representation of the underwater landscape.

Rayat recognized it. He recognized the type of weed and the dark red things clinging to the rocks that might have been plants or shellfish or anything in between.

So they see the world pretty well as I can see it.

Rayat experienced a disturbing and profound sense of connection. His scalp tightened and he found himself looking into the bezeri's mantle to seek eyes. Terrestrial cephalopods had eyes, eyes made the same way as a human's.

Oh God. It was hard to tell in a creature that was almost transparent and full of swirling lights. *Oh God I have to stop thinking this way.*

Rayat's next thought was that this was a remnant of Shan Frankland's memories, her unsettling ability to blur the line between the value of man and cockroach, the same world-view that the wess'har shared. And *c'naatat* had brought with it elements of every host it had passed through.

She's in my bloody head. Bitch. The bitch is in my brain. I don't even know which thoughts are my own anymore. Bitch, bitch, bitch.

He found he was gripping the azin shell map far too tightly and he slackened his grip, struggling to keep calm. If he didn't have his inner core of certainty, he had nothing—and he would never last down here.

But he couldn't die; he'd end up insane.

It was the first time in his life as an intelligence agent that he'd come adrift from the internal anchor that he had learned to seize when he was alone and terrified and in pain. You had to have that core. Without it, you *broke*.

He concentrated on his fear and reminded himself that if Frankland could survive in space—and that had to be far,

far worse—then he could handle an existence like this. Humans had evolved from the sea. He'd simply come home for a while.

The bezeri examined the maps with slow, elegant care. One of them picked up two shell sheets in its tentacles and appeared to gaze at them, and Saib reached out and stroked one almost lovingly.

Our map makers are gone, said Saib. *We are the last of the clans. We shall be gone when the last of us dies, because we have found no others.*

"You've survived this far," said Lindsay. "You have enough of a population to start over. Humans nearly died out completely too. We bounced back."

Sometimes Rayat just wanted to slap her. "We declined to a few *thousand,*" he said wearily. "You're thinking of cheetahs. They're the ones who got down to single figures."

"But they still *bred.*" Lindsay stood her ground. "God, all the things *c'naatat* can change, but it lets you carry on talking. *Now* tell me it's smart. Just shut up, will you?"

Saib rippled with deep blue light so saturated that it almost became black.

But he is right. We cannot produce young ones among ourselves.

"Why?" asked Lindsay.

Most of us are old. We escaped the contamination because we did not go to the spawning grounds near Ouzhari.

"Are none of you young enough to reproduce?"

A few. But they are all of one family. They cannot breed. It is unthinkable.

Rayat hadn't even thought about the bezeri when he decided to salt the tactical neutron bombs with cobalt. He knew next to nothing about the species. There was a certain irony in the fact that Surendra Parekh had been executed for causing the death of just one of them, but his actions had led to the deaths of thousands—and here he was helping the survivors file their archives, like a murderer allowed to work in the prison library for good behavior.

Saib gathered up a stack of azin shell maps in two of his tentacles and held them against his body.

We have many maps to collect, from many locations. If nothing else, we will have our history.

Rayat thought of terrestrial octopuses opening jars and solving puzzles, and his solid view of the universe began to tilt and tear like a quake zone. He wondered if Earth's squid had histories, and if he had simply never seen the obvious.

Jejeno, Umeh

In daylight, the scale of the damage to Jejeno was visible even from the ground. Eddie opened the airlock and stood outside Umeh Station, surprised at the relative quiet.

"Off you go." He took the bee cam from his pocket and flicked it into the air, sending it out on its own beyond the defense shield. "Urban damage, bodies, emergency measures. Go get it."

He prayed that the isenj weren't jumpy enough to shoot it down. It was only the size of a tennis ball but he didn't know if their systems could detect it. He didn't even know if it could pass through the Eqbas defense shield that formed a network of invisible corridors linking the ship to Umeh Station and parts of Jejeno itself.

Yeah, I'm trapped under an upturned glass. Like a spider.

Eddie couldn't shake the analogy. Spiders seemed to form a sizeable chunk of his mental imagery at the moment. Isenj were spiders with piranha mouths, and he was a spider too, a soft pink one, and he wasn't sure who was outside the glass or within it, and whether the glass was a trap or a haven.

But there was one significant improvement in his situation: and that was a negotiated time slot on the ITX, thanks to Esganikan, or—to be more specific—thanks to the efforts of the Australians at the UN. He could guarantee getting hold of the BBChan news desk at least once a day. In

Jejeno, that meant sunrise for the time being. It was nause-
atingly early and his stomach churned with fatigue.

Silly bastards. Anyone in the FEU with three brain cells
should have realized that he was the only neutral out here
and attempted to sweet-talk him into a spot of informal intelligence gathering. It wouldn't have been the first time.
But they hadn't even tried. He had his price ready if they
ever did; unlimited ITX access.

He opened the ITX link that Livaor had managed to build
into his handheld and comforted himself with the knowledge that he could at least conduct his business in private
now—or at least as private as a shared comms link could
ever be. None of the species in the Cavanagh's Star system
had any concept of secrecy or encryption.

" 'Morning, Mick." Eddie doubted if the duty news editor
slept much these days. He was gray-faced and unshaven.
"You doing double shifts?"

"Might as well make the most of it." Behind Mick, the
newsroom looked as if the cleaning staff hadn't been around
for a while. Cups and other detritus littered the desks. "I'll
be retired by the time the Eqbas show up. Dead, even."

"You're always so upbeat."

"Have you been watching the output at all?"

"I've been a bit busy with an air raid."

Mick rolled over his comment, oblivious. "We had another hurricane. We lost backup power for six hours and the
roof came off the staff restaurant."

"Okay, you win. That trumps my personal disaster." It
was a few weeks before Christmas back home. The climate
had shifted an awful lot since he'd left Earth. "Look, things
are going pear-shaped. Are you up to speed with the
geopolitics here?"

"I have a hard time keeping up with the Earth side of
things at the moment, mate."

"Well, it looks like we've got a real shooting war. One of
the neighboring states took exception to the Eqbas arriving
in Jejeno and sent fighters into Northern Assembly airspace
to take a crack at them."

"And?"

"I've got the footage. And in retaliation the Eqbas wiped a town off the map. Buyg."

"You got footage of that?"

"No, just the dogfight over Jejeno, but—"

"Oh." Mick's personal amazement threshold seemed to have racked up a few notches overnight. Alien dogfights in the skies of exotic distant planets weren't big enough to shift his needle now. "Okay, send it down the line."

It was a challenge. "If I can get some footage of Buyg . . ."

"Great."

"Mick, are you listening? The Eqbas are heading our way in a few years and it'll be sobering to show the viewer what they can do."

"We had anti-European riots over that last Eqbas piece we ran."

"Are you being leaned on by the Foreign Office again?"

"Not anymore. It's just that we've got an immediate killer weather story with a domestic body count and something that might happen in thirty years is way down the menu today."

"Point taken," said Eddie, teeth gritted. *Sod you, mate.* But it had taken decades for the media to get excited about climate change, too, and by then it was too late: the seeds of inevitability were sown early. The Eqbas were coming. Nothing would divert them. "Look, the new Defense Secretary is going to want to see this. You might be able to trade it for a favor sometime."

Eddie had done this before; he'd shared footage of wess'har vessels with the FEU. Somehow they felt they were getting something useful beyond a warning, but he doubted it after what he'd seen last night. It was just a reminder that they had thirty years to catch up technologically on a million-year-old civilization.

Mick's mind obviously wasn't set on *receive* today. "Are you okay, Eddie? Generally, I mean."

"Well, if I'm not, you can't exactly send a car for me, can you?"

"Just checking. Manager's duty of care and all that."

"I'm fine." *I'm scared and I'm lonely and I'm excited and I wouldn't want to be anywhere else right now.* "Don't worry about me. I'm a local celeb. They even give me decent coffee. Do you want this footage or not?"

"Check in tomorrow. Jan's on duty."

Eddie closed the link and marveled at how short the attention span of a news editor could be. But the isenj war was 150 trillion miles away, and its consequences decades in the future, and the problems of Europe were happening to Mick right now.

Eddie would have made the same call.

He recalled the bee cam and tracked it all the way back to the dome, watching what it could see via his handheld. He caught a glimpse of blackened buildings. The cam was programmed to search for specific shots, matching them against typical templates—large areas of certain colors and shapes—so it was a relief to find that bomb damage looked the same across the galaxy. The cam knew what to go for.

But it wasn't bomb damage. It was the destruction caused by a military vessel exploding and sending debris, hot metal and undischarged ordnance ripping through a heavily populated city.

It was an academic point. It was a *politician's* point.

The bee cam appeared in the distance, a dull gray sphere streaking head-on towards him through the heat haze tunnel of the defense shield, looking disturbingly like an incoming missile trailing turbulence. It slowed and he caught it in a practiced move.

"Well held, that man," said a woman's voice.

It was Sofia Cargill from *Actaeon,* a lieutenant who was now the ranking officer in Umeh Station. The senior officers had died when Nevyan had launched the attack on the ship: Lindsay was dismissed the service for her actions on Bezer'ej. That left Cargill, a conspicuously young, sturdy redhead who had accepted responsibility without a murmur.

"I'm up for the first eleven if we can make enough room to play a game," said Eddie.

"The lads are talking about clearing some space in the dome." "Lads" was a unisex term they all used. Cargill stood at the airlock and squinted against the rising sun, Ceret, a star the isenj called Nir, and humans, in their erasing way, called Cavanagh's Star. The politics of names fascinated Eddie. He opted to call it Nir for the time being. "So what's happening out there?"

"Aftermath." He thumbed the bee cam's controls and tilted his handheld for her to look at the screen. "But it just bounced off us."

"Bloody hell."

"Better to have the Eqbas on side than not."

"I hate sitting here not knowing what's going on."

"I'd lie low and say nothing, love. Leave it to Shan and Esganikan."

"Not much choice."

"Anyway, you've got more to worry about—keeping that dome in order."

"Only for a few more months."

"Something you're not telling, me?"

Cargill shrugged. "No secret. *Thetis* picks us up in ten months and fifteen days. We turned her back by remote."

"Oh, that. You're going home, then?" *Thetis,* the ship that had brought him to Bezer'ej, was much slower than *Actaeon,* which had been built nearly fifty years later. "Bit of a disappointment for the ussissi and isenj embarked in her when they wake up."

"They decided to cancel the Earth trip anyway. We're evacuating—well, some of us."

"But it'll take seventy-five years to get back. You know what home is going to be like then, after the Eqbas have finished with it?" Eddie calculated, boggled by relative velocities and light-years. "They'll still get there more than forty years before *Thetis.*"

"Might be better."

"Might be *worse*."

"Whatever it is, it'll all be *over.*" Cargill looked remarkably cheerful. It seemed to be the navy way of coping. "Seventy-five years, twenty-five. We'll sleep through the lot, and it's a case of ten months here or nearly five. A lot of people have opted to go sooner rather than later." She rubbed her eyes. "And it'll relieve the pressure on the station's systems. Good compromise all round."

It removed leverage, too. But Eddie suspected the public didn't give a shit what happened to a few hundred FEU and Sinostates citizens out here. They were old news. They were a long way from practical assistance: a minimum of twenty-five years, in fact.

"I'm going for a walk," said Eddie.

"You be careful, then," said Cargill, and Eddie regretted that she was not his type.

He began walking down the invisible corridor, crossing the service road that ringed Umeh Station like a moat, and glanced up to check that the incongruously pretty Eqbas vessel was still on station above him. It gleamed bronze in the early morning sun, a little lower than it had hovered last night when it batted away incoming missiles like a casual pre-game badminton knockabout. Jejeno looked unnaturally deserted.

The last time he'd walked alone in this city, he'd nearly been killed in the crush. There were traffic rules for pedestrians here, and very few vehicles. That was a measure of the crowding. He paused on the perimeter that shimmered faintly like a very clean sheet of glass in front of him, only visible as a hint of substance at certain angles.

Eddie slipped on his transparent breather mask and reached out cautiously. He wasn't sure what he'd touch. But his fingers penetrated the barrier with a slight resistance, like pressing through water.

"Ah, sod it." He stepped through.

When he crossed the first block and turned the corner, he found himself among crowds of isenj; not as tight-packed as he had seen before, but busy and moving fast enough for him to have to match their pace and stick to the pedestrian traffic rules.

Isenj had quills. That made him careful, too. But he had walked much more dangerous streets on Earth, feeling somehow safer than he really was because he had a camera and a tabard marked MEDIA.

He stood at least a head taller than everyone else, looking down on dark heads. Isenj were subtly different shades of chocolate and umber and charcoal, and the clicking and whirring sounds—conversation, or just movement?—made him strain to hear patterns and understand them. Their scent of damp wood and the continuous movement only served to reinforce the impression of a living, dark forest floor alive with insects.

Eddie went with the flow of pedestrians, mindful not to make a sudden change of direction this time, and recorded a few landmarks to help him find his way back. A run of burned-out buildings and a deep crater that ran fifteen meters at an angle across the road told him exactly where last night's debris had landed. In the blackened rubble, water still fountained from a burst pipe, surrounded by isenj clutching tools.

Could the Eqbas protect the whole of Jejeno? Would they even want to? He hadn't worked out their mindset yet. If they were anything like their wess'har cousins, he suspected he might get a few unpleasant surprises.

This is not your species, and it's not your morality. Stop judging them. You intruded here.

Ahead of him, isenj started moving to the sides of the road, crowding together with sporadic shrill sounds, but the pace remained constant. He couldn't see why they were parting. Then he risked a glance behind him—no simple feat while trying to keep pace—and saw the top of an official isenj ground car just visible above the carpet of dark velvet heads.

The vehicle managed to make progress. As the sea of isenj parted, Eddie was suddenly aware that the road surface wasn't a uniform color, but covered in intricate, vivid designs like the ones that covered many of the buildings. Just as he was wondering if it was some kind of traffic sign or merely decoration, the vehicle drew level with him and he heard, *"Eddie!"*

It almost stopped him in his tracks, or it would have done if isenj hadn't started crushing into the back of his legs. *Shit.* He tried to step clear and get to the cleared space in the road, but he lost his balance. Hands grabbed his jacket and he was jerked off his feet and into the car so hard that his shins scraped along the running board and he swore loudly.

"Daft sod," said Ade, and hauled him into a sitting position. "What are you doing off-camp without an escort?"

Eddie rubbed his leg ruefully. Shan and a masked Serrimissani stared down at him, somehow with matched expressions of disapproval despite the huge species gulf. It was the narrowed eyes that did it: two stroppy women.

"I can handle it, Ade."

"Not on my watch."

"I've been an embed before. I know the drill."

"Yeah, and I've scraped people into body bags before." Ade's expression was more intense than angry. Eddie noted that he was wearing gloves. "I don't want anything happening to you, mate. I haven't got a clue who regards us as targets and who doesn't, and neither have you."

Yes, they *were* mates; Eddie, Ade and Aras. They'd shared a house after Shan's apparent death. They were his friends, the last left alive in the universe. And he hadn't worried much about catching *c'naatat.* Funny, that. Every time he shaved with a simple razor told him he was still mortal.

"Sorry." Eddie felt stupid. "You didn't come out just to find me, did you?"

"We're seeing the ministers, remember?" said Shan. "Esganikan's making her own way there."

Eddie felt suitably chastened and turned to Serrimissani. An isenj ground car wasn't designed for humans, although the ussissi seemed happy with their saddle-like seats. "And what's your interest in this, doll?"

"To report back to Nevyan." Serrimissani never showed signs of a thaw but he counted her as a friend too. The females tended to be aloof. "To decide if F'nar should be involved in restoring Umeh, as it affects the security of a wess'har protectorate."

Eddie wondered if F'nar had minded bearing the burden of looking after Bezer'ej. He hadn't yet worked out how one city took on interplanetary responsibilities. There was plenty about the mutual aid and communality of wess'har society that was still invisible to him.

But parts of Jejeno were familiar country.

The ground car stopped outside the ministerial building where he had first had coffee—for want of a better word— with Ual. Inside, the pale aquamarine stone walls and echoing floors were both familiar and sad.

Ping.

A quill with its decorative corundum bead had fallen to the floor.

Ping.

He heard it as if it were happening now. Ual had handed it to him, thinking he wanted the sapphire bead, but it was the isenj quill that was the prize—the source of DNA to help the wess'har create an isenj-targeted pathogen to stop them from ever settling on Bezer'ej again.

You slimeball, Michallat.

Ual had known and still forgave him. The minister said it saved him from being forced to make a dangerous decision, but Eddie didn't feel any better about it.

Rit appeared in the doorway of the adjoining chamber with Ralassi at her side, far too like her dead husband for Eddie's comfort.

"The cabinet is waiting," said Ralassi, and for once it didn't sound as if he was interpreting for Rit.

There were eight isenj in the adjoining chamber, some with beaded quills and some without. They'd settled on the floor rather than on the dais-like seats Eddie had expected to see, and Esganikan sat looking a little uncomfortable on a slab of black stone. Like all wess'har, Eqbas preferred kneeling and sitting back on their heels.

"You may record the meeting," said Ralassi.

Eddie sat cross-legged on the floor against the nearest wall, feeling like a kid in a school gymnasium. Shan and Ade sat down without hesitation, arms clasped around knees. It made them look oddly innocent.

"I am Par Shomen Eit," said the isenj in the center of the group. He spoke *English*. In fact, he spoke English just as Ual had done, sucking air through a gap and somehow articulating sound like a laryngectomy patient. It was painful to listen to, but the words were intelligible. "My responsibility is infrastructure and supplies. Par Nir Bedoi governs home affairs, and Par Paral Rit deals with off-worlders."

Only in a crowded, resource-limited world like Umeh would a utilities minister have the whip hand. The Northern Assembly had no head of state, just a cabinet committee dominated by Eit.

"The Maritime Fringe has breached our airspace to fire upon you," said Eit. "And now that you have retaliated by attacking Buyg, they hold us responsible for harboring you and so have formally declared war on us."

Esganikan studied him, head cocked like a baffled dog. "And what is your response?"

"We moved troops down to our southern border and attacked their defense installations overnight."

Whoa, thought Eddie. *I hope that's bloody audible on the bee cam.* Isenj had no news media. How the hell was he expected to find out about these things? It was like covering the battle of Trafalgar by standing at Greenwich and waiting for someone to row ashore weeks later with a dispatch.

"This will not affect our timetable," said Esganikan. "But it might hasten the process of population reduction."

Shit.

Ralassi listened intently to Rit. "The minister asks whether that is ours or theirs."

"In the end, it makes no difference." Diplomacy wasn't exactly Esganikan's strong suit. She said exactly what she thought, like all wess'har. "But we would prefer this planet to be populated by the responsible and the environmentally frugal. So those isenj who cooperate will receive our help."

Eddie found he was clenching his hands tightly into white-knuckled fists, utterly embarrassed. Shan didn't show any reaction.

"Minister Rit asks if that extends to helping us defend the border. Land has always been an issue between the Northern Assembly and the Maritime Fringe, and they seek every opportunity to encroach, although never by violent means before now."

"Defense is very resource-intensive," said Esganikan.

"We need your help." Ralassi had that disembodied tone of all interpreters. There was no "we" about it for her. "What are your plans?"

"It seems clear that our original plan to limit the population by mass contraceptive measures has been overtaken by events."

"What does that mean?" asked Eit.

"You have a war. We cannot restore your planet while fighting. So you must bring the war to an end." She took something from the folds of her green and gray tunic, a hand-sized block that looked like a bar of transparent soap. Lights flickered within it. "There are no species other than isenj living in their territory, am I correct?"

"None, except the food crops they grow."

"Do you feel your forces could subdue the Maritime Fringe?"

"If we did, we would have done so already. We require military support from you."

Esganikan paused and did the head-tilting ritual that could have been anything from curiosity to suspicion. She was studying Eit. "I will not commit ground troops here. Aerial bombardment, perhaps."

"I was thinking of weapons that are unique to the wess'har. Targeted bioweapons."

Sometimes Eddie had the sense of being present at pivotal moments; sometimes he thought that he might look back on them and identify them as such, not knowing them for what they were at the time. It was a journalist's privilege. And sometimes he saw them anyway, and was unsettled by them. He glanced at Shan, but she was watching the exchange with only the occasional blink, as if concentrating on every syllable. She wasn't used to hearing isenj articulating sound like that: he was. But Ade looked as if he had no trouble understanding, because his jaw muscles twitched. He knew what was coming. On the level playing field of the unknown, Ade's intelligence was suddenly visible.

"Drastic," said Esganikan mildly.

"No more drastic than targeted contraception. And you can do this, can you not? If you can tailor something to a specific genome for those purposes, then the same must apply to bioweapons."

"The pathogen would need containment within your borders, or it would drift into the Maritime Fringe's legitimate territory."

"I did not mean it as a deterrent." Eit had definitely shifted from "we" to "I" even if the Northern Assembly had no individual head of state. It wasn't a slip of the tongue in an unfamiliar language. "I mean as a *weapon*. To be used across their border."

"You plan to annihilate your enemies in their homes, yes?"

"Before they annihilate us."

"Annihilation will take some time if they continue to fight street by street."

Esganikan waited, silent. Rit said nothing in response to Ralassi's interpretation.

"The Maritime Fringe believes the Jejeno government is risking isenj sovereignty and has given in to wess'har aggression," Eit said at last. "It has pledged to attack Wess'ej, reclaim Asht, and end wess'har dominance once and for all."

"Is a nation capable of that if it struggles to deal with its own neighbor?"

"Our own citizens are divided over your presence here. If

this government fell, and a less sympathetic one took our place, then they would probably ally with the Fringe and the rest of the nations and make a more concerted attempt at reclaiming Asht than they did nearly two years ago. And we cannot defend Umeh Station."

So, save us, or the wicked enemy will attack you next. Eddie was unpleasantly impressed by Eit's maneuvering, but he couldn't see any wess'har responding to blackmail or scare tactics. Eit seemed to think that Esganikan cared what happened to the humans here: the legendary isenj memory had let him down badly, then. Esganikan wasn't wired to respond to manipulation and she was immune to pleading. Eddie watched the exchange and had to keep reminding himself that he was watching a cabinet minister openly bidding for a genocidal weapon without the slightest hint of embarrassment.

Esganikan obliged and lived up to Eddie's wess'har stereotype.

"If any isenj attack us, we will retaliate. And they will all die." That fluting tone always sounded reasonable, and this time it was a great sound-bite. "If isenj manage to land on Bezer'ej, they will *certainly* die, because of the pathogen seeded across the planet for that specific deterrent purpose. They are no threat to us."

Eddie tried to reconcile the reluctance to fight on the ground with the confidence he'd just heard. But Eit didn't look like he was giving up yet.

"We asked you to help us. We *invited* you here."

"We agreed to help you restore your ecology. We did *not* agree to fight for your territorial ambitions, or anybody else's. We will, however, pacify any who attack us."

"How do you expect any nation to voluntarily reduce its population now? The Maritime Fringe has focused other governments on your presence as the major threat facing Umeh."

"Then reduction can only take place by force."

"We invited you, and so we are your allies, but we might not win a conventional war." Eit paused for effect. *Ah. He picked that up from Ual.* Eddie desperately missed the dead minister's benign influence right then. "Would allies not make your task easier? I believe wess'har care only about outcomes, not intention or motive."

"If we did agree to giving you bioweapons, we would need to assess which genome variations we could exploit. And this takes time—in which you may yet be invaded. In the meantime, I would like to speak to the Maritime Fringe leadership."

"We still have diplomatic channels," said Eit. "What do you plan to say to the Fringe?"

"That if any isenj in that territory want to co-operate with the restoration of your planet, we will assist them." Esganikan looked down at the transparent chunk in her hand as if she was receiving messages. "If they resist, they will become part of the consequences of restoration."

Eddie wondered how even a force the size of Esganikan's—and a ship that could separate into different assets was a force in itself—could subdue a region. But he'd seen the whole planet's infrastructure. It was precariously balanced wherever he looked. It was wholly managed, *artificially* managed, because the environment was shot to hell. Maybe a few strikes in the right places could do far more damage here than on a world with more room to maneuver and recover.

Earth's governments really needed to start taking notes. Eddie wasn't even sure where to start.

"I shall visit the Maritime Fringe," said Esganikan. "Some things are better demonstrated that spoken."

Mar'an'cas island, Pajati coast, Wess'ej

"So you came back," said Deborah Garrod.

She stood on the beach with the wind whipping through her hair, arms folded tight across her chest. Aras pulled the boat up onto the shingle and decided it was time he used his human influence to temper what he said.

"I want to see if the colony can sustain itself through the winter." Pajat was almost as far north as his birthplace, Iussan on the Baral Plain, a far less clement place than F'nar. "Perhaps you should reconsider the marines' offer of help. They're very capable."

Deborah beckoned him to follow her. The last time he'd visited, the colonists had greeted him with a hail of stones.

"I think it might be too soon," she said. "They're still upset about Jonathan."

She didn't mention Josh, so Aras decided not to mention a few hundred thousand dead bezeri. He regretted having to kill his lifelong friend. But he didn't regret the execution, and that was a hard thing for a human to understand.

The refugee camp on Mar'an'cas was a sea of tents made of patterned blue Pajati fabric. Composite crop tunnels and patches of tilled soil filled the space that wasn't taken up by accommodation. The island was inhospitable, and even more so compared with the quality of life that the colonists had made for themselves in Constantine back on Bezer'ej.

But I created the biobarrier and the terrestrial conditions within it that helped you grow crops. I labored with you and excavated the underground settlement where you lived. I even helped build your church. I made its stained-glass windows. You were my family.

Deborah seemed less hostile towards him for executing her husband Josh than the rest of the colonists who had been forced to flee Constantine. Aras hoped she finally understood why he had to do it, but he suspected it had more to do with her acceptance of the thing they called God's will. It seemed to be a self-comforting reaction to tragedy. If this god really intended the bezeri to die to cause the colonists to return to Earth with the gene bank, then Aras doubted the deity's claim of omnipotence. Influencing humans to manage their own world properly and avoid the need for a twenty-five light-year exile seemed a more obvious course of action.

Perhaps God—if God existed—enjoyed sadistic games.

Ordinary wess'har didn't grasp divinity. Aras very nearly

did, but every time he thought he had the measure of forgiveness and atonement, humans would do something that set him back to square one again.

The colonists treated him as one of them for five generations. Now he walked through the camp and none of them acknowledged him, although some stared.

Perhaps they were staring at Deborah, widowed by him and yet walking at his side as if nothing had happened.

She stopped in her tracks. She was a small woman, much shorter than Shan and much less strongly built. Eddie described her as "oriental"; humans came in many varied forms. She dropped her arms to her sides and turned to face a couple who were rinsing clothes in a bowl outside their tent, John and Catherine: Aras knew them well. He'd made glass pens for them.

"If I've forgiven Aras," said Deborah, "then so can you. Don't forget what we are." She was aware she had quite an audience: she turned around slowly, addressing every colonist within hearing distance. There were no doors to shut out the sound in a camp of tents. "Do you hear me? Let's put an end to this. Without Aras, none of us would be here today and we'd have lost the gene bank. We're going home to restore Earth and that's thanks to *him*."

Aras wasn't embarrassed. It wasn't a wess'har reaction. He wasn't ashamed of what he'd done. He was simply bewildered. He had wanted to kill when he thought Shan was dead. He wanted revenge; no, he'd wanted *balance*. Pure revenge was a human emotion. But here was Deborah Garrod putting aside her human desire to see someone punished for her husband's death, and looking at . . . outcomes. *Like a wess'har.*

Deborah seemed to resent the silence. "I want you to find it in your heart to forgive him." She looked around. "*This* is what our faith is about. *This* is where it gets hard. Going without a few comforts isn't a test. Neither is being persecuted. Putting aside personal hatred—*that's* the test."

Aras could smell the reaction of the colonists closest to

him. Their scents of agitation and discomfort carried on the wind; what she had said had hit them hard. Aras wished he understood the complexities of faith. But he understood, at least, that Deborah Garrod had stepped without hesitation into the role that Josh had left as the colony's leader, naturally and without effort.

"You said you would never understand why I did it," he said.

"I think I understand why all these events had to happen, though," said Deborah. "And that's close enough for me to carry on with what I have to do."

Aras understood matriarchs. It was the natural order of things. Deborah seemed to think she had made her point to the colonists, and walked on. The Garrods' tent was in the center of the camp and she was heading in that direction.

"So some bezeri survived," she said.

"Fewer than sixty."

"We pray for them."

"Will my presence upset James?"

Josh's teenage son had been bitter and angry about his father's execution. His little sister Rachel only seemed to understand that her father wasn't coming back—in this life, anyway. Their faith in noncorporeal existence was somehow both literal and symbolic. It kept them happy and restrained in their actions, so Aras saw no harm in the delusion.

"James and I have spent a lot of time talking," said Deborah. "I won't pretend it's been easy. But he's reached some degree of understanding."

"And Rachel?"

"She misses Josh, and she misses you."

"Have you told her what I did?"

"Of course not. One day I will, though, so that she understands."

Despite generations spent among humans—more time than he had even spent among his own kind—Aras still found it odd that human children couldn't absorb reality in the same way as wess'har youngsters. Giyadas could reason much as

Nevyan could; she was simply aware of fewer things, and as she experienced them, she absorbed them. Human children existed in a state of semi-sentience for years.

Deborah's tent was strewn with branches painted red and green. A candle stood on a saucer, its flame guttering occasionally as a draft caught it. It was nearly Christmas and Aras knew how much time they spent preparing for the religious festival. They took it seriously. It was some kind of birthday event, although Shan insisted it was just a Pagan midwinter ceremony dressed up in a new theology like many others. Aras didn't mind. It was all untruth to him.

"Rachel painted all these branches," said Deborah.

"Where is she?" Aras missed the child. She'd always drawn pictures for him, strangely stylized and wholly inaccurate, and he wondered if that was how she perceived the world. "Where's James?"

"We've set up a schoolroom in one of the horticulture tunnels. It solves a few heating problems." She handed Aras a cup and poured some liquid into it. The scent of sage tea filled the tent and briefly overpowered the smells of the camp—garlic, sewage and burning. "James teaches in the mornings and works on the crops for the rest of the day."

"And you've taken over the leadership."

"Not intentionally."

"I don't recall women leading the community before."

"That always confused you, didn't it?"

"My society is run by matriarchs, just as the Eqbas and the ussissi are." He sipped the tea. "Will you do things differently? What do you intend to do when you return to Earth? I know you'll be planning."

Deborah looked lost for a moment. "We're discussing that."

"And?"

"We've served our purpose when we return the gene bank to Earth and the Eqbas begin restoring the environment. All we can do is carry on living a respectful life in the service of God."

Aras groped for a focus in that. *We've served our purpose.* Life without purpose alarmed him. "But how will you live?"

"As we've lived here." Deborah reached for an old data device, the kind that they no longer used on Earth. It was even older in design than Shan's swiss. She displayed a map on its small screen. "I believe we'll end up in Australia. We've been wondering where we might settle. At least we speak the same language, more or less."

"Earth has changed a great deal since your ancestors left."

"Yes, we know. That's why we're going back."

The colonists seemed to take upheaval relatively calmly. A few had resisted the evacuation of Constantine, but it was just two families, and they'd succumbed to the pathogen that the wess'har had released on the planet to make it uninhabitable for humans. Aras was sure this had something to do with the colonists' unproven belief in a more desirable life beyond death. It was a strange gamble.

"You have a great deal of catching up to do."

"Ah, so has Earth," said Deborah. "It'll be a time of huge change for everyone."

Aras fought with his curiosity for a moment. He'd never seen a whole ecology restored before. At the back of his mind, fragments of Shan's memories of Earth nudged him and told him he wanted to see the planet and the changes the Eqbas would make. He felt a passionate responsibility; and although it was an emotion transferred from Shan's memory, it was still powerful, so close to his sense of stewardship of Bezer'ej that it felt like his own.

He thought of the macaws that Shapakti had restored from the gene bank.

"The Eqbas have re-created some species."

Deborah's face relaxed and for a moment she looked much as she had been three years ago, before the *gethes* had arrived in *Thetis* and the chain of destructive events had begun. "It worked?"

"Did you think it wouldn't?"

"I shouldn't have doubted. But it was always possible that we hadn't maintained the storage conditions properly." She seemed distracted from her loss for a moment. "What did they re-create?"

"Blue and gold macaws."

"Oh."

"They're extraordinary. They're so *vivid*." Aras felt that sense of amazement again at seeing life from Earth that was utterly unlike *gethes,* independent of humans and with its own way of life. "They use human language as well as their own."

Deborah's eyes filled with tears but she smiled. She seemed to be at that tipping point of intense emotion where humans either laughed or cried, and sometimes did both.

"Josh would have been so excited." She clasped her left fist in her hand. All these humans had seen of their home-world was food crops, a few pollinating insects and rats. Earth's ecology was as alien to them as it was to Aras: and according to Eddie there were no wild macaws left on Earth. "May I see them?"

Aras didn't feel guilty, although he would always regret that Josh had to die. He missed him. And Deborah was a friend, and not responsible for what Josh had done. So making her a little happier was *not guilt.* "Of course," he said. "I'll talk to Shapakti."

"It's real, isn't it? It's really happening."

"Yes. It's real."

"Without the Eqbas, could we have carried out that degree of restoration?"

Aras thought of *gethes* and their technology, and their political will to change their greedy, destructive habits. "No," he said. "I doubt it."

"Then the intervention of the Eqbas was essential."

Where is this leading? "I would say so."

Deborah's face was fine boned and her eyes were dark and slanted. Her point of focus now seemed to be to one side of him, on nothing at all.

"This helps me make sense of Josh's actions . . . and yours."

"Why?" *No, don't ask. You won't understand.*

"If Christopher Island hadn't been bombed, the Eqbas would never have come here. It's part of a purpose."

Aras was right. He *didn't* understand. He drained his cup, fighting hard against his wess'har instinct to explain that she was wrong and that there was no greater plan in all this. Humans were superb at pattern recognition and prediction. They were so good at it, in fact, that they saw patterns where none existed and imposed them for comfort, to convince themselves of some benign plan unknown to them that would explain one day why life was so painful. They were still content not to know that imagined purpose. And sometimes they were led by the recognition of patterns that proved to be utterly wrong and totally destructive.

A coping mechanism. An evolutionary quirk, not a perception of reality.

Aras wanted to tell her that events happened because they were consequences of other actions and that only causality connected everything. Some humans seemed not to know where they were in linear time. But he knew Deborah believed that God intervened and placed events in order to offer humans choices and consequences as incentives.

"It's fortunate that the Eqbas have expertise in genetic manipulation," he said carefully.

"But you left Eqbas Vorhi ten thousand years ago. They would never have come to this system, would they?"

"That's true." *And delusional.* But if this helped *gethes* make restrained choices . . . did it matter how they reached them? *Outcomes.* Motive was irrelevant. He ventured into her framework of logic. "The destruction of Ouzhari was a catalyst. If you want Earth restored sooner rather than later, the involvement of Eqbas Vorhi is the best way I know to achieve it. And your God isn't omnipotent after all, perhaps he recognized a need to enlist their intervention."

If that helped her deal with Josh's death, that was fine

too. Aras didn't require that *gethes* thought as he did. He just wanted them to act in a responsible and civilized manner. How they managed that was up to them.

Deborah's discomfort at his doubt in her God was visible, though. She changed tack. "Tell me, how did Lindsay Neville cope at the end? She seemed to find some peace in prayer."

There was no point in deceiving Deborah, and for all his recent practice, Aras was still a literal wess'har with no fear of the consequences of knowledge.

"She's alive," said Aras. "And so is Dr. Rayat."

Deborah's expression was a total blank and her lips parted a little. Aras waited for her to speak again. She just stared at him. Eventually he filled the silence.

"The bezeri wanted someone to live among them and help them," he said. "Lindsay and Rayat seemed appropriate, and *c'naatat* enabled them to do it."

"You *contaminated* them."

"Yes." Aras waited for her to ask why Josh had to die but they were spared. He had his explanation ready, including the shockingly altered life they would lead, which would no doubt fit her ideas about eternal damnation. He didn't need to mention Vijissi as well. "It was deliberate."

She closed her eyes for a moment. "I'm glad you didn't do that to Josh."

It surprised him. Sometimes he didn't know humans as well as he thought. But Deborah thought Josh was now with God, which was where they all wanted to be in the end. Aras hadn't felt that at all when he believed Shan was dead. She was simply gone, and the world had been too painful to bear without her.

"If I acquired some food supplies, would you accept them?" he asked.

"That's kind of you, Aras."

"And contact me when you want to visit the macaws." He took Shan's swiss from his pocket. He hadn't returned it to her yet. "I can receive your messages."

There was nothing more to say. They looked at one another

and Aras found he had no more questions. He turned to go, disappointed that he hadn't seen Rachel, and ducked to get out of the tent.

"I'll walk you back to the boat," said Deborah.

"No need." The worst he could face was abuse. "And let me know if you want help from the marines."

Aras strode down the foot-worn path between the tents as the fabric snapped and whipped in the wind. He knew every one of the colonists in the camp; now he had fallen from grace with them, and it bothered him not because he wanted their approval but because he didn't like to be reminded of how fragile humans' affections were. Wess'har didn't have feuds or abandon their families. Attachments were for life.

You're still worried that Shan's the same. You're still worried that she'll do what humans do and choose between you and Ade, instead of accepting you both like a real isan *should.*

Aras's human side, scavenged by his *c'naatat* from viruses and bacteria and skin cells, was a little nagging voice of doubt. He ignored it. Shan was, he knew, as good as her word. She would never abandon him again.

"Aras." The voice came from behind him. "Aras!"

Movement caught his peripheral vision. He wouldn't let the colonists' hatred touch him. That was their problem to deal with: he made himself immune, thinking of Shan and Ade.

"Aras!"

The man's tone was urgent. Aras turned. It was John, John for whom he had once made glass pens, John who had earlier turned his back on him. His wife stood beside him.

"We're sorry, Aras," said John. "And we're sorry for what happened to the bezeri. Go careful, my friend."

Deborah's words had hit their target. Humans were at least capable of change with sufficient motivation. Aras suspected it was more to find favor with their god, the one who said they had to forgive, than out of a genuine change of heart.

But that was motive. And motive didn't matter.

These had been his friends. He liked them, and he felt better when they weren't hostile towards him.

"You too, John," said Aras. "You too."

7

So the Federal European Union accuses Australia of breaching UN treaties by unilaterally inviting the Eqbas Vorhi mission to its territories. Is this the same FEU that issued a unilateral invitation to the isenj delegation less than two years ago? And would the FEU explain the difference? Perhaps it's that superpowers can flout international treaties with impunity. Let me just say this. Any act of economic or military aggression against our Muslim brothers and sisters in Australia, New Zealand, Australian Antarctica or any of the Pacific Rim States will be treated as a hostile act against us, too.

JEAN ARLENE,
President, African Assembly
in an interview

Bezer'ej: near Ouzhari island

Lindsay stared at the squirming translucent tubes clutched in one of Saib's tentacles.

I have to get through this.

She was ravenous. That was *c'naatat,* she knew: all that cellular remodeling expended a lot of energy. She felt hot, even though the water was cold, and her body demanded calories. And she could adapt to anything. And that meant . . . she could *eat* anything.

Oh God.

Saib shimmered with radial streaks of violet and gold and the lamp's audio boomed. *You must learn to trap your own. You might prefer the weed.*

Lindsay was sure she would. Rayat reached past her and grabbed one of the tubes. "What is it?" he said, and hesitated for a second before shoving it into his mouth and chewing hard.

She was sure he'd vomit up. His eyes screwed up for a reflex second as he gagged on the thing but he kept it down.

Rayat always had to win, even against tubes.

It grows on the rocks, said Saib. *It is perhaps a weed but it acts like an animal. It moves between rocks.*

"Fine," said Rayat. "Because if I don't eat something solid then *c'naatat* is going to make me filter krill or mud or something. I want to keep chewing, thanks."

Lindsay steeled herself and reached for a tube. *Do it fast.* It felt horribly cold and gelatinous in her mouth but it tasted of *nothing.* Somehow that was the worst part. She swallowed hard and struggled against her gag reflex.

"How much of this do we need to eat?" she asked.

"Eat when you're hungry and stop when you're not."

"Thanks, doctor. Great. I might never have worked that out on my own."

But he was right. Her instinct told her to eat as much as she could when she found food. Whether it was her human hypothalamus telling her to gorge in an emergency or *c'naatat* making the decisions for her, she decided to obey it. Clustered on the rocks were writhing translucent gold tubes like the ones Saib had gathered. She made her way over to them—and it was becoming far more natural to move in the water now, a combination of swimming and touching down on the seabed every few meters—and reached out.

She expected them to shrink from her hand like anemones. But they *scattered.*

She lunged at them and managed to grab a handful. *Plants,* she told herself. *Plants, plants, plants.* She crammed them into her mouth and shut out every conscious thought that said food had to be dead and cooked.

She'd eaten oysters once and vomited.

"I'll stick to chasing weed," said Rayat. "Until I develop the ability to move efficiently in water."

"You reckon you will?"

He nodded emphatically. "You can see how this thing works. It fits you to survive in your environment. It wants you to stay alive, because it depends on you in some way. It optimizes you."

"It survives in soil. Why does it need us?"

Rayat was a pharmacologist, a scientist. He would be useful at last. "Lots of parasites need a host for certain phases of their life cycle. Some even need hosts for transport, nothing else."

"Maybe I shouldn't think about this."

"Maybe you should. I want *c'naatat* to give me those damn lights so I can talk to the bezeri without the lamp. It probably won't last forever."

"Shan picked up the bioluminescence. She couldn't speak the language, though."

"Did she ever try?"

"I don't know."

"How exactly did she acquire it?"

"No idea."

Saib moved, shooting a powerful jet of water and sending silt pluming in clouds. *Hurry. If you do not want to eat, then work. Fetch more maps. The podship will come soon.*

Rayat held his hand out for the signal lamp. Lindsay paused for a moment and then decided that if he tried to keep it, Saib would probably take it from him anyway. The bezeri needed to communicate with them too.

She put it in his hand. "Go ahead."

Rayat aimed the lamp at Saib. "How can I get some cells from you?"

I do not understand.

"I want to be able to use light like you do. I need some cells from you, but I mustn't break your skin or I might infect you." Rayat was looking over Saib's mantle, searching at a careful distance. "Can you scrape off any skin?"

Saib didn't respond. He hung in the water motionless for a moment, and then gathered up his tentacles tight to his body and shot off with a powerful jet of ejected water. He disappeared into the darkness. The two remaining bezeri waited.

"Okay, you've pissed him off now." Lindsay kicked up into the water and swam for the repository again. "Come on, let's shift those maps."

It was hard work. Lindsay *wanted* it to be. She'd brought these creatures to the brink of extinction, through her own stupidity, and she didn't deserve a second of respite. And the harder it was, the less she thought.

Lindsay wondered for a moment how long her clothing would survive immersion in saltwater. At least she didn't have to worry about hygiene and latrines any longer. The things she found comfort in now astounded her.

How long have we been down here now?

She had a sense of it being the first day, maybe the second. Her watch had stopped. Her hunger didn't mark time by telling her when she had missed regular meals: it was constant.

Ignore time. Just keep moving.

She stacked up the azin shell maps and records, passing Rayat in a silent relay. It must have taken an hour, maybe two—maybe three. The podship Saib had referred to turned out to be a five-meter translucent gel sac that maneuvered by pulsing jets of water. At first Lindsay wondered if it was a living creature. But it had a hatch that opened, a hatch with unnaturally straight edges, and a bezeri emerged from it to gather up the shell documents and place them in the craft.

The next time she returned to the cache of shells, she found Saib waiting with something in his tentacles. Rayat settled on the silt beside her, staring.

Saib was carrying a small body.

My kin, he said. His light display pulsed deep blue, almost purple in its intensity. *He is recently dead.*

Lindsay had no idea whether *kin* meant son or nephew or grandson; but she knew exactly how Saib felt. She could still taste the pain of David's death, such an unfairly short life after months of carrying him. Without the numbing influence of the mood enhancers she'd been taking, the grief was now rushing back to fill the voids, triggered by seeing that small body.

Let's get the poor thing tidied up. Lindsay could hear Shan's voice even now. Lindsay was instantly back in the *Thetis* camp on Constantine, standing over the dissected corpse of an infant bezeri after Shan had punched Surendra Parekh to the floor for disobeying the order not to take organic samples. It had been the start of the chain of slowly unfolding disasters.

Take what you need, said Saib. *Will he live on in you?*

"Let's see," said Rayat.

There was no bioluminescence in the body. But that didn't mean the cells were useless. It was worth a try. And if Rayat could develop the lights faster, then Lindsay wanted them too.

Saib laid the body on a rock and Rayat fumbled in his pockets, growing more impatient. Then he found a piece of plastic—a tag of some kind—and scraped it along the inside of his wrist.

"Don't look," he said to Saib.

Rayat kept scraping until he drew blood. Lindsay hoped there weren't predators with the senses of sharks in these waters.

"Okay," he said. "Let's try it with the body. The photophores are between the skin and the mantle muscle in terrestrial squid. You know how complex they can be? Lenses, reflectors, even color filters. Amazing."

Lindsay gathered up the child's body—a child, a life like David's, whatever the species—and was surprised by how heavy it felt. Rayat hesitated before hacking into the mantle and scooping out chunks. Then he braced his arm and gouged into his own skin, working in the bezeri's tissue like a paste. That was the problem with *c'naatat*: it healed wounds almost instantly so it was hard to keep the blood flowing. Rayat pounded away at his arm making little grunts of effort for a period that felt like long minutes. It was hard to tell. He opened up three wounds. By the time he stopped, there wasn't a mark on his skin.

"My turn," said Lindsay. She held out her arm.

"You sure?"

"Of course I'm bloody sure. This might be the only chance

we get to try this." She stared at him. *Oh my God I'm living under water and I'm trying to develop bioluminescence and I have to stop thinking about this*—"Oww—"

Rayat stabbed into her arm. The edge of the plastic was blunt and it hurt like hell, shocking her out of her thoughts. Did it matter that he was working photocytes into her bloodstream? Wouldn't any tissue do the job? Maybe he knew something she didn't. It was as good an idea as any.

"Okay." Rayat picked up the lamp and turned to Saib. "How do you dispose of your dead?"

Under stones.

"Is this place appropriate?" Rayat laid the child's body down on the seabed in a space between outcrops of rock. Then he gathered some stones. "I'll do it."

Saib said nothing, but he coiled one tentacle around a rock. The other bezeri followed him. Lindsay joined in the burial party and they covered the body a stone at a time, forming a cairn between the outcrops.

I will make a memorial later, said Saib.

Yes, they carved stone: Lindsay remembered that. They had memorials at the high-water line on Constantine, single carefully-shaped stones with inscriptions commemorating podship pilots who had breached the barrier to the Dry Above, a place as remarkable to the bezeri as space once was to humans.

"You do have some decency in you, then," said Lindsay.

"One thing you need to learn about monsters," said Rayat, "is that we're not monochrome. Saints aren't, either."

He swam back to the repository. Lindsay paused to grab some red weed and chewed it. It tasted like wet salty leather, but it was better than chasing plants that might have been worms.

She looked up towards the sunlight, filtering through the water in shafts like a woodcut from a family bible. That was an image she couldn't shake now, not since she'd seen it on Christopher Island. And she knew where she was; she was close enough to Christopher—Ouzhari—to find Constantine, or what was left of it.

She wanted to see David's grave. She wanted to mourn properly for her child. Aras had made a glass headstone that threw brilliantly colored light on the grave in the sunshine.

She would find it. She knew she would.

But she had time, and these aging bezeri didn't. She had to do her duty first. She had to look for more survivors.

Umeh: Maritime Fringe airspace

"They don't piss about, do they?" said Shan.

Ade stared down between his boots at a fire-blackened, shattered landscape that had been part of a Maritime Fringe city called Buyg. Shan was back to being the detached copper again, and he wondered if the kind of violence she was used to seeing before she went to EnHaz made it easier to deal with this war. It was hard to tell. She'd just switched off; it was more than just her scent signals. She'd battened down all the hatches. Even her eye contact felt like a stranger's.

The devastation extended as far as he could see from the transparent deck of the Eqbas ship. He was almost used to walking on nothing now: as long as he concentrated he felt perfectly safe. But the minute he let it slip from conscious thought, the primitive part of his brain took over and he jerked back as if he was falling into a deep, deep pit. Eddie seemed to have solved the problem by kneeling on all fours and resting on his folded arms. Maybe he was just getting a better look, though. Sometimes he looked as if he had no sense of danger at all, as if he shut down simply to cope.

We all do it sooner or later.

"I'm glad Lin's dead," said Eddie. "I don't think she'd cope with knowing she started all this."

Ade decided not to even breathe. Shan didn't meet his eyes. "Yeah." Then she glanced at Esganikan and warbled in eqbas'u. Ade took a guess that she was telling her Eddie didn't know Lindsay was alive, and to keep her mouth shut about it. Judging by Esganikan's rapid head-tilting, she had.

Eddie could never leave anything alone. "How did she go in the end?"

"Calm," said Ade. He had that down pat now.

"Rayat?"

"Same."

"Did she say anything?"

"Eddie, shut the fuck up about her, will you?" Jesus, everyone wanted to know how people died. Sometimes it was better not to. It definitely was this time. *Change the subject.* "Was that a single missile?"

Ade avoided Eddie's eyes but he glimpsed his startled expression. Esganikan took no notice of the spat and seemed engrossed in studying a mist of small lights that shimmered in the bulkhead.

She prodded one and the display changed. "Yes, with twenty dispersing warheads."

"And how many do you carry?"

"Fifty," she said. "But we make more on deployment."

Make more. Ade wasn't used to that. It skewed his sense of logistics and supply chains, chains that could be broken to cripple an enemy. He was glad he wasn't fighting them.

"I bet that got their attention." It was hard to get a sense of scale because the buildings—or at least the stumps of them—had no familiar ratios that he could latch onto. "What's our altitude?"

Esganikan paused for a second. It always took her a little longer to convert to Earth metric. "Twenty thousand meters."

Shan stood with her feet slightly apart as if bracing for impact, looking down, turning the ring around on her finger. She didn't seem used to wearing rings; Ade had never seen her wear any jewelry. But she hadn't taken it off yet, and that was reassuring.

"Looks lower," said Ade.

The ship suddenly seemed to drop. Buyg loomed much larger, closer. Shan's intake of breath was audible and she put her hand on the nearest bulkhead. Ade's gut flipped and Eddie jerked back onto his heels. The ussissi nearby didn't move a muscle: Ade always kept an eye on them.

"Shit," said Eddie. "What was that?"

"Magnification of the image," said Esganikan wearily.

The deck behaved almost like a lens, then. Ade's brain had told him he was falling.

Shan seemed reassured. "This is the same technology as that electron microscope sheet you had on Ouzhari, isn't it?"

"The image projection is similar," said Esganikan. "But that was a particle-force scope."

It meant little to Ade. Shan raised an eyebrow. "If you ever want to raise capital when you get to Earth, auction that tech."

"Do we need to?" asked Esganikan.

"No."

"Good. Giving technology inappropriate to the user causes problems, I find."

Ade was starting to form a picture of how they handled knowledge. They didn't have secrets. They didn't shove information down anyone's throat, either, but they had no concept of confidentiality and they didn't encrypt their comms. But even if you knew they were coming, there was sod all you could do about it. Stealth was redundant when you had overwhelming force.

Even a ship like this wasn't enough to hammer a planet on its own, though. That was interesting.

"So would you *tell* humans how to make one of those particle things?" asked Ade.

"We would answer questions." Esganikan seemed totally unwary of interrogation. "There would be no reason not to."

"But you wouldn't give them the kit."

"Probably not."

"So what if they asked you how to make one of those dispersing missiles?"

"We would ask *if* they could make it."

"And?"

"If we decided they could, we would refuse to tell them." Esganikan cocked her head and her vivid red plume bobbed. Eddie was right: she reminded him of a parrot, as capable of taking a chunk out of you as Shapakti's macaws.

"No, Sergeant, we are not as secretive as you, but neither are we stupid."

Ade felt his face burn. Shan put her hand on his back, reassuring and protective. He liked that. So she hadn't switched off completely after all. "He's got a point. Your relaxed attitude to security concerns me sometimes, too."

"It's sufficient."

Eddie, still on his hands and knees on the transparent deck, chuckled to himself. "You missed your vocation, Ade. The art of political semantics."

"I learned weasel-speak from you, mate." *Yeah, I know what* semantics *means.* Eddie knew better than to patronize him, but Ade was still conscious of being undereducated. But at least he'd diverted Eddie from the subject of Lindsay Neville.

Esganikan pointed down through the deck. "The blast area is nine square kilometers and the firestorm damage extends to twice that."

"Jesus. Not nukes, though." She'd already said they didn't use them. "I mean, it's not like I can tell what you were firing last night—"

"The nearest equivalent appears to be your fuel-air device. Destruction without persistent contaminants."

"Depends what your fuel is."

"The explosive is nearly all combusted. And nontoxic. There is little we can do to stop debris being ejected into the atmosphere, but this can be cleaned up too."

Shan snorted. "Well, it looks pretty bloody toxic from here. If you tried that on Earth you'd release so many pollutants from the built environment that you'd poison the place anyway."

"That may well occur here, of course. Bioremediation will be necessary anyway."

Ade made a note to look up *bioremediation* later. He could guess for the time being.

"You getting all this, Eddie?" Shan squatted down and fixed the journalist with her listen-to-me stare, oblivious of the bee cam. She seemed to ignore it now, and Ade remembered what Eddie said about people eventually becoming far too comfortable with a fly on the wall. "What do you think the folks back home will make of this, eh?"

"It *ought* to have a highly laxative effect," said Eddie. "But it's *not* back home, and it's not now. And it's not happening to them."

"This is not our usual mode of operation." Esganikan seemed a little offended. "But there's no other species or natural environment here that we need to avoid harming."

"You're going to be a sucker for the fluffy bunny shield, then," said Eddie. "Or the strategically placed tree."

Esganikan appeared to understand *bunny.* "That's why we prefer species-specific measures. Your distaste for some weapons and not others seems almost irrational."

She said it mildly, as if explaining to a particularly dim child. Ade thought bioweapons sounded tidier. He'd seen the aftermath of enough fuel-air bombs and other conventional ordnance with huge overpressures; it was ugly. But, like Shan always said, dead was dead, and shoving a knife in someone was pretty ugly too if you were on the sharp end of it.

This wasn't his war. He couldn't stop it happening. It made him think of things he wanted to keep out of his mind, memories he wished would just leave him alone, and so he switched off.

The ship moved towards the coast. Ade had worked out that the illuminated display on the bulkhead was a chart and he started to marry up the colors and symbols with ground features; the meandering yellow line was the coast. The Maritime Fringe seemed to be precisely that, a corridor all along the southern edge of the continent. No wonder they were paranoid. They looked as if they had their backs to the ocean, ringed on three borders by the Northern Assembly.

The ship passed over undamaged city made up of buildings without end that were light gray, cream and ochre. They ran right up to the edge of a rusty coastline and a dirty pink-tinged sea.

Esganikan clicked audibly. Ade wasn't sure if that was annoyance or regret. "They had more land before the ice caps receded."

"That sounds familiar."

"And as on your world, they found the climate change could be unpredictably rapid. It saddens me that we see this repeated so often."

They were a long way into Maritime Fringe airspace now and nobody had opened fire on them. Maybe the Fringe had learned its lesson last night. But Ade was sure they hadn't, because people who felt that threatened tended to carry on lashing out. And isenj were definitely people. Once you looked past the quills and the absence of eyes, the English-speaking ones were very . . . human.

Esganikan was *much* more alien.

She turned to one of the bridge crew, who sat in niches as if they were dozing, glancing at lights in the bulkhead. Ade tried to find parallels with the ships he knew; maybe if an Eqbas had walked into the citadel of an FEU vessel they would have thought the crew was watching entertainment as they stared unmoving at bright fast-changing displays. Esganikan warbled in eqbas'u in her double-voice, just like Nevyan's, and one of the crew began touching lights on the bulkhead with long multijointed fingers. Sometimes he could see they were cousins of the Wess'ej wess'har, and sometimes they looked totally different, as if they had no common roots. He wondered how they looked to Nevyan.

"Hayin, open communications with the Maritime Fringe government," said Esganikan, leaning over a crewman at his station. She beckoned to Aitassi. "Interpret for me."

Hayin handed a *virin* to Aitassi, who settled back on her haunches and held the communication device in front of her. Shan looked as if she was concentrating hard.

"*Pirb,*" said Hayin, nodding.

"Minister Pirb," Esganikan said carefully, in English. "Minister Pirb, this is Esganikan Gai, commander of the Eqbas Vorhi adjustment mission, and I require your cooperation."

Ade wondered if the English was for Eddie's benefit again, but maybe she just wanted to be fluent by the time she had to have the same surrender-or-else conversation with Earth. They were good at picking up languages. He was certain that she could have spoken the isenj language if she'd had the right throat to make the sounds.

The sound of isenj rattles and whirrs filled the bridge. Aitassi turned her head slowly to the commander as if choosing her words carefully.

"Pirb says he is *President,* and that he cannot cooperate with an invading army."

"Tell him that any of his citizens who want to cooperate with the new environmental measures should present themselves at the border with the Northern Alliance for instructions."

"He tells you to remove your ship from his airspace, and that you have a minute to withdraw."

Esganikan seemed utterly relaxed and unmoved. Ade had been around wess'har long enough to read their body language—the freeze reaction when startled—and now he knew their scent signals. No, Esganikan really *didn't* give a damn. She had her objective and she was going to stick to it. Sometimes her kiss-my-arse attitude was so much like Shan's that he almost liked her.

"Tell President Pirb," she said, "that if he attempts to carry out his threat to attack Wess'ej and Bezer'ej, I will respond in kind. Tell him, too, that I am *not* a Wess'ej wess'har, and my definition of balance is not as liberal as theirs. I will destroy his cities, and kill his citizens, and those of his allies if they attempt to threaten our kin."

Esganikan was totally calm. There were people who made threats, and people who made promises, but Esganikan was just telling Pirb what was going to happen. It was much more chilling. Ade felt a surge of familiar adrenaline and caught Shan's eye. She didn't even raise her eyebrows.

But there was no answer from Pirb. Esganikan didn't seem concerned and exchanged conversation with crew at another station on the bridge. Lights danced across the port bulkhead and on the chart. "Aitassi, are any ussissi still operating vessels within the Ebj region?"

"No. After the attack on this ship they suspended commercial duties here." Ussissi took a threat to one of them as a threat to all. Ade approved of that degree of camaraderie. "But all ussissi across the planet are stopping work."

Esganikan kept her eyes on those bulkhead lights. Ade was still looking down at the terrain beneath his feet when a brilliant white light and a trail of vapor streaked up to fill his field of view and exploded in a blinding sheet as if it was filling the bridge.

Incoming—

His instinct was to throw himself flat. He crashed into Shan, cracking his temple against her head and all he could see for seconds was a dark green disk across everything while his seared retina tried to cope with the overload of light.

"Jesus Christ." Shan sat up awkwardly and rubbed her head. "That's not funny."

Eddie nodded, apparently calm. "It's not, is it? I've seen incoming before, and it makes me nearly shit myself every time."

Esganikan gestured to them to get up. Ade wasn't sure if she was amused or baffled, but none of the Eqbas looked as if they'd reacted to the attack. "You *know* that the defense shield will hold. The missile exploded fifty meters beneath us."

"Yeah, but we're pretty basic models," said Ade irritably. "We've got reflexes. We normally say *missile incoming brace brace brace,* just so nobody has a nasty surprise like *that* one."

"The target light was illuminated." Esganikan indicated the bulkhead array. "Pay attention next time. There is clearly no point talking further with Pirb, so now we withdraw."

Only an Eqbas could make *withdraw* sound so ominous.

Shan got to her feet and made a conspicuous point of standing right in the middle of the transparent section of deck. Warbling chatter passed between two of the Eqbas crew at bulkhead consoles. Streaks of light flared beneath the deck like tracer rounds and Ade watched the ground lift visibly with the chain of explosions, flame and gray clouds rising until all he could see was a billowing carpet beneath his boots.

"You okay, Boss?" He caught Shan's arm again.

"Fine." The shock just seemed to make her more aggressive and determined to force herself into a show of strength. She *had* to be the bloody alpha female. She had no scent at all now. "Esganikan, what did you just do?"

"Returned fire. What would *you* do under the circumstances?"

"Jesus, how big a chunk have you taken out?"

The Eqbas commander tilted her head as if calculating. "The entire ground battery and roughly a thousand meters around it."

"But they can't damage your ship."

"They fire upon us. We fire back. We will continue to suppress attacks."

"But a thousand meters covers a lot of civilians too. You're going to trigger a surge of refugees. They'll self-evacuate across the border, and that's bad enough where I come from, let alone in a place this crowded. Did you think about that?"

"Your priority as a police officer was probably to ensure that as many of them survived as possible. Mine is not. My task is to restore the ecology of this planet as far as anyone can, given that all non-food species have been driven to extinction, and that is not a task for the squeamish."

Esganikan gazed at Shan, unmoved. Shan stood stony-faced, fists on hips. It hadn't crossed Ade's mind that she might have a problem with collateral damage: she certainly had no trouble killing people. She could use her fists, too. Violence was far from her last resort, and frequently her first. He had enough of her memories now to prove it.

"You're right," Shan said. "This isn't my business. I'll stay out of it."

"I meant no offense."

Shan held up her hands in acceptance. There was still an edge to her voice. "No problem."

"Do you want to observe further?"

She shook her head and glanced down through the transparent deck. "I've seen what I came for. We'll head back to Wess'ej."

"I'd like to stay," said Eddie.

"Yeah, you do that," said Shan.

There was an awkward silence and then the ship turned slowly, skewing the image in the deck through 90 degrees and Esganikan trooped off with Aitassi, followed by the bee cam and Eddie.

"Good call." Ade caught her hand and squeezed it for a second, just long enough to remind her that he was hers without embarrassing her in public. "It's some other bastard's watch now."

"I can't afford to get in a ruck with her. If that bloody dominance pheromone kicks in and she cedes to me, I'm in trouble."

It was messy politics between creatures neither of them fully understood. "War's dirty, Boss."

"Yeah. Don't think I underestimate the difference between us." She blinked rapidly, hit by either realization or embarrassment: he wasn't sure which. "Remember I'm just a copper."

"When are you going to tell Eddie about Lin and Rayat?"

"Not yet. I think Nevyan needs to know first, and that's going to be hard enough."

"I think word will get around."

"I know. It's hard to decide which pile of shit to tackle first, really."

"And we ought to call Aras and let him know we're okay. He frets."

"I'll do it." Shan took the *virin* out of her pocket. She held it awkwardly. It really was like a bar of transparent soap; operating it needed finger placement on a par with guitar fretwork. "I miss my swiss. First thing I'm going to do is to get it back off Aras and have Livaor modify it for me so I can use it on the ITX. He did it for Eddie, so he can do it for me." She seemed to be making an effort not to look at him. "I'm not good bystander material."

"You can't run the universe."

"I know, I know . . . ," Shan fumbled with the *virin* and held it in front of her in both hands as if it was going to lunge for her throat. "But I can't remember a time when I wasn't responsible for putting things right."

"First things first, Boss. Let's get our own house in order."

"That's what I'm doing now."

The lights shimmered inside the *virin* and Shan's hands reacted, pulsing violet light back. Ade couldn't shake the impression that the bioluminescence was trying to communicate. Aras's voice was projected from nowhere.

"Are you safe?" he asked.

"Of course we're safe, sweetheart. Just wanted to let you know we're on our way back. Seen enough here. The shooting's started."

"I have news for you."

Shan seemed focused on the *virin's* lights. "I've got a surprise for you, too. Garlic—"

"Vijissi has been found alive."

Shan stared at the play of violet light in silence, expressionless. It was one of those pieces of good news that looked great on first glance and then came horribly unraveled when you thought about them carefully.

"Oh *fuck*," said Ade.

8

*We understand the Australian position on hosting the Eqbas
Vorhi delegation. It's Australia's sovereign right to deter-
mine who enters its territory and who doesn't, a precedent
established by the FEU when it invited the isenj delegation,
and for which we thank them. Like Prime Minister Pho, we
look forward to the Eqbas contribution to solving our environmental issues even if that solution lies decades in the future. We will support any and all of the Australasian States
if their sovereignty comes under threat.*

IRNIQ SATAA,
Canadian Peoples delegate,
United Nations Security Council

F'nar: clan home of Mestin, former senior matriarch, mother of Nevyan

"Where is he?" said Shan.

"This way," said Mestin. "I thought you would want to be notified."

"You bet. It's my fault he ended up like this."

"I was the one who told him to stay with you."

"Why does everyone want to get into a guilt contest with me?" Shan followed her down the warren of passages cut into the rock. "Sorry. Trying times."

The flagstones were polished smooth like the foyer of an upmarket hotel, bathed in gold light from a system that gathered sunlight and channeled it deep into the tunnels cut into the caldera: another piece of desirable wess'har tech that would have made them wealthy had they wanted to sell it to Earth.

They didn't. Commerce wasn't part of the way they thought.

Shan took a deep breath at the entrance to the chamber. It was like every raid she had staged, every door she had smashed down to make arrests, every closed portal that threatened to hold nightmares behind it. But wess'har didn't have doors, and all she had to do was steel herself to enter and see a creature in the same terrible state that she'd been in when Nevyan recovered her from space. Mestin gestured for her to go in, then walked away.

Vijissi looked like a little dead animal that had been hit by a vehicle and left to decompose and dry out at the side of the road. There was absolutely no flesh on him; he was just minutely pleated light brown skin shrink-wrapped onto bone. A tube hung from the corner of his mouth. From time to time his eyes fluttered open and their matte black surface simply added to the impression of roadkill. *C'naatat* had used every scrap of tissue it could spare to maintain life in hibernation in the most hostile of environments and the result was something akin to mummification.

Jesus, thought Shan. *I looked like that once.*

She was aware of the members of Vijissi's pack now waiting at the door of the chamber, a dozen or so adults and their young. Ussissi had a distinctive scent, like feathers. Their claws made skittering sounds on the stone as they milled about outside, and they were anxious: they wanted him home, but they feared *c'naatat* more.

If he had a mate, no female had come forward. Shan had little idea of the family lives of ussissi and she wondered why she'd never asked.

"You poor little bugger," said Shan. Would he remember drifting in space like she did? There was no telling how a ussissi experienced *c'naatat* because the parasite seemed to have a new plan of improvements for every host it colonized. It was certainly imaginative. "Can you hear me, Vijissi?"

He stirred but didn't wake. A faint scent of powdery musk and fruit alerted her: Nevyan was coming, and Shan decided it was as good a time as any to try to repair the growing rift.

You saved me, Nev. You didn't give up looking for me when everyone else thought I was dead. Damn, if you're not my friend, who is?

Nevyan sat down beside her by the makeshift bed. Wess'har preferred to sleep in alcoves, a remnant of their warren-dwelling origins. "I insisted on returning as soon as we found you. But Serrimissani wanted to carry on looking for him anyway. She was right."

Shan knew guilt all too well. But it was rare for a wess'har because they dealt in outcomes, not should-have-beens. "He's alive now. You couldn't have known he had *c'naatat*."

"I hope he forgives me."

It was a remarkably human sentiment and Shan wondered if Nevyan meant it the same way.

"Three months, six months . . . you've no real sense of time out there." Shan hoped that was true of Vijissi. "You're not even sure who or what you are."

And what had Vijissi come back to? Aras and Ade had been at her bedside when she regained consciousness—both *c'naatat* like her, with no fear of holding her or sleeping with her. She returned to a life that was possibly a hell of a lot better than the one she would have had on Earth. But Vijissi was the only one of his kind—just as Aras had once been. And she knew what that isolation had done to him.

"Still," she said, continuing her thoughts aloud, "I know what he's going through and I'll give him whatever support he needs to get through this."

"I think there's a limit to how much support a human can give a ussissi," said Nevyan.

"Yeah."

"We fed him exactly as Ade fed you, with a tube."

"That's all you can do."

"Are you going to tell me how things went on Umeh?"

"How do you *think* they went, Nev?"

"I can't smell your scent. I assume they went badly."

"Let's just say I found it sobering."

Nevyan put her hand on Shan's sleeve and tugged gently. Shan followed her outside, wanting to say something of meaningless comfort to Vijissi's pack; a large female, chest-high to Shan, stood in their way.

"What will happen to him, *Shan Chail*?"

"He'll recover." She slipped effortlessly into her Superintendent Frankland persona, adept at breaking bad news to next of kin. "You know what *c'naatat* is. I won't pretend it's easy to deal with. But I've managed it, and so will he. He's alive. That's all that matters."

Liar. How could she trot out platitudes so easily?

"But he is my *son*. Does this mean he cannot father young? That he cannot mate?"

The answer was out before she could stop it. "Yes. I'm afraid it does."

Does it? Really, does it? Yes, or else everything you've done is for nothing.

Vijissi's mother sank down on her haunches, visibly defeated. Shan hadn't realized Vijissi was so young and it stunned her for a moment; ussissi had none of the visual clues she used to gauge a human's age. *Shit, he's just a kid.* She'd thought of him as an elder statesman of some kind, a diplomat: but he wasn't. For some reason his lost future crushed her.

She wanted to be optimistic and say that Shapakti might be able to do for Vijissi what he couldn't do for Aras, and remove *c'naatat* from ussissi cells. But if he couldn't, it was a cruel false hope. She swallowed hard.

Damn, I didn't even tell Nevyan about that. It was my own private dilemma. It'll have to stay that way.

"I'm sorry," she said.

Nevyan waited until they reached the terrace before resuming conversation. It was hard to know where to begin. And Nevyan, just like Vijissi, was far younger than she seemed, too, dealing competently with situations for which she was hardly equipped. There was nothing like seeing an old head on young shoulders for making you feel inadequate.

"When we found you alive, it was a cause for rejoicing," said Nevyan. "Now we find Vijissi, and it's a source of unhappiness."

"Ask Aras how well I reacted when I found I was infected." Shan thrust her hands deep in her pockets and stared out into the pearl bowl of the city. On this cloudy late afternoon it looked more like newly polished pewter. "And I got used to it."

"With *jurej've*. With males who bonded with you."

"What are you saying? That we make Vijissi a little *c'naatat* friend and it's all okay?"

"No. That wouldn't be the answer."

"Aras coped with being alone for centuries. Somehow, Vijissi will too."

"Let's resume our talk about the Eqbas."

Shan decided now was as good a time as any to blurt it out and get it over with. "No, let's stay on the subject of *c'naatat* for a few more minutes. It's not just Vijissi. The bezeri wanted assistance so we gave them Lin and Rayat. And to make sure they survived to do the job, we gave them a dose."

Nevyan's scent of agitation was suddenly as strong as if she'd sprayed grapefruit oil in the air. She stood absolutely still in that wess'har alarm reaction.

"After all that happened to you, all that you did, you infected them *willingly*?"

"Yes."

"*We.*"

"*Yes.*" Shan was aware of her reflex of bracing her shoulders and dropping her arms to her sides when she was cornered. She found she was doing it now. "We did."

Nevyan cocked her head to one side. Shan stared back at her, waiting for all hell to break loose. *Great way to mend fences. This kid's a real friend, remember?*

"I am . . . *surprised* that you took that decision so easily and without discussion."

Wess'har always said what they meant and had no concept of tact or kind little lies. Shan wasn't sure if Nevyan's show of unwess'har diplomacy was actually shock. It didn't matter. What was done was done.

"But I did," said Shan. She hated herself for defaulting to the don't-argue-with-me Shan in an instant. "And I'll deal with it. Esganikan's aware of what's happened. So you don't need to worry about it, okay?"

They stared at one another for a few more silent seconds.

"I'm still disappointed," Nevyan said at last. "And I will *remain* disappointed. How did Esganikan react, since you told her before you told me?"

"She's responsible for Bezer'ej now. She needed to know."

"That wasn't a rebuke."

"Okay, she didn't seem bothered."

"And yet you find something in common with the Eqbas."

"Yes. Yes, I do."

Nevyan fixed her with that topaz stare, pupils snapping flower-cross-flower. Shan didn't notice wess'har pupils these days any more than she noticed Ade's or Aras's, but now they seemed suddenly so alien for a few seconds that she found herself wondering whose eyes she was seeing this through. It was almost like the moments of brief consciousness when she was drifting in space, waking and seeing but not knowing who or what she was.

"Shan, do you *want* to see the Eqbas invade your world? Is that what you want?"

"*This* is my world."

"Now you know why I wanted the Eqbas to leave Wess'ej. It wasn't easy asking them to move their camp to Bezer'ej after I summoned them, but we admit when we're wrong and seek better outcomes. Why don't you see that the Eqbas are wrong to interfere with Earth?"

Nevyan was ignoring the problem as long as it wasn't in F'nar's backyard. Shan couldn't stop herself. "Whoa there, you wanted the human threat contained. You wanted balance for the destruction on Bezer'ej. That's *interference*."

"But proportionate. The balancing of those responsible."

"*Those responsible* will all be dead or senile by the time we get there. Working by your rules of guilt, the stupid bastards who equipped *Actaeon* with cobalt and neutron ordnance aren't even responsible. That leaves Rayat, Lin and one spook minder back at base who authorized Rayat to deploy nukes, and anyone who fails to use their authority to bring the guilty to justice. So you go twenty-five light-years to sort out fewer than perhaps twenty people?"

Nevyan's pupils were a perfect black poppy on a gold field. She was utterly still. "We?"

"Figure of speech." *Yes, it was. Wasn't it?* Ussissi trotted past them on the terrace, making their way back to the settlement just outside F'nar. Shan waited for them to be out of earshot; it wouldn't do for them to see her arguing with the senior matriarch of F'nar.

"Generalization. Wess'har. That's what I mean by *we*. Here's what I see. We fucked a chunk of Bezer'ej and the bezeri with it. *C'naatat* is something humans will always want, no matter how hard it is to get at, and if we got here once, we'll get here twice sooner or later. Add the fact that we've screwed our own planet, and that some people back home want radical intervention, then I think the Eqbas have made the right call."

"You're wess'har. You live Targassat's philosophy."

"Eqbas are wess'har too."

"If they don't act as we do, then regardless of their genes, they are *not* us."

It was ironic that the wess'har view of identity seemed so liberal—that you were what you did, nothing more—and yet was so beset by orthodoxy. Shan reminded herself that she had to choose which mindset to think in at any given moment, wess'har or human, because the two didn't mix. They never would.

"Nev, let's just say that they have a view of right and wrong, and they live it," she said. "What's the point of believing something if you don't act on it? *You* do."

"Intervention for the sake of it is not justified."

"You *summoned* them."

"And the isenj needed only to be confined."

"Ual invited them in just like you did. What are you doing,

imposing your definition of appropriate response? What did your ancestors do when they realized the bezeri were asking for help to kick out the isenj? You responded. *With force.* You defended Bezer'ej for five centuries—with force. You're not native to this system, so how does walking into someone else's system with a new rule book fit Targassat's teaching? Where's the line?"

"I see a line, though, and I draw it."

"Just tell me where your line is, then."

"Intervening in a world where there are no people being exploited." When wess'har said *people,* they meant any species, *all* species; there was no distinction for them between man and animal, intelligent or otherwise. Shan had never been sure what the opposite might be of *intelligent life.* "The isenj only cause themselves problems—except when they stray off their world."

Shan felt a *but* forming. "I don't imagine the aquatic life that's still alive on Umeh would agree with you."

"I agree that the line's often hard to see."

"Here's my problem with it. There was diversity on Umeh once. They wiped it out. So, according to this logic, all you have to do is knock off anything alive that's likely to call for help, and the Targassat statute of limitations kicks in—bang, you're only hurting your own kind now, so we leave you to it."

"I never said this was easy or absolute. Only that I feel uncomfortable with the way the Eqbas do things, and that I wouldn't do them."

"You still haven't said what you don't want me to do if we're to remain friends."

"This isn't an ultimatum."

"Just tell me. I've never known a wess'har afraid to speak their mind."

"I fear for the erosion of this society's founding principles, and that this will escalate. I don't want to see a friend become an instrument of that."

Nevyan had a point about culture shock. The wess'har life here was quite specifically agrarian, and in a contrived way: it was a blend of high technology—still way beyond humankind's for all its antiquity—and deliberate simplicity. They could have used machines to plant, tend and harvest crops, and they could have had elaborate cities and roads and factories, but they opted for manual labor, minimal facilities and sinking everything they could below ground level. It wasn't real. She'd once thought it was like Marie Antoinette's shepherdess act, but that the wess'har really did rely on their agriculture to survive. Shan had never seen any automation beyond the nanite-maintained fighter craft and the underground transport system. If she hadn't seen that and the ITX comms links, she'd have thought this was a pre-industrial civilization. She hadn't even seen a doctor or a hospital or a street-cleaning team.

"I'm not leaving," Shan said. "So I'm not going to be invading anyone and getting them to clean up their act the hard way. Does that reassure you?"

Nevyan smelled perilously close to the edge of confrontation but she stopped short. Shan detected the faintest hint of ripe mango, the *jask* pheromone of dominance, but it didn't develop further, and she wondered what it would be like to face the full strength of it and be triggered into subservience. *Am I wess'har enough to experience it?* She was certainly wess'har enough to out-*jask* the matriarch Chayyas by accident, and that was why Nevyan was in this spot now.

It's my fault. I screwed the pecking order of the matriarchs by throwing my hormonal weight around. Accident or not, this is my doing.

"I need your support, Shan, not your hostility." Nevyan stepped back a few paces and her head-tilting indicated she was more bewildered than angry. "You know you have misgivings."

"Yeah, and I'm going to do what Targassat suggested and keep my bloody nose out of it." What did she know about Targassat? Not a lot. Isolationist, minimum-impact lifestyle, big on personal responsibility. It was the definition of the last bit that gave her all the problems. "I just *observed.* Jesus

Christ, what do you expect me to do? Talk Esganikan out of it? Out of what, exactly? Tell her to leave Umeh alone? Forget about Earth?"

"As long as the isenj are confined to Umeh, they are no threat."

"As long as they have population pressures, they'll want to colonize." Shan turned to walk away, crushed to be losing something that she never thought she even needed—a friend. Where was the matriarchal consensus now? "And what about Earth? I was tasked with bringing the gene bank home. Forget that I was set up, forget that they never planned on me actually doing it—I did what I was tasked to do. Now I want Earth put back *right*. That's one thing I can trust the Eqbas to do that my own species can't."

"You could take control of this."

"I don't *want* control."

"We made her cede before."

"Oh no, not that. No *jask*."

"Combined, neither of us has to take her position. It's just persuasion."

"No. Sorry, Nev, but *no*. Look, I've got to get back home. We'll talk later."

Shan walked away, not actually sure that she should go home yet. She was a seething mass of conflict. Rayat and Lindsay were loose on Bezer'ej, Vijissi had just come back from hell, Nevyan was locked in an all-too-human ideological struggle with the Eqbas, and all Shan wanted to do right then was lock the door and curl up with Aras and Ade. It was needy. She couldn't go home *needy*. She had responsibilities. She had to get a grip before she opened that door.

Shapakti might be able to sort Vijissi. I'll ask him. I'll take a tissue sample. He can have a go at removing c'naatat, *and then the poor little sod can—*

A distant howl of pain stopped her and raised the hairs on her nape. F'nar was a natural amphitheater honeycombed with passages; sound was carried and magnified. The sound was pure animal, a wailing, inarticulate scream of distress.

Vijissi had regained consciousness.

She turned on her heel and broke into a fast walk, the stand-off with Nevyan forgotten. The two of them pushed through the ussissi at the doorway. Under stress, ussissi turned into one single chittering, anxious animal, mirroring each other's movements, teeth bared, and Shan found herself instantly wary of them. But they kept well back from Vijissi. The warning about infection had been heeded.

Why did every bastard have the sense to avoid c'naatat *except humans?*

Vijissi's eyes were open and a thin trail of foam emerged from the corner of his mouth. Shan leaned over him, ready to pull back. *Shit, I bit Ade's hand when I was coming around, didn't I?* The terrified howl had been replaced by rapid, panicky breathing punctuated by little whimpers.

"It's me," she whispered. "Vijissi, it's Shan. Can you hear me?"

He *creaked.* She could describe it no other way. He turned his head towards her and the dry *ak-ak-ak* sound from his mouth was like cane bending and breaking. He was shaking with the effort.

Jesus, I looked like that. Less than a corpse.

He was in this state because he wouldn't abandon her, and she remembered—as she remembered most days—that she hadn't helped a gorilla desperately in need of her aid. She had no excuse now that she didn't understand what was required. Vijissi needed her, and there was no walking away from this.

Put it right.

Shan fought down her revulsion and did something she had rarely done to anyone in her entire life. She folded Vijissi in her arms and cuddled him like a frightened child. Nobody else here dared: and nobody else in creation had experienced what he had. Only her.

"We'll get you through this," she said. His finely pleated skin looked like short fur and felt like corduroy stretched over a frame so frail that she almost lifted him without meaning to. "*I'll* get you through it."

Stupid little sod: he should have let her go, should have let her step out that airlock alone, should have—

But he hadn't, and she would deal with it, because it was the right thing to do.

Umeh: Northern Assembly airspace

"What you watch?"

Hayin wasn't quite the linguist his commander was, and Eddie wondered if he could trade language lessons for future favors. A ship's comms officer was a handy pal to have for a man who always needed an ITX link to Earth.

Eddie gestured at the transparent section in the bulkhead where it joined the deck. A haze of smoke was visible in the distance across the Maritime Fringe's border. "Funny how all wars look the same."

"Why funny?"

"Another word for *odd*. Not *amusing*." No bloody laughs here, that was for sure: he had the same sense of predatory voyeurism as when he'd watched wars from hotels across borders on Earth. There was something disorienting about sipping a beer while artillery flashed and boomed a few miles away. The only thing missing was the beer and the genuine danger. "What's happening?"

"Isenj fight overnight. Many die on both sides. You want see better?" Hayin tapped the bulkhead with his spidery fingertips as if he was drumming idly on a table. The bulkhead thinned to transparency level with Eddie's eyes. "See? This creates visible field."

It was a very good view of the horizon. The sky, amber with smog, faded into gold as Nir set. Tall buildings, packed like pine forests, created a silhouette of spikes and domes and asymmetric roofs. Hayin tapped again and the image magnified times ten.

"Amazing," said Eddie, meaning the optics.

"They become mad," said Hayin. "Calm to cope with crowding, but any trouble—then they *tip*." He made a gesture with his fingers, splaying them like an opening flower. Eddie took it as a mime of an explosion: it was the equivalent of human finger-snapping. "They are unused to fight, too."

And you are too, mate. The Eqbas hadn't taken a casualty yet and Eddie got the impression they never would. Vast superiority of that kind cushioned you against the reality of destruction. Asymmetric force didn't even come close.

"How do you feel when you see death on that scale?" How-do-you-feel questions were professional anathema, but there was no other way to phrase it for Hayin that wouldn't be a leading question. Eddie wanted to understand him, not get a good quote out of him. "What do you think when you see isenj dying?"

Hayin did the rapid head-tilting of a wess'har contemplating a fascinating object. "I regret they get like this. I regret they not stop breeding sooner. Sad, but life is sad. All worlds, all die."

"Sorry?" Jesus, did they wipe out populations? *Try plain English.* "You mean you kill everyone?"

"No. Life ends. Life ends for all, one day." His almost-flat brown face—not at all like the long-muzzled local wess'har—seemed to relax into a humanly satisfied expression. "Even *c'naatat.* They end too, yes?"

He was a laugh a minute, this one, just like Shan. "They can be killed. But it's not easy."

"Useful," said Hayin. "There new ones now. Maybe too many."

"Shan's no risk, mate, believe me. You must know *that* by now. Nor Ade."

"Not Ade." Hayin froze and looked baffled for a moment. Maybe the syntax was too complex for him. But when they froze, something had caught them off guard. Eddie waited for him to carry on, but he simply went back to his station without another word.

Ah well. You must sound bloody strange to him too.

Eddie wandered down the length of the ship, trying to orient himself the same way as he had on board *Actaeon.* It was hard. The bulkheads were filled with displays he couldn't read, shifting panels of colored light that sometimes seemed set in the material of the hull and sometimes floated above the surface. The lack of solidity disoriented him. Warships were supposed to be gray and functional and full of straight lines, not a cross between a hall of mirrors and a nightclub.

That was how it felt. He had the analogy nailed down now. A fluid, shifting illusion, and he was probably missing a lot of the detail because his eyes were just the regular human trichromat kind.

Eddie took his bearings as best he could; there was no guarantee that the features he memorized would still be there on the way back. The Eqbas ability to manipulate matter and energy was beyond his comprehension. Any ship that could melt and reform into separate vessels was the product of a wholly different mind.

He could now hear Aitassi so he followed the sound. She spoke eqbas'u complete with the overtone that he'd tried to reproduce for so long: higher pitched than the Eqbas around her, but an equally complex descant to her own voice. Was there a separate ussissi language? He'd only heard them speak the language of the species they worked alongside, and they seemed to absorb that effortlessly. His original view of them as smart, co-evolved companion animals like dogs had vanished.

He wasn't sure what an animal was any longer. If push came to shove, he wasn't even sure that he could define a plant, either.

Esganikan knelt on the deck of her cabin surrounded by translucent hand-sized slabs of material, and Aitassi was peering at one of them as if mesmerized by the display of green lights. When Eddie leaned into the open hatchway a little—it still surprised him when he felt the hard, solid, warm material of the frame—he could see that some of the slabs actually held images of maps and charts. He assumed they were of Umeh.

"Commander," said Eddie. "I was wondering if you could spare some time to talk to me."

Esganikan bobbed her plume. "Now?"

Aitassi's matte black stare tracked him. The charming image of the almost-meerkat gave way to the reality of an aggressive pack animal with disconcertingly dead eyes. Somehow the eyes bothered him more now than the array of close-packed teeth.

"Whenever's convenient for you."

"Now."

She didn't seem to be one for making appointments. Everything was *now* for her.

Threat is now.

That was one of their phrases; it made more sense the more time he spent with them. Suddenly it struck him that he knew more about aliens than any human alive except Shan and maybe Ade, and that was quite something for a man with a degree in anthropology. It would have been a wonderful thing to ram down Graham Wiley's throat, but the snobbish bastard was almost certainly dead now. He felt like digging him up to make the point.

See, you tosser, I did it. It was worth the one-way ticket after all. Shove that up your syndicated arse.

"Okay," said Eddie. He just wanted to talk, not record. He made a point of taking out the bee cam and placing it back in his pocket but Esganikan seemed never to care whether she was being recorded or not. "Is your approach to dealing with the Maritime Fringe indicative of your strategy for Earth?"

"Not in all respects," said Esganikan.

Phew. "So how does it differ?"

"Earth still has a mixed ecology. It also has humans who actively work to maintain environmental balance. We will be much more *selective* if we need to obtain cooperation."

"What do you mean by selective? Bioweapons?"

"Not necessarily. The Northern Assembly wants us to give them bioweapons to target their enemies. If we use a pathogen that specific, it will not take account of an individual isenj's state of mind. But I see no isenj that are *militant greens,* as you call them."

Eddie should have been used to this by now. But old taboos died hard. "We have long-standing bans on the use of biological weapons on Earth for moral reasons."

Esganikan looked fascinated; Eddie could tell by the slow sideways tilt of her head. It was always a bad idea to use the word *moral* in any cross-cultural conversation, let alone one with a real alien, and he'd been brought up short by ussissi and wess'har about moral relativity too many times. Just when humans thought they had adopted moral absolutes, the bloody wess'har pulled the rug out from under them. Eddie could already feel it moving now.

"Your proscription only involves your own kind. You have no ban on using biological agents against other species when they become too numerous."

Here we go. "No. You know we don't."

"And you helped secure isenj tissue samples to create the pathogen now deployed on Bezer'ej."

That was different. It was to save Bezer'ej from invasion. Eddie wanted to blurt that out, but he couldn't. He had no idea now if it *was* any different: he was starting to lose all sense of what was right and wrong because he'd seen the wess'har point of view once too often.

"I know you're only stating facts and not rebuking me," said Eddie.

"No, that was a rebuke." Her echo of a voice was level and unemotional. "Did I not make it clear? I think you have inconsistent standards."

"*Double* standards."

"When the task force reaches Earth, we want to talk to those with *one* standard."

Yes, she really meant *task force.* She had all the military jargon down pat, she was a *soldier.* He looked into her eyes; she had the same petal-like lobes of pupils as Giyadas except the cruciform iris was more deep olive green than gold. There was something utterly focused about her that reminded him so much of Shan that it scared him. They'd both come to environmental enforcement from tough jobs;

they were both ruthless and uncompromising. There seemed to be a universal type of hard-arsed female that transcended species, and for a moment Eddie thought that someone had got the phrase *earth-mother* horribly wrong. This wasn't the embodiment of maternal fertility and the source of all life, but the implacable ruthlessness of nature itself, a mother who devoured her weakling young without pity.

Females scared the shit out of him. He was trapped in a universe of matriarchs at the mercy of warrior queens.

"Are you going to show the Australian PM what you've done here?" asked Eddie. "I'd like to see his reaction to civilian casualties."

"You recorded it. It is no secret."

Wess'har don't bluff. They don't understand it. They're literal. But it was just the kind of saber-rattling any human government would indulge in, and journalists were a convenient vector for that message; both sides walked the line between using and being used.

"How much contact have you had with him so far?"

Esganikan rumbled faintly in her throat. "Not as much as I want."

"Well, if you show him images of deep-fried isenj, he's going to panic."

"And what do humans do when they panic?"

"They overreact. They can get aggressive." *I'm trying to be helpful.* "They don't always give in."

"You have observed what happens when isenj overreact."

"You're very confident about your ability to deal with Earth on a military level."

"We know your current capabilities and unless your mindset and skills alter out of all recognition in the next thirty years, then you have neither the engineering capability, infrastructure or the political will to match our technology by then."

Eddie maintained eye contact. Wess'ej wess'har respected that, so he assumed Eqbas did too. Like her cousins,

Esganikan might simply have been speaking literally; or she might have been warning him. Either way, she had grasped English and a great deal of subtlety about human semantics in a frighteningly short time.

"Personal question, ma'am," he said. "Are you typical for an Eqbas, or are you what we'd call a high-flier? Someone who has exceptional talent."

She'd be immune to flattery. She'd take it as the literal question it was and give him a straight answer. He wanted to know if she was normal for an Eqbas, although he suspected he already knew the answer.

"I was selected for strategic skills," she said. "I am suited to this work so it is my obligation to do it."

"Ah." Just like the F'nar matriarchs, power was thrust upon those with the skills. Ambition wasn't one of their failings— not ambition for power, anyway. It was almost conscription. "You and Shan have a lot in common, then. She was drafted too. So, do you want my footage—my images—to show Canh Pho?"

"We recorded all our actions here. We keep records."

Boy, that sounds familiar. "What next?"

"We decide if giving biological countermeasures to the Northern Assembly will achieve anything positive."

Eddie wondered how he would report *that.* He was talking about an automatic war crimes rap.

What am I? If someone asked me what I was, who I'd defend, whose side I'm on now—what would I say?

He feared for Earth. No, he feared for *Europe,* and just the corner of it that was his home. The rest might as well have been another planet, like Umeh.

Maybe biological weapons would rekindle News Desk's interest in the situation out here. Eddie thought of the rioting and conflict that followed his first revelation that an Eqbas task force was coming, and wondered if the latest development would do far worse.

He still wasn't certain if that made it his fault. His mind went back to Hayin for some reason, and it occurred

to him that it was the first time he'd seen any wess'har clam
up on him.

Odd, that. Very odd.

F'nar

Ade opened his eyes and was briefly aware of smooth
hair against his mouth. After a couple of moments he realized he was still curled up against Shan's back, face buried
in her hair, his knees slotted neatly into the angle of hers.

It was still wonderfully strange and new. He didn't move,
and listened half-awake for any sound of activity in the
main room: there was no sign of Aras yet. Ade slipped his
arm a little further round Shan's waist and luxuriated in the
fresh realization that he had a woman, a *wife,* an utterly reliable and loyal and unpredictably physical soul-mate.

Mine. She's mine. Aras's claim on her didn't spoil the
gentle filter of bliss one bit. *She's alive and she's mine.*

That was all that mattered. The world was going to rat shit
again, but he was working hard on not letting it touch him.

He drew his head back slowly, far enough to look at her
back. If he drew his fingers down . . . yes, it worked again:
the bioluminescence pulsed zebra-stripes of rainbow light
in waves radiating from her spine. And she smelled *delicious.* It was a scent of ripe tropical fruit, cedar and a pleasant musk. He wondered if the fruit component was what the
matriarchs referred to as *jask.* It certainly made them scared
of her. But it had a different effect on him, and it wasn't
fear, not at all.

Shan stirred.

"Dirty bugger," she murmured, and pressed her backside
further into his lap. "Sergeant Todger's up early, I see."

"Hi baby." She didn't sound disapproving. "You've got
lights down your back now. Did you know that?"

"Jesus. That's new." She made a vague effort to look over
her shoulder but settled back into the pillow with a grunt. "I
can go to fancy dress parties as an airport runway."

"It's the same pattern as Aras's stripes."

"Sometimes I think *c'naatat* gets bored and starts messing around for a laugh." She sighed as if she'd remembered something, and of course she had. "Oh God. Poor bloody Vijissi."

"Yeah."

Ade kept wondering exactly how *c'naatat* made its choices. It hadn't synchronized their sleep patterns. "Does Aras always wander around all night?"

"You've shared this house with him for the best part of a year. Didn't you notice before?"

"Not really." Ade slipped his hand over hers and checked she was still wearing the ring. "I'm usually out like a light the second I hit the pillow."

"Wess'har don't sleep like we do. They keep taking naps. Wakes me up *every* time."

"I understand their sleeping arrangements a lot better now."

"Yeah, the bedroom furniture business wouldn't make much money here. Look, about Vijissi—"

"How far back does this memory thing go?"

"Jesus, Ade, you've really picked up that wess'har habit of jumping from subject to subject."

"Sorry. I've got your memories and some of Aras's. Shouldn't I be getting isenj ones? And what about the other hosts before that?"

"You want to think like an isenj?"

"Why not?" He was curious. "Do you?"

"I don't know. When I was coming round from the coma, I had some weird flashes of memory that I couldn't even identify by species." She twisted her head to look at him and studied his face as if she hadn't seen him before. "I don't get it much now."

"Your memories are pretty repetitive."

"Thanks, Ade. I'm a disturbed girl."

Ade often saw the sheet of liquid flame cascading down a riot shield right in front of his eyes; that, and the gorilla making the hand signals, and the peeling blue door she kicked open, and a persistent sense of desperately trying to do something. He didn't know what yet. "You had a shitty job."

"We all did."

"I loved being in the Corps. Whatever happened, I still *loved* it."

"It upset you getting kicked out."

"'Course it did." Being a Royal Marine had been his life, his only family and solace since he was sixteen years old. "Not fair on the detachment. I want the verdict quashed, Boss."

"I know, sweetheart. I hope Esganikan can get some diplomatic pressure applied. It was supposed to appease the wess'har but they don't need appeasing now. Not by the detachment, anyway."

"Thanks." This was one of the reasons he adored her. She knew what comradeship and honor meant in ways that a regular civvie didn't. She'd been in uniform and taken lives and been shot, and when the past crowded in on him, she was one of the handful of people he knew who understood what that really meant and what it did to you. "Nobody will even remember who we were, but I want the history books to get it right."

"You're a sweet naive boy, Ade Bennett. Go and talk to Eddie about truth sometime."

He rested his forehead against the nape of her neck and basked in the comfort for a while.

"How do you think Vijissi's going to cope, then?"

"Dunno. It's hard at first. Christ, I remember going off on one when I found Aras had infected me without asking." She meshed her fingers with his and squeezed slightly. "I never asked how *you* coped, did I?"

"It was the least of my problems at the time."

"You take everything in your stride, don't you?"

"Paid to. Well, *was,* anyway."

"Maybe you can help Vijissi more than I can. Or Aras. He had a lot of practice at being alone too." She paused. "Ade, how did I get from being EnHaz and hating anything to do with gene mangling and bastard scientists to being okay with bioweapons?"

"Circumstances."

"Means justifying ends?"

"Life's not as clear-cut as we think, is it?"

"I always thought I had a solid sense of right and wrong."

"You went native with eco-terrorists you should have busted. I reckon that shows an appreciation of gray areas."

"You know I carried on using them in EnHaz, don't you? Handy for unofficial enforcement when I couldn't get charges to stick on a company. Come home to a nice roaring fire. That kind of stuff."

"You were a bad girl, weren't you?" He knew just how bad sometimes. It was disturbing to be briefly in the head of someone who was doing the punching when your own memories were about being beaten. "But don't blame yourself about Vijissi."

"Well, that makes six *c'naatat* now."

"Shit. Clocking up the numbers, aren't we?"

"It's okay. I'm not going to start another fight."

Ade bit back an apology. That just wound her up: his efforts were better spent on making sure she had nothing to worry about on Bezer'ej. He molded himself around her again and buried his face in her hair.

"So . . . do you mind if we have a proper Christmas?"

"You don't need my permission."

"But Pagans don't observe it."

"I'm a *very* lapsed Pagan and I like eating to excess as much as anyone."

"Y'know, I always dreaded Christmas. Dad was a lot worse when he was drunk. They say suicide rates and domestic violence are worse at Christmas because families get cooped up together. Bloody true in our house. Fucking awful."

"Then we'll try and have a good one."

As a boy, Ade had always planned his escape just to stay sane. When he was old enough to leave home, he'd join the Marines and get as far from his dad as he could. He'd meet a nice girl, and they'd have kids who'd never have to lie about how they got the burn marks on their hands, or spend the night sleeping in the bus station because they were too scared to go home.

He'd met the girls; but they never stayed. And he never had the kids to give the childhood he'd never had. But he'd finally found his nice girl, even if she was very different from his boyhood fantasies, and it didn't matter one bit that there was now absolutely nothing normal about his life or hers.

He had a wife and he had a brother. And that was enough for any man.

9

*Our future lies with the Eqbas. If we cooperate with them,
we become the dominant force on Umeh. We don't have the
military capability to achieve that ourselves. What do we
want? To slide inexorably towards the collapse of the infrastructure of the whole planet, with no guarantee that the
Northern Assembly will survive the chaos that follows, or to
embrace change and become the new world order?*

MINISTER PAR NIR BEDOI

Bezer'ej: near Ouzhari

Sand castles. They're sand castles.

It was Rayat's first thought when he saw the bezeri settlement. The buildings were cones, columns and domes, clustered together like an asymmetric jelly mold. They looked
as if a single wave would sweep them away. Colored stones
were set into grooves and depressions in the walls.

And the settlement was deserted.

He followed the faint, pulsing green light in Saib's mantle. There was no sound coming from the signal lamp and
he took their green light to be wordless noise, as if the bezeri were humming to themselves. But it might just have been
the equivalent of a heartbeat.

Rayat was starting to notice pattern in the light sequences.
The intensity seemed to convey emphasis like volume in
sound. Saib swam ahead of him in rhythmic, explosive
bursts, propelled by a jet of water, his green light more no-
ticeable as he slipped into shadow from filtered sunlight and
back again. The bezeri appeared to be comfortable swimming at any depth, just like cephalopods on Earth, but it

seemed they chose to live nearer the surface in the shallows around the landmasses.

Maybe they could have avoided the fallout from Ouzhari if they'd chosen to live deeper and further from the shoreline. But, like humans, they lived in places where it wasn't always safe.

Lindsay swam parallel with Rayat, hair billowing just like it did in zero-g. He'd given up conversation with her for the time being. He felt feverish even in cold water. He was sure the sea around him would boil sooner or later.

I have to sleep tonight. And I have to eat.

Eating. He'd steeled himself to that. His instinct— somebody's instinct, anyway—took over. He swam through fanlike white growths on the rocks and caught a ribbon of it between his fingers. If it was the one thing that *c'naatat* couldn't handle, it was too bad. Maybe Lindsay would note that it killed him and identify it as a way of stopping the parasite from spreading if it ever did fall into the wrong hands. She wasn't wholly incompetent: just impossibly *subjective.*

So whose hands are the wrong hands?

Rayat didn't know if that was his own thought or that bitch Frankland's. He broke off a piece of the white ribbon and chewed it. He was now an animal on the brink between survival and death, and it was wonderfully focusing in the way it shut down all his long-term planning. *Can I eat this?* It tasted metallic and salty.

His body said *yes.*

He snapped off more of the white growths and swam on to catch up with Saib and the other bezeri. He'd never been an animal before. There had been brief moments of pain and danger in his life when he'd glimpsed his primal self for a few seconds at a time, even minutes, but this felt indefinite and the way he might be forever if he didn't keep his mind sharp.

They passed more molded mud villages. The groups of sandcastle buildings became a strip and then what could only be described as a city with buildings curved around rocks and slopes, some of them stacked one on top of the other. If you swam, you needed no horizontal roads. There was none of the decay in the water that he'd tasted near the map repository.

Rayat made his way towards Lindsay and gestured for the lamp. Her eyes had that flat, dead look that a barrier of water created but she showed no dissent and handed him the device.

"Saib?" He caught up with the patriarch and moved in front of him, treading water. "Saib, tell me about this place. What is it?"

A city we once lived in before the isenj came and killed us with their pollution.

"How long has it been abandoned?"

For generations. There were many millions of us once, spread across this part of the world.

Tens of thousands had died after the detonation of cobalt devices on Christopher Island. That gave Rayat a good idea of how fragile bezeri biochemistry was, and how long it took them to recover their population numbers from the last disaster. They hadn't; they'd still been struggling back to strength after the isenj occupation when the bombs detonated. Five centuries, and that was all they could manage— a few hundred thousand. Now there were around fifty, the few of breeding age all from one family.

They were doomed to extinction. They had passed the point of recovery.

"When things are normal, how many young do you produce?" It was a brutally zoological way of putting it, and he hoped it didn't come across as dismissive. "How fast do you breed?"

One child every six, seven years. Our eggs mature for many seasons. We must be thirty years or more before we can reproduce.

"Yeah, think about that, you bastard," said Lindsay.

Bezeri had very little in their favor in survival terms. Against the fast-breeding isenj, they were the universe's losers.

Rayat thought of the impact that *c'naatat* would have on

Earth. You did right. *You didn't have much choice.* Yes, he
still believed that.

It was the nature of his job. Collateral damage was inevitable and it didn't take away the need to get the job done.
Rayat handed back the lamp and Saib directed him into one
of the mud cones.

Concrete might have been a better description than mud.
When he ran his hand down the walls, they were smooth
and hard, dotted with inlaid colored stone and fragments of
shell. The floor wasn't packed silt but the same hard material. He grounded himself and walked on it.

He was so engrossed in wondering how they'd made
these structures that he almost didn't see the three bezeri
huddled in an alcove until one uncoiled and its bioluminescence flared in a pulsing pattern like chaser lights. He
flinched instinctively. Saib glided between them and
wrapped his tentacles around one of them. The exchange of
lights was a conversation that Rayat couldn't understand.

He wasn't looking at cephalopods now: he was looking at
people.

Get out of my head, Frankland. Get out, you bitch.

But it wasn't a fragment of her memory; it was his
own painful revelation, and it was different. He could feel it.
He'd met aliens. He'd encountered four intelligent species
and seen many more alien life-forms in this system. But
each time his rational mind had noted them and their characteristics, he'd never had that pang of recognition, that vis-
ceral realization that there was *someone just like him* inside
them.

Rayat had too many questions now. He needed desperately to communicate without using the lamp. He *had* to.
The more he knew, the better his chances of getting home.

Lindsay squeezed through the opening and settled beside
him. She had a firm grip on the device and didn't look ready
to surrender it.

"Okay, you've got the talking stick," said Rayat. The room
had openings at apparently random points in the walls, some
set high off the ground and he assumed they were connecting

doors. *Bezeri live in freefall, dummy; they swim. Think zero-g spaceship architecture.* "Who are they? I need names."

Shafts of aquamarine light pierced the gloom of the chamber. Rayat looked up; the roof of the building was dotted with inserts of the same transparent shell that sandwiched the sand maps. He was getting a sense of how bezeri lived and what they liked. They liked light. But they could function at extreme depths, and they had bioluminescence, so they didn't *need* light. It spoke to him of beings that wanted to explore, and he knew that was as much an emotional reaction as a scientific one.

Rayat concentrated on everything *but* emotion. He wanted his scientific rationality, or his animal survival instincts; he didn't want regret or empathy or any of the other unreliable, weakening elements of being human to make his time down here any harder than it had to be.

"Take the bloody thing, then." Lindsay thrust the lamp at him. "I need to eat." She backed out of the chamber. Saib uncurled a tentacle in her direction. "Just going outside to find some seaweed, okay? I'm not running away. I've got nowhere to go."

Rayat took the lamp. "*Rye-aht*," he said. "Rayat." Nobody called him Mohan; he'd always been just Rayat. He couldn't remember the last person who had called him by his first name, let alone *Mo*. For some reason that crushed him for a few seconds. "My name is Rayat."

"Ooorrrrrrr," said one of the bezeri in a stream of bubbles. "Oooorrrrrraaaaaa . . . ."

A talking squid. And I'm not even surprised.

If bezeri could manipulate air and water in their body cavity, maybe he'd learn to use light—if he developed bioluminescence. They rippled with rainbows, living liquid opals, and the lamp's translation systems took over.

I am Pili, a mother. She is Seem, mother of mothers. He is Keet, father of fathers.

"Where are your children?"

Dead. All of them.

Rayat laid the lamp aside as Saib deposited armfuls of

azin maps in front of Pili and the others. They seemed far more interested in fondling the maps than in his questions. Their light patterns changed into repetitive concentric circles of violet, ruby and gold that welled up from bright central points all over their mantles. It was a pattern he hadn't seen before.

Their maps were their past. They were looking at their history. For a moment Rayat imagined browsing through a picture album of relatives long dead and had a brief, awful glimpse into what the bezeri might be thinking.

He shook it off. *You came here to secure* c'naatat *for the FEU and to stop any other government getting hold of it. That's all: nothing else. Don't forget that.* Sentimentality was dangerous.

The bezeri appeared to have forgotten him. He slid down the smooth wall and rested his head on his folded arms, knees drawn up, and the moment he closed his eyes, reality crowded in on him again and he was *drowning*.

He jerked his eyes open again and found he had braced both hands on the floor of the chamber. The more he looked at his right hand, the more disoriented he felt.

It didn't look the same any longer. Something wasn't quite right. He thought for a brief elated moment that he saw a colored spark, but it was something more bizarre even than that. The faint play of light came from the floor.

His hand was becoming translucent.

"I wanted lights," he said. *"Lights."*

Maybe *c'naatat* could hear him. There was no harm trying.

F'nar, Wess'ej: experimental rainforest habitat

Shan had to hand it to Deborah Garrod. For a woman whose husband had been decapitated, she was being very polite to his executioner.

Aras walked beside her, pointing out objects of interest on the plain as they approached F'nar. The transport could have taken them straight to the city, but Shan knew why Aras had opted to walk the last two kilometers. He wanted to see Deborah's face when she caught sight of F'nar.

The City of Pearl left humans stunned. Shan wasn't steeped in Christian mythology, but it had left her reeling the first time she saw it; she could only guess what impact it had on people who thought their heaven looked like that.

Deborah inhaled sharply and put both hands to her mouth.

"It's exquisite," she said. She paused for a moment, eyes closed. Shan assumed she was praying. It didn't seem the right time to tell her the nacre coating was insect shit. "I had no idea."

"You should see it on a nice summer evening." Shan walked on, hands in pockets. Aras walked alongside Deborah. Her two kids hadn't come with her. Shan's last encounter with the teenaged son, James, had involved slamming him against a wall and backhanding him to get him to tell her what his dad was doing, so maybe that was just as well. *Dad's just helping Commander Neville bomb Ouzhari. Thanks, kid.* "How does everyone feel about going back to Earth?"

"Apprehensive, but happy."

"It's an alien planet for you. Big upheaval."

"A sense of fulfillment, though. For both of us. This was your mission too."

"Yes." *I only* thought *it was. That's what you get for trying to stitch me up, Perault.* "Well, when you see the macaws, it'll put it all in perspective."

Shan wanted to get it over with. Somehow it felt like taking a relative to identify a body, and she was more concerned with getting back to visit Vijissi to check on his progress.

She didn't mention him to Deborah. It couldn't remain a secret forever, but the longer it took for the colonists or Eddie to find out, the more time she had to maneuver. Twenty-five light-years wasn't distance enough to reassure her that *c'naatat* was out of reach of Earth.

Deborah slowed down as she drew closer to the F'nar, and when the sun came out from behind thick cloud and illuminated the top level of the terraces in fierce white light she stopped again. Shan and Aras waited, silent. Then Deborah gathered herself and walked on.

Da Shapakti was waiting for them at the top of the flight of steps that led down into the tunnels beneath the city. He kept rolling his head slightly, a preening gesture almost like the re-created macaws he was so proud of: he'd even delayed his departure for Bezer'ej so that he could show off the birds to Deborah.

Deborah peered down into the stairwell. "Just like Constantine. Everything's underground."

Shan hung back to let Shapakti lead the way. The enclosed rainforest environment that he'd created was nestled between the dimly lit hangar bays of fighter craft, built thousands of years ago and maintained by nanotech, and still capable of taking out a FEU warship like *Actaeon*. The more intrusive aspects of city life—the utilities, generators, storage and manufacturing facilities—were housed down here. F'nar might have been less rigorous about making minimum visual impact on the natural landscape than the stricter Targassati wess'har further north, but it still kept its industrial side carefully concealed. Even a meticulously agrarian society needed some ugly technology. It was the only hidden aspect of this transparent culture that Shan had seen.

Shapakti opened the double airlock that sealed the terrestrial environment. Warm, humid air rolled out and Deborah inhaled audibly as she stepped through the portal. Shan knew how she felt. The oxygen-rich air and smell of Earth, of familiar things, was almost shocking.

But Deborah had never smelled the air of Earth, and she was the fourth generation of settlers habituated to lower oxygen levels on Bezer'ej. She wasn't remembering. She was *imagining*.

"You grew all this from the gene bank?" she asked.

Shapakti held out his arm and the two macaws plummeted like raptors from their favored roost a few meters above him to land on it, squabbling over the best position. They were more than bright: they were *luminous*. Shan saw them in ultraviolet, as they saw themselves, with all their vivid patches.

Deborah gasped, even though she saw only in a human's narrow spectrum.

"These birds, yes," said Shapakti. His English was perfectly clear despite the overtone. "I get the plants from Umeh Station, already growing. I accelerate their development."

Deborah had never struck Shan as a demonstrative woman. As a guest in the Garrods' house, Shan had catalogued her as the stoic sensible type, a frontier woman in every sense, a dispenser of tea and first aid when disaster struck. But now she burst into tears and stood staring at the macaws, one hand to her mouth. The birds shrieked at her.

Shan felt a pang of embarrassment and for a moment she envied Deborah her loss of control. *I had no idea how much emotion these people invested in the gene bank. But they think they're doing it for God, don't they? That must ring the bell for them, all right.* But where Deborah saw pearls and the fruition of dreams, Shan saw insect shit and just the beginning of a long struggle—one she wasn't going to be part of.

"What are you going to do with them?" Deborah asked.

"Take them back to Earth," said Shapakti.

"How many species are you going to revive before you reach Earth?"

"Few. Only plants. The macaws are experimental."

"But you think you can do it?"

"We restore ecosystems. We do this."

"Yeah, I think Shapakti knows what he's doing." Shan gave the macaws a wide berth in case they took a peck at her. *C'naatat* made her wary of every possible accidental contact. "Now all the Eqbas have to do is get the Earth governments to behave and let them do the restoration. That's going to be the interesting bit."

Deborah raised her chin a fraction. "There's no point my telling you to have faith, is there?"

"I've got faith in Shapakti."

"I shall never see Earth," he said. "My mission ends here. I go home."

He didn't seem disappointed. Shan knew he missed his family; he had an image of his home on the bulkhead of his ship, a little indication of homesickness that was touchingly . . . human. *Poor sod.* But once you'd restored one world, maybe you'd restored them all. Even miracles palled in time.

Deborah wiped her eyes with the heel of her hand. "Josh would have been so happy to see this."

Aras didn't react. Shan couldn't smell any agitation. He seemed to be checking out the dimensions of the tropical hothouse, no doubt sizing it up for terrestrial crops.

Deborah held her arm out and one of the macaws studied it for a moment before edging onto her hand a step at a time. Aras paused in his inspection of the raised beds of soil to watch. There was no sound either from macaw or woman. It eyed her, head cocked on one side in a disturbingly wess'har way.

"*Uk'alin'i che,*" it said, almost with an overtone. *Feed me.* It rustled vivid turquoise feathers. Deborah laughed, but the tears were still welling in her eyes.

"So what are you feeding them?" asked Shan.

"Synthesized nutrient pellets. When we relocate to Bezer'ej, I will grow fruit and seeds for them."

"How much of the habitat are you removing?" Shan kept a careful eye on the parrot. "We could grow crops here."

"Your marines have already planted some. Look." Shapakti reached into the raised bed and indicated small plants each with a pair of ovate glossy leaves. "I will avoid disturbing the seedlings when I remove the foliage plants."

Aras *urrred.* It was a sound like someone riffling through a wad of paper sheets, and he only did it when he was relaxed and happy. Shan hadn't heard him do it for a long time; it was a good sign. Having Ade around as a housebrother and the prospect of interesting new crops seemed to settle him down. Aras was, at heart, as much of a pragmatist as she was. For the first time she felt that—with effort—her life might settle down too and become like anyone else's, except for the fact she was light-years from Earth, living with two genetic chimeras and pretty well indestructible. But it was a lot more normal than her previous existence.

As soon as she sorted the problems in hand—those two bastards on Bezer'ej, and Vijissi—she'd count her blessings as carefully as she could, and not look an inch beyond them.

"Bananas," said Aras. "And grapes."

"Not many grapes like tropical conditions."

"I didn't realize you were so informed about grapes."

"I'm a mine of information," said Shan. Her father had wanted to swap city life for a smallholding, but the only soil he got was a conventional burial. It was the best she could do. "And most of the horticultural stuff was useless up to now."

Deborah still stared at the macaw. "You're not going back to Earth with us either, are you?"

"No," said Shan. "My home's here now."

"After coming so far and giving up so much?"

"You forget one small detail." There was no point telling her that *c'naatat* could probably be removed from humans but not from wess'har. It couldn't be removed from her mind, and that was where she had been changed most. The months she spent drifting in space, sporadically conscious, hardened further by every momentary realization that she was alone beyond imagining with only her inner animal core to rely upon, had left her a stranger to herself at times. And then there was Aras. She promised she wouldn't abandon him, and her word was *everything*. "I think it's best that *c'naatat* stays here."

If you're not going back to Earth, then what are you going to do for Wess'ej? What's going to become of Umeh?

The macaw appeared to decide that Deborah wasn't a source of food and swaggered back along her arm to climb onto Shapakti's. Deborah let her hand drop to her side. "What happens to you at the end of time, Shan?"

Don't. Stop it. "Who says *c'naatat* hosts live that long?"

"What if they do?"

"I'll have some interesting snapshots, then, won't I?"

Shapakti interrupted, showing extraordinary tact for an

Eqbas. "Let me show Deborah how I achieve these things. You go."

Shan took it as a hint to leave; maybe Shapakti was as sensitive to her discomfort as Aras. The parrots took off from the scientist's arm in a flurry of bright feathers and settled on a branch again.

Shan watched them and then took note of the small tree beneath. The leaves were green and glossy, rather like giant bay leaves, and the spikes of small cream flowers reminded her of bay laurel.

"What's that plant?" Shan asked, hoping for some kind of aromatic bay. Herbs mattered. They were right up there with chili and garlic in the familiar food league.

"Dwarf avocado," said Shapakti.

The thought of a new and exotic addition to the menu temporarily erased any nagging worries about how *c'naatat* hosts finally met their maker. "I'll *definitely* visit you on Bezer'ej, then. Can I take a cutting later?"

"I leave this tree for you."

"Thank you." *Vijissi. Ask him now.* "One more thing— would you mind taking a look at a tissue sample for me some time?"

"Which time?"

Be specific. "When are you leaving for Bezer'ej?"

"Perhaps two more days."

"I'll bring it to you." She managed a smile and didn't expect one back. Like Aras, all wess'har struggled to mimic that distinctly simian expression. "You're a star, Shapakti. Thanks."

He understood the meaning if not the phrase, because he *urrred* just like Aras—praised, pleased—and beckoned Deborah to follow him deeper into the forest habitat that extended thirty meters into the tunnels.

"I don't know if Ade even likes avocado, but I bloody well do." Shan walked back up the tunnels with Aras and climbed the steps towards real daylight. "And they produce lovely green oil. Think of it. Soap. Salad dressing. Fry-ups."

"Shapakti's tissue sample."

"So, I was thinking of dispensing with speech completely and just relying on telepathy," said Shan. "Am I that bloody obvious?"

"You once told me that police are very good at getting people to do things for them. You appear to have two modes of doing that—violence and exaggerated charm."

"Ouch."

"And I know your preoccupations. I have your memories." Aras took her hand gingerly in his as they walked. "You need to *clear your decks,* as Ade would say."

His hand was cool and the skin like fine suede. Something wess'har in her felt solidly happy inhaling his sandalwood scent. "I hate unfinished business hanging around. We have three *c'naatat* now outside our control."

"Is that how you think of Vijissi, *isan*? Something to be controlled?"

"Okay, so I'm a callous bitch, but why did you quarantine Bezer'ej for centuries if you didn't see it the same way?"

"I didn't say I disagreed with you. And I know Vijissi's survival is both joy and despair for you."

"And what about *you*?"

"I have no sense of guilt about his condition as you have."

"Just answer the bloody question."

"I think he's a complication, and I believe he will be very unhappy."

Shan inhaled the sweet sandalwood musk that surrounded Aras and felt inexplicably good when she should have been distracted by worry. She squeezed his arm, wondering if this was actually biochemical bonding and not love. Sleeping with Ade had placated her, too. Maybe it didn't matter: the love and bonding were the same thing in the end. Aras had struck a chord in her long before he'd infected her.

Infected. It's a funny word to use to describe someone saving your life.

Shan couldn't pretend to understand the biochemistry of *oursan*. But she'd seen Nevyan take on an entire family of males and their offspring out of duty when their *isan* died, and become utterly devoted to them in a matter of days. *Oursan*—and Shan still thought of it as sex, even if it wasn't reproductive—really did bond wess'har, males to females and so males to their housebrothers. They had no concept of infidelity and the urge never crossed their minds, and without the constant genetic repair of *oursan*, males sickened and died.

C'naatat put her odd little clan beyond that. But the instinct remained.

"Hey, I'm sorry about Black," she said. "But he was very old for a rat. He had a good life."

"Did he? What's a good life for a rat? It was an unnatural one as far as I understand, not at all how rats live in the wild."

"Well, we'd know all about unnatural, wouldn't we? And so will Vijissi. So let's see what Shapakti can do."

Shan hung on to her weird life even though she knew how to end it. *I tried once.* But here she was, living with *c'naatat* when there was no absolute need to because she knew how to end it. They all did. If Shapatki couldn't remove *c'naatat*, there was always one way left.

You're used to it, you stupid cow. And now you enjoy it, don't you? Hey, look! I was serious, I tried to once, I failed. Can I live now? Please?

Aras *urrred* again. If she was distracted from the growing *c'naatat* roll call, then he was no longer devastated by the near extinction of the bezeri or killing Josh Garrod. Life went on, the life you liked and would hang on to grimly until you couldn't hang on any longer.

But I'm not like that. I stepped out the airlock. I'm above all that—aren't I?

"Ussissi are not *gethes*," said Aras. "They have no wish to misuse *c'naatat*."

"That still leaves Vijissi. What if he changes a lot, like

you did? What if he expresses human genes, or wess'har ones? Everything that was in me?"

"He'll live with it, as I did."

There was a point at the top of the terraces, at the highest point the stairways reached, where she could look down and enjoy F'nar laid out beneath her like an iridescent bowl. Whatever the weather, whatever the light, it was always absorbing. Shan stopped now and took in the view. Bezer'ej, Wess'ej's twin, was visible as a huge but faint crescent moon.

"Jesus, it's a steep climb, isn't it? No wonder my arse is my best feature." Aras didn't laugh. She often expected him to be more human than he was. "I hope I never take this view for granted."

But her eyes were fixed on Bezer'ej. And she wasn't thinking of the exquisitely alien skyscape, or even recalling a year spent there: she found she was now thinking of bloody Lindsay Neville, the stupid destructive *selfish* little cow, and that bastard Rayat.

I can't rest until I see for myself. I can't forget them and get on with my life until I know they're never going to be a risk.

Aras sighed. He could read her like a map. But he didn't scold her.

"I'm pleased that you walked away from Umeh," he said. "You've accepted that some things are not yours to resolve."

But some still are. Just one or two, or even three, when they happen on my watch.

"The problem is that I don't know what *resolved* means anymore, sweetheart." She turned her back on Bezer'ej and longed for the days when an arrest, a charge that stuck, and a good stiff sentence meant the case was closed and she could move on.

"We mustn't forget to tell Ade about the avocados," Aras said. "Food delights him."

Ade had that solid sense of proportion common to all sergeants. So did Aras. But Shan found it much harder to lower her sights to the here and now. She thought of Bezer'ej, and knew that sooner or later, the need to settle matters would overwhelm her.

Northern Assembly border with the Maritime Fringe, Umeh: Eqbas Vorhi ship 886-001-005-6

Isenj were harder to fathom than Esganikan had thought.

Beneath her, palls of smoke drifted south from a clearly defined corridor of burned-out towers and buildings. There was no artillery activity: nobody opened fire on them. It was like the aftermath of a battle, not the start of a war.

Esganikan nodded at Hayin to open the communications link with Eit. It was convenient to use a neutral language like English and Aitassi no longer appeared offended by being bypassed as interpreter. She simply observed. "What is happening, Minister?"

"We appear to have a local difficulty."

"Define difficulty."

"The local population is cooperating with Fringe troops."

Eddie had been sitting quietly in an alcove, fiddling with his bee cam, his small mobile recording device. Esganikan was suddenly curious about bees. "Shit," Eddie said.

Esganikan took that as surprise. "Minister, are your troops repelling the Maritime Fringe invasion?"

"They are not responding to our orders to do so."

"So your army is in revolt, and your citizens are aiding your enemy."

I thought a nonviolent method might be preferable. I was wrong. And I have no need to commit ground troops.

"My priority is to keep order inside our own borders with those troops who remain loyal."

"I thought that isenj were cooperative," said Esganikan. "I believed that your crowded conditions encouraged order and consensus. That means they should do as their government has asked."

Eit didn't answer. The image of him displayed on the

bulkhead was of no use to her, because she couldn't deduce anything from his expression—if he had one. His scent would have told her nothing anyway. She glanced at Aitassi, rocking her head in silent irritation.

In her peripheral vision, Esganikan saw Eddie stand up and walk slowly towards her. His bee cam hovered at his shoulder.

"I fear a coup," said Eit. "Our invitation to you created huge rifts within the administration at every level, national and local. When Minister Ual first suggested it, there was uproar and violence that cost him his life. I admit I was among those who saw it as an act of treason."

"But you changed your mind."

There was no clear objective for Esganikan here. She'd responded to the isenj appeal for intervention, exactly as her duty required; but when it came to their internal disputes, all her guidelines deserted her. There were no other land species to consider, and the remnant of aquatic life would probably be better off if the isenj were eradicated completely. There was no target for her act of balance; and no group she could single out and hold responsible for Umeh's current condition. It was outside her experience.

She regretted agreeing to intervene. Even bioweapons wouldn't solve the Assembly's internal dissent. But complete annihilation seemed *wrong*.

"I must consider this, Minister," she said. "Be aware that genomes tend not to stop at borders. If we agree to give you a pathogen, you might have many casualties among your own citizens. As Eddie Michallat would say, that would play badly to the electorate."

Eit's quills were definitely raised a little. "Then I await your decision—as long as this government survives."

Hayin closed the link and the bulkhead screen flipped to transparency. The comms team resumed listening to the audio chatter of the isenj networks—neighbor calling neighbor, city calling city—and appeared fascinated. The ussissi crew interpreted: the information was largely irrelevant gossip and panic, but this was a new species for the Eqbas, and they were curious.

"You're wess'har," said Eddie. "The average isenj doesn't give a damn what their government tells them to do, because you're the ancient enemy embedded in their genetic memory, and you've invaded as far as they're concerned."

"And yet the Assembly cabinet can stomach our presence. Eit can, anyway. Some of the others seem indecisive."

"Well, there weren't many who thought like Par Paral Ual either," said Eddie. The human probably understood isenj better than any wess'har: the two species thought in similar ways and seemed to enjoy each other's company. "Maybe it's only Eit that's holding it together. And although isenj aren't as blatantly dishonest as we are, they're fast learners."

"As are we," said Esganikan. *And we need to learn to lie, Hayin. Foolish slip.* "If they want a sustainable environment that does not require increasing climate management each year, then they must cut their population by three-quarters. Until they accept that, I cannot restore this planet. The fact that Shomen Eit appears to be dragging his cabinet colleagues into a power grab—that is the phrase, yes?—does not alter that."

Eddie licked his lips, agitated. He had a talent for taking over discussions. Esganikan would normally have silenced a presumptuous male with a cuff around the ear, but he was a useful source of insight.

"And now you've started, you have to finish, don't you?"

"No," said Esganikan. "We *can* withdraw completely, although we rarely do. This is a wholly artificial environment. I remain concerned about whatever marine life remains, but the isenj are now only harming themselves. Earth is my priority."

"You'd walk out now, after the war's started?"

"They choose to fight."

"Are you going to give them the bioweapons?"

That depended on the definition of *give*. "We are not omnipotent. This is just one ship, and pathogens require far fewer resources than bombarding the planet."

"What a bloody mess." Eddie didn't seem to grasp her point.

Esganikan turned to Aitassi. She was aware of the whole crew watching her. "Do we have ussissi in Umeh Station at the moment?"

"Yes."

"Offer them evacuation. In fact, offer all ussissi evacuation from Umeh if they are unhappy with the situation."

"What about Umeh Station?" asked Eddie.

"We are not your defense force. You chose to build a base there." Where did he expect her to find room for evacuees with specific alien food requirements? Ussissi could go to Wess'ej. But she couldn't unload more than three hundred *gethes* on F'nar without asking, and she knew that Mar'an'cas couldn't provide food for them anyway: and no wess'har city could, either. Human biochemistry was unequipped to handle wess'har food. "There is nowhere that can accommodate them all."

Eddie looked at his bee cam and then reached out to retrieve it. She couldn't imagine what was going through his mind: perhaps he felt he had been denied dramatic pictures that he needed. He might have feared for his fellow humans in Umeh Station. He was certainly agitated.

"It's interesting to see that you get in over your heads sometimes," he said, and began walking away. "You might want to read some Earth history about what happens when you start a war between two factions and then leave them to slug it out."

"There are many deaths," said Esganikan. "I know."

"And that's part of your population reduction policy?"

Esganikan understood the tone of human rebukes now. She felt a tingle of irritation, and the crew inhaled discreetly and watched, waiting.

"Every army of occupation has to withdraw sooner or later, Eddie. There is never an ideal time, and as long as one person with old grievances remains, there will be an aftermath."

"Hence your scorched earth policy."

"The isenj have choices. This is simple causality." *He has to learn. He isn't stupid. But* gethes *simply don't see the obvious.* "They can choose to live differently, and they can also choose not to fight. *All* of us can make choices. You cannot want one thing but do another, and still expect the situation to resolve."

Eddie looked thoughtful, in slight defocus. Then he shook his head as if disagreeing with himself and left the bridge.

Aitassi watched him go and the bridge crew emitted a communal hiss.

"Earth is going to be fascinating," said Hayin. "Humans don't connect their actions with what befalls them. Don't they perceive time as linear?"

"They do," said Aitassi. "They just don't see why they should do anything *individually* to change their future to the one they want. All eight billion of them."

Hayin and a few of the bridge crew looked utterly bewildered.

The isenj were much simpler to understand in most respects. They knew what they wanted: they simply didn't have room to carry on doing it without escaping their planet and its moon. Something had to give, and that, Esganikan reminded herself, was the reason for being here: to ensure they never became a threat to Wess'ej and Bezer'ej as they had in the past.

She almost wished they would launch that threatened attack. The solution would have been very much simpler then. Even Eqbas Vorhi had rules of engagement, although Eddie seemed not to notice. They were not his rules, and so they didn't count.

"Set a course for Tivskur," she said. "I'd like a closer look."

"The reconnaissance remotes are detecting seagoing vessels in harbor with drives operating," said Hayin. "Tivskur appears to be preparing its navy."

Umeh's nearest continental neighbor also had plans, then. Maybe it would go to the aid of the Maritime Fringe: Esganikan was still uncertain of the politics of the four landmasses that made up the surface of the planet, but if they were readying ships then an Eqbas vessel wasn't their target. Did Jejeno know what was happening? Did she have a duty to tell Eit?

Would it change anything?

She was supposed to be able to operate independently, guided by the broad and unchanging principles of balance. But she wanted to excel. She wanted to be able to finish her term of service and go home with honor and self-respect intact. She wanted *jurej've* and children at last. If she didn't do her duty and maintain balance and order, she had no right to contentment.

And she would have failed her crew. They had endured a long separation from home too, a few of the males even leaving families behind in suspension, medicated to maintain their health, a rare and desperate thing. She was the commander and that made her their acting matriarch, with all the expectation of competence that went with it.

The ship climbed and pushed through cloud. From this height, Umeh could have been any planet covered largely by ocean. It was only from orbit or beneath the cloud layer that the dying seas and land almost entirely obliterated by building were visible as patterns of pink and gray and rust. The surveillance remotes penetrated the layer from orbit and relayed images of a continent that could just as easily have been Ebj, the continent dominated by the Northern Assembly.

There was no natural landscape in Tivskur to indicate how far north they had flown. It was simply a different coastline. Its capital, according to the F'nar archive, was Tivsk; and the outskirts of the city—how did they know where one settlement ended and the next began?—had been hit by debris from the *gethes'* warship *Actaeon*, destroyed in orbit on the orders of that nervous little matriarch who looked to Shan Frankland for direction.

Nevyan. Nevyan Tan Mestin. She had no idea how lucky she was to opt out of the duty of balance and never leave home. She even had a clan of four males, all with children, and she was barely an adult. Esganikan envied her anew.

I'm failing. Nevyan asked us to remove our camp from Wess'ej. Umeh is collapsing into war. So I have to get Earth right. I can't go home and have a family until I do my duty.

The ship dropped back through the clouds and Esganikan

stared through the transparent deck at the long finger of harbor that cut deep into the eastern coast. She pondered Targassat's words about the futility of selecting the point of equilibrium for any planet. It was a good argument. But taken to its logical conclusion—like the timing of troop withdrawal—it meant sitting back and doing nothing while species died and never had a chance. There was a single point in time at which to act, or not act: and inaction had its consequences too.

Esganikan had discovered a human called Charles Darwin in the *gethes'* archives that were duplicated in F'nar, and a view based on his findings that had become a revered ideology among scientists. Darwinism said that only the best-fitted survived. Yes, that was bound to be a popular philosophy for a species that claimed it couldn't help the disgraceful things that it did; humans felt that their nature was wonderful, bold, soaring, and free, and that their rapacious side was just a price to be paid—although not by them, generally. *Gethes* took refuge in the apparently inevitable nature of their superiority. They couldn't help but be on top. Somehow, though, they managed to ignore the fact that being the dominant species on Earth meant that absolutely nothing about their position was inevitable or beyond their control.

Those having choices must make them.

Targassat taught that, too. She was a most inconsistent *isan.* What might she and this Darwin have discussed if they could have met?

Esganikan had made her choices as every Eqbas had for millennia. She wasn't ashamed of them.

Bezer'ej

Every time Lindsay woke now, she wanted to scream.

It took a few seconds for her to remember that she wasn't drowning but *surviving.* That bothered her: humans had a swimming reflex and all the signs that they remembered their primeval aquatic origins. Her brain should have dealt with the new reality.

How long have we been here?

It wasn't months, she was sure of that now, or even weeks. They'd settled near enough to the surface with their bezeri captors to see the daily cycle of light and dark. And the lamp was still working. She examined it and wondered about its power source. With its hemispherical case and its flat lens, it reminded her of the headlamp of an ancient car.

But she hadn't had many conversations with Saib and the remnant of his people. They'd gathered in the deserted ruins, a ragtag community of the elderly and a single family, fifty or so individuals in all including a few very young infants.

They couldn't rebuild their species from this; it might have been kinder if they'd all died. Now they would watch their civilization—their entire race—disappear in the slow fullness of time.

She couldn't let that happen.

"I'm going to get some more maps," she said.

Saib shimmered. *You should clear the repository today. We believe we have found more records south of here. But we must examine and put in order what we have retrieved so far.*

She glanced at Rayat and laid the lamp down. "He'll help you sort them."

The bezeri appeared to trust her to go off on her own now. It wasn't as if she had anywhere to run. She'd expected abuse and torment, but the bezeri were far more concerned with gathering their history around them than exacting revenge on her. Perhaps they thought they had their vengeance. Every time she ate weed or reminded herself that she was stuck here for the rest of her infinite life with a man she loathed, she knew they had.

In the repository, she examined the faced stone and the intricate detail of the carved images. Animals she didn't recognize and plants that she did chased up the walls to the vaulted ceiling. Bezeri had the same ability as human artists to reproduce exact images, and everything she saw reminded her that she had helped destroy the remnant of an ancient and fragile civilization.

She gathered the last of the maps and took off her shirt to make a temporary bag, knotting the sleeves and fastening the front. The weight slowed her down. She resorted to walking along the seabed in a bouncing motion.

I can handle this. I can survive and I can do something for these people.

Gathering their maps wasn't much in the scheme of things. Maybe she could locate other bezeri communities so that they could breed. Most bezeri had gathered in the ancient spawning grounds around Ouzhari. But this small group *hadn't* gone; she found it hard to believe there weren't others like them.

Eqbas based here had found Saib and his group. Maybe they could find more in time.

Bezeri were vulnerable to land-living species: they had no technology that could stand up to the hard metal and ordnance of a spacefaring, terrestrial civilization.

So that's my job. That's my mission. Save them—somehow. Whatever it takes.

Lindsay needed a focus, and now she had it. When she got back to the settlement, Rayat was squatting over a pile of shell maps in one of the cone-shaped houses and examining them with Pili.

Then she realized his attention wasn't fixed on the maps but on his own hands. She'd rarely seen him look shaken; but he did now.

He was examining his hands with rapid, frantic movements, flipping them over palm to back to palm again, and his gill slits were opening as if he was panting.

Oh shit. Gills. I've got gills too.

She looked at her own hands: nothing, and no lights. She settled beside Rayat and grabbed his fingers.

"Oh my God, you're turning *transparent*." She could see the purple and red snaking branches of blood vessels near the surface of his skin, and the hint of pale bone. "Like *them*."

Rayat's eyes were wide and horrified. But he pressed his

lips together in a thin hard line and his gills flared. "Very scientific analysis, Commander. I can always rely on you for a rational view."

Lindsay knew she would now be checking herself every few minutes for signs of translucency. *Why is that so much worse than gills or echolocation or whatever other weird adaptations* c'naatat*'s giving you right now?* It *was* worse, because she could *see* it. Without a mirror, her other changes were visible only in the expression on Rayat's face.

Shan never changed, of course. Shan just became more of Shan than she'd been before. Suddenly Lindsay both envied and hated her with renewed venom for her absolute iron certainty in herself and the way the world should have been.

Lindsay had to find that certainty, too.

Saib drifted towards them and hung there with his lights on what Lindsay now thought of as tick-over—a steady speckling of green. She waited for the lamp to translate but there was nothing. Then he drifted away again, mantle pumping slowly like bellows.

"I'm going to look for food," said Rayat.

Lindsay grabbed the lamp and followed him outside. She sat in the filtered light and picked fronds off a rock to chew them. Rayat tried them too. Pili swam towards them and appeared to watch.

They will poison you, she said, shimmering a rainbow of urgent colors.

"We can't die," said Lindsay. "Haven't you noticed?"

It was the first time she'd realized that bezeri had individual levels of intelligence, exactly like humans. Wess'har seemed uniformly intelligent and . . . superior. Pili hadn't quite worked out what was happening; but then she'd never seen humans before, and a human confronted with a bezeri would have no idea what degree of adaptation was normal for them, either.

Lindsay felt an odd kinship, and wondered if it was the bezeri tissue worked into her open wound, or a genuine moment of epiphany.

Or maybe it's because I know how it feels to lose a child.

She chewed on the fronds, concentrating on the satisfying texture, and found she was working out the bearing and distance to Constantine. She was thinking of David's grave and its stained-glass headstone.

I can visit it now.

She never questioned that she could emerge from the sea and that her lungs would take over again. She wondered if she was placing too much faith in *c'naatat*.

No, Shan survived space without a suit. You can be amphibious easily enough.

"Are we going to adapt the same way, do you think?" she asked Rayat.

"How do you mean?"

"Shan didn't end up looking like Aras. Nor did Ade. It's not as if this thing works to a template."

Rayat didn't answer. He just looked at his hands. Pili picked up a map and examined it lovingly, running tentacles over the smooth surface. There would be a lot of time to fill, and Lindsay wondered when she would eventually become used to her new existence.

For a moment she saw endless black void with a speckling of white hot stars and felt as if she was falling forever. The spit second of boiling pain was incredible. She put her hand to her mouth.

It took her a few moments to work out what it was, and that it wasn't a random image but a memory—Shan's memory.

Lindsay wondered how much of her acceptance of her situation was Shan's grim obsession, and who else's memories and characteristics would emerge.

Even my bloody courage might not be my own. I'm never going to be out of her shadow. When she said I envied her guts, she knew that'd eat away at me for the rest of my life.

Rayat laughed. For a moment Lindsay wondered if she was thinking aloud. But he was laughing at something else.

Somehow his speech had sounded normal to her underwater, but the laugh was booming and unnatural. She turned, wondering if he was cracking up at last. But his face was all delight and triumph. She hated that expression. It bore no resemblance to a normal human being's happiness.

"Look," said Rayat. He held out both translucent hands as if demonstrating steadiness and sobriety. "Look. Lights. I've got bloody *bioluminescence!*"

His hands flickered blue and violet like a lighting fixture about to break down. Pili watched. The lamp spoke.

What are you saying? Pili asked.

"No idea," said Rayat. "How do I control this?"

Pili was silent. The other bezeri emerged from the cone house to watch. Lindsay waited for some expression of surprise from them.

Saib moved into the range of the lamp. *I don't know. We simply speak.*

Lindsay examined her own hands, bitterly disappointed that she had neither lights nor transparency. Rayat stared at the lamp and turned it to look at the display.

He put his hand flat on the lens.

"This is a test," he said slowly. "This . . . is . . . a . . . test."

The lamp flickered into color. Rayat counted up to ten and then began reciting Tennyson's "The Kraken."

There hath he lain for ages, and will lie
Battering upon huge seaworms in his sleep,
Until the latter fire shall heat the deep;
Then once by men and angels to be seen,
In roaring he shall rise and on the surface die.

It was a depressing choice. Lindsay fought an urge to punch him. "Are you going to keep that up all day?"

"I'm encouraging the formation of neural pathways," he said. "How do bezeri kids learn to talk? Probably by imitation. Whatever makes me light up might react the same way."

Lindsay hoped he was right but said nothing. She wanted bioluminescence too. She wanted to understand the bezeri, just as she wanted there to be new bezeri infants who would learn to speak by imitating their parents' kaleidoscope displays.

It was a forlorn hope but she held on to it. She would find

survivors and rebuild the bezeri, and somehow train them to defend themselves—or she would find nothing, and spend her days looking after a store of dead and beautiful maps that would be all that was left of a unique civilization she had helped destroy.

The first option wasn't her idea of heaven, but the latter was certainly close to hell. In the uncertain gray lands of fragile faith, Lindsay Neville prayed just as Deborah Garrod had shown her, desperate to hear an answering voice.

Umeh Station, Jejeno: a few days before Christmas

There were just over five hundred ussissi in Jejeno and they traveled light.

Eddie watched them boarding the little droplets of ship-stuff and ascending to the main hull of the Eqbas vessel. The bee cam covered every angle while he sat on the curb-stone that bordered the access road, pretending it was a sunny day on Earth. The shadow of Esganikan's ship sliced across the biodome and the surrounding isenj neighborhood, as eloquent an icon of invading menace as any historic B movie could have created.

He thought about Lindsay. He tried to recall his last words to her, and he had a feeling that they were along the lines of wess'har not forgiving or forgetting. He definitely didn't say goodbye. He could forget about her for days, and then suddenly she'd be on his mind, making him feel be-reaved and guilty.

I ought to ask Hayin what he meant by too many c'naatat. *Not exactly a plague.*

"So, going home for Christmas?"

Eddie turned at a familiar voice he hadn't heard for a while. Kris Hugel, the doctor from the *Thetis* mission, am-bled out of the main doors and sat down beside him. Her knees cracked alarmingly.

"You ought to see a doctor, doll," said Eddie.

"Quacks. Can't trust 'em." She was trying to make eye contact: he tried to avoid it. He was in his own head, thinking, and he didn't want interruptions. "Not going to sit it out here?"

"I need to go back to Wess'ej." He missed Giyadas. The kid was always pleased to see him, never bored by his stories, seldom less than fascinating. "Things to do."

"Why don't they evacuate us?"

"Where would they take you?"

"Where the colonists are."

"They can barely feed themselves. You're better off here."

"But can't they leave the defense shield in place?"

"Generated by the ship."

"Well, if the fighting reaches here, we're finished. No protection apart from rifles and hand weapons. The dome's hardened, though. Designed for all hostile planetary environments. I hope that included angry natives."

"Make sure you keep the warranty . . ."

"I'm scared, Eddie. I don't scare easily."

"I've been shitting myself nonstop for the last few years Kris. Eventually you just run out of shit. Try it." He stood up and held his hand out for the bee cam, and it plummeted back to him like a trained falcon. "The fighting's all on the border, and it's not about humans. Isenj have genetic memory so they haven't forgotten the wess'har wars in *any* sense of the word. We're a sideshow."

"So what's actually happening?"

Eddie stared at the bee cam in his palm. "Civil disobedience. Revolution. The citizens on both sides of the border want the wess'ar out. It's bloody knee-jerk with them, and isenj have more knees than us."

He wondered if Esganikan had decided to pull back to let things calm down but didn't want to look soft in front of him or her crew. But wess'har didn't have any concept of saving face. She was doing it for the reasons she stated: she could do nothing useful here.

"We still don't have comms links with Earth, you know," said Hugel. "Transmissions in, but nothing out. Except through you."

"Ah. Here we go."

"You haven't told anyone back home that Shan survived, have you?"

"I did the back-from-the-dead story once. Then she makes a habit of it. News Desk gets bored."

"For Chrissakes, Eddie."

"No, it doesn't matter any more. We've all forgotten what started it. The conflicts have moved on to bigger stuff—who controls Umeh, and who controls Earth."

"You reckon that's a bigger deal than immortality?"

"Indefinitely extended life. *C'naatat* can be killed." He had no plans to mention how. "Yeah, I do."

"That means it's potentially controllable."

"You don't give up, do you?"

"If any of us had been the giving up kind, we'd never have spent seventy-five years in the freezer getting here."

Eddie rolled the thought around in his brain. Shit, he really *had* become blasé about *c'naatat:* how could he criticize 'Desk for yawning at more alien war footage when he'd burned out on immortality? He couldn't even feel anxiety for Kris Hugel because he was back in war mode and switched off to everything except the narrow focus of elusive adrenaline.

"Kris, if the Eqbas don't like what they see when they reach Earth, *c'naatat*'s going to be irrelevant." He leaned over and patted her head emphatically. "These people redefined regime change."

"Can you get us out of here?"

"What?"

"Me, Vani and Olivier."

Oh yes: he'd all but forgotten them. Vani Paretti and Olivier Champciaux, two of the scientists from the original *Thetis* mission, were stranded here too. The rest of the payload, as the marines called the research team, were either dead or working on a deal with God among the colonists. Eddie imagined Nevyan's reaction if he walked back into F'nar with a microbiologist, a geologist and a way-too-curious medic.

"I can't," he said, knowing that he probably could. "Sorry."

"We were *crew,* Eddie. We went through a lot together."

Eddie wasn't a crew-minded man but he thought of all the people he couldn't take back to Wess'ej, like Cargill and the civilian engineers. If he took one, he'd have to take all of them, or else spend the rest of his time battling guilt about those left behind.

"I can't take humans back to Wess'ej uninvited," he lied, remembering doing exactly that with the Royal Marines. "You're *gethes* as far as they're concerned. Carrion eaters. And there's no carrion or much else there that you can eat."

"Okay. Great."

"You know Lindsay's dead, don't you? And Rayat. Wess'har don't do prisons. They do executions. Like I said, you're safer here. Keep your head down and I'll see you after Christmas."

It was as meaningless a thing as he'd ever said, but that was how it escaped his mouth. Hugel just stared, and he walked back into the biodome just to end the conversation. But this was how he'd lived his life—a visitor to disasters and violence with a first class ticket home. He'd been stranded a few times too; jailed, bailed out by BBChan, stuck behind borders, abandoned by minders. Hugel was facing no worse then he had. Tough shit.

But I can leave.

He felt bad about it and made a conscious effort to stop what he thought of as "fixing." When something unpleasant happened, he could feel the image boring into his memory, noting all the inconsequential things around at that very moment and marking them as a trigger for full recall of itself. The moment had a real physical sensation; he was convinced he could feel the neural pathways snapping together. *No no no.* He had a game for stopping it happening, too. He'd see or hear the utterly unconnected things—an orange coverall, a sack trolley, the sound of a fountain—and try to stop the bond forming. *No no no.*

It rarely worked. Now he practiced overload instead, recalling the awful moment over and over until he was sick of it and it lost some of its ability to make his stomach pump acid. Right then he thought of Lindsay and couldn't imagine affable Ade Bennett pushing her into the sea to die, alone and terrified.

Distraction. There was always a coffee to be had if he asked nicely in the main refectory area. He might even get a real one and not the synthesized flavoring processed on site. He set course for it. He needed to get that image out of his mind.

"Our man on the scene, eh?" Cargill was ahead of him in the queue for the drinks dispenser. "Don't forget we don't have comms back to Earth—or anything else outgoing for that matter. We're not getting any information except what the ussissi say. Maybe you ought to file a report back to BBChan so they can transmit it back to us."

The isenj had blocked outgoing ITX relays—not his, it seemed—when they feared loose human lips would cause the wess'har to sink isenj ships. Like any self-respecting human government, they were slow to open them again. "The spider boys are ripping chunks out of each other," Eddie said quietly. "The Eqbas decided not to fight a ground war because they couldn't think of a good reason for it."

"Jesus. And they're going to invade Earth?"

" 'S'right."

"About fucking time. We could do with politicians like that."

Cargill guffawed, apparently unconcerned. Eddie wished that he fancied her. He'd work on it if Izzy Qureshi wasn't interested. She extracted two coffees—synthetic—from the dispenser and pressed one cup into his hand.

Eddie had a sudden urge to test a theory.

"Sofia, do you want to leave the station? Evacuate to Wess'ej?"

She dropped her chin slightly and looked up at him. "Where you going to put three hundred and sixty-one bodies? And feed them?"

"I meant you."

She stopped blinking. "Thanks, but it sort of goes with the

uniform, staying with the doomed ship and all that. If you could get the civvies moved, though, that would be handy."

"Can't do bigger numbers." He wasn't sure he could do *any,* and he wasn't sure if he was just testing now. But one or two individuals wouldn't salve his conscience, and staying around out of some misplaced sense of solidarity was just as self-indulgent. He had a job to do: so did she. "Just asking. Just in case."

"Am I reading you right, Eddie?"

"Forget it. I'm rambling. Someone made me feel guilty for not taking them back to Wess'ej with me."

"If they're essential personnel, they bloody stay put." She lowered her voice. "Nobody in uniform leaves here until all civvies are evacuated. That's the navy way."

She looked at him as if expecting a name, but he shook his head. Yeah, Umeh Station needed all its medics. "When you put it like that, I feel a lot better."

"Wouldn't mind seeing that pearl city before *Thetis* shows up, though," said Cargill. "Shame to come all this way and not see the sights."

Eddie made a mental pledge to grant her wish. He collected his bag and walked back to the staging area where the ussissi were embarking for F'nar. Cargill hadn't even been tempted. Leaving was out of the question, and he knew she'd be the last out.

He wedged the bag between his feet, clasped his hands in front of him and waited in a sea of grim-faced chest-high meerkats. When they stood still like that, all looking the same way, all perfectly still, it was impossible not to see them that way.

He almost smiled. Cargill had reset his switch. It was good to know that order and a certain nobility survived in an outpost so isolated that cannibalism wouldn't have surprised him. Kris, who he'd quite liked in a superficial way, had fallen instantly from grace simply by asking him for a way out. In his mental filing cabinet, there were people who had a certain quality—Cargill, the marine detachment,

Shan—and people who did not, and they might as well have been two different species for all the attitudes they shared.

Maybe they really *were* different. The wess'har definitely seemed to think so.

Eddie's turn came to embark. He stood watching a bubble of blue liquid composite with a dozen Umeh ussissi who appeared never to have seen metamorphosing vessels before, and wondered whether Lindsay met her fate like Shan, or like Kris.

He suspected Ade would never tell him, and nor would Aras.

10

*You know in your ancestral memories that this is true: the
Northern Assembly is not the enemy. Our foe is, and always
has been, the wess'har. They invaded this system and imposed their laws on it. They took our territory on Asht. Turn
your arms against the Eqbas, brothers and sisters, and reclaim Asht. If your government stands idle, depose them.
And when we have reclaimed Asht, we will root out the contagion on Wess'ej.*

President PIRB of the Maritime Fringe,
appealing to Northern Assembly troops and citizens
to oppose the arrangement with Eqbas Vorhi by force

Ussissi settlement, outside F'nar

The eggshell domes of the ussissi settlement just outside
F'nar had lost their Fabergé look.

They were never meant to be permanent, a summer's
decoration at most. Their brilliant colors and intricate designs had faded to the weather-beaten shades of ancient
stucco and the hemispheres almost merged with the soil.
Others had already crumbled back into fragments like pot-
tery shards. Shan was reminded of the bubble domes of
Constantine again, Aras's re-creation of discreet Wess'ej architecture on Bezer'ej. She wondered how much it hurt to
see a colony you shaped over generations reduced to dust
by your own hand.

She glanced down. "Are you sure you're okay?"

Vijissi tottered unsteadily at her side. Eventually he gave
up walking bipedally and dropped down onto four of his six
legs, bring him to below waist-height. Shan slowed down
again and debated whether to simply pick him up and carry
him. There still was nothing much to pick up except skin
and bone.

"I have been unable to walk for many months," he said. Ussissi had oddly childlike voices at the best of times: Vijissi's pressed all the human buttons in Shan that said *look after me*. "Walking aids my recovery."

"Sitting down and eating plenty does that too."

Vijissi didn't respond. He panted occasionally and sometimes slowed so much that Shan simply stood still and waited for him. The half-hour stroll from Mestin's home to the settlement had stretched into a slow hour but he was determined to walk unaided into his home village.

"I never said thanks," said Shan.

"For what, *Shan Chail*?"

"For staying with me. Even when . . . it killed you. More or less."

"You were my responsibility," he said. "*Mestin Chail* said I was to look after you."

"I'm sorry. I really am."

"You're as restricted as I am. Don't be."

A few meerkat faces appeared at the portals of the egg domes and watched them approach. They synchronized their movements and the effect in Shan's peripheral vision was like watching a wave breaking. Vijissi straightened up onto his hindlegs as if determined to put on a brave face.

Last time I came here with him, they just stared at me.

Shan waved, a brief display of the palm of her hand, and waited. "Remember, anytime you feel it's too much, I'll take you back to Mestin's place." She glanced down at him, anxious to help: since she'd realized how young he was, she felt doubly guilty. *I never even asked. I never treated him as a person.* "A step at a time. Don't overdo it. I know how it feels."

More ussissi came out into the central clearing of the eggshell village. When they were excited or agitated, they matched their movements perfectly and there was a very real sense of dealing with one entity; Shan never lost sight of the fact that they probably attacked that way, too. Vijissi swayed slightly as if he too was trying to mimic that movement.

A large, dominant female—all the females were larger than the males—broke from the group and trotted forward, the tan beaded belt across one shoulder slapping against her bright yellow robe. She stopped in front of Shan and stared at Vijissi.

"If we didn't know this was possible, we would be more shocked," she said. "Are you infectious?"

They didn't believe in a bunch of flowers and a basket of fruit for the convalescent patient, that much was clear. Shan concentrated on restraint: ussissi could detect *jask* as well as any wess'har. Vijissi craned his neck to scan the small crowd.

"Binissati, where is she? Where is Talissari?"

"She believed you were dead. She went to Pajat to find another."

Shan knew bugger all about ussissi culture even now, but she knew a *Dear John* when she heard one. Vijissi's head drooped a little. She didn't know he had a female.

"I came to greet you all," he said. It was almost a whisper. "But I am tired. I will come back later." He looked up at Shan, his eyes black voids like a blind, pleading dog's. "We should return now."

Binissati narrowed her eyes. "Are you planning to return here for good?"

"Where will I live if I do?" Vijissi leaned forward slightly, just a fraction, and Binissati drew back. Shan winced. That display of caution sealed Vijissi's status: *leper*. "I will come again when I feel stronger."

"I want him back in bed and getting some rest." Shan found herself almost squaring up to the ussissi matriarch. *You callous bitch.* Where was his mother? "I'll bring him back when I feel he's fit."

It probably wasn't the best thing to do to preserve Vijissi's dignity, but she scooped him up in her arms and strode away. *I'm evacuating him. This is what coppers do. He'll understand.* She'd always seen ussissi as close and clannish, but Vijissi had hardly been welcomed home. They hadn't even asked how he was. Clannish didn't always mean inclusive. Where *was* his mother? Shan was certain now that she'd recognize her.

Shit, however scared the wess'har had been of *c'naatat,*
they'd never treated her like an unwelcome freak. Theirs
was physical caution, nothing more. Ussissi weren't like
wess'har at all. There was a joylessness about them that she
occasionally glimpsed in the females.

Takes one to know one, of course.

Vijissi made no protest as she carried him. As soon as
they got close to F'nar, she set him down and kept a careful
eye on him, ready to grab him if he stumbled. Sometimes the
lack of a private vehicle system in F'nar was a pain in the
arse. He was making a brave show of trying to walk straight,
but his muscles were barely more than threads at the moment and he'd worn himself out on the walk. She knew that
feeling too well. *C'naatat* had a brutal list of priorities for
keeping a body alive in space without a suit: it mined fat,
then muscle, then organs to keep the brain intact for as long
as it could. When it began to restoration process, leg muscle
preceded organ tissue and then fat was the last to reappear.

*I looked like a fucking lab specimen. Mummified, Eddie
said. Nothing but skin and ribcage.*

"Sorry." For a moment she wasn't even sure which language she was speaking. "They're all in shock. They'll settle down."

"She's gone," said Vijissi.

Shan tried to remember the female's name. *Talissari.*
That was it. "When they brought me back, it wasn't exactly
a bundle of laughs either."

"But you had Ade and Aras, and they could touch you."

"It's not that easy to transmit. Wess'har are susceptible,
but—"

"Touch has many meanings." Vijissi struggled to his feet
and stretched as tall as he could on his hind legs, looking
like he intended to walk back into F'nar with his dignity intact. "I meant mating. We were intended for each other
when I came of age. What will become of me? How can I
ever return to my pack when I have no role? When they're
afraid to come near me?"

There was absolutely nothing she could do for him but

maybe Shapakti could. *Don't get his hopes up.* "Time to eat.
Let's get you back to Mestin's place, shall we?" Somehow,
she had to take a sample discreetly. Ussissi weren't furred,
for all their illusion of having a short coat, and a buccal
swab was going to be tough to explain away.

I could just give it to him straight. Tell him.

Vijissi looked in the direction of the village and lifted his
muzzle to sniff audibly at the breeze. The sniff turned into
staccato panting, and then he let out a long, thin wail that
grew into a wild keening note. Shan didn't need to know
anything about ussissi to realize that he was grief-stricken.
He took a few steps and tipped forward onto all fours.

"That's it," she said. His dignity could take a back seat.
She picked him up in her arms and cradled him. "Home."

Shan took off her jacket and bundled him in it to give
him a little privacy, but there were few wess'har out and
about in F'nar today to see them: it was too chilly. When
she reached Mestin's home high on the terraces she pressed
her backside against the pearl-coated door to force it open.
But it wouldn't yield. She turned around to give it a kick
with her boot—not her forced entry kick, just a push—but it
swung open with more force than she expected and Sevaor,
one of Mestin's husbands, stood staring.

"It was a bit too much for him," she said. "He needs a rest."

It was a good opportunity. Sevaor stood back to let her
carry Vijissi down the passages back to his room and she
laid the ussissi on the bed. It was simplicity itself to feed
him the flatbread waiting on the bedside table and then wipe
his mouth carefully with a piece of cloth. He even coughed
obligingly. He produced plenty of spit.

*I was always pretty bloody good at getting DNA outside
rules of evidence.*

Shan folded the cloth carefully and placed it in her breast
pocket inside a fold of hemp paper. Mestin intercepted her
on the way out.

"How did the clan greet him?" she asked.

"They didn't," said Shan. "They didn't roll out the red carpet at all."

She was halfway to Shapakti's underground rain forest before she realized that she'd kicked open a door without triggering memories of all the doors she had smashed open in her police career to find vile things inside, things that haunted the moments before she fell asleep and that never went away, and that always came to mind when she saw doors.

It was the first time that no memories had triggered. It was a small but significant victory. She fumbled for the saliva sample in her pocket and hoped—but not prayed, *never* that—for good news for Vijissi too.

Bezer'ej: Bezeri camp

Rayat knew the power of obsession and it was all that stood between him and purgatory.

He willed his hands to do something—*anything*. The lights they emitted seemed random, responding to the lamp in a chaotic flurry of color. If there was any communication taking place, it wasn't going via his conscious brain. Frustration nearly overwhelmed him. His hands suddenly burned with yellow and amber pulses.

You are angry, said Saib.

I didn't think they could read human expressions. "How can you tell?"

Your incoherent signals.

"Like a baby screaming," said Lindsay quietly. "If you can't talk, you vent your frustration any way you can."

The revelation was blinding and almost joyful. *I'm having a tantrum. I'm having a tantrum with lights.* That meant the photophores were somehow connecting to his brain, to his speech centers. *I'm a baby again. Oh God.*

"Lin, let me keep the lamp for a while, will you?" He hated asking her for any concessions. She had a lot more steel in her backbone than he'd given her credit for, but she still thought she was in command in some petty managerial way. *Okay, whatever it takes, sweetheart. I'll humor you.*

"I'm making headway here. Once I've cracked it, then I might know how to activate it in you."

Lindsay examined her hands. They remained steadfastly unilluminated. "Why can't I shake the feeling that you're manipulating me again?"

It was possible to plant an idea in her mind and nurture it. He'd talked her into helping him bomb Ouzhari. He'd set her thinking about acquiring *c'naatat* long before she took the decision to ask Ade Bennett to contaminate her. It required restraint and subtlety, because she wasn't stupid, but if he was patient he could persuade her, and she never seemed to learn.

All he wanted was to hang on to the signaling lamp for a few hours and see if his bioluminescence could be taught to speak. There could be bezeri memories of language in him now, and he might be able to reinforce them.

Saib coiled a tentacle around the lamp and rocked it vigorously back and forth as if he was shaking a tin of paint, creating eddies in the sea around them. Rayat wondered if he was making a protest of some kind. But the bezeri set the lamp down again.

The lamp must be moved to keep it alive, he said.

Rayat struggled to make sense of the words. "You shake it? Why?"

So the lights continue.

"I get it." *Clever buggers, the wess'har.* "It charges mechanically. How do you know that?"

Many talked of the visits by Aras and how he used this.

"At least we don't have to worry about power cells," said Lindsay. She held one hand up to the filtered light as if checking something. "Why doesn't *c'naatat* have a consistent pattern?"

"I don't know. Try not talking and see if that forces it to do something."

Lindsay turned her head slowly, hair billowing like a malevolent version of Botticelli's Venus. "Funny, aren't you?"

"I'm serious. If you can expose it to new environments

and force it to adapt you for survival, then silence might just make it express the photophores."

She looked if she was weighing the theory and was about to spit it back at him. But she just shrugged and settled on a rock to watch the lamp.

Rayat spent the next hour holding his hand in front of the lamp while he repeated basic words—*shell, azin, sea, weed, rock.* There *had* to be simple signals for those. The bezeri drifted back and forth with shell maps, pausing occasionally to check his progress. Pili edged into a crevice as if she was settling into an armchair and watched him.

Rayat could see her eyes now. They were more opaque than the rest of the mantle, round and slightly domed. There was a great deal to be said for convergent evolution; life set about solving engineering problems and did it pretty consistently. He hoped *c'naatat* took the hint. Then he noticed the shadow of something teardrop-shaped set lower in Pili's mantle, and when he thought about terrestrial cephalopods— the best parallel he could imagine—he remembered they had lethal beaks.

Bezeri were carnivorous. He marveled that a hunting species could also have villages, written records and vehicles. Intelligence manifested itself in remarkably uniform ways.

Hungry, he thought. *Hungry.*

It was the kind of animal-level message that any organism could express. He concentrated on it. He imagined food. His hands still seemed to be shimmering at random, trying out colors and patterns, and if they could manage to express his frustration then they could form more specific concepts. He was certain of it.

It was just a matter of time.

"I'm going to have a look around," said Rayat, and got up. Saib, passing with maps clutched to his mantle, paused in front of him. "I said, I'm going to have a look around and see what else I can eat. I'm not trying to escape."

You could find land, and we could not follow you far into the Dry Above, said Saib.

It was an observation; Rayat wondered if he would have made it, because it also sounded like a suggestion. Did Saib know how *c'naatat* adapted its host? Or was he just making the assumption that if humans could survive in the ocean depths, then they could switch back to breathing air again?

Either way, the bezeri was right. But Rayat didn't want to alienate him. Swapping an existence down here for one on land might not have been a better move, because at the moment the only creatures he could learn from were down here. And he needed to know more before he could formulate a plan for getting off Bezer'ej and back to Earth.

The same thought seemed to be going through Lindsay's mind. She gave him an unblinking stare.

"Don't even think about it," she said.

But she had no way of implementing her vague threat. There was nothing she could do to him, or he to her. All they could do was bitch at each other.

"If I find a kebab shop, I'll fetch you one," he said. "Want hot sauce with it?"

"Sod off," she said.

Rayat set off towards the repository. The store lay in the direction of Ouzhari. If he got his bearings from there, he could work out where Constantine was, because he'd studied the map of the chain of islands when he was on board *Actaeon* for so long that he could re-create the image in his head at will. Ouzhari—Christopher Island, the Small Mountain to the Dry Above, whatever name it wore—was the southernmost island of a chain of six named for saints; Constantine, the one that had given its name to the colony, and Catherine, Charity, Clare, Chad, and Christopher. It was somewhere between ninety and one hundred kilometers to Constantine.

Rayat swam, distracted by the sporadic lights in his hands each time he used his arms.

The colony had a mothballed ship—also called Christopher—and one more shuttle somewhere: they'd taken one to transport Shan Frankland when she was captured. The wess'har had released nanites within the colony to break down every artifact and manufactured substance to its component minerals, but there was always the chance that the ship or something else spaceworthy had been laid up outside the warren of tunnels and had survived intact. And there were small seagoing boats, too; he and Lindsay had used one. They'd left it on the shore.

It was a slim chance. Even slim chances had to be taken.

I swear I'll get home somehow. I've come this far and I can go a lot further. I won't be beaten.

Maybe if he said it to himself often enough he'd believe it. Right then his body was going through the motions and he crammed his head full of numbers and plans and lists again to stop the little voice inside that kept telling him this was a strange, cold alien sea and he had no life here at all.

Rayat passed different weeds and growths and paused occasionally to sample them. They grew more sparse as he swam and that told him he might be getting closer to the blast zone. The seabed began to slope and he could see the feet of submerged mountain ranges.

Yes. The Mountains to the Dry Above. It was easy to see the world through bezeri eyes now.

The sea around him became paler and brighter with the gradient. There was a bright sunny day above him, and that was where he should have been—on dry land. He was so close to Ouzhari now that the temptation to make for the shore and wade up the beach was almost overwhelming.

It's still a hot zone, you idiot. Cobalt-salted neutron devices, remember?

It wouldn't kill him. If Frankland could survive hard radiation in space, a stroll along an irradiated beach would present him with no problems. But he might take the contamination back with him when he returned to the bezeri. He had no way of measuring his exposure. And he needed them alive.

No. You don't, actually. Admit it. You just want them to survive.

He paused and decided not to go any further. He knew

where he was, and he also knew the Eqbas had embarked on a clean-up mission here.

And you've got time. That's the one thing you've got plenty of.

As long as he planned to go back and live with the bezeri, he had to steer clear of contamination. But once he made the final decision to run for it, that would't matter.

And he didn't have to walk on Ouzhari and pretend he felt no remorse. He could make his way straight to Constantine as long as he got his bearings. The bezeri were obviously good at making maps, and that meant they could show him how to interpret their charts. He'd know where to go and how long it would take him, so now he could *plan.*

It's a slim chance. There might be nothing left on Constantine. But the alternative is turning into God knows what down here for . . .

How long? He had no idea. He had to stop thinking in those terms.

He looked up, distracted by shadows and movement. Above him he could see dark shapes silhouetted by the sunlight and they were traveling at a steady speed that suggested a powered craft. But he couldn't see the outline of a vessel. He was looking at the foreshortened view of a biped standing on what looked like a sheet of glass.

It had to be the Eqbas. He knew they were operating here; and they had extraordinary technology. The glass raft paused over him, and for a moment he thought something had been poured into the sea. A column extended from the underside of the raft almost like gin being poured into water, swirling with barely visible variations in density. He felt the change more than he saw it.

Have they detected me?

He had no idea if they knew he was here anyway. He waited, motionless, and the raft picked up speed and moved on.

Rayat took a slow meandering route back to the bezeri settlement and stopped to collect samples of vegetation, chewing fragments experimentally before shoving them inside his shirt. *Look at me. I can do this. I haven't freaked out yet.* The intelligence services had trained him to be resilient but nothing could have prepared him for this. So he was doing fine. He would *win*.

When he got back to the settlement, Lindsay was surrounded by a small group of bezeri, all clustered around the signal lamp and pulsing light. He watched too. She looked up.

"Look," she said.

She held up her hands, palm out, and then rotated them slowly. There was a flicker of violet light.

"Welcome to the squid club," said Rayat. "But can you control it yet?"

"Can you?"

Rayat concentrated and tried to shut everything out of his mind except his hands and his immediate thoughts. He'd been trained to visualize to control pain and to focus himself in tight spots so he fell back into the techniques he'd learned. He could still slow his breathing, even with gills.

Food.

He simply thought of food. He saw a chunk of warm bread; he could smell it and taste it.

Food.

He heard the word in his head.

He looked at his palms. For a moment he felt as if he was reciting the *salaat,* hands cupped in front of him in private prayer, but he hadn't been to the mosque since he was a kid. God hadn't played a part in his life but observing prayer times kept his grandfather happy when he visited.

It was a long time ago. His family never knew what he really did for a living, but his mother had been proud of the part she knew about. *My son, the scientist.*

My son, the spy.

But Rayat now lived in an age of explicable miracles. In his palms a distinct pattern of green, red and blue dots of light swirled about a common center. Saib drew up his tentacles in a sudden whoosh of water and the signal lamp boomed.

You ask for food.

Saib understood the lights.

"Alhamdu lillah," said Rayat. He didn't realize he still knew the words. *All praise be to Allah.* "It's a start."

No, it was a miracle. And it wasn't diminished by the fact that he had a good idea how it had happened, and that he would one day be able to demonstrate exactly how his neural pathways connected his speech centers to alien photophores and enabled him to talk with cephalopods.

Being a scientist and a spy didn't stop you being amazed by the universe.

Eqbas Vorhi ship 886-001-005-6, Northern Assembly airspace: hangar zone

Esganikan and the detached combat specialist Ki Joluti kept one focus on the images from the surveillance remotes and one on their calculations. The Maritime Fringe forces were on their way across the Northern Assembly border, pushing towards Jejeno.

There were fewer than she expected, but they made their way on foot and in vehicles along the narrow canyons of roads that led north towards the capital. The head of the column was already in Northern Assembly territory: the tail was back in Fringe territory. From one angle they glittered like a muddy river in torrential flood. Ahead of them by a kilometer or so, refugees made their way out of the area.

There was no sign of resistance. Some of the Northern Assembly army had fallen back to defend the capital and some had defected.

"They could launch an air attack on Jejeno again," said Joluti. "What's your view on why they haven't?"

"They want to gather popular support from Assembly citizens as they go, not kill them. Numbers are the weapon they need." Esganikan watched as a fighter tailored for Umeh's atmosphere extruded itself from the hangar deck and began forming into a copper and blue ovoid. Eddie had gone home too soon: he would have been very excited to record the process. "They're not a violent species."

"I think that they don't have the resources to sustain both an attack on Jejeno and launch against Bezer'ej, so I speculate that they're saving what assets they have for us."

Esganikan didn't understand why isenj would commit forces to battles they knew they would lose. It seemed almost a reflex: not unlike the *gethes'* great admiration for hopelessly outnumbered last stands, in fact. Losing well seemed to matter more than winning. Esganikan believed in successful outcomes, and heroism was only *motive*. She made a mental note to talk to Shan's *jurej*, the human soldier Ade, about the ritual of human warfare. He seemed very competent. They said he was a hero, and an official one at that, and so he would be best placed to explain it.

She glanced at the surveillance remotes' output again. The Maritime Fringe forces were within seventy kilometers of Jejeno and it was time to act. She opened a link to Eit with her *virin*.

"Do you want me to act? Your army failed to do its job, which is to carry out your lawful orders. The Fringe forces are within hours of your offices."

Eit made a sound like a box being shaken. The image floating in the *virin* was small but she saw his beads rattle dramatically, amber ones this time. "The elected government of the Northern Assembly is about to be removed by force by a foreign power. Yes, Commander, if you were inclined to act to defend us, now would be a very good time indeed."

Esganikan thought she understood sarcasm when she heard it. The humans used it copiously. "There will be collateral damage."

"So be it."

It would probably have made little difference if she'd spelled it out, but like humans, the isenj dealt in euphemism. They said that Eqbas did too, but she hadn't noticed.

"The target is the Fringe column and the armor accompanying it. We begin immediately. Order your remaining troops to stay clear." She turned to Joluti. "Battle stations, my friend."

Even for Esganikan, the sight of her ship preparing for combat was still an impressive experience. The squadrons of fighters had now formed fully on the hangar deck and pilots gathered from around the ship to slip into the cockpits. The ship's resources were diverted to reassembling the materials suspended in the massive hull and shaping them into the particular template that was needed at that moment. Metals and composites linked and built into airframes and ordnance; the rest of the ship reshaped into different vessels and separated, some becoming forward air control positions, some becoming escort vessels.

It wasn't just a ship. It was a collection of building blocks for any number of assets that could be reconfigured at will and deployed anywhere. An Eqbas warship was a fleet and an air group in itself. Even its ordnance was formed from the materials present in its liquescent, nanite-directed structure.

Some worlds that had seen the application of Eqbas technology thought the ships were organic, even sentient. But the only organic tools in Esganikan's armory were the specialized bacteria that carried out bioremediation, devouring pollutants and making toxins and metals harmless. Eqbas drew the line at harming living creatures, like all wess'har.

"*Gethes* want *c'naatat*," said Esganikan. "And yet they overlook the technology we have which would be more useful to them?"

Joluti checked the state boards: the squadron was ready. "They'll have difficulty ignoring these if we need to use them on Earth."

The steadily rising note of the drives almost drowned out his voice as the transparent deck shield rose to protect the hangar from the backdraft. Two hundred fighters slipped out the aperture in the ship's stern in an orderly sequence. However routine the technology, the thrill of seeing them deploy never palled. Esganikan enjoyed her job. It had a purpose and a lasting value. At least a part of the galaxy was better for it.

"I'd watch this up forward," she said.

She walked back up the long center axis of the ship to the bridge, noting features that had been temporarily diverted to become other assets for the attack. *Modeling clay.* That was what one of the human soldiers had called it. He said it would *amaze the fuck out of the people back home*. Barencoin's English was different and fascinating, and quite unlike Eddie's.

The bulkheads of the bridge were now devoted to observation screens. Joluti directed the squadron as air group commander, and Esganikan needed only to watch. It was unhappy viewing; nobody could take pleasure in death, although she heard talk that some *gethes* did.

The bridge always fell silent at times like this. It was important that the crew saw the consequences of the warfare they unleashed, so that their relative invulnerability never let them lose sight of what they made happen.

Lights and targets on tracking screens had their advantages because they removed data that complicated decisions and added others that couldn't be seen: a cloud-shrouded, complex city could be stripped down to grids and icons, and invisible detail like buried utilities could be superimposed. But when there was no need for precision, then the crew had to see the real detail of war so they never forgot that it wasn't a game or a training exercise.

"Pay attention, please," said Esganikan. "And remember that we don't take this action lightly."

Three remotes had been linked to provide a close aerial perspective and a high-level icon view of the progress of the Maritime Fringe column. The advance was split into three lines because there was no single road wide enough to take both the armored division—truncated flat pyramidlike ground cars, rectangular in plan with tubby artillery pieces mounted on top—and troops on foot. The roads ran almost parallel: isenj, logical engineers that they were, built on slightly angled grids that reminded Esganikan of some insects' hive-building templates.

She estimated there were two thousand vehicles moving in the central road at less than ten kilometers an hour, a deliberately steady procession. Perhaps they thought Jejeno would surrender. If it did, she wondered if she should abandon the mission as a lost cause.

We've never come across a planet in this state of balance before. If it weren't for the oceans, and the fact that some do want change, I think now that I'd leave them to their fate.

Her options and reasoning were clearer in her mind now.

"Oh. *Oh.*" Churutal, a very young *isan* about the same age as Nevyan Tan Mestin, reacted to the sudden change of perspective from the aerial remotes to a head-on view of crammed buildings from the cockpit of a fighter. "I can feel the crowding. How can they live like that?"

"They think they have no choice," said Hayin.

There was a sudden synchronised ripple in the column to the left of the screen as if all the isenj troops had looked up at the same time. The movement appeared as an uneven wave: they'd spotted the first fighter. But there was nowhere to run. The view switched to a fighter at the rear and Esganikan saw the tails ahead breaking into three lines. Several of the armored units swung to train weapons on the aircraft, but the pilots were fast, and shielded, and already wreaking havoc on an army that was trapped in three narrow canyons of roads.

At this speed Esganikan found it hard to tell which view she was seeing. The images chopped and switched from speed-smeared walls streaking past on both sides to blinding white flashes and balls of rising flame and black smoke. There was no sound: the images were as silent as the bridge crew.

It was seconds. Just *seconds.* The squadron ripped into the columns of troops and vehicles like a knife.

The lead image tilted to become open yellow-tinged sky as the fighter climbed. The rest of the squadron was hidden by smoke, and only the navigation sensors and the plot display Joluti was managing showed the full picture of the raid as a schematic on a calmly neutral chart.

At one point one fighter providing a viewpoint—and there were many—banked to give Esganikan a moment's glimpse of a shattered street framed by a break in the palls of smoke: armored cars at odd angles, some overturned, others with their turrets blown off to reveal the cockpit inside: flames licking out of buildings; and bodies.

She only spotted a packed patch of corpses, but she had seen enough fighting to extrapolate from that to the full scale of carnage. No, she didn't take this casually at all. She glanced at the repeater panel showing the battle chart that Joluti controlled. The attack concentrated on the head and the tail of the column, the textbook method of stopping an armored advance. The armor behind the lead section couldn't move forward and it couldn't reverse past the burning wrecks of the rearguard: it couldn't turn around either, although some units might manage to work their way between buildings.

She didn't look at the routes where the troops on foot had packed in ranks. She knew what that would look like, more or less. And she could calculate the casualties in the buildings that flanked the routes, but she didn't—not yet.

A single tight-packed city where the national boundaries were simply deep conduits and high walls meant high casualties. She was relieved that she was fighting this from the air and not trying to subdue the area house-to-house on the ground.

Now she'd seen enough. She left the bridge crew staring at the screens and made her way back aft to the hangar deck. Aitassi trailed after her in silence. Joluti indicated a group of icons clustered on the tracking screen moving away at high speed from the ten kilometers of destruction.

"Two targets we would be advised to take out immediately," he said. "Vessels tracked from Tivskur are landing troops at two points of the Fringe coast."

If the Eqbas—and the Northern Assembly—hadn't been at war with Tivskur before, they would be now.

"Let's give Shomen Eit an overview of the situation," said Esganikan. "If he hasn't worked it out from his own intelligence people."

She fought every engagement as if she risked losing. She never took an enemy for granted. The smoke took hours to clear from the streets, and the main section of the ship took up station over the area to survey it. She'd seen worse, but only once.

"It's probably best that Eddie Michallat wasn't on board to see this," said Aitassi.

"I was going to give him images," said Esganikan.

"Would he understand them?"

Esganikan tried to imagine how a human, with his rules and concept of what was fair in war, would come to terms with obliteration on that scale. Humans always had wars somewhere in their world, he told her. Perhaps their rules were why they never settled anything.

"We have no secrets, apparently." Esganikan stared through the transparent section of the bridge deck. Beneath her, a group of fighters looped back to return to the hangar. There was a shallow crater about a hundred meters wide at a crossroads, probably where an armored vehicle and its ordnance had taken a direct hit. "He finds our openness odd."

She could see bare soil in the crater; she was sure of it. She came from a world where open space made up most of the planet, but here there was almost none, and she felt the emergence of this little scrap of the natural planet for the first time in probably centuries was a landmark moment.

"Look, 'Tassi," she said, and pointed. The ussissi dropped onto her four hind legs to peer down to the ground. Esganikan tapped the bulkhead to magnify the image. The transparent hull now brought the ground to fifty meters instead of five thousand. She found her eyes drawn to the chassis of a groundcar with half a body still sitting in the driving seat as if the whole top half of both vehicle and driver had been sliced horizontally.

Soil. Earth. Esganikan pulled her attention back to the commonplace that had suddenly become exotic here.

"They still have native trees on Tasir Var." Smoke was still rising from lumps of rubble but the dark velvety patches were definitely soil. Whatever had been blown up hadn't had deep foundations. "Detach a vessel and see if we can acquire one to plant here. We can remediate this site as soon as we secure the area."

"Why start here?" said Hayin.

"It creates an open space. Show the isenj something they haven't seen for generations, a patch of soil with a living tree growing in it that isn't solely for their benefit. Something they have to learn to share their world with on its own terms. We'll see how they react and if they can be motivated by seeing things that are achievable."

Hayin jiggled his head in dissent, but he despatched a section of ship to Umeh's moon. The isenj there were far more cooperative, but then they had a much more pleasant lifestyle and far more to gain—and lose.

"I've never heard of this before," Hayin muttered. "Haphazard restoration."

"It is new," said Esganikan. "I learned it from the *gethes*. It's an area of plants where nobody can build, something pleasant and unspoiled for those who live in sterile cities. They call it a *park*."

11

If you believe everything you read, then better not read.

Japanese proverb

F'nar, Wess'ej

Shan sat and stared at the ESF670 rifle on the table.

It was an interesting piece of kit. It did a lot of different things, but she wasn't sure if it did any of them really well. She knew her handgun better than she'd known some men; and it was a lot more reliable. But the kind of target she now had in mind needed a lot more than stopping power.

C'naatat needed fragmentation.

"Shit," she muttered. "Shit."

Her only experience of a 670 was waiting one shaving of a second too long on the brink of blowing a hole in Lindsay Neville's head and getting taken down herself. Did Ade open fire, or Mart Barencoin? She still wasn't sure, and even if she used it spitefully against Ade in arguments, she felt no real anger or betrayal at being shot. It was drilled reflex rather than deliberate violence; God knew she'd done it often enough herself, and it was—*c'naatat* excepted—why she was alive today.

The 670 had a grenade launcher, and high yield grenades fragmented very well indeed. But if she couldn't get Lindsay or Rayat out of the water, then she needed an explosive harpoon. And that was beyond her right then.

She was still trying to clip the launcher attachment onto the barrel when the door swung open and Ade strode in, breathless from his morning run. He leaned on the table, charmingly disheveled. Sweat welded his lovat T-shirt to him and he wiped a drop from his nose with the back of his hand.

"It's not waterproof, Boss."

Shan leaned back and fixed Ade with a glare. "Have I got *no* fucking private thoughts left?"

"I promised you I'd sort some kit out for you, remember? Besides, I don't need to absorb your memories to know what you're thinking." Ade peeled off his shirt and began washing it in the sink. His routine rarely varied. "Does it bother you?"

"What, every bastard knowing what I think?"

"Not every bastard. Me."

"No. Actually, it doesn't. Not at all. But I know you're humoring me. Stop pissing me about and let me get on with it."

Ade rubbed the misshapen bar of soap on his shirt with slow deliberation. He ran in boots and sometimes even with his Bergen loaded, with *full fighting order* as they called it; it was a mad Royal Marines kind of thing and sometimes their insistence on ferocious training and discipline made her feel inadequate, which was no mean feat. Right then she felt ashamed of her amateur transparency and short temper.

"Sorry. I've got to go to Bezer'ej sooner or later. You know I have."

"Well, you *can* immerse the 670, but then you might as well just lob the grenade in as an underwater charge. Explosive harpoon, that's what you really need."

"I know."

"Fresh out."

"You're taking the piss now, aren't you?"

"I'm just thinking it through with you."

Don't take it out on him. You were the one who took your eye off the ball. "I *have* to tie up the loose ends. Once I neutralize the risks we can get on with our lives."

"Boss, what are you going to do if the bezeri say they need them down there?"

She'd thought about that. It tested her ethical logic to the limit. The copper in her said to finish the job, but if the wess'har weren't subject to her morality, then the bezeri definitely weren't. Shan found herself constantly locked in a loop that said *c'naatat* was bloody dangerous and would lead to terrible consequences.

But for whom? *Humans.*

Rayat was evidence enough. Government departments wanting to control it, pharmacorps gagging to exploit it: and every last fucker on earth never wanting to die. But so far she hadn't found another species that didn't dread it or treat it with wary indifference—just like the isenj, whose colony on Bezer'ej had picked up the parasite by accident.

"The war was over genocide," she said. "Never *c'naatat.* The bezeri called in Aras and his troops to wipe out the isenj for killing them with pollution. The isenj wanted Aras tried for war crimes and they wanted their territory back. But they didn't want *c'naatat.* None of them."

"Yeah. Looks like it's us that's the problem."

"Does stopping humans getting hold of it and shitting everything up with it outweigh the wishes of the bezeri?"

"Why are you asking me?"

"Because you always have a different take on things."

Ade wrung the water from his shirt as if he was strangling it and shook it out with a whiplash snap. "On their turf, it's their business."

"But the complication's Rayat."

"Last time I looked, he couldn't fly."

"Let's not rule out anything, shall we? This is a highly resourceful spook with *c'naatat* we're talking about."

Ade pegged his shirt on the rail above the heating vent and disappeared into the washroom. The bath itself was more or less a sheep-dip but the toilet was the real deal, aquamarine glass, custom-made to human plan by an obliging wess'har when Shan simply couldn't stand trying to use a wess'har latrine any longer. A vent halfway up the wall took some using for anyone with human anatomy. Ade emerged fastening his fly.

"I know you're right," he said. He sat down astride the bench next to her, frowning slightly. His eyes weren't the mid-brown she had once thought but deep honey-gold flecked with chocolate and olive; she couldn't imagine why she had ever thought of him as forgettable. "But work this through with me, will you?"

"I just hate uncertainty."

"What about Vijissi?"

"What about him?"

"Do we frag him too? And then what about us? Where does it stop? Maybe it never will."

Ade had a talent for asking truly demanding questions. He cut the crap and asked the basic stuff, *copper's* stuff: in a way, a child's questions. She admired both the clarity and the courage needed to ask them. "Okay, perhaps Shapakti can remove *c'naatat* from Vijissi."

Ade's gaze flickered over her face. "Here's the deal. I'll sort something to do the job if you promise me not to go yomping off on some half-arsed crusade without me." He paused. "And Aras. And that you ask the bezeri what *they* want, 'cos this is about them."

For a moment Shan had that out-of-body moment when she looked down on herself as a stranger and saw an obsessed woman planning a cold-blooded assassination. *Is that me? Is that what I am?* She wanted to be sure why she was doing this, even if motive was irrelevant.

"Okay," she said. "Deal. You reckon a harpoon will do it?"

"Depends on the charge, I suppose."

"What injuries do you get with underwater explosions?"

"Lots. Ruptured guts and stuff, but that won't even slow down a *c'naatat*, will it?"

"Right."

"Look, I said I'd sort something out for you, didn't I?"

"Does it bother you that I'm planning to liquefy Lin and Rayat?"

Ade pursed his lips. "If it did, that wouldn't stop you."

"I'm that much of a selfish cow, am I?"

"I'd never call you selfish. Inappropriately independent, maybe."

She forced a laugh. It stung her a little because like all painful revelations, it was true. "Didn't take me long to fall

from walking on water to just being the missus, did it?" Ade
looked suddenly mortified. She realized how vulnerable he
still was in relationships: even now he walked a knife edge,
trying not to provoke his dead, hated dad and never quite
knowing what would earn him a good hiding. He seemed to
treat his women with the same fearful reverence. "I'm
sorry. I always snap at you. About time you saw me for what
I am, though."

"Oh, I see you just fine. So, how about a bit of training
before Aras gets back?"

"Okay." Ade liked doing things as a couple. She doubted if
he'd ever had a woman whose idea of shared fun was combat
training. "But let's try not to break anything. And no ten kay
runs."

"How about knives? Know how to use one?"

Shan shrugged. "I know how to disarm someone *armed*
with a blade, if that's what you mean. Basic training."

"No, I mean *use* it as a weapon."

She reached down the back of her belt and took out her
9mm. "What, when I can blow someone's brains out with
this from a nice safe distance?"

"But what if you needed to do the job *quietly*?"

"Silencer."

"Come on." He gestured to the door, instantly the experienced sergeant sorting out a new junior officer. "Out on the
terrace, Boss."

It kept him happy, and for all she knew she might even
need the skills one day. Ade bounced his knife in his hand a
couple of times by the ribbed handle; it was a timeless design, a keen edge both sides of a plain, tapering blade that
was designed to kill and not much else.

Shan considered the knife and Ade's expression. The
combination of the little boy desperate for approval and the
sheer killing power of a commando disarmed her every
time. The reaction told her something about her original
species that wasn't flattering, but there was no mystery in
what she'd found so instantly attractive; he looked good, he
looked fit, and he would look out for her.

"Now, class," he said. "Just because we can't be killed, doesn't mean we can be careless. Okay?"

"I've had a few blades stuck in me before. So your dagger—"

"Fighting knife, Boss. Not a dagger."

"Okay. *Fighting knife.*" She stood with her arms loose at her sides, not sure how an elite commando went about teaching someone to kill, and feeling that little fizz of adrenaline that went with preparing to square up to someone. "Have you done it? Have you ever killed someone with that thing?"

"Yes." Now his eyes weren't quite fixed on hers but focused slightly past her. He was remembering. "Three. Two textbook. One not."

Stabbing someone wasn't a quick way to kill them, not unless you got a good deep slice across the trachea and took out the jugular or carotid, and then it was messy. She'd investigated too many stabbings. "I'm not judging you, Ade."

"You have to be decisive or they make too much bloody noise." He wasn't a violent man. He was just prepared to do the job, and she admired that. She didn't want him plagued by yet more nightmares just because a squeamish society expected him to do its dirty work.

"Okay, grips and stance." He demonstrated with the knife, flicking between styles. "Reverse . . . ice-pick . . . fencer . . . and hammer. There's only one correct answer as far as we're concerned, and that's *hammer.* Then we'll do stances—"

"What about walking up behind the bloke and cutting his throat? Shoving the blade in the base of the skull and—"

"You get the basics right first and then you can try the figure skating." He'd snapped back into role as the instructor sergeant. This was another Ade, the man who really, *really* knew his business, a man at the top of a hard game, not the heroic victim that Shan saw him as a little too often. "And forget all that police shite with your free hand out in front. This is to kill or disable, not arrest." He slapped the knife in her hand and fumbled in his pouch belt for something. It turned out to be a pocket knife. "Okay, shield hand—free hand—close to your vital bits and knife held like *so.*"

And it *was* an education. Shan had dealt with a lot of bastards carrying knives in her career, but if they'd been marines her career might have been a lot shorter. It was just as well that most of the lowlife she came across had learned their technique from the vids.

I can't cause permanent damage. Neither can he.

Stab wounds felt like a punch. She knew that. She had a long knife scar in her calf from a man she'd brought down with her baton in a riot. It was odd: she had no sensation of being *punctured,* just hit.

"Come on," said Ade, beckoning with his free hand. "Do your worst."

She'd never get past his guard to his torso. *Face. Facial injuries demoralize.* She went for it. He jerked back and—*oh shit*—she spun around to grab his blade with her free hand as he aimed for her torso. She hung on to it for grim death; he tried to drag it from her. Then he slackened his hold on it and stepped well back. If he'd been trying, she was sure the blade would have been embedded somewhere serious by now.

"You do all right for a civvie." He took her hand and looked at the wound. It stung. Blood welled briefly in a line the width of her left palm and the cut faded to a pink line. "Well done. Right instincts. You okay?"

"They trained us that it was better to have a cut hand than a blade in your guts. Fine as long as you keep a tight grip."

"Just remember to keep your hand in front of your vital bits. It's not called your shield hand for nothing."

"Can I try again?"

"I don't like seeing you hurt."

"It's only pain."

"That's my line."

Shan didn't like seeing Ade hurt, either. She fought her instinct to win—blind, indiscriminate and sometimes embarrassing—and concentrated on him. She was so engrossed in learning something new that she didn't catch Aras's scent as he walked onto the terrace. She didn't even hear him. She certainly hadn't smelled Shapakti. The two males stood staring at the spectacle.

"Is this a game?" Aras stood wiping his hands on a cloth. The mud suggested he'd pulled some root vegetables. Shapakti did the sensible thing and watched. "If so, it's foolish."

Ade's shoulders were set and he exuded a delicious scent of sandalwood, just like Aras; it was the first time Shan had detected a hint of challenge between them. Nevyan's husbands did it all the time, establishing constantly shifting pecking orders. "Just teaching Shan the finer points of fighting knives."

"Put the knives away. Shapakti wants to talk to *isan*."

Aras didn't like knives. Shapakti's gaze darted from Shan to Ade and back again and she realized that any wess'har could smell that she was aroused. She wasn't sure if she was turned on or just ready for a fight, and maybe the two were one and the same. But she felt good at an animal level, good enough to be able to forget Bezer'ej for a moment. Ade grinned, a blush starting to color his cheeks.

But Shapakti was the bucket of cold water thrown over two amorous dogs.

"I have been busy," he said. "I apologize for the delay."

"It's okay." *Busy on Esganikans's bioweapons, no doubt.* "Any luck?"

"I have attempted a number of procedures with the ussissi sample." He clasped his hands in front of him in a gesture that looked like prayer but was just a comfortable neutral position for wess'har. "I failed to separate the parasite from the host cells."

"Ah."

"That doesn't mean it's impossible."

"Just that you haven't done it yet."

"Yes. But the only cells I've performed separation upon so far are from the first sample. Yours."

"Why? Gender? Species?"

"I'm hesitant to express my speculation, because it sounds odd."

"If I were Eddie, I'd be beating it out of you by now. He hates a tease."

"I don't understand."

"I meant that I'd rather hear it and make allowances for its being a theory."

"I believe *c'naatat* might have *learned.*"

Shapakti looked as if he expected disbelief. Ade shrugged. "We know that. Look how fast it moves. Next time it comes across the same problem, it sorts it faster. Remember when you were first shot in the head, Boss?"

"Yeah. It patched me up a lot faster the next time."

"Well, then."

"All organisms adapt to survive," said Shapakti. "But *c'naatat* may have learned how *not* to be removed. And that intrigues me. I need to carry out more research."

"I'll see if I can get you a couple more samples." Shan's brief diversion was over. "Aquatically adapted ones."

It was bad news for Vijissi. It was reassuring news in an odd way for her, though. It meant that removal was a choice she might never have to make now.

Something else was nagging at her, like a Suppressed Briefing, but that box of psychopharmaceutical tricks was out of her system for good now.

She'd forgotten it, whatever it was. There were bigger things on her mind.

Bezer'ej

The diurnal cycle had become meaningless for Lindsay in a matter of days.

She wondered if it was her own determination to forget what she'd been, simply to be able to cope, or if *c'naatat* was making subtler changes to her. The lights in her hands spurred her on. And she had a clear focus now; she was determined to help the bezeri survive. She had to find others.

Saib gave the impression that he respected her zeal. He let her wander off alone to explore the surrounding area after warning her to stay clear of the hard-shelled carnivores that patrolled the nearby reef. They looked like half-meter long whelk shells occupied by creatures with jointed tails and clawed front feet almost like terrestrial raptors. If they approached too close, loud noises were enough to scare them off; they showed no stomach for tackling anything as large as a human, especially a noisy one.

A rattle seemed like a good idea. There was plenty of raw material. Lindsay searched for flat shells, and then sat down on an outcrop of textured lemon stone—a coral, perhaps—to string them together with strips of fibrous weed. She rattled them like castanets, and the tumbling noise of a small avalanche was satisfying.

What are you making? asked Pili.

"A rattle to scare off the things with the claws."

Pili shot off in a jet of water. Lindsay wondered if the signal lamp had misinterpreted something. The lack of resentment among the bezeri bewildered her more than anything, because for all their appearance of wanting balance, of wanting the same harsh justice that had ended in Parekh's execution, they remained civil; mostly distant, yes, but sometimes quite friendly. And nobody who'd helped bring them to extinction deserved friendship.

Pili reappeared with something held in a tightly coiled tentacle. She unfurled the arm and deposited a glossy black T-shaped object in Lindsay's lap.

For when the noise does not work. I made this.

It was a polished stone hammer. Lindsay hefted it in her hand and ran a fingertip along the almost-invisible joint where the handle slotted into the head: a thin band of a reflective substance circled the end of the grip. Bezeri had no fire and no metals, and Lindsay had started to see them not as stone age technologists but as a cold manufacture society. They could certainly work stone and manipulate organic materials well enough to create a sophisticated array of goods.

They *had* to survive. They were too important to let slip into extinction.

"Thank you."

Leenz, if you hit them on the back, even the most aggressive irsi *flee.*

"I'll remember that."

Lindsay had formed an image of Pili as a slightly dotty grandmother, none too bright, but now it occurred to her that she could be anything: a sculptor, a mason, even an engineer. She enjoyed the moment of revelation. Even this odd friendship that was more of a polite cease-fire boosted her motivation.

Irsi taste bad unless you are very hungry indeed, said Pili.

Lindsay smiled out of simian habit and realized it meant nothing to a cephalopod. If she developed bioluminescence— *when* she developed it—a bezeri smile would be near the top of her signals to learn.

She didn't want to find out how irsi tasted. It was bad enough getting used to defecating under water, but her body seemed to be adapting her for that, too. When she finally decided to discard her clothes, life would become much simpler.

Rayat was engrossed in signaling with Keet, holding up his hands so that the bezeri could see the signals. The old male appeared to be happy to teach him the language, and judging by Rayat's occasional grin they were making some progress. Why weren't the bezeri venting their rage and grief on the two individuals responsible for their misery? Lindsay knew how she'd react. She'd want vengeance. She was sure of it.

But humans often developed odd alliances; hostage and captor, prisoner and guard. Maybe that was happening here. And how much energy could you devote to actively hating someone if you had to live alongside them in desperate conditions?

"Saib, do you have any information on where your people were when it happened?" *It.* She couldn't quite say it yet. She wondered what *nuking* looked like in lights. *It.* Neutron and cobalt irradiation might have defied translation anyway. "I know most of them would have been around Ouzhari, but are there any other places some might have gone?"

The spawning weeks are important to us. Everyone goes to the small mountain, except those who are ill or too weak.

"I'd like to search for more survivors."

Do you think we will forgive you if you succeed? There are none. We would detect them.

She was still reliant on the lamp to understand Saib. Rayat was a long way ahead of her in using bioluminescence. "I don't think I can be forgiven. But I can try to be useful."

You said your child died.

"Yes. He was born too early."

Did you make a memorial for him?

She almost had no words to frame her answer that wouldn't have involved a long explanation about friends who became enemies. She opted for literal simplicity. "A wess'har made one for him. On Constantine." She struggled for a description in English. "The Largest Mountain to the Dry Above."

So far from your home.

Did Saib mean the grave or her? David would have been two: walking, talking, exploring the world. Lindsay had managed to keep the pain under control with medication, but she didn't have any to numb her now. It wasn't so much pain as fear of letting herself speculate on what David might be like today had he lived. Somehow that hurt more than the fact that he was dead. She would be destroyed, she knew, if she let herself think too much about what he was *not*. It was the loss of a *lifetime,* not just a life, a loss of not only his potential but all of hers too.

Yes, she was pretty sure she knew what the bezeri were going through. She had no future; all that she had ever loved was dead; and she had no familiar society around her. She was living their lives. It was both punishment and education.

"Yes," she said. "Far from our home planet. But I'm here, and my child's here, and that will have to be enough."

Saib hung motionless in front of her for a while, flickering with faint green pinpoints of light.

Why did you come so far to be here?

"It was my job," she said.

But that explained nothing. She remembered thinking it would enhance her career prospects no end when she finally got home, even if she'd been out of circulation for 150 years by then. It never occurred to her that she might never go home and yet still be alive.

Saib disappeared into the mud buildings, reminding her of a woman gathering up long skirts and running into the distance. The town's size emphasized how very few bezeri there were left. She joined Rayat and watched the exchange of lights between him and Keet.

"You can have the lamp back now," she said.

"Don't need it," said Rayat. "I make faster progress if I can't use it. It's almost as if the frustration speeds up the neuron growth." He looked away from Keet for a moment, seeming distracted by an idea. "I wonder if *c'naatat* responds to stress hormones? Smooths things over?"

"If it did," said Lindsay, "I'd enjoy eating raw seaweed right now. And I don't."

She didn't feel specifically angry towards him right then. She just felt tired somewhere in the depths of her soul.

"How can you miss someone you only knew for a few weeks?" As soon as she said it, she regretted exposing her vulnerability. Rayat didn't have any compassion and he wasn't her buddy. "Forget it. Doesn't matter."

"Who, exactly?"

"David."

Rayat flickered a pattern of blue and red lights back at Keet. She thought he was ignoring her.

"Nearly ten months," Rayat said suddenly. "That's how long you knew him."

It was such a conciliatory comment that it stunned her. Sometimes Rayat exposed the man within and for a fleeting moment she saw someone who did a dirty job whose grim detail he could never discuss with anyone. It had either destroyed his capacity for trust, or he had none to start with and being a spy had been a natural career choice for him.

Either way, she could never imagine him having feelings. Like Shan, he was an efficient machine for getting the job done. And she couldn't love machines.

She wondered if this was the first glimmer of compassion, or just another of his careful, patient, Byzantine strategies to achieve something. But maybe he was just scared, lonely and racked by remorse. Perhaps *c'naatat* had changed more than his physiology.

"Nice hammer, by the way," said Rayat. "Very pre-Columbian. Mind your fingers."

Lindsay drifted across the silt plain and moved between rocks, blsck stone hammer in one hand and feeling oddly primeval. She paused in a submerged canyon where the sunlight hung in a perfectly vertical shaft through the water like a pastel tourmaline crystal. There was something uplifting about it, almost a reassurance that she wasn't confined here.

Possibilities were replacing inevitable misery. The Eqbas stationed here had the monitoring technology to comb the ocean for other survivors. If she made contact, the Eqbas might help her. With more survivors, she could help the species rebuild: and she could train them to defend themselves. She was an officer, dismissed or not. She could give them a defense force, which was more than they ever seemed to have had in their history.

Lindsay considered how the Eqbas might react to a stray *c'naatat* with a history of war crimes, and somehow she doubted she'd be feted like Aras. It didn't matter. For the moment she had a little bit of hope.

F'nar, Wess'ej: Mid-December

"Jesus, Ade," said Shan. She peeled off her jacket, accompanied by a draft of cold air. "Santa's grotto or what?"

Ade thought he'd done a pretty good job of decorating the house. Shredded strips of his foil survival blanket hung

from the walls and the tub of lavender that usually stood on
the terrace was now in the corner nearest the sofa festooned
with tiny hemp paper chains. He looked at her expression
and felt instantly, totally and irredeemably stupid.

"I just wanted . . ."

He had no idea how to finish the sentence.

Her surprise melted into an embarrassed grin, which was
unusual in itself. "It's lovely. Really, it is. I'm just amazed
that you managed to come up with all this." Her glance fell
on the table. "Is that a cake?"

"Yeah," he said.

He'd had no idea before today how to bake and he had almost no ingredients that matched what it said in the recipe,
but he was set on having a Christmas cake, a real one. Aras
occupied himself feeding the rat colony and offered no comment.

Shan leaned on the table and placed a careful fingertip on
the cake. "Still warm," she said. "I'd estimate time of death
as two or three hours ago, but some rigor's already set in."
Then she grinned and gave him a playful shove with her
hip. "Bloody clever. You're really into this, aren't you?"

"I thought it would be fun."

"It's great. What about icing?"

"No idea."

"Tofu maybe. A kind of whipped cream frosting."

"I'm never going to hear the end of this from Mart."

"Big roughy-toughy Bootie baking cakes, eh?" She
sniffed it. "Can they eat it? I mean, is it all safe for humans?"

"Aras checked out the ingredients."

"What if we can score some alcohol from Umeh Station?
Then you could soak it."

"Marinate?"

"Stab some holes in it and pour it in, if I recall correctly."
Women didn't have cooking genes, then. If they did, Shan
must have been on leave when they handed them out. She
looked at Aras. "What do you reckon, sweetheart? Does this
do anything for you?"

Aras, gloved as a precaution, held a couple of rats in his arms. They really had taken to him. Sometimes he made that rumbling noise deep in his throat, the one that wess'har dads used to get their kids to sleep, and the rats gazed mesmerized at him until he stopped. It had that effect on humans, too. He placed them back in their cage with a tidbit.

"I've seen more than a hundred and fifty Christmas festivals," said Aras. "I believe you need lights too."

"Does that mean you're getting into the spirit of the thing, then, Ras?" Ade wanted everyone to have a good time: no arguments, no disappointments and no sense of dread. He was aware of how desperate that was, and he knew where the urge came from. But it didn't make it any less important or exciting. A normal, happy, stable family gathering: something everyone else seemed to have and that seemed distant and magical when he was a kid. No hiding from Dad, no avoiding the other kids at school because he'd have to explain his bruises: no listening to them looking forward to the holidays and talking about experiences that were as alien to him then as the isenj were now.

Aras looked thoughtful, head on one side like a dog. His dark braid flopped forward over his shoulder as he leaned forward to join the cake inspection. "If you mean that a biologically impossible act gives me hope for noncorporeal existence, no."

"Bah, humbug," said Shan, and burst out laughing. She was in an unusually good mood; Ade had never heard her laugh so much. She wasn't *demonstrative*. He liked that word. "Sod Tiny Tim, eh?"

"I enjoy communal celebration," Aras said stiffly. "I just prefer to be clear about its purpose."

"Well, we're still alive, we've got food, and we've got each other." Shan picked a crumb off the cake and chewed. "Not bad at all, Ade."

"I was thinking of asking the lads over. Can I?"

"You don't have to ask my permission."

"Your home."

"Aras's house."

Aras shrugged. It was one of the things that made him look very human. "This is *our* home. I despair at your fixation with ownership."

"Maybe we can get Eddie to front up, too," said Shan. "And Vijissi, if he's up to it. Yeah, let's have a few laughs. God knows we need some. What's the alcohol situation?"

"Brewing," said Aras. "Ade has planned ahead. And I think I shall make lights."

Shan flexed her fingers. "I've got my own."

"So have I," said Ade.

"Let's see you hang *that* on Christmas tree, smart-arse."

Things were improving, definitely. Ade savored the glimpse of the life that everyone else took for granted. Aras went in search of lighting equipment at the Exchange of Surplus Things and Shan picked another crumb from the edge of the cake.

"He's going to rig million-lux arc lights, isn't he?" said Ade, moving the cake to higher ground for its own safety. "Captain Overkill rides again."

Shan smiled. "How do you want me to play this?"

"What do you mean?"

She shrugged. "Your mates haven't seen us together socially since we became an item. How do you want me to behave in front of them?"

"Sorry?"

"Professional distance or all over you?"

"They know we're shagging." *Oh God, I didn't mean it to come out like that.* He checked discreetly to see she was still wearing the ring. "That we're . . ."

"Well, then?"

Ade took her hand and squeezed gently. "All over me, please. And thanks for checking." She was perfect: she understood every anxiety a bloke might have. "I'll deck Mart if he says anything out of order."

"It's the thought that counts."

His stomach knotted and that luscious weight settled on his chest, making him catch his breath. He loved her to distraction. Being with her was effortless: there was no mystery to her, no game with hidden rules to work out. He felt secure despite her occasional anger.

"I was really worried you'd be embarrassed to be seen with me."

Shan shook her head with an exasperated snort. He knew when she was having difficulty broaching a subject and she was close to that now. "Shit, Ade, I love you. What makes you think I'm ashamed of you?"

She'd never said it before: love. He knew she didn't like saying the word. It caught him off guard and he found his mouth working independently of his brain. "I'm just so ordinary."

"Oh, yeah. I forgot that. Everyone freefalls from space and shoots aliens. When are you going to do something *different*?" She edged up to him on the bench and gave him a ferocious hug. "Ade, you'll never be ordinary as long as you've got a hole in your arse. You're a commando, for fuck's sake. I'll smack anyone who even looks at you the wrong way, okay?"

That was all he needed to hear. Being stranded twenty-five light-years from Earth among warring aliens with some parasite living in his guts was nothing, absolutely *nothing*. He was home now; and he had never been home before. When he thought she was dead, he'd made himself stop thinking about what might have been, but now he could stand on that edge and imagine what he would have lost. There was no other word for it: he *mourned* her at last. It was a frightening, bittersweet, unbearable panic. He threw his arms around her and pressed his face into her neck, feeling like he'd just been reunited with her after a long absence.

"What's up, sweetheart?" she said.

"Just feeling normal," he said. "And I don't take normal for granted."

He thought of what lovely kids they could have had—fierce

and clever daughters, loyal and protective sons—and put the idea out of his head.

Bezer'ej

Rayat rejoiced in the simple pleasure of learning a new skill. He couldn't recall the last time he'd had such uncomplicated joy; but talking in light was probably on a par with learning to walk, if only he could remember how that had felt.

Share? he asked. He offered a handful of what he thought of as glass worms to Keet.

You are not what I expected, said the patriarch. *I expected you would try to kill us again. We heard about the infant too. The isenj killed us accidentally. You sought us out to kill us.*

Infant? He probably meant the juvenile bezeri that Parekh had thought was dead. She found it beached; she dissected it. She ended up in a body bag because she ignored the warning not to take organic samples. So humans were not only genocidal, they were child-killers. It was a tough image to improve.

I can't put this right, said Rayat. *And sorry won't help.*

Keet slipped the worms up into his mantle. There was a beak in a fold of the flesh at the front, not within the ring of tentacles as it would be on a terrestrial squid. Somehow the arrangement seemed more like a mouth and made him that much more . . . human.

Saib says Leenz says the same thing. Sorry does not help. She grieves for her child buried here. There is no sorry that can stop the grief.

Rayat watched but he couldn't see the progress of the worms into Keet's digestive system. Lindsay was doing her mourning late. That was the trouble with mood enhancers; you had to stop taking them sooner or later, and the reality that had driven you to them was still waiting patiently, drumming its fingers, happy to pick up the conversation of misery again.

How did people complete the grieving cycle?

Seeing where their loved one had died was important.

So was seeing the grave.

David Neville's grave was on Constantine, and Rayat *needed to go there.*

It was an opportunity. He felt both satisfaction at its convenience and the slight worry that he'd already blown his credibility with Lindsay the last time he maneuvered her into doing his bidding. She was remarkably malleable. Most people were, once you worked out their motivation. He'd talked her into taking nuclear weapons to Bezer'ej and he'd talked her into acquiring *c'naatat*, and she knew it. Now all he wanted to do was have a legitimate excuse for visiting Constantine; a pretty harmless act for her to collude in, but she was twice bitten. She might refuse this time.

He'd try anyway. He had to. He turned to see where she was.

Lindsay had taken an interest in the maps and Pili held them in front of her, caressing the smooth surface of the shell with one tentacle as if pointing lovingly to familiar features. Rayat could make out words in the lights that shimmered in her mantle: *my clan, my home, our hunting grounds.*

And this town had a name. He couldn't translate it into English; he could have used the signal lamp, but suddenly he didn't want to. He wanted to understand one bezeri word as a bezeri did, simply by feeling the resonance of that pattern in his mind. At a deeper level the word became *town;* he left it at that and savored the pattern and color and movement.

Town.

The rest of the bezeri came out of hiding now and moved around the settlement. The more Rayat explored it, the more it looked like russet clay jars thrown on a potter's wheel and then piled up while still soft so that they sagged together in a random honeycomb. And now that he'd started to find positive elements in life underwater, he started to appreciate the beauty of his new environment. It was the blues and pinks and violets that struck him most. The carnival colors almost glowed; they painted everything from weed and coral-like growths to a surprisingly wide variety of animals.

There were no large predators, according to Keet. The biggest seemed to be what Lindsay called the killer whelks, *irsi*. One of them edged into the settlement on its own, skittering along the silt on its front claws and gouging a wake behind it with its long tail. It looked more comical than menacing. But Rayat could imagine what a pack of them might be able to do. He swam up to it and it shied away from him, propelling itself off the seabed with spurts of water jetted out beneath it. Then it paused on an outcrop, testing the water with a fringe of bright orange projections as if it was playing an invisible piano.

"They don't have a lot of bottle," said Lindsay. "You can scare them off with a bit of noise." She shook her rattle hard. The whelk took off like a missile. "See? They're all mouth and trousers."

"Odd that there aren't any big predators."

"The whelks from hell are big enough."

"But water supports big bodies. There ought to be something that fills the niche of sharks and orcas. Even whales." Rayat thought of the land animals of Bezer'ej, or at least the creatures he'd seen on Constantine. "Maybe a marine version of the *sheven*."

"Great," said Lindsay. "They'd be fun."

"I'll ask Keet."

"I don't like the idea of a carnivorous plastic bag at the best of times, let alone a whale-sized one."

Lindsay was almost chatty. Bezer'ej had a number of species that were no more than transparent sheets of digestive material that enveloped their prey; *alyats* could fly, and *sheven* lived in the bogs and streams. Yes, the idea of a bigger marine version was unsettling. Being engulfed and digested was a terrifying thought.

"Perhaps the bezeri will teach us to pilot those podships one day," said Rayat.

Lindsay's tone hardened a little. He could hear it even under water. "I didn't think we planned to do any traveling."

"Face it, you're going to want to visit David's grave sooner or later." He planted the idea almost without thinking. But he was certain it must have crossed her mind. "And it's almost a hundred kay to Constantine. That's a bloody long swim, and you don't know what's out there."

She stared at him. It must have been sunny on the surface; the colors around him were vivid and Lindsay's uniform pants looked navy blue again rather than black.

"Since when did you worry about my welfare?"

"You think I want to live on my own down here? Fascinating as the bezeri are, I'd prefer to have human company, even if it tends to get a little whiny at times." There was no point in looking too friendly. She'd get suspicious. "Lin, we're stuck here. Let's try to get on."

Too late. She had that wary look, head tilted back a little. "Why didn't you refuse *c'naatat*?"

"Because I didn't want to die. It's a pretty consistent motive in organisms. If you recall correctly, we were about to be tipped off a raft into the middle of the ocean at the time."

"Yeah."

"And why did you insist I come along to do the undead thing, then?"

"It was time you paid for what you did."

"Well, then we both know why we're here, then. Let's cut the crap and concentrate on being productive."

They looked at one another in silence—both sound and light—and then Lindsay dropped her head. It was odd to watch someone's body language under water; it was as if they were moving in air, but slowed down and exaggerated.

"You're right," she said. "I *do* want to see David's grave, if there's anything left of it."

"The nanites were probably confined to the area within the bioscreen. It'll still be there, probably." What was it like to lose a kid? Rayat looked for the worst experience he could recall, his greatest pain, and tried to superimpose his grandfather's death on the situation. *Think how she thinks. Feel how she feels.* That was how you got to know a target and deal with them, by thinking as they did. Lindsay needed to feel David's death wasn't her fault. "If you'd had a termination, you'd feel just as bad. At least you gave him a chance."

"Well, you seem to be making progress with Keet. I'll leave you to get around to the subject of how we visit Constantine."

We.

So far, so good. She needed support. Damn, sometimes he felt he did, too. He thought of patting her on the shoulder but reconsidered, and went back to sit with Keet and exchange illuminated words while the other bezeri went through the stack of *azin* shell records.

One of them had two sheets of shell and a collection of small pots the size of cups. She coated one slice of shell with something sticky, spread from one tentacle, and then sprinkled sand in very fine lines with another arm. As Rayat watched, a sand image grew before his eyes.

So that's how they do it.

The bezeri's precision astonished him. But this was how they had written in ancient times, and this one still had the skill. She was making a record; maybe she was tallying the retrieved maps, listing them. Or maybe she was recording how alien air-breathers came to the Dry Above and destroyed them and all hope.

Rayat didn't want to ask. He just watched, mesmerized by seeing an intelligent squid create a document as a child might have glued glitter to a greetings card. When the shell sheet was covered in symbols and color, the bezeri wiped the sticky substance around the edge of the shell and pressed the two layers tight together.

Rayat still thought the price had to be paid, but he genuinely regretted wiping out a species like this one. He withdrew to the rocks to collect food, and wondered again why there were no other large animals in this part of the ocean.

F'nar, Wess'ej: Nevyan's home

Nevyan's library had become Eddie's edit suite.

It was quiet, it had a comms screen set in the wall, and she'd let him keep a table and chair in there. The jury-rigged furniture was square-built and very unwess'har, but made out of old vegetable crates he'd hammered together, so it was recycled and therefore *admirable* according to Giyadas.

She was very pleased to have him back. She sat with him for hours, simply absorbing whatever it was she absorbed to be able to stun him with her perception.

It was a comfortable den; with the lighting dimmed, and his various screens, cams and keyboards spread out, it felt just like editing footage back home. All he needed was a big mug of coffee and a stack of pizza and he could have forgotten he was 150 trillion miles from Earth. When the marines from the detachment dropped in for a chat, sometimes with beer, the place almost had a real buzz. He missed working in an office. You could work from anywhere in the galaxy, and he'd proved it, but he was one of those people who liked a crowd around him. There was only so much monkey that technology could take out of you.

He imagined a pizza and wondered how he was going to cut the rushes from Esganikan's attempt at diplomacy into something fresh enough to tempt a jaded news editor's palate.

"Eddie." Giyadas stood at his elbow. "Eddie, I have something for you."

"Pizza, doll? With extra mozzarella?"

"That's cheese."

"Yes."

"Coagulated excretions."

"Don't ever get a job waiting on tables, will you? You're not cut out for it." He gave her a hug and she seemed not to mind. "What is it, then?"

She reached forward and touched the screen to activate another ITX feed. "Esganikan sends this. She says she's sorry you weren't there and she hopes this is enough." Eddie was used to Eqbas recordings now. He tried to work out the orientation of the static image and decided it was an aerial view and needed rotating 90 degrees right. He tapped the icons on the control strip and the image flipped and began to play.

"Oh shit," he said.

It was the ten seconds of perfectly steady on-board footage from what had to be a fighter's cockpit that most disturbed him. It showed nothing graphic. The craft was making a straight run down a road flanked by typical isenj high-rises, solid and continuous as canyon walls, and the dark river flowing between them resolved into masses of isenj troops. But although he didn't see any missile strike in those ten seconds, his memory and imagination filled the gaps in advance. He knew what was coming.

The fact that isenj blood was straw-yellow plasma and their body parts were hard to recognize in the debris didn't save him from that jolt when the unidentifiable image he was looking at snapped suddenly into something called *person*. He felt that same awful combination of revulsion and reluctance to look away. For a second, he saw Minister Ual's thin blood on his clothes again. The columns of troops and vehicles had nowhere to run: they couldn't even turn. Had the footage been of a human war, BBChan would never have transmitted it.

Giyadas said nothing. It crossed Eddie's mind several minutes too late that a kid shouldn't see that kind of footage, but she was wess'har. They had strong stomachs.

He had one of those once, too.

"Your bastard news editor won't be angry with you now," said Giyadas primly. Oh yes, she absorbed *everything* he said. "You missed nothing."

He looked down at her, certain he'd protect her like she was his own, and hoped he'd never see her vague resemblance to an Eqbas.

"No," he said. "You got it all."

12

*FEU Defense Minister Margit Huber today refused to com-
ment on allegations that she wanted to stage a military
strike against Australia over the Eqbas crisis to "effect
regime change." Civil service unions claim a leaked memo
shows that Sinostates president May Yi Jun threatened to
withdraw FEU access to Sino airspace and bases if it went
ahead. An aide now faces charges connected to leaking
information.*

BBChan 557, December 24 2376

Eqbas ship 886-001-005-6; in detached fleet mode, Northern Assembly airspace south of Jejeno

President Pirb repeated his call to arms as the Eqbas
fighters pounded his military bases. Esganikan couldn't understand it, but Aitassi translated the audio message that
was being relayed across the messaging system in each of
Umeh's four landmasses.

"He repeats his plea for other nations to commit forces
to attacking Wess'ej and reclaiming Bezer'ej." One of her
clan wandered onto the bridge and gave her a bowl of fried
fruits: it had been a long watch. "I wonder if he knows his
range and limits."

"In which order of priority?"

"It varies each time he repeats it. Either way, it's academic."

The *gethes* had got it right with mass media. Esganikan
wished for an isenj version of Eddie, with news program-
ming she could tap into for the state of play across Umeh
quickly and easily. Isenj preferred their complex network of
personal links, only some of which bothered to use images.
The nearest they had to media was the collective gossip of
loosely defined groups.

"Where exactly does Umeh space begin?" asked Hayin.

"Where I say it does." Esganikan stood with her hands clasped in front of her. She found herself trying Shan's resting stance with hands on hips, but it was uncomfortable for wess'har shoulders. "No isenj vessel needs to go beyond Tasir Var. Beyond that, if they head towards Wess'ej space, open fire. Tell them so. They're confined."

It wasn't *if*. It was *when*. She knew it; isenj liked gestures.

Joluti kept an eye on the displays that monitored the locations of the detached ship components. A squadron of fighters was formed in the hangar, ready to intercept isenj long-range craft heading off-world, and a small shuttle was inbound from Bezer'ej and Tasir Var. It carried a tree.

"How many variants of the pathogen was Shapakti able to create?" asked Joluti.

"Seven distinct strains."

"Guesswork."

"Without a complete genome record, how can we know who lives where? Isenj must interbreed to some extent."

"They do realize they'll have to accept the risk of deaths among their own people, don't they?"

"I've explained that to them."

"A sad fate for the civilization that spread an entangled photon network." Joluti reached out and grabbed a chunk of vegetable from Aitassi's bowl. "To be reduced to this."

"It must be hard to live with faded glory when your ancestors' memories are part of you. I imagine it makes for bitter personalities."

"And delusional ones, perhaps."

"Why?"

"In their minds—in their genetic memory—they're still a powerful imperial army that took on the wess'har and almost won. In the flesh, they don't appear to have had any substantial military experience in many generations."

It was a telling comment. The military capacity of Umeh surprised Esganikan by its inadequacy. Isenj did something

Eddie called "talking a good game": their threats were more impressive than their actions. She realized she was fighting the equivalent of police and civil emergency teams on Earth. Isenj weren't a particularly aggressive species, and the Northern Assembly didn't even have a specific minister with sole responsibility for defense, as the *gethes* always did.

And the isenj were no longer the galactic engineers who built and deployed the communications networks that the *gethes* called ITX: they didn't even have the resources to maintain them across light years now. The glory days of their civilization were over, eroded by environmental pressures and the increasing need to manage every aspect of their climate. They were already long in decline. But—like their faith in their military prowess—their genetic memories were those of a colonial power who believed its engineering skills could solve any problem. That illusion was probably the basis of their undoing.

If Eddie Michallat wanted to demonstrate to Earth what would happen to it if it didn't mend its ways, it wasn't Eqbas military strength he needed to show: it was the decline of the isenj themselves.

Joluti took his *virin* and stared into its layers. "ITX was superior to our technology in many ways at the time. They must feel bitter to think we benefited so much from it."

"Knowledge can never be owned for long."

"Eddie thinks we're too open about our military capacity," said Aitassi.

"Then perhaps he should stop reporting on it, if it troubles him."

"What if the *gethes* were to acquire countermeasures?"

Esganikan's confidence was based on the knowledge that Earth's technology was a civilization's history behind her own. They probably knew that too. Perhaps they were hoping that if they tried to repel the Eqbas task force rather than cooperate, then a computer virus, terrestrial bacteria or even a simple element like water would strike down her personnel: they seemed to believe these things, or at least fantasize about them in their myths to comfort themselves that they were special and that fate would always spare them.

"It would be a technical advance on an unprecedented scale," said Esganikan. "But we have the blueprint, as they call it, for nearly all life on their planet, including their own species." She glanced at a remote surveillance image of the remnant of Tivskur's shattered fleet, half-submerged in its harbor. "And they do not have *ours*."

The surveillance remotes continued to show space-capable vessels from the Sil and Tivskur continents gathering on Pareg. The build-up was far smaller than she expected, no more than three thousand fighters: a large nation's air force, not a planet's combined forces.

"I never expected them to be so inadequate," said Joluti. "But even if they had the resources, I doubt if they could use them effectively."

"I hear the Wess'ej matriarchs never attacked Umeh even at the height of the wars." Esganikan could imagine their polite, non-interventionist agreement. "And the isenj never targeted Wess'ej."

"Bezer'ej was always the disputed territory."

"That explains why they're not equipped for planetary defense."

"We could destroy most of the aircraft on the ground," Joluti looked hopeful. "Do I have your permission? There's something distasteful about knowing their inadequacy and waiting for them to make a move that justifies our action. Let's end it now."

"How long before the shuttle is inboard?"

"Half an hour, no more."

"Very well. Put the air group on alert."

Joluti was right. There was something tragic about it. The isenj have been left in peace to decline and die. Esganikan wouldn't have felt uneasy and could have concentrated on planning the Earth mission.

But Par Paral Ual had asked for her help. If one isenj could change, it was worth the fight.

Library, Nevyan's clan home, F'nar

"They either think it's the Second Coming or the end of the world," said Barencoin. "That's the trouble with aliens visiting Earth. Every dingbat and loony this side of the Black Stump is going to be out in force."

He slurped his tea and watched the BBChan feed on the ITX with Eddie. Some evangelist group was hailing the Eqbas visit as the beginning of the time of judgment, a wake-up call to repent. The story was buried with the novelty features like water-skiing squirrels and people who set records for eating glass.

Eddie wondered when to show Barencoin the footage from the Eqbas raid.

"Maybe it *is* the end of the world," said Eddie. "You know the isenj in Jejeno want the Eqbas to give them bioweapons to use against their neighbors, don't you?"

"I lose track of the NBC ordnance these days, mate. There's so much shit around this system."

"Doesn't it bother you? Tailored biological weapons? Target-by-genome?"

"What, like on Bezer'ej? Courtesy of Eddie Michallat?"

"That's defensive."

"Oh, that's all right, then." Barencoin flipped his knife from his belt. "So's this. And I can only use my powers for good. Christ, you fucking civvies. You can't create a weapon and use rules as the safety catch."

"They'd have acquired isenj DNA in time anyway, without my help."

"We had no business interfering on Bezer'ej." Barencoin replaced his knife. "And no business telling aliens how to run their affairs when we can't even run our own."

"Okay, Mr. fucking Isolationist," said Eddie. His language

got steadily worse in the company of marines. "We've got more than three hundred people still in Jejeno."

"Agreed. We should be over there. Just in case."

"Five marines and a few billion isenj. What do you think it is, Rorke's Drift?"

"Six. And isenj don't have a problem with humans."

"Collateral damage. They don't *have* to have a problem. And Shan will have something to say about it if you try to get Ade over there."

"Yeah, I thought she might." Barencoin looked defocused, as if calculating. "I bet the ladies here could lend us a ground-to-air defense system."

"Anyway, you lot were fired, remember?"

"That's just technicalities."

"Could Mar'an'cas cope with just the civvies? That's just over a hundred."

"What about the naval personnel? Don't blue suits matter?"

"I'm just thinking aloud. By the time we work out how to find enough food for them there could be fighting in Jejeno anyway."

Barencoin didn't answer. He looked a threat at the best of times, a very big man who never looked clean-shaven however often he used a razor. The news footage absorbed him for a few moments.

"Let's watch the main topics," he said, and Eddie didn't argue.

However abrasive Barencoin could be, Eddie admired and liked him. He still did the job, fired or not, and took his responsibilities seriously even when stripped of his status and honor. Eddie stifled the reflex that made him want to garrote politicians with rusty razor-wire.

"What do you fancy doing when you get back to Earth?" asked Eddie.

"What, if it's not a smoking pile of slag by then, you mean?"

"Assuming that, yes."

"I have a Master's in international law and my first degree was politics. I don't fancy doing either for a living."

"Sorry?"

Eddie's shock must have been visible. Barencoin's jaw clenched a little. "I'm just a mindless grunt right?"

"No, I never—"

"Liar."

"I just didn't have you down for a lawyer." But it was true: he really was shocked that Barencoin had an academic background. He'd taken his smartness for rat cunning. "You're a bit . . . direct."

"Anyway, being dismissed the service doesn't look great on your application, does it?"

Eddie suspected there'd be a lot of security work for special forces troops with no place to go in about thirty years' time. The FEU forces already had enough trouble keeping their personnel, faced with the lure of better pay outside for the same risk of getting your head shot off, or worse. He had a sudden image of Barencoin in some vile foreign jail and it upset him. He deserved better. They all did.

"I wish I could be some help, Mart."

"You're not my mum."

"Media always needs security minders overseas."

"Well, got time to think, haven't we? Five years to do some distance learning course. Flower arranging, maybe."

"Want to evaluate some reconnaissance footage for me?"

"Is this like your little job of getting us to snatch Rayat and Neville from the isenj?"

"Not really. I just need to show someone."

"Okay."

Eddie loaded the file and leaned back to let Barencoin watch the uncut footage from Esganikan's operation.

The marine scared him. If any of them were capable of random violence, it was him; just like Shan, he had *nasty bastard* written all over him and it would come as no surprise if he punched you in the face from a cold start. He watched the recording with an occasional tilt of the head as the cockpit view skewed, and didn't turn a hair.

"Those things can really move," he said as it finished. "So, what else do you want to know?"

"Does that disturb you?"

"No. Should it?"

"It got to me."

"How many conflicts have you covered, mate?"

"Five. Six if you count this."

"Then you must have spent your time in the hotel bar. Because that's what it's always like. Except they've got better kit than us. *Lots* better."

"Okay."

"What do you *think* happens when there's an air strike on ground troops?"

"In a civilian area."

"Oh, yeah, I forgot. We've never done that, have we? Jesus, Eddie."

Barencoin was an elite commando and it was his job to get it done before someone did it to him. Eddie found himself increasingly adrift in a world where physical aggression was part of his own community's rules and not just something he reported in disapproving terms.

"The Eqbas scare me."

Barencoin snorted. "Esganikan just loves you. You're Eqbas Vorhi's favorite spokesman."

Spokesman. Eddie always had a feeling it was true, but he wanted at least to be in denial rather than suppressing the instinct to blush and nod. Mart was definitely far from a grunt.

"I'm editing this to file later."

"Have you looked at the situation developing back home?"

"I'll say. On the hour, usually."

"The Aussies and the Canadians can't wait to gang up on the FEU. The African Assembly's pitching in and nobody knows what the Sinostates are going to do. The veggies are fighting the meat-eaters. Somehow, I don't think they'll notice *Attack of the Parrot Woman.*"

Eddie did his maths again about the return to Earth, and it was the numbers that always made his stomach churn. Twenty-five years was a long, long time, and fifty was unthinkable: and that was how long the round trip to Earth would take, plus however long it took for the Eqbas to complete their restoration—an unknown period that might be anything from a short and catastrophic war to a permanent occupation.

There was no guarantee that it would be a round trip at all. The prospect of permanence on Earth scared him now, standing on a balcony somewhere back home and looking up at the stars, and trying to pick out where he had lived, and where his friends were.

He dreaded waving goodbye to Giyadas and leaving Wess'ej knowing that if he came back, she'd be a grandmother. Nevyan would still be alive: wess'har lived to a good age, longer than humans, but it was a lifetime's separation.

Barencoin stared at the news output, arms folded across his chest. Eddie wondered how it felt to have only a uniform to wear, and for that uniform not to be yours any longer. Everyone who'd made the journey from Earth—whether in *Thetis* or *Actaeon*—was now permanently displaced not only from location but from their culture.

"I'll miss F'nar," said Eddie. "I like wess'har—the ones here, that is."

"You got a few years to go here yet, if you're heading back with the Eqbas. What's brought this on? Wangled a private flight or something?"

"Y'know, if I could transport back to Earth instantly right now, I'm not sure I could fit back in."

"I'm worried about you, Eddie. You used to be gung ho and up for anything."

"Yeah."

"What changed?"

"Me," he said. "Because I used to be able to choose when dangerous adventure was over. If I could get transport, I could go back to a nice, safe home. But there isn't a safe home anywhere now. And I've reached the stage where I'm not sure if I should get morally outraged over biological weapons. If that's not fucked, I don't know what is."

Barencoin leaned over him, voice dropping to a whisper. "I got one more bit of bad news to break to you, then, mate. There's no hamster heaven either."

Barencoin could always make him laugh. The marine probably despised him, but he hid it well.

"Mart, if we have a war with the Eqbas, would you fight against them?"

Barencoin shrugged. "If I did, it wouldn't be for long." He walked to the door. "Beer and small eats tonight at Frankland Towers, okay? Be there. Be festive."

"I will."

Eddie spent a while trying to work out why there was so much conflict over Australia's invitation to the Eqbas and yet his reports were slipping further down BBChan's list of priorities. It was like the warnings of environmental disaster over the centuries: somehow they were of more use as an excuse for an international brawl than as a warning to do something before it was too late.

And it *had* been too late.

After a point, nobody wanted to hear unending bad news. And that was the only kind of news he had to offer.

F'nar: December 24, 2376

Eddie looked like shit.

"You need a drink," said Shan. He slumped past her as she opened the door and there was no smart-arse greeting or any sign of the old Eddie who always had to reduce everything to one-liners. His face was etched. There was no other word for it. Lines she'd never seen before formed a fine net around his eyes.

"I brought one. A large one."

He reached inside his jacket and pulled out a clear industrial container of equally clear liquid and handed it to her. About two liters, she estimated: she popped the cap and sniffed. It seared her sinuses like cleaning fluid.

"Shall I just put a straw in it for you?" She turned to Aras and tilted the bottle in mute request for a glass. "I take it that this anesthetic is connected to what you wanted to talk about."

"It's been an educational couple of weeks."

Aras held out two heavy glass cups, clear deep amber with swirls of purple in them. Shan slopped in a respectable amount of the unidentified spirit and thrust it into Eddie's hand. She poured a little for herself anyway, pointless though it was.

"You should eat something first," said Aras. "It won't reduce the toxicity of the product, but it might make you feel more comfortable."

"He never quite got the hang of hospitality training," said Shan, but Eddie didn't laugh. She exchanged a discreet oh-dear look with Aras. He inhaled by way of comment and went back to join Becken and Qureshi, who were laying out food on the table with all the bowls and plates at a precise distance from each other.

"The whole gang's here, then." Eddie hung his coat on the nail by the door one-handed with all the unconscious familiarity of a man who'd lived here while she was temporarily dead. "How are you . . . three?"

"We're fine. You? Okay, bad. I know."

He took a pull at the glass. Shan couldn't tell from the smell what it had been distilled from and it probably didn't matter: Eddie could do one thing denied her by *c'naatat,* and that was to get as pissed as a handcart. She'd always taken a dim view of getting drunk, but the fact it was now beyond her always made her a little wistful.

"If I blurt all this out it's going to screw the evening. "I'll tell you later." He looked around. "Well, this is festive."

"Ade's handiwork."

Barencoin interrupted by fetching Eddie a plate piled with chunks of cake and flatbreads. "It looks like pita," he said. "But it doesn't taste like it. And there's a bowl of something suspiciously like dip on the table, but it's beans menaced by a bit of garlic. Oh, and beer. Get stuck in, and for Chrissakes cheer up, you miserable sod."

"It's such a *convivial* time of year," said Shan. She steered Eddie over to the door that opened onto the rear terrace, bottle under one arm. However cold the wess'har thought it was, the

weather was mild by human standards, mild enough for a barbecue later. Ade insisted; he'd built that bloody barbecue and
he was going to get the most out of it if it killed him. Eddie
cradled his glass and stared at it in a way that suggested he
wasn't seeing the glowing embers on a jury-rigged trestle of
pipes and metal sheet but something else entirely.

"Okay, spill your guts before that stuff destroys too many
neurons."

Eddie transferred his glass to his left hand and fumbled
in his pocket to extract his handheld. "That's the rushes.
Cued up."

"Rushes of what?" Shan pressed the pad one-handed,
clutching her glass in the other. *"Oh."*

Eddie said nothing. She watched. The images were long
sequences of steady shots from a high aerial position. It had
to be Umeh, but some of the more conspicuous buildings
were a different style of architecture; it might have been
from the Maritime Fringe, although she hadn't seen many
intact buildings on her brief visit. It definitely wasn't Jejeno, though.

The aerial shots were interspersed with much faster,
more chaotic images at low level across gray water and over
pale canyon cities that looked like a fly-through simulation.
It was only when the point-of-view appeared to do a loop to
the right that she realized it was the output from an aircraft
recce camera. The craft must have been retracing its flight
path because it was passing over towering palls of black
smoke and flame. Something white-hot flared to the left
hand side—*port,* Ade would tell her, it's bloody *port*—and
the ahead view wobbled briefly. Had the craft taken a hit? It
was still flying straight at stomach-churning speed.

She was instantly in a cockpit, flying through flame that
had burned five centuries before, about to smash her face
against the controls. She'd relived this several times: she
was seeing through Aras's eyes as he crashed on an island
called Ouzhari. She shook the memory aside and concentrated. There was more random footage: vehicles exploded
in a firecracker sequence on the ground while tiny scuttling

figures that had to be isenj scattered in all directions and didn't get far.

Shan could watch anything. Coppers often had to sit down and sift through footage that was a few miles beyond a nightmare. After the initial revulsion you could put your shock back in its box and suddenly all you saw was detail, the detail you needed to investigate a crime; movement, injury, spatter pattern, distinguishing features, background that would pin down time or place or vehicle or witness, and any of the scraps of knowledge that made up the jigsaw of nailing some bastard.

Shan imagined that Eddie had grown used to doing the same. Maybe he hadn't. Maybe it was all linked to the trauma of having Ual shot dead standing right next to him, blood spatter and all. Ade's memory was headlined by an incident like that: Dave Pharoah's brains splashing his face at Ankara. If it could mark a veteran Royal Marine, it could mark anyone.

Eddie's swallowing was audible as he stared out over the caldera with his back to her. Shan pressed the key again and the carnage froze on the little screen, a ghastly vidgame. "So what did I just see?"

"Esganikan and chums removing an isenj army and assorted civilian bystanders." His glass was half empty now. "The Fringe and Tivskur have decided to gang up and launch a strike on Bezer'ej."

"They must be fucking suicidal. They know what the wess'har will do."

"Like the last time."

"They haven't got anything like a credible spacegoing force. They can barely manage enough craft to bomb each other."

"Maybe genetic memory makes you think you're better than you are." Eddie held out his glass for a top-up. "What happens if I send that to Earth?"

"Gut feel? Won't make the four AM update." Shan felt disoriented, part of her now having flashbacks of agony and being pulled from a burning cockpit, and part of her running screaming from white flame rolling at her like a ball. The fragment of isenj in her was reacting: that disturbed her more than developing claws or wings. "It's just aliens killing aliens. About as relevant to the folks back home as a wildlife show."

Eddie turned and looked slightly bewildered. "Okay, carry on and look at the cut package. Imagine you're sitting eating your cornflakes tomorrow and *that* pops up on the screen."

Shan pressed the key again. This was the edited piece; it opened with a shot of Esganikan's ship blacking out the sky over Jejeno. Eddie's voiceover began: *"It's a scene from a B-movie: a gigantic alien spaceship looms above a city . . ."*

There was nothing inaccurate in the report as far as she could tell. He made it clear that the Eqbas were effectively guests of the Jejeno cabinet. He had fabricated nothing: *twisted* nothing. Eddie never did. He'd even cut in some of the isenj archive footage of previously "adjusted" planets, the material that Ual had given him and that had so alarmed the Northern Assembly parliamentary meeting.

But it still set her teeth on edge.

"Want a frank answer?" she asked.

"Why do people like you always ask that?"

"All right, the Eqbas ship as a harbinger of doom has a high shock value but it's . . . misleading. Bit too *War of the Worlds*."

"Tell me how."

"You might as well have said that it's all the Eqbas's fault. I think the B-movie line sets the tone."

"You think I should cut that bit."

"I don't think anything. It's not my job. I just told you how it made me feel."

"Is it *scaremongering?*"

"Overall . . . well, if you're asking if it gives the viewer a true flavor of the Eqbas M.O. then I'd have to say yes."

"So, given the level of sphincter pucker on Earth right now, what with the tension between the Australasian states and the FEU, would *you* transmit that piece?"

Oh, so that was it. Eddie was losing his nerve again. He saw the direct connection between what he reported and what happened 150 trillion miles away, and he was scared he'd kick off a full-scale war this time, not just riots.

She sympathized. The truth was noble and lovely, but it had consequences just as much as lies and stony silence. *No, your husband didn't suffer. He died instantly. No pain. Wouldn't have known a thing about it.* She'd lied kindly more than once when she was breaking bad news to families. As long as the truth didn't need to come out for an investigation, no harm was done.

"Come on, Eddie, get a grip." She hadn't seen him quite like this before, not just agonizing aloud but asking advice. "If you haven't worked out your personal limits by now, quit. You either send every bloody scrap of information you've got, or you don't. Once you omit bits, you shape it. You can't fart around about where the line gets drawn. Evidence. It's *evidence.*"

Eddie, still staring out over F'nar into the gathering light-speckled dusk, managed to wag his index finger at nothing in particular with his glass in the same hand.

"See, Shan, that's the problem," he said. "I'm paid to define that line. I'm paid to interpret without distorting. To make things clear for the viewer."

"No chance of that," she said. "Is showing this to the public going to make any difference to what happens when the Eqbas show up? No. Will it make humans behave any better? I doubt it. Does it matter when you send it, then? No. Just sit on it like you've done before. Maybe the decision becomes clear, and maybe it doesn't. But either way you're not solely responsible for what's going to happen down the line. If there's one thing I've learned from wess'har, it's that *everyone* in the chain of consequences has a chance to stop something happening."

"That's rich coming from you, Shazza."

He had to be a bit drunk to call her that. "Okay, then, learn from my mistakes."

"I have real trouble working out whether the wess'har are

wrong or we are. Ethically, I mean. Sometimes they make so much sense, and then I see them roll in like the Mongol hordes and I just don't know what's right and wrong any longer."

"You can't mix the two philosophies," said Shan. "It's like trying to work in Imperial and metric. You can do one or the other and it's fine, but try mixing them and everything goes wrong. Take guilt and responsibility. The wess'har logic on who's guilty makes perfect sense to me when I'm in it. Then I step into the human moral framework and that makes sense too. But I can't mix the two. It doesn't work."

Eddie sipped. "Like the way they fight."

"What, that they just decide what they're going to do without any sense of maneuvering the other side into conceding?"

"Yeah."

"Culturally psychopathic in human terms."

"But ordered and predictable in their own."

"Human psychopaths make perfect sense until they mix with the majority of humans who work on escalating threat warnings and consider other people's reactions." A pool of yellow light spilled onto the terrace: someone had opened the rear door. "God knows I met enough of them as a copper."

"Is that why you're so good with aliens? That you're used to dealing with nutters?"

"No, it's because I'm as fucking mad as they are." She sipped the bathtub eau de vie; no, she couldn't even guess what it was made from. She concentrated on the placebo effect. *Change the subject.* "It was nice of you to fetch the booze, Eddie. Thanks."

"See? Scientists do come in handy sometimes. If only for making moonshine."

"Yeah. Just don't tell me what they made it from. I've seen the recycling facilities, remember."

Eddie didn't seem soothed. In fact, he seemed more agitated. They'd lived in one another's pockets for two years, and he was nowhere near as good at poker as he thought—not in

front of a seasoned police officer who also had a wess'har olfactory advantage, anyway. He was working up to something
bigger.

"I need to ask you a *really* hard question now," he said.

"Harder than asking me if you should drop another
bombshell on the people of Earth? Jesus, Eddie . . ."

"What happened to Lin? I suppose I should ask about
Rayat, too, but the twat deserved what he got."

Oh, shit. Why was he back on that? She hoped he'd forgotten, or at least moved on. It was a naïve hope. Like her,
Eddie needed to close his cases. "Like Lin didn't?"

"She was a stupid cow, I know that. Tactical nukes are
fine but cobalt is a no-no. Yeah, that sort of puts her in the
twat league too."

"Are you asking how she died again? Come on—"

"Yes, and I'm asking *if* she died."

Shit. That was straight out of the blue. "And why do you
think she didn't?"

"Did Ade back out of handing her over?"

"Still not with you." *Oh yes, I am.*

"He overreacted when I mentioned her. I just can't see
him handing her over. Aras, maybe."

Shan hoped her face was blank. "Leave it, Eddie. Don't
start."

"Don't piss me about, Shan. *Is she dead?*"

Shan didn't have the guilt now about lying to him. But
she wasn't sure if he really did know the answer, and then if
she lied she'd lose all credibility. She'd never lied to him
before; she'd ducked the question as only a copper could,
but an outright lie . . . no, she hadn't. As Aras had told her
in the early days, before they really knew one another, she
wasn't cut out for lies.

"Ask yourself this," Shan said carefully. "If you find out,
will you want to deal with the answer?"

"She's alive, isn't she? They didn't do it, did they?"

Shan simply stared back at him. She could do that; she
was even better than him at the silent routine, waiting to see
who would blink first. She'd stared down a lot of suspects

during interrogations. Some got so mad about it that they
took a swing at her, which was always a mistake that she
dealt with robustly.

"This is where it gets awkward," said Eddie.

Oh God, Eddie, just keep drinking and shut up, will you.
"You tell me."

"She's not in F'nar. Or Mar'an'cas. I'm pretty sure I'd
hear about it if she was."

"This isn't *Twenty Questions.*"

"So where is she?"

"What did I say, Eddie?"

His face went oddly blank for a second, and she knew
that look: it was sudden revelation, like he'd put a few
pieces of the puzzle together with a satisfying snap. "She's
on Bezer'ej isn't she? And if she's not dead, and there's the
pathogen, then—oh, that's what Hayin meant, isn't it?"

She put down her glass on the balustrade and stood
square on to Eddie, a little too close for his comfort.

And she was a couple of inches taller. That always had a
salutary effect on men. She was back to being Superintendent Frankland for a moment, and never far from that persona at the best of times.

"Eddie, you stop right *now.* Okay?" She kept her voice
low. "You're my friend, and I'll never forget what you did
for Aras when I wasn't around, but if you go down this path
then I'll have to stop you. And I stop people hard."

Eddie didn't flinch but she saw his pupils dilate and he
smelled scared. She didn't think he was afraid of her. He
was afraid of what he now knew.

"Oh shit," he said. "Oh shit, it's true, isn't it? Her *and*
Rayat?"

"Are we clear on this, Eddie? No speculation, no stories,
nothing. We've just had a chat about consequences, haven't
we? I don't have to draw you a picture, not after last time."

"Hey, I know what I did. I regret even asking questions. If
I hadn't talked to Kris Hugel, the rumor about you would
never have developed the way it did. And the bezeri would

still be here, and *Actaeon*. That's a lot of deaths for me to live with. So I'm not going to file any more *c'naatat* stories."

"But you can't *un*know things. They eat away at you. Better not to know in the first place."

"Well, right now, I *don't* know anything."

"That's a good place to be. Stay there."

"Just answer this, if I—"

"No." Shan kept her voice hushed. "No. Okay?"

Eddie never gave up. She admired that more than he'd ever know. "If I did anything irresponsible, you'd do a lot more than smash my cam, wouldn't you?"

"I'd do what I had to."

"You'd put a round through me."

"For Chrissakes, Eddie . . ."

"Shit, what else could I expect from someone who spaced themselves to stop Rayat getting the bloody thing?"

"Look, let's forget we had this conversation." Shan picked up her glass again and reached for the bottle to top up his. "You know you need to."

"Jesus, you must be really pissed off about it after what you went through. How the hell did it happen?"

Don't remind me. Don't rub it in. "How *what* happened?" She knew how to say *what* in a way that shut people up. She didn't blink. "See, Eddie, if I told you anything then I'd have to *trust* you. And I recall asking you to trust *me* and walk away from a story about two years ago on Bezer'ej. When you thought I was a mule for a biotech company. Remember? When you put two and two together and came up with six?"

"And don't you think I regret it?" Eddie had a heart and a conscience, and it was now pretty easy to get a clear shot at both. "How do you think I felt when you *killed* yourself? After all I'd said?"

"I don't want your guilt. I just want you to understand what happens when someone tells you that it's better not to know and it's actually *true*."

"See," he said. "You edit *all* the time."

Too right. If she told him, she'd have to watch him for the rest of his life, and even then she'd worry that he'd passed on the information. Neither of them said it, but they both knew the unsaid subject was *c'naatat.*

Eddie didn't look so hard-arsed now. Tired and drawn, he seemed to have aged more than a few years; high gravity, limited food and—there was no other way to put it—stress that few humans had ever experienced had all taken their toll.

"Oh, balls to it," he sighed, and tipped the eau de vie down his throat in one gulp, screwing his eyes shut for a second or two. "I just want to know she's okay."

"Truth is, Eddie, I *don't* know. I really don't. Now let's change the subject."

Ade's personal radar never failed. He strode out the open door with a tray of lumps on skewers—*evem,* probably—and laid them on the barbecue, at once both friendly and making it clear that he was interrupting. He was a natural sergeant. He *sorted* things. He looked after her. Except for Aras, nobody else had ever been that protective towards her, and she *liked* it even if she didn't need it.

"Party pooper," said Ade. "Come on, mate, stop talking shop. Make yourself useful and get everyone a beer."

Eddie just looked at him, and Ade stared back. Shan prepared to step in: but Eddie's question—and he definitely had one—dried on his lips. "Okay, Ade," he said, voice artificially calm. She could hear the effort.

"Mart wants to play charades when everyone's tanked up," said Ade. "It's always funnier when you're pissed."

Eddie either took the hint or he really did want to forget what he thought he knew. Shan watched him disappear into the house.

"Thanks." She gave Ade a quick kiss on the cheek. "Very diplomatic."

"What's his problem? You looked bloody furious with him."

"He's worked out that Lin and Rayat aren't dead, and he's not stupid. Process of elimination and a bit of journo maths, as he calls it, and bang—he's reached the right conclusion."

"Shit. Is he going to keep his mouth shut? Maybe I need to relieve him of his cam because if he's had a bit too much of the old firewater, and he decides to file . . ."

"Ade, I've picturized him. He knows what'll happen if he lets that slip out on air."

"I'll educate him if you like."

"No, leave it. But maybe I *ought* to crimp his ITX link." *For how long? You can't erase his brain. You're going to have to trust him. Shit, shit, shit.* "Anyway, it's my problem and I'll deal with it."

Ade looked as if he was going to say something. He didn't. But Shan heard it anyway; he thought it was all his fault.

It was. But she was looking for reasons not to feel betrayed by him, because she loved him and he was a good, decent man. She'd never allowed herself to look beyond the crime to the criminal before. She was very conscious of how unwess'har that feeling was, and this bore no resemblance to the ferocious sense of self-sufficient completeness she'd felt after surviving raw, cold space for so long.

I don't need any bastard. Not Ade, not Aras, nobody.

But it was a better life with people you loved than without them. If that was weakness, she'd have to accept it.

Eddie reappeared with a tray of beer, flanked by the marines and Aras, who was carrying a large *efte* fiber drum. Shan met Eddie's eyes, unblinking, and the silent warning was heeded.

"You really did put some time into this, Ade," said Eddie. "Nice job, mate. Thanks." He recovered his glass and checked its absence of contents. "Cheers. Merry Christmas."

Aras shook the drum and it rattled invitingly. "A slow process, but this is sweet potato sliced and roasted to a crisp as you suggested."

The marines turned to the box of crisps with military focus. You could never overestimate the morale-boosting power of familiar food—or its close approximation—a long way from home. It even distracted Shan for a moment, but the moment didn't last. She thought of Lindsay and Rayat again and what Eddie might let slip.

"Bloody brilliant," said Becken. He dug into the crisps. "I'm so impressed that I'll do the dishes."

Eddie didn't raise the subject of Lindsay again that evening. Shan concentrated on behaving as if she was having a good time, which she wasn't, because she didn't know how to. But it mattered to Ade that she looked as if she was, because he needed a normal family Christmas for the first time in his life and she was determined to give it to him.

Normal.

It wasn't the planet or the alien neighbors or even *c'naatat* now that were abnormal. It was being an *isan,* a matriarch, and having to find a new reason for being.

What if I'm hanging on to the policing role here and worrying about Lin and Rayat because I don't know how to do anything else? Am I creating crises to keep myself busy?

They drank the beer and ate far too much. Ade was right: Barencoin was very funny with a few drinks inside him and the charades degenerated into the kind of vulgar mime session that felt just like being back at the police social club, all raucous laughter and barracking. Shan wondered how the marines coped with celibacy, or if she'd missed something and there were relationships within the detachment. She'd never seen the slightest sign of that. They couldn't still be taking suppressants. Perhaps they might have been better off back at Umeh Station after all; they might have had a better social life.

Ade got up to take his turn at charades and Aras slipped into the spot he'd vacated beside Shan on the sofa.

"You're fretting," he whispered. "You mustn't worry. Eddie won't betray you and Bezer'ej is beyond the reach of humans."

"You're a bloody telepath," she said.

"You have always been transparent, and I have far better hearing than you imagine."

She watched the game, hoping she wouldn't have to get up and perform. Ade gestured, acting out a book and tapped three fingers against his arm. The detachment watched in silence, utterly focused despite a full tank of beer.

"The Mahabharat," said Barencoin, swilling his beer around the bottom of his glass.

"Smart-arse," said Ade. "*Three* syllables. Can't you count, you dinlo?"

"You've got a lot of mouth for a bloke with a neon dick."

The detachment roared with laughter, even Ade. Shan felt a pang of regret that Ade's condition put a permanent barrier between him and his comrades; she felt she'd robbed him of something precious. Bonds in uniform could be closer than family. But at least they could still enjoy that brutal humor. She cringed at the thought of what Barencoin might say about her.

And they didn't know Lin and Rayat were still alive, either, or that Ade had infected them. She wondered what Barencoin would make of it.

The beer and the eau de vie were soothing everyone who could be soothed by alcohol and for a few hours, in a warm and dimly lit room, reality was confined to another place. The laughter blurred into a restful white noise. She found herself wedged between Aras and Ade on the sofa, conscious of the difference in their body temperatures and sinking in a delicious haze of sandalwood-scented wess'har male musk, while Sue Webster demonstrated an extraordinary ability to mime the titles of pornographic vids. It made Shan laugh; she was suddenly aware that she didn't laugh much, even now.

See, you can do this. You can relax.

But she couldn't take part of her mind off considering what it might take to make a fragmentation device that operated under water. The Eqbas team would have to help her locate Lin, too. This needed planning.

She was conscious of someone staring at her. She glanced up and Eddie gave her a sad smile. He seemed to be forcing it. Maybe some of his thoughts were where hers were.

"Merry Christmas," she said.

"You too, doll," said Eddie. He raised his glass halfheartedly. "Here's to knowing where to draw the line."

If he'd know how hard she found it to find that line sometimes, he'd never have believed her. Shan savored the extraordinarily reassuring sensation of being settled between
her *jurej've,* certain of their loyalty if nothing else. *Yeah,
that's changed. I'm starting to trust them unconditionally.
Either I'm getting sane or I'm going soft.*

There was a scrabbling outside the door. Chahal looked
up. "Let the bloody dog in, someone," he said, and they all
laughed.

Qureshi hauled herself to her feet accompanied by barracking and slid the catch on the door. Serrimissani shot
into the room as if she'd been booted up the backside.

"Hi, doll," said Eddie. "Come in and play charades."

"When we have dealt with the matter in hand, then you
can explain what that is." Serrimissani could chop Eddie to
size with a slit-eyed glare. They seemed to enjoy the
double-act of flippancy met by disapproval. "*Shan Chail,*
the Eqbas Vorhi attacked a combined isenj air force on the
ground. Most vessels were destroyed. I think we can regard
them as confined to Umeh for the time being."

"I expected that," said Shan. "A bit preemptive, but it
was going to happen sooner or later. Has this come from
Esganikan?"

"Yes. She's returning to Bezer'ej."

"So what's she doing about the bioweapons?"

"She's asked for a meeting with the Northern Assembly
cabinet to discuss them."

"Boy, she's getting all pissy and formal, isn't she?" Out
of the corner of her eye, Shan saw Ade hang his head for a
second and straighten up again. "Okay, thank you."

Shan didn't know how to ask a ussissi in for a drink
and Serrimissani slipped off without a word. She closed the
door and turned back to a room of grim-faced marines. Eddie was rubbing his forehead.

Barencoin folded his arms and elbowed Ade. "The first
person to say, 'It'll all be over by Christmas, Sarge' gets my
boot up their arse."

A nice, normal Christmas; maybe next year, maybe never. This one would have to do for now.

Eqbas Vorhi ship 886-001-005-6: en route for Bezer'ej

Eit was slow off the mark to respond to Esganikan's request for a meeting. But she could wait.

She went to her day cabin just off the bridge and knelt down for a few moments' rest, taking advantage of the lull to watch the link to Surang set in the bulkhead.

Being able to see her homeworld and snatch views of it from the global network of imagers gave her a sense of peace. Surang was basking in a summer day; Jipay was in darkness, the islands of its natural harbor picked out in pinpoints of colored light.

Earth did this, too.

She switched to the Earth ITX node and watched the output that Eddie's organization generated. There were many channels, but they seemed irrelevant, and the one he called the Filthy Enemy—his employer's rival—seemed to be the most absorbing even if it was repetitive. Humans fought wars; their leaders argued and were disgraced; and their climate punished them with ever fiercer storms and floods and droughts, the symptoms of a badly managed planet.

That wasn't news: it was predictable. It was fairly typical of the kinds of world the Eqbas visited. The bulletins were dominated by spectacular images of a ferocious tropical storm that was whipping whole trees out of the ground and sending them tumbling. It should have been a terrible thing: but the landscape was lush, wet and green. It was *alive*.

It was these images juxtaposed with the last few days' fighting that gave Esganikan some comfort. Earth was everything that Umeh wasn't. It might have been badly damaged, but it looked diverse and full of potential.

Earth was perfect for Eqbas intervention. The benefits to all species would be enormous, even if individual humans, with their belief of their unique worth to a universe that didn't even know they existed, would suffer in the short term.

Culling. They even had a word for it, and thought it humane and beneficial as long as it happened to other species and not to their own. She knew that much about them already.

Hayin had shown her how to find the feed from the cameras that watched the coastline of Australia. She switched to see a late afternoon and a storm brewing beyond massive flood defenses. She switched to the output from the capital city, a place called Kamberra, and the image was a pleasant one of a lake with humans wandering along its margin. They were dressed in brightly colored clothing and it looked as if it was a very hot day; the heat haze shimmered visibly.

She quite liked the appearance of Australia. Even the red arid heartland looked beautiful, clean and wild in a way that the city of Umeh beneath her was simply *not.* The Australians had started to build their cities underground, too.

Humans could change. And, unlike Umeh, millions of humans wanted it to happen; knowing that would get her through the hard times ahead for Umeh.

13

Spacefaring societies have their limitations. We think of them as infinitely powerful, able to solve anything, masters of their destiny if only they apply enough will. The isenj are a useful lesson for us. They had spaceflight and an unimaginably sophisticated artificial ecology; they were, and still are, superb engineers and one of the pioneers of ITX. But they took on a much more advanced civilization, and rode out like the Polish cavalry facing German tanks. Because the wess'har had never attacked their world, they concentrated their military assets into easy targets. And they forgot that no amount of engineering can triumph over the formula of consumption against available resources. In the end, it's easier to let the planet do it.

EDDIE MICHALLAT's Constantine Diaries

Bezer'ej: December 26, 2376

The podship was a far simpler vessel than Rayat had imagined.

He eased through the hatch and found himself slipping involuntarily into a horizontal position as if he was settling into the cockpit of an old sports car, legs outstretched. It was built for bezeri so there was plenty of legroom but not much clearance above his head. And he could see through the translucent bulkheads as if he was in a plastic bag.

Transparency began to overwhelm him. In the last two years, it had become the first thing he noticed, and he saw it everywhere; from the translucent *alyats* and bezeri to the wess'har use of glass for building, from the clear composite dome of Umeh Station to the almost-invisible but very real barriers both the wess'har and Eqbas could deploy, everything here was a window. He hated it. He felt exposed: he liked solidity. And he hated the hint of translucency that had spread from his hands and up his arms and threatened to alter the tissue of his whole body. It seemed to have stopped. *C'naatat* had almost responded to his anxiety.

He wasn't alone. Lindsay's flesh had become much more insubstantial in appearance than his—and she had developed lights.

She no longer looked human. He could see her moving outside the vessel and for a moment he wasn't sure if he was looking at a bezeri or not because the outline was hazy and only the strong bioluminescence was visible.

"How can they manufacture things like this?" asked Lindsay. She thrust her head through the hatch. She could still manipulate sound well enough to speak. "This *has* to be something they breed."

"That isn't what I need to hear right now."

She was still bipedal, four-limbed, and far from a cephalopod, but it was as if somebody had taken a lump of gel and made a human shape out of it in an art class. He could see the liquid pulsing outlines of major organs, like staring into the sheer depths of a jellyfish. The change had been shockingly rapid. He wondered how the marines would have reacted if they could see her now.

It didn't matter. He'd reached a truce with her, and a tolerable but cold relationship with the bezeri. What else you could expect from the people you almost wiped out, he couldn't imagine. It was . . . tolerable, no more.

Rayat lay back and considered the deckhead above him. The hatch was to protect the occupant rather than to keep the water out, and he found something strangely disorienting about a submarine that was *designed* to fill with water. He raised his hand and the controls—just two gently domed areas the size of a melon on each side of him—shimmered into life. He still wasn't sure if this was just organic technology or something alive in some way. He made an effort to put the thought out of his head; there were too many digestive connotations and for a moment he had a brief flare of panic that made him want to swim for the surface and find air. That was becoming much less frequent now.

Rayat composed himself, concentrating on what kept him human; memories, articulated speech, a future back on dry land one day. *I haven't turned into a squid. I can turn back into a man. I can become anything I need to be to do the job.* And his job was to get home with his prize intact and exclusive.

Saib drifted alongside like a ghost, his lights visible through the ship's membranes.

"How do you do it?" Rayat called, mirroring his words with light signals. He had to keep talking to stay in touch with his humanity. It struck him that using light and sound simultaneously had given him a kind of overtone just like the wess'har, albeit one that was partly inaudible. "How do you make these?"

We grow them, Saib said. *They are seed cases that propel themselves great distances when exposed to light. They respond to our lights because we have bred them selectively over the years. We have bred their propulsion jets to more powerful and their size to be greater, too.*

Lindsay turned to him and lights pulsed through her in response. *Very clever. Are they actually alive?*

They no longer live. The response to light is a mechanical reaction.

Saib slid into the hatch. Like an octopus, he seemed able to squeeze through any gap that could accommodate his rigid mouth-parts. He flowed into the vessel.

"May we go to Constantine now?" Rayat asked.

You wish to see Leenz's dead child's memorial.

"Yes, I would. And I want to see what's become of the colony and the camp, and if there's anything left to salvage." Well, that much was true; he just didn't mention a space-worthy vessel. "Is there anything you want us to do on the way? We could make contact with the Eqbas mission and see if they've located any more survivors."

Saib had been unwilling to let them venture further north than Ouzhari. Rayat made a point of coming back earlier than agreed and bringing food with him; he wanted Saib and the others to trust him. They almost did. But whatever they felt about Lindsay, they believed her sincerity. She'd thrown herself into helping them with slavelike devotion. She'd make sure he didn't try to escape.

He'd have to play this carefully. A recce, no more. He couldn't show his hand in front of Lindsay, either. She was determined that he'd stay here and serve his sentence.

They're finished, he thought. *If I really believed I could do something to help them survive, I'd do it.*

Saib withdrew from the cockpit like a cork being pulled from a bottle. *Return in three cycles. Bring back whatever you see fit, but news of survivors will be preferred. Now practice.*

Lindsay slipped beside him, almost becoming one gelatinous creature with the pod. "I can do this," she said.

"You were a pilot once, weren't you?"

Not that it gives me any advantage flying this, she signaled. *But I'm used to orienting myself.*

"Can we stick to audio?"

Tiny bubbles like a stream of champagne issued from her nose. "Sorry."

She placed her palm against one of the light receptors and the pod lurched a few meters. Saib billowed like a sail, caught by the rear jet, and shimmered with an irritated display of amber and lemon light. Then Lindsay seemed to get the hang of it and the pod lifted and skimmed low across the silt. In a few minutes they were out in open water and threading through the rocks to the north.

"You really want to fit in with them," said Rayat.

"I think I owe them something, yes."

"Apart from the first few days, they didn't need us at all, did they?"

"I think they wanted prisoners and then they weren't entirely sure what to do with us. We're all so certain we know what we'll do when we get hold of our enemies, but it's not always so simple. Even for bezeri."

"They're not geared up for punishment. Execution, maybe."

"What's happening to us must seem like punishment to them."

"Seems like it to me, too."

"That's the idea."

"Are you religious?"

"Why do you ask?" said Lindsay.

"Mortification of the soul."

"I'm not into that. I've prayed. Anyone who's been under fire manages to find a prayer just in case someone's listening. Even atheists."

"Just wondering." Rayat didn't enjoy traveling in a prone position. He'd never been a good passenger; he always wanted to steer. "I know Deborah Garrod gave you some spiritual support."

"How about you?"

"Only when my granddad was looking. No virgins waiting for me in paradise. I could never work out the demographics of that."

"What a cute kid you must have been."

"I always found comfort in reality. Not teddy bears."

"Is that what made you such a bastard?"

"Yes. That and the fact that someone has to do it."

They teetered on the edge of humor. It seemed easier for her to cloak it in abuse; she was that kind of woman. She never wanted to climb down from her outrage, as if she enjoyed the exercise of free anger so much that she was afraid she'd never be allowed to do it again. She was an inverted image of Frankland, who seemed scared that if she let her rage loose she'd never regain control of it. Lindsay wanted desperately to be like that bitch, whether she admitted it or not. It told Rayat a lot about Lindsay's relationship with her mother.

Conversation died. Rayat wished for a crystal clear window so he could stare at the astonishing array of life that he knew had to be out there somewhere. It was all tantalizing smears of color and movement. Either life here was more resistant to cobalt than he'd thought, or the spread of the fallout had been limited—or the Eqbas were cleaning up the area at a rate close to miraculous.

Don't use that word. Stick with the science. Learn.

"Where are we now?" Lindsay asked.

"I was under the impression that *you* were the naval officer."

"You've got the charts. I've still got a compass, for what it's worth. Let's try working together."

"All stop, then." Rayat peered at the sand within the azin shell, then eased the soft hatch open and slid out to get his bearings, comparing the landscape to the sand images. "The seabed looks about right."

"We're still heading north."

"You could surface."

"Won't help. I don't remember the landmarks from last time. And my watch shattered, so we can't do the old submariner's trick and time between features, and I don't know what speed this thing is making anyway."

It was easy to forget that Lindsay Neville was actually *Commander* Neville—fired or not—and that she'd had to satisfy the FEU navy of her seamanship skills before being trusted with warships. Eventually the sea in front of them grew darker and a cliff loomed and filled their field of view.

This was why the bezeri called islands Mountains to the Dry Above. From this perspective, it was *exactly* what they were.

"I think this is it," said Lindsay. She took the podship into a climb, holding parallel with the slope, and it porpoised on the surface, falling back to float with just a fraction of its bulk above water. Rayat could see the fierce sunlight. He realized how much his perception had changed in a matter of a month. Yes, he was sure it was about a month now.

"Okay," she said.

"What?"

"I'm going to beach this. I hope I get it right, or it's a bloody long swim back."

Neither of them said they were worried about breathing air again. Neither of them mentioned David's grave, either.

"Get on with it, then," said Rayat.

Lindsay dropped her shoulders as if limbering up for

something and then her lights flared. The pod responded and shot forward like a speedboat, silent except for the weird hammering of the jets' bubbles under the hull.

"Good God, woman—"

"Shut up."

"Steady on—"

The darkness ahead—a blurred slice of black and gray and amber—expanded rapidly and suddenly the impact beneath him lifted him bodily and slammed him against the deckhead like he was landing on a trampoline facedown. His teeth smashed together and he tasted blood. He was totally disoriented.

You can't die.

You'll heal.

Shut up.

He didn't know what podships used for brakes. He found out.

Friction.

"Oh God . . ." Lindsay groaned.

But the podship was stationary even if the water inside was still attempting to move forward, making the bulkheads bulge and pulse as it slopped back and forth.

Water. Bloody good impact bag.

He waited until all movement around him died down. They were still in a bulb full of water.

"Who's first?" he said.

"Doesn't matter."

"Okay, me." Rayat put his hands against the soft catches—little interlocking projections—that held the hatch closed. "You realize that once we readapt to air, we have to drown all over again, don't you?"

"Oh, for God's sake, just do it," she snapped.

He counted to three and pushed. The hatch opened with a faint ripping sound like a zipper and water spilled out, but his head was still submerged. There was nothing to do now but to just sit up and put his head above the water.

And *breathe.*

It was agony.

Rayat drowned in oxygen and nitrogen and carbon dioxide and traces of other gases. Bezer'ej's atmosphere had once been inhospitably short of oxygen by Earth standards, but now there was far too much and he *couldn't get it into his lungs*. He could hear his gills slapping as they opened and closed in frantic attempts to glean oxygen from the dry air.

He drew a long agonized scream of breath and his chest felt as if it was exploding. Ribs creaked: lungs blossomed. He felt every single cell changing and tearing loose.

Oh God. Oh God, oh God, oh God.

He fell out of the pod and his face hit pebbles, cold wet pebbles. Water poured out of his mouth and he coughed and choked. And he was suddenly *heavy*. He could hardly move.

And then heat seared through him.

You think this is bad? Think what space was like for Frankland. Body fluids boiling. Lungs rupturing. Desiccation and cryogenic freezing, all at once, fully conscious.

He hated thinking of her but it was inevitable. For all he knew, her memories were surfacing in his brain and this wasn't what was happening to him at all, just her nightmare intruding for a few moments.

Lindsay might well have been scrambling clear of the podship too. He didn't know and he didn't care, because he was . . . a fish.

Rayat swore—yes, he swore *to God,* to Allah, that when he got back to Earth he would *never* take up angling because now he knew what it was to be a fish plucked out of water and left to drown helplessly in air.

People who wouldn't dream of drowning a puppy in a barrel of water think nothing of killing a fish the same slow way.

Was *that* his own thought? It could have been Shan's. Or Aras's, come to that. Rayat never had those kinds of thoughts before. He lay on his back, staring up at the blue sky and scudding white clouds, heavy and wet and gasping, and he was a man again, a mammal that breathed air.

C'naatat was terrifying, magnificent, beyond his imagination. His mind raced with possibilities for it. And as soon as he conceived them, the dread chilled his stomach.

No, this couldn't ever be trusted. He was more certain than ever that he would do whatever it took to keep this out of the wrong hands. It was more than his mission. It was his duty.

"That was . . . worse . . . than I'd imagined," said a voice he barely recognized.

Lindsay Neville was standing over him. She sounded very different in air. She was a ghost: the sunlight penetrated her like a stained-glass window left to grow filthy in a neglected church, her photophores and reflectors providing brilliant splashes of color.

"If we find a mirror," he said, "try not to look."

F'nar, Wess'ej

The steady influx of ussissi evacuated from Umeh had made little difference to F'nar. Shan was surprised how effortlessly they blended into both the city and the landscape. Where did you hide hundreds of stroppy chest-high meerkats?

They melted into the little settlements half-buried in the plain. Some stayed in F'nar: a few went to Bezer'ej with the Eqbas.

Shan walked along the terraces to Nevyan's home, twisting Ade's ring on her finger and savoring the slow surprise of managing to feel comfortable with two males. Neither Eddie nor the marines had said a word about it. But she knew damn well that there had to be some prurient interest and comments she never wanted to hear.

It didn't feel weird or kinky or even thrilling. It was *normal*. She wasn't sure whether that was because Aras wasn't human, and so didn't count as an extra, forbidden man in the part of her brain that told her monogamy was right and anything else was wrong, or because *she* wasn't human any longer.

Either way, she was comfortable and so was Ade. Aras—she had never doubted that Aras would settle into a marriage like that because he'd wanted a housebrother so badly. No, Aras was happy. He *urrred* a lot, that oddly appealing little variation on the paternal purring that wess'har males did when they were pleased with life, like a human humming tunelessly. *Marriage:* Jesus, *that* was the weird bit. Humans needed events and markers in their life events. Ade needed to put that ring on her hand and she'd needed to wear it, and that caught her by surprise.

She felt guilty about that. She felt weak because she enjoyed thinking of herself as someone's wife, and wondered if she'd ever admit that even to Ade. They were happy now, as happy as three fucked-up, exiled, badly damaged people ever could be. She'd make sure it stayed that way. It was part of her self-imposed therapy to steer her away from tackling anything—world-saving, crime-busting, avenging, the bigger the risk the better—rather than face the fact that she was a piss-poor excuse for a human being most days.

She rapped on Nevyan's door with her knuckles, counted to ten and pushed it open.

"I'm glad you came," said Nevyan.

Giyadas sat at the table beside her, every inch the workshadowing student matriarch, mane bobbing as she cocked her head. Shan wondered if she'd ever get to know the three sons in Nevyan's adopted family: they always seemed to be out working or learning in the communal schoolroom beneath the city.

Nevyan smelled agitated. Shan swung her leg over the bench and sat astride it, facing her. "What can I do for you, Nev?"

"The Eqbas are handing over bioagents to the Northern Assembly."

"I heard they were going to *discuss* it." Shan was aware of Giyadas staring intently at her, so she suppressed her scent slowly and tapered it off to nothing. "I seem to recall we did that too. DNA donor number one here." Jesus, if you couldn't trust Eqbas to know what they were doing with biohazards, there was no hope for anybody. Then her next careless comment simply hijacked her and she marveled that she could say it and mean it. "What's the problem with that?"

What's the problem with biological weapons? Did I say that? Well, dead's dead. Don't be so bloody prissy.

"I hope they've made sure they can't reverse-engineer it."

"Do you want to talk about regret, Nev? If so, I'll join you." Shan held up her hands to indicate she wasn't up for a fight. Without a scent cue, it was probably hard for Nevyan to tell from her voice these days. "I don't know how I got from EnHaz to being Biobomb Woman. I told myself you were the good guys and that I could trust you to use science responsibly."

"As I trusted the Eqbas."

"Have they actually betrayed your trust yet?"

"No. No, they've just done things that I would never do myself, and I have no rational argument beyond the fact that I think they've gone too far with the isenj."

"Once you start messing with this stuff it's really hard to work out where the line lies between far enough and too far."

"I *can* see that line," said Giyadas. "One requires the isenj to do something wrong for them to be killed. The other doesn't."

Shan paused for a moment. It was sobering to argue moral relativism with a child, especially one who actually understood it better than most human adults.

She hoped she wasn't going to find herself outgunned at the end of the debate, because the core of her self-respect was that everyone else was less intellectually able than she was. *Thick bastards, most people.* She'd found it hard at first in F'nar because—unlike on Earth—she wasn't feared, and she wasn't stronger, and she wasn't more ruthless, and she wasn't smarter: she was pretty average by wess'har standards, except for her aggression and capacity for taking massive risks.

Well, that's too bad. If the kid's smarter than you, you learn something. Deal with it.

"Okay," said Shan. "The wess'har view is that the isenj have no right to be on Bezer'ej."

"Yes." Giyadas had cocked her head to the right, fascinated. Her pupils were fully dilated. "They're despoilers. Polluters."

"But they were there before you. They'd had a colony there for some time."

"But they killed bezeri by their irresponsible increase in numbers and their pollution and the bezeri *asked* for our intervention."

"So Aras and the army wiped them out and restored the planet. So how is that different to the Eqbas responding to the isenj request for help?"

"We were not *asked* to intervene by those suffering."

"I think Esganikan asked me once if I waited for a murderer to ask for justice for his victim before I would arrest him. What if the victim can't ask you?"

Giyadas considered the statement carefully. Shan had a sudden, powerful sense of being as fascinated by the kid as the kid seemed to be with her. She was watching the development of a mind of astonishing capacity; what Giyadas would be like as an adult was frightening. The sheer elation of fencing with her verbally and of being close to defeat didn't demoralize her, as she'd expected, but made her want to encourage the child, nurture that mind, look after her . . .

Oh, fuck.

Shan didn't have a maternal bone in her body. But she suspected this was an insight into what *parents* felt. It was massively seductive.

Nevyan watched, scent neutral. Giyadas appeared to finish ruminating. "It happened before we arrived here. How far back do we look to decide if a species is in need of balancing?"

"Wrong's wrong. Why does time make a difference?"

"Nobody asked *us* to intervene there."

"Okay, Targassat taught that Eqbas Vorhi was wrong to force its view of a balanced environment on other worlds, and that your ancestors couldn't take it on themselves to police the galaxy." Shan thought it was interesting that the nearest wess'har had to a religion was the thoughts of an *economist*. Targassat had been an analyst of resources on Eqbas Vorhi 10,000 years ago. "But she also said that if you have a choice, you *have* to make it, and those with most choice have most responsibility."

"Responsibility for *restraint*. Just because the Eqbas *can* make a world do what they want, it doesn't mean they *have* to. Because how do we know that the people on that world want what we think they want, or what we think is best?"

"What about creatures who can't ask? Nonhuman animals on Earth? The gene bank. Wess'har and Eqbas agree on that."

"No people . . . no *animal* wants to die or be used or to suffer pain." Giyadas struggled with the word: wess'har had no concept of a division between species like humans did, and no word for animals except *people*. "It seems obvious that we should help them."

"Okay, but what about plants? Plants on Earth try hard to avoid being eaten. They defend themselves with poisons and spines, so they probably don't want to be eaten. But we all eat plants here. Where's the line now?"

Giyadas chewed that over visibly. "We have to eat to live. We don't *have* to eat other people."

"Some animals *have* to eat others."

"*Gethes* don't. We don't. *We* make the choice because we have one."

"So, the line is necessity?"

"The line," said Giyadas, "is *necessary*." Shan thought for a moment that the child had just stumbled over an unfamiliar word and then realized where she was heading. She felt as if someone had poured ice down her neck. "Because if we don't place a line somewhere, then anything is acceptable. There's an excuse for any excess. We draw a line so that we'll always be able to see there should be one."

Shan sat back and almost forgot she wasn't in a chair. Without even thinking, she applauded. Giyadas and Nevyan stared at her clapping hands.

"Amazing," she said. The child had put Shan's moral gyro back in balance. Giyadas had reminded her what she'd always lived by. "Thank you, sweetheart."

Shan had never actually liked a child before. The kids she'd known always needed a good kicking to point out the error of their ways. They were little evil versions of adults who got away with murder because some whining liar of a lawyer said that kids needed to be given a chance to change. But they would never change, and she knew it.

And now she was sitting with a kid who she actually felt affection for, affection that—whether she wanted to face it or not—was maternal in its intensity.

Giyadas was still staring at her, head so far on one side that it looked comical. Nevyan seemed less taken with the diversion and fixed Shan with her hard citrine stare.

"Do you feel Esganikan has the situation under control?"

Shan shrugged. "She's given the isenj a good hammering."

"I knew little of the World Before when I asked for their aid, and I admit that I was expecting—greater *power*."

"Well, one ship blatting a continent is pretty good going. It got my attention for a start."

"Have you asked her how many resources Eqbas Vorhi is committing to the Earth adjustment mission? How many vessels?"

"Not really." *Now that's a bloody oversight: how did I miss that one?* "If she said ten ships, how would I know if that's enough? I don't know the first thing about their capability, other than it's overwhelmingly impressive and it looks like magic to humans."

"I feel the Umeh readjustment is needlessly destructive because she has insufficient resources to do the job properly, by degrees."

Nevyan often surprised Shan as much as Giyadas did. She was a strategist, of course: wess'har females were.

They were the planners, the ones who saw the big picture. Nevyan had learned a lot being at Mestin's side in the Bezer'ej garrison.

"Well, she said as much." Shan wondered if she was defending Esganikan because there was no case to answer or because she was afraid Nevyan might be right. Shan wanted the Eqbas to be omnipotent too. "There was no way she was going to mount a ground offensive. Don't forget she was diverted from another mission, like Shapakti's team. They weren't equipped or tasked for this. And they've met resistance, so they fight back. What else do you expect?"

Giyadas was watching intently. Shan was careful not to set a bad example: the kid learned like blotting paper.

Nevyan rocked her head from side to side in mild annoyance. "This is my point. If the Eqbas don't commit enough ships, then the same thing might happen to Earth."

"It's not like Umeh. It's biologically diverse. They know that. Esganikan said so."

"But if they miscalculate, the consequences will be enormous. Even with bioweapons, the destruction that might cause could make matters worse for Earth, not better. If you can't subdue humans, and you wipe them out in a conflict, what happens to all the processes that must be maintained to remain safe, like your power stations? Why did you want a duplicate of the gene bank held in reserve if that thought hadn't occurred to you?"

Ah. Good point. "Because I'm a copper, and I don't trust any bastard."

"Umeh has not gone as planned. While I feel no pity for isenj, I do fear for Earth if the World Before finds itself under-resourced. They do not retreat."

Shan felt the ice effect again. She'd become used to seeing the Eqbas as invincible. But there was no such thing. Shan began to see Targassat's fears, at least from an economist's point of view. It was a massive commitment to occupy a world twenty-five light-years away from backup.

"You have good relations with her," said Nevyan. "I think

you should ask to discuss this before we allow Esganikan to take the gene bank, even if there is a duplicate now."

"Okay. We'll go and see her, then. On Bezer'ej. I'll call her."

A good reason to go to Bezer'ej. Shan thought the timing was perfect. Her satisfaction made her feel guilty, because her private war with Rayat and Neville was becoming obsessive. She was just like Esganikan: charging in, and imposing her view of what was best.

Yeah, and I know my own kind, and what'll happen if this bloody thing ever gets loose, and it'll only take one little slip, one small chance . . .

"Targassat's objection to policing other worlds was partly based on the difficulty of exit strategies without the total annihilation of the dominant species," said Giyadas, a miniature professor. Shan was speechless. Did wess'har kids ever mess up the place with finger paints? "While they remain, they hate. It requires extermination or constant management."

It was sobering to hear a child define your own planet's geopolitical history without even knowing it.

But Shan was utterly smitten. No wonder Eddie doted on the kid. Now that the shock of identifying a maternal urge had begun to subside, she saw it as a pleasant but slightly sad thing; but she'd never wanted kids anyway. Giyadas was a one-off, an alien novelty. It didn't mean she was getting broody at all. Shit, she was way too old for that kind of crap anyway. If she had a hormonal reaction, it was as a grandmother, and everyone knew grandmothers loved kids because they didn't have to look after the little bastards.

Grandmother. That's a cheering thought. Thank God Ade doesn't see that in me.

"How about taking Vijissi with us?" said Shan. "I haven't seen him in days. How is he?"

"He stays in my mother's home. He's very distressed, especially now that other ussissi have come to F'nar. He feels very excluded."

"All the more reason to get him to come with us." Poor little sod: she should have been spending more time with him. She'd promised to be there but events had overtaken her. "It takes some getting used to, *c'naatat.*" It was time to tell Nevyan in case the same solution had crossed her mind. "For what it's worth, Shapakti tried to remove *c'naatat* from one of Vijissi's samples. Didn't work."

"He can do this?"

It was all coming out now. *What the hell.* "He removed it from some of my cells, but it didn't work for Aras."

Nevyan didn't freeze but her flaring pupils betrayed her intense curiosity. "You considered reverting back?"

"Shapakti tried it out of curiosity. Once he said he could do it, I had to think about Aras's chance to be a father." Shan paused, remembering, and wondered why she had ever been angry with Aras or Ade when they were everything to her. "An antidote to *c'naatat* would have changed the course of events in this system too."

"You put Aras first. I was wrong to think Esganikan had changed you, wasn't I?"

"Hey, we don't know the removal works on a live subject and I'm buggered if I'm volunteering."

"But you would have let him go if it had been possible, even to another *isan.*"

"Yeah."

"That would be distressing for you."

"Yeah." Shan was squirming now. Even with Nevyan, who'd seen her at her best and her very worst, the whole love thing embarrassed her to the point of pain. "But if he wanted kids, he could have gone with my blessing."

She wanted the floor to swallow her. It was everything she was used to suppressing. Nevyan drew Giyadas to her—an adopted child, Shan reminded herself—and exuded the powdery vanilla-like musk of matriarchal contentment.

"You set my *isanket* a good example, my friend," said Nevyan. "As you also set me."

Things were getting back to normal, one by one. Mending

fences with a friend was a new experience for Shan, and being able to tick one crisis off her list gave her fresh resolve
for the rest of her tasks. She contemplated the meeting with
Esganikan with renewed confidence.

14

*It's very odd to have dreams of fire and burning buildings
when you wake up and find yourself in fifty meters of water.
They're someone else's memories.*

*So far we've lost ten more bezeri. They were old and frail,
and I can't help thinking they lost all hope, as unscientific
as that is. There are only forty-four left now.*

MOHAN RAYAT,
from personal records etched on an azin shell tablet

Bezer'ej

Rayat found he could walk faster than Lindsay. Once
they'd oriented themselves he set off along the beach with
her trailing a little behind him, a glass figure of a woman
with a solid belt around her waist. If he looked at her a
certain way, the belt appeared to be making its own way to
Constantine.

Now that they were back on land she seemed to represent
all his fears: he didn't want to end up like that, disappearing
from humanity.

"Why are you going this way?" Half squid or not, she
could still manage to gripe like her old self. "If we go up
that cliff, we're due south of Constantine. That's where the
grave is."

"I want to avoid running into the Eqbas patrols."

"Do you think they know about us?"

"Does Shan?" Oh, that'd stick in her craw. It'd *choke* her.
Sometimes hate was a better driver in adversity than the
prospect of happiness. *Look on the really black side: there's
always someone more pissed off than yourself.* "We know
Ade and Aras know, so to speak. Aras will tell the Eqbas if

he's the . . . man I think he is. He'd warn them to steer clear.
He wouldn't want anyone else contaminated."

"Yes, but the Eqbas are capable of shelling us. Fragmentation, I think Shan said."

"Afraid to die? You got used to immortality pretty damn fast."

"Work to do," said Lindsay.

Me too, he thought.

The beach route took them to the west of the Constantine
site. It wasn't a big island, perhaps less than four hundred
square kilometers: if you made an effort, you could walk
around the coastline in a day, and definitely in two. He'd
hung on to his shoes for this. The excuse that underwater
rocks were too sharp for him to walk on seemed to adequately explain to both Saib and Lindsay his insistence on
keeping them.

It was why he'd kept his clothing, too, and it was holding
up to immersion pretty well. But it was also the last remnant
of privacy he had other than his thoughts, and even those
were contaminated by the memories of others.

By the time they ventured from the shore to the interior,
scrambling over dunes of brown sand interrupted by tussocks of blue-gray grass, the sun was overhead. Lindsay
consulted her compass. She'd hung a collection of tools on
her belt, including a rock hammer: her primitive compass
was proving its worth too. Simple kit sometimes had its advantages over sophisticated technology.

"This way," she said. "Constantine's about an hour's
walk. Find the site, then turn south and we'll reach the grave
in about another half hour."

The grave. She seemed to be detaching from everything, talking like an officer and not a bereaved mother.
Rayat understood.

"I want to stop off at the colony site," he said.

"Souvenirs?"

"If there's anything useful left there that we can haul
back, yes. A bag might be useful. Did you bring a bag?"

Lindsay fumbled in her belt. It had a little tack-zipped

pouch. She drew out a ball of gossamer and shook it like wet laundry so that it snapped out into a string bag of glassy filaments.

"Don't tell me how to go shopping," she said. "Pili makes these."

"Could have given me one when we were collecting the bloody maps, couldn't you?"

"Only discovered them a couple of days ago."

He hoped she wasn't lying. The last thing he needed was to sustain an exhausting and counterproductive feud at a time like this.

He'd thought it was a hot summer day, but it was his *c'naatat* burning extra calories to feed its adaptation activity. The landscape told him it was early spring; he could see short trees like cycads with newly unfurling orange leaves that said *autumn fruit* to his brain and reminded him just how disorienting an alien world could be. A transparent sheet of—

Blue plastic. *Blue.* He knew what it was: it was an *alyat,* another of the carnivorous sheets of membrane that roamed the planet, a flying one this time, but it had always looked colorless to him before. Now he saw it as blue, vivid peacock blue and dappled with faint patterns. His eyes had changed. Somehow that startled him, even though it paled to insignificance alongside the vast changes *c'naatat* was making to him every day.

"The trouble with buried cities," said Lindsay, taking no notice of the *alyat,* "is that you can't find them."

They'd always been able to see evidence of Constantine if they looked hard enough. Small domes of glass—barely visible, less than a meter tall—dotted the landscape like blisters and channeled light into the subterranean colony. But the nanites seemed to have done their work in a matter of months. There was nothing.

"Right spot?"

"I think so."

For the next hour they scuffed around the short violet-gray grass that had overgrown the land since the biobarrier was shut down. Eventually, Rayat nearly fell into a gaping hole big enough to swallow a truck; the entrance to the colony. He couldn't believe it had been so hard to spot.

"Here we go," he said.

The last time either of them had been here was when they captured Shan, or at least when the marines had. It seemed a very long time ago: but it was just months. The tunnels could have collapsed by now. The nanites the wess'har had introduced to break down all traces of human settlement and artifact had been devouring the braces and props even while they were down there hunting Shan. He needed to search the warren. He needed to find the mothballed ships, *Christopher* and its remaining shuttle: one shuttle had been airworthy just months ago, because they'd used it to escape to Umeh. The nanites might not have reached them, or they might have found them too big a meal to digest. There was a chance. His job was to exploit every last opportunity.

"I'm going down there," he said. "You go ahead and find the grave. Meet me back here. Can you find this again?"

Lindsay was checking her compass and looking around the landscape. He read her body movements because he couldn't quite see her eyes. "Getting my bearings," she said. "Yes, I can. But I'll wait all the same, thanks. I don't think we should separate."

Smart-arse. She thought she was being canny; she thought he would sneak off and take the podship, or approach the Eqbas, or whatever. It was a reflex action of mistrust. If she'd thought it through, she'd have realized that there was nowhere he could go and no way she could be stranded on the island.

But if she'd thought about it enough, she'd have remembered the spacecraft.

"I'll try not to take too long," he said, and started down the overgrown ramp. "I'll bring back anything I can carry."

"Tools," she said. "Tools and waterproof textiles."

Being a squid clarified your priorities.

The underground colony had once been bathed in light and it had been easy to forget that it was excavated into the rock unless you looked up to the top of St. Francis spire—a church, a Norman-style church here of all places—and saw not sky but a vaulted ceiling. Rayat's eyes compensated for the darkness by feeding him images of density differentials and surfaces mapped by sound and magnetic signature. There was no color, but there *was* astonishing detail.

The caverns and galleries were largely intact. All structures that hadn't been cut from the stone had vanished, and there were piles of fallen masonry here and there where something had been robbed of its supports by the nanites. The carvings, arches and round windows were untouched. And there was the church of St. Francis: no doors, no glass bells, no gilding on the notice board on the front. It looked for all the world like a building that had been carefully bombed into ruin and then scrubbed clean of scorch marks.

GOVERNMENT WORK IS GOD'S WORK.

The inscription was still crisp and visible on the stonework. They said it was part of the original tympanum constructed by the advance mission of automated bots long before the colonists arrived to take up residence. It had been built on Ouzhari: Aras had moved it here and this was where the colonists had come.

Whose god? Whose government? It had been an arrogant colonial claim of the British Raj five hundred years ago, but governments had never stopped citing God as their authority, including those who'd once been the colonized. Humans never learned. Shan was right, the bitch.

Rayat didn't go inside the church. He checked occasionally in houses and storerooms as he went, finding nothing, but this was a sideshow. He was after transport. He lost track of time, partly because he had no urge to urinate; *c'naatat* seemed to want to retain as much of his body fluids as it could while he was on land. He followed the route he remembered from last time. There *was* a shuttle down here.

Eventually he reached a series of chambers whose ceilings were progressively higher, and then he stepped through into brilliant light that confused his adapted eyes for a second. He looked up; there was no ceiling and he was looking at sky again, seeing in the visual spectrum. The weather covering had gone. But this was a hangar.

Yes, *this* was it. *This* was where he'd come. *This* was where Ade Bennett had found the shuttle last time. He carried on to the next connecting doorway.

The roof was blown back when we lifted. The fact that it's not there now doesn't mean the nanites got it. We're a long way from the hub of the colony. They might not have penetrated this far.

He stepped through and the light ahead seemed much less intense. *Intact hangar roof. Oh God, yes, please let it be there . . .*

Rayat found himself staring at the dust-caked but distinctive gunmetal gray hull of spacecraft more than two hundred years old. No, there were two of them: beyond this one, he could see a much smaller shape, a shuttle. This was *Christopher*, the original colony ship, and it was enormous—bigger than three through-deck carriers. *How the hell did they excavate a structure to house this?* The wess'har were more beneficent than Rayat had imagined.

He had no idea how to gain access. He didn't even know how to start the drives. He'd bloody well worry about that when he needed to. Right now, he needed to get *in.*

He sprinted down the port side of the vessels, scanning frantically for a ramp access. They were set too high; he couldn't find a gantry or even a ladder. He looped around the stern of *Christopher* to check the starboard side.

But he needn't have worried about access.

The entire side of the ship had dissolved.

Not ripped, not blown apart, not even rusted: the whole starboard hull was just *not there.* He was staring into a vast shell—no transverse bulkheads, no decks—that faded into gloom. It was a tunnel, not escape. It was the carcass of a whale picked clean by scavengers.

He heard himself gulp air and sob once.

That was all he allowed himself. He wasn't giving up now. He stepped over a dune of gray dust and ran the length of the ship looking for something, anything he could make use of: if he couldn't fly out of here, he could find some comms kit and get a message out, link into the ITX somehow, call base and tell them what had happened.

And what are they going to do about it, then? Send a cab?

Yes, they could. Extraction might be decades away, even centuries, but he could wait that out now. The nanites couldn't have eaten the lot. They'd left the port side, hadn't they? There was a chance.

His eyes gave up searching as he went deeper into the hull, and he slipped back into echolocation and senses taken from the lightless depths of the ocean. But there was nothing. The ship was empty in a way that no wreck had ever been. *Christopher* was a blown, broken eggshell.

Rayat made his way back up the ship, suddenly conscious that he was coughing. He put his hand to his neck and found his gills had clamped shut. The air was thick with dust that he'd kicked up by moving around, and he'd defaulted automatically to breathing through his nose again. When he looked up at the hangar roof that had given him such hope because it appeared intact, he saw that it was simply festooned with thick vines and runners that had somehow made a mesh across the huge void. Almost all the manufactured structure was gone.

There was still the shuttle, though.

Stupid bastard. It's gone too, you know it is.

He walked the length of the shuttle. It seemed intact and he knew how to open the hatches on one of those, so he reached out and took the yellow and black recessed bar of the manual override in both hands, bracing to jerk it up and out.

But as he squeezed tight, his hands filled with powder. He clutched striped talcum. He shook the dust from his hands in a disgusted reflex and as his fingers caught the frame around the hatch, the whole structure crumbled like a sandcastle. The collapse continued along the length of the shuttle leaving him staring across a gap at the starboard bulkhead.

There was *nothing* inside, the absolute scoured nothing of determined invisible destroyers.

"Shit." He stood with his hands on his hips, head down, crushed. "Shit, shit, shit, shit, *shit!*"

His voice echoed. And he did something he hadn't done in a long, long time: he began crying.

The walk back to the surface felt twice as long. On the way he made a few half-hearted searches for things to scavenge. But the nanites had already swept through. He composed himself at the entrance, not wanting to look an idiot in front of Lindsay, and walked back to her as casually as he could. She was sitting on the grass cross-legged, a weird life-sized ornament.

He should have been thinking of alternatives, of other plans to implement. Instead he just nursed numb defeat. It would pass. But not yet.

"You look pissed off," she said. She stood up. "No joy?"

"Nothing," he said. "Bloody *nothing.*"

"It was a long shot anyway." Lindsay began walking south. "I'm bracing myself to find the gravestone eaten, too. But I need to see."

David Neville, thirty-one days old, lay in a grave outside the colony boundary in the unspoiled wilderness. Aras had made him a headstone of stained glass because Lindsay didn't want the body left for the rockvelvets in the same way the colonists disposed of their dead, and Aras was a skilled glassmaker who saw no harm in marking the grave.

They reached the top of a hummock. Lindsay pointed. "Oh my God, it's still there."

She broke into a strange rolling run. Did she still have bones? Rayat jogged after her.

It was amazing how bright the colors were even at a couple of hundred meters. The slab was beyond the reach of the nanites and the glass shapes looked as piercingly vivid as gems in sunlight. Aras was a master craftsman.

Rayat didn't know what to do with bereaved people so he stood at a discreet distance while Lindsay knelt down and placed her hands on the grave, caressing the ground and then the headstone—head*glass*—itself. He wasn't in a hurry. He sat down to avoid skylining himself in case Eqbas troops had orders to solve the human *c'naatat* problem the hard way, and occupied himself by racking his brains for a Plan B. It displaced his embarrassment too.

You really ought to feel some sympathy for the poor bitch.

Eventually she sat back on her heels. It was odd how she didn't *look* naked; there were none of the hard-wired visual cues in a jellyfish shaped like a human female.

"I have to take something back," she said.

Oh no. This was getting uncomfortable now.

"Lin, tell me you're not thinking of . . . exhuming the body, are you?"

"No." If she was crying, he couldn't see it. Could she lacrimate any longer? She sounded as if she was, but it was hard to tell in a transparent woman. "As long as I'm here, he stays here too. I just want something to take back below with me, something to remember him by." She stood up and unhooked the stone hammer from her belt. "Sorry, Aras. You did a beautiful job."

She grasped the hammer in both hands and swung it, an excessive amount of force to break glass. But this was wess'har glass and it was tough enough to make the church bells in St. Francis. The colored panes flew apart, scattering in a rainbow storm. Two thirds of the panel—peridot and emerald terrestrial grass, topaz daffodil, ruby poppy, amethyst *chirte*—remained standing. Lindsay bent down and gathered up the other pieces. None of them had broken: it was the leading that had yielded to the hammer blow, releasing pink and red fragments of roses.

"That'll last under water," she said. She separated out the pink petals and folded them in a sheet of clear membrane that might have been a flat piece of weed. "That'll do. Let's go."

Rayat wished the metal of *Christopher* or one of its shuttles had lasted quite as well. He followed her back to the

shore for the long walk back to the podship, bereft and
wholly without a Plan B.

Temporary City, near Constantine island,
Bezer'ej: January 1, 2377

The good thing about visiting Bezer'ej was that the anti-
human pathogen made it off-limits to Eddie.

Ade was fond of the bloke but there were things that were
best kept away from him. It wasn't that he couldn't be
trusted: he hadn't gone public on Lindsay and Rayat, and he
hadn't even mentioned their names since that Christmas
Eve session. But, like Shan said, once you knew things, it
couldn't be undone. Even if you never mentioned them, you
still *knew* them and they ate and nagged and clawed at you,
sometimes until they drove you to do something about
them. It wasn't fair on Eddie to expose him to the possibility of new stories that he couldn't tell or live with.

Ade scanned the horizon. "This takes me back."

He folded his arms and superimposed a memory—his
own, nobody else's—on the landscape. He'd looked for
bezeri survivors among the corpses washed up on the
Ouzhari beaches: he'd tracked isenj infiltrators on Constantine with Aras, and he found out that wess'har didn't take
prisoners, quite literally. Their military code of conduct
was nothing like his. But he saw nothing wrong in what
they did. This was their society and they could play by their
own rules, and if he said he'd never wanted to slot some
bastard there and then instead of taking them prisoner, he'd
have been lying. Aras did okay. Ade had no complaints.

Shan and Aras contemplated the heathland with him.
"You can go exploring while Nev and I do the business with
Esganikan," said Shan. She jerked her head in the direction
of the discreetly plant-shrouded entrance to the half-buried
Eqbas garrison. Only the occasional solid outline of a blue
blob of shiplet gave the game away. "No need to sit in unless you want to."

"I want to," said Aras.

Ade got the impression that Shan was finding it hard to get used to taking her men around with her. "I think we ought to have a nice walk," he said. "Frankly, Boss, I'll be bored shitless, and anyway, I haven't had my run today." He gave Aras what he hoped was a meaningful look. "Come on, mate. Let's thin out."

He set off at a brisk walk and then broke into a run, his rifle shuddering on his back at each pace. He knew the terrain: he remembered it better than he thought, and it might have been Aras's memory of the place he was drawing on. He'd been around here for five hundred years, after all. A steady thud-thud-thud behind him told him that Aras was close on his heels. After a couple of hundred meters he slowed to a stop and Aras paused with him.

"She needs a bit of space, 'Ras." Ade watched the Eqbas troops wandering around the blue heathland like tourists. "We'd put her off."

"I would have liked to have heard what Esganikan had to say about developing a bioagent for the isenj."

"Shan will tell us."

"And I want to know if Esganikan encourages her to return to Earth."

"Jesus, mate, she said she isn't going, okay? It's over. She's done what she came to do, and we're all *hors de combat* now."

"What does that mean?"

So Aras's knowledge wasn't encyclopedic. "Means we're out of the game. Not our fucking problem any more."

"I would like to visit Constantine."

Wess'har jumped from one subject to the next without warning. Ade was used to it. He changed gear with equal speed now. "Let's blag a raft off the Eqbas, then."

"You miss the sea."

"I'm a marine. Can't take that out of me." Ade had seen more land engagements than anything, but he liked ships and boats. He certainly missed the exhilaration of skimming up a river or slipping into an enemy harbor in a rigid inflatable with the spray peppering his face. There was something about quiet speed across the face of the water that was more thrilling than flight or freefall. "Come on, let's go and charm a vessel out of our chums over there."

"If you spoke wess'u or eqbas'u, you could do the charming."

"I'm too thick to learn a language."

"You talk complete *bollocks* sometimes."

Ade burst out laughing. He was never sure if Aras was playing the naive alien or having a laugh too. *No, you're the alien here, not him.* They trotted over to a group of Eqbas and Aras warbled at them. A few minutes later they hauled out a white cube on straps, about thirty centimeters square, and dumped it in Aras's arms.

"Boat on a rope," said Ade. "Just add water. Bloody handy."

"*Niluy-ghur.*" Aras repeated it carefully as they jogged towards the shoreline carrying the cube between them like a picnic basket. "*Nee-loor-ee-khoor.*"

"I can't do two voices."

"Try."

"Can't."

"Try or I'll be angry at your lack of interest in culture."

Ade didn't even know where to start. He hated looking stupid. He was totally confident in his soldiering skills and what his body could do but he was going to screw this up and Aras would know he was a thick useless bastard after all. He found he was licking his lips nervously. He broke the seal on the raft—*nee-loor-ee-khoor, nee-loor-ee-khoor*— and dropped it into the shallows, hanging onto one of the straps to stop it making a getaway.

The cube unfurled and flattened into a clear sheet as it settled on the water. A column rose out of it like a snail extending eyestalks. The edge—he couldn't call it a gunwale—extended to form a solid platform with the shingle so they could just walk on board. It was *brilliant;* Ade was as mesmerized by it as he'd been with his first handheld as a kid. It had been stolen property, and his dad smashed it against the wall in a drunken rage as usual, but he still remembered the sense of amazement for the short time he had it.

Aras let him take the con. "You're thinking about your father," he said.

That shook Ade. He felt suddenly naked. "You're not telepathic, are you?"

"No, but you always look the same way when you think about him. Hatred and fear. You never have that expression at any other time."

"No shit?"

"If that's a request for verification, yes. It's true."

Ade contemplated the fact that he was an open book to Aras and that his dad still haunted him. The raft—*nee-loor-ee-khoor*—skimmed towards Constantine at what must have been fifty knots and yet there was no sensation of wind or spray or even movement: it was like he was in a simulator. *Shame.* He liked the raw experience of a wess'har powered craft, which was pretty well an old inflatable Raider except for the controls, with a proper solid hull where you couldn't see the water and weed churning in some weird air pocket beneath your feet.

The raft was just like the see-through deck of Esganikan's ship. He settled for a different kind of thrill. Aras nudged him.

"Say it."

Ade took a breath. *"Nee-loor-ee-khoor."* It was just a single tone, his only voice. *"Nee-loor-ee-khoor."*

"Hum."

"What?"

"Hum. One note."

Ade felt like a complete pillock but he did it anyway.

"Now say the word and keep humming."

"Yeah. Okay." He was going to crash and burn. *"Nee-loor-ee-khoor."*

The sensation made his ears ring and for a moment he wasn't sure what was happening. He did it again. He could hear—no, *feel* an overtone. He giggled helplessly.

"You can learn," Aras said grimly. "You just fear you won't

be as excellent at language as you are at warfare. You don't
enjoy being average."

Being average was all Ade had ever thought he might as-
pire to. He was happy that he managed that, and when the
Corps had shown him he could excel, he fell in love with
the approval it showered upon him. Yeah, maybe Aras was
right. He could hardly stop grinning as he kept up the overtone all the way to Constantine.

Aras nudged him in the back. "I think it's urgent that you
learn some new words, if only for my sanity."

Ade tried to beach the raft but it clung doggedly to the
shoreline and gave every sign of waiting for their return. He
wanted to learn more words now and impress Shan, and by
the time they reached the site of Constantine colony, he could
manage a few basic phrases. He was too embarrassed to ask
Aras to teach him the one he most wanted to learn.

Aras went unerringly to the entrance to the buried colony,
now almost hidden by grass. "I want to have a look around."

"Mind if I stay here?" Ade's memory of the complex was
unhappy, one of emptying his clip into Shan to drop her. It
wasn't the kind of thing a man wanted to recall about the
woman he loved. "Seen enough."

"I know," said Aras. "I've experienced your flashbacks of
the event."

C'naatat could give you complete understanding of
another person. Sometimes it made Ade feel invaded, but
occasionally it was a comfort. He didn't have to articulate
difficult things. The worst stuff did him a favor and explained
itself in Shan's or Aras's mind.

"Good," he said.

He stretched out on the grass, completely at ease with the
fact that it was a dusty blue, and practiced wess'u unself-
consciously. Part of his mind rambled through past events
and things he was planning while he surrendered himself to
the resonance vibrating through his skull.

*Umeh Station. Best thing we can do is help them evacu-
ate. I'll be okay, but Barkers and Izzy and . . . fuck it, why
should they bother? Bastard government.*

He sat up and rummaged in the pouches on his belt. He still had his camo kit so he opened the tin and looked in the small mirror to check that he still didn't need to shave. *C'naatat* had taken a dislike to body hair for some reason. It had its advantages. Then he was looking at someone he didn't know, like catching his reflection of a shop window and wondering who the hell it was. The sensation didn't go away.

For several seconds he was looking at himself through Shan's eyes—yeah, it was her, he *knew* it—and wasn't seeing ordinary Ade Bennett at all, but some bloke he would have given anything to be: capable, respected, attractive, desired, and heroic.

And *loved.*

Ade snapped the camo tin shut and felt as if someone had walked over his grave. It scared him because it was alien in every sense, but it also left him feeling secure in a way he never had in his life; he knew, absolutely *knew,* how Shan felt about him without the filter of wondering if she really meant it. He found himself sitting with the fingertips of both hands resting on his lips, shocked by the intensity.

"There's nothing left down there," said Aras.

Ade nearly leapt to his feet. "Jesus, don't creep up on me like that—"

"I apologize. Are you all right?"

"Just startled."

"I built it."

"What?"

"I built Constantine. I built it with my hands, alongside them. And now it's empty and dead."

Poor sod: Ade wondered what five hundred years of loneliness was like. He got to his feet and gave Aras a rough hug. That took him by surprise too. He *never* did that.

"It's okay, mate," he said, and dropped his arms to his sides, embarrassed. "It wasn't for nothing. You kept the gene bank going, and the colony would have been dead in the first year without—"

"Last time I touched you, you slammed me against the

wall." Aras's tone was mild, not at all accusing. "This is unusual."

Ade didn't have an answer. He didn't have to think too hard to work out the connection with his dad, and Aras probably didn't either. "I've been seeing my shrink," he said, and laughed it off. "Anywhere else you want to go?"

Aras didn't blink. "David Neville's grave."

There wasn't any answer to that, either. They set off in silence, and Ade felt they'd reached a . . . *profound* understanding with one another. *Well, that's not a word I would have used a year ago.* Maybe it wasn't just overtones and seeing yourself through your lover's eyes that *c'naatat* sneaked into your head while you weren't looking.

The grave was marked with a colored glass headstone like the windows Aras had made for St. Francis church. In bright sun, you could see it a long way off. Aras pointed.

"Something's wrong," he said.

Even from this distance Ade could see that the stained-glass headstone had been smashed. On closer inspection he found the upper third had been broken away cleanly, leaving the leading twisted and empty. The rest of the slab was untouched. There was no debris on the ground, not a scrap.

"Bastards," said Ade.

Aras stared down at the grave. "Why would anyone do that?"

"People do it all the time back home. Mindless twats."

"Eqbas would never do this."

"Well, it didn't break in high wind, mate. Someone's ripped this apart."

"I'm . . . bewildered."

Ade was angry and upset for his housebrother, and disturbed by the desecration of a grave. Losing a kid was even worse than wanting them and not having them; Lindsay might have been a stupid cow and a bezeri killer, but he could still feel pity for that part of her, the grieving mother.

"Well, she's not here to see it, so maybe we can fix it up. Out of respect." Ade turned to walk back. "Let me ask my little chum Shapakti. He'll find out for me, one way or another."

Aras was upset. Ade could smell his agitation all the way back across the strait to the Temporary City, and he was reminded that wess'har experienced powerful emotions, however calm or callous they appeared to outsiders.

He had wess'har in his head as well as Shan and things he didn't even have names for, thanks to his parasite. Ade knew things in a way nobody but another *c'naatat* could know.

Temporary City, Bezer'ej, command and control center

The ussissi in the Temporary City milled around the chambers, making Shan think *pack* and not *team* again, and she made a point of keeping clear. She'd been on the brink of an attack by challenging ussissi before, and this wasn't the time to prove how hard she was; but they were a different kind of creature now, and her initial assessment of them as savage rather than cute was being verified. The teeth were a clear advert for their ferocity but she noticed something she hadn't seen before. The finely pleated skin that made them look like corduroy toys had changed. The thousands of little ridges were now prominent, more like razors. The sooner they felt reassured enough to return to Umeh, the better she would like it.

It was good to be back here. Even the Temporary City held some memories for her, but she wanted to walk on the blue plains again and recall a time when she thought her commitment was a year here and then she'd head home.

She turned to Esganikan. Nevyan maintained a stony expression, head jiggling occasionally, and she smelled irritated. *At least hear her out.*

Shan opted to talk in eqbas'u. "Don't you think that giving the isenj a biological weapon is asking for trouble?"

Conventional pressure didn't work on wess'har, whether Targassati or Eqbas. There were no insecurities to play on and nothing they wanted to hide.

"In what way?" Esganikan asked.

"Are they going to reverse engineer it and develop an

antidote to the bioagent here? If they get good at it, they could develop a counter-wess'har version."

"They have no expertise in genetic warfare and no chance of developing it. Their bioagents are designed to kill their neighbors."

"You're very confident."

"If they could manage it, they'd have attempted it by now. They had access to tissue samples from your *jurej* many years ago, I understand." Esganikan wasn't being a smart-arse. Shan had to remind herself of that. She was just stating facts. "Nearly all of their resources are devoted to simply maintaining a survivable environment so research of that kind is beyond them, even if they had a core of expertise—which they don't. And the pathogens are nonpersistent. They don't have the dormancy that the bioagent here has."

"So it's a black box for them."

"I don't understand."

"They can use it but they don't know how it works, and they can't open it to find out."

"Exactly."

"And are you going to have a meeting with the Jejeno cabinet about this? Can we come?" The good thing about Esganikan was that her default setting, while not naive, was yes-why-not. It was a striking reminder of the gulf between their cultures: Shan's first reaction would have been to ask why.

"I think that would be especially useful for Nevyan," said Esganikan. "These are her reformed neighbors."

"You're rather optimistic about rapid change in the isenj mindset," said Nevyan, suddenly her old self again, earnest and unafraid. "In five years' time, the main task force arrives and you embark for Earth leaving us to deal with whatever comes out of Umeh. They'll be bitter and resentful. If all goes well they might even rebuild their fleet. Where does that leave us?"

"We'll maintain a permanent base here."

Shan caught a whiff of *jask* rising from Nevyan and she

reached out to jog her arm. *Don't.* A couple of Eqbas crew paused to look at them.

"That's new," said Shan. "When did you decide to make it permanent?"

"Curas Ti feels that Bezer'ej is a unique environment that needs protection. There are still bezeri and when Ouzhari is remediated, they might well let us help them."

"How many are there?"

"The numbers have fallen, judging by the traces in the water samples. Possibly forty or so."

"What happened to the others?"

"We don't know."

It was wrong, Shan knew, but she had a personal task and this was as good a time as any to broach the subject. "And have you evidence that Lindsay Neville and Mohan Rayat are still with them?"

"The Ouzhari remediation team saw Rayat in the shallows recently and we find traces of human DNA and excreta in our sampling."

"So you can locate them?"

"Usually. Within a few thousand meters."

Nevyan, Umeh and a future with Eqbas neighbors were totally forgotten as Shan wondered what form Lin and Rayat had taken. Shit, she might not even recognize them now: she hadn't thought enough about that. She could take a raft out and hunt them but they might be the first aquatic life she passed and she wouldn't know it.

But there were more ways of hunting them than by sight.

"Just checking," said Shan. "I want to be able to visit this place when I need to. Is there any problem with that?"

"None. Shapakti is keen to talk to you on Earth habitats and the gene bank."

"I'll make this a regular run, then." Shan glanced at Nevyan. "Let us know when the meeting is scheduled with Eit."

Nevyan and Shan walked around the perimeter of the Temporary City and recalled old times that were only a year ago.

There were no *alyats* flying but Shan spotted the outline of a stabtail wheeling high on a thermal; this was still a beautiful wilderness full of extraordinary wildlife and the bombing of Ouzhari hadn't reached far beyond the southernmost islands.

And they were walking on land that had been restored. It was easy to forget that. This had been Umeh overspill before Aras and the Wess'ej army had done here exactly what Esganikan had very nearly done to large parts of Umeh. The moral loop was hard to untangle; only the motive—that most fragile of concepts between human and wess'har— was different.

But it wasn't the time to tell Nevyan that, and Shan liked having friends at the moment. She shook aside a vaguely disoriented feeling like the start of a illness and wondered what the hell they put in the Eqbas snack she'd eaten.

"It'll work out fine, Nev."

"Statement or wish?"

"Bit of both."

"Your preoccupation with Rayat and Lindsay is visible to say the least." She looked into Shan's face, blinking with concern. "You let it keep you awake too many nights. Even a *c'naatat* needs rest."

The grass ran into a shingle beach that fell away sharply, creating a low cliff. Shan and Nevyan watched the water for a while. There was a time when standing here and swinging a signal lamp would bring bezeri to the surface, and even summon a pilot in a podship.

The sea looked as it always had, but something had vanished from it forever. The only lights to be seen now were coming from Shan's own hands. She moved to the very edge of the cliff and stared out to sea, ignoring how hopelessly vast the search area was.

They were out there somewhere, the last of the bezeri she'd failed to protect and the two humans who all but wiped them out.

"I'm coming," she said. "I'll find you."

15

*Humans' greatest asset is recognizing patterns. It gives
them predictive minds, which is a great survival advantage.
Unfortunately, it also makes them prone to see only what
they want to see, and the patterns they are used to, and not
what is actually in front of them. It makes it hard for them
to analyze anything dispassionately: they are both the center of their world and the lens through which they see it.*

Matriarch Historian SIYYAS BUR

Bezer'ej: January 2377

Lindsay laid the glass petals on a slab of stone in her bezeri cone house and arranged them as they'd been before, a
perfect rose.

It had been worth the double agony of adapting to air and
then enduring the few minutes of drowning again. The tran-
sition back to being aquatic had been much quicker. If she
ever wanted to visit land again, she knew her body would
do that faster, too.

She might even make herself fully amphibious, although
she wasn't sure yet what use that might be.

Pili drifted behind her. *What's that?*

Lindsay held one piece of glass up to the shaft of sunlight that pierced the roof of the chamber. *It marked the
grave where my son is buried. I'll make a memorial to him
down here, without the body.*

Pili flickered violet agreement patterns. *It's good to have
something to help you remember.*

Rayat would probably tell her it was a shrine and that she
was a fool. But maybe that was a harsh judgment. He seemed
very subdued: the visit to Constantine had set him back just

when she thought he was doing a good job of accepting his fate. But it wasn't supposed to be fun. It was partly his punishment, and partly to help the bezeri.

She laid the glass petal back on the slab in the space left for it, re-creating a whole rose, and wondered whether she would use her *c'naatat* if David were dying in her arms now. She'd been alternately sure that she would and sure that she wouldn't, and now she was sure again that she *would*. It didn't make it right or ecologically responsible: it would probably have brought him misery eventually, either as a freak and a source of samples for the pharmacorps or the military, or as a man who couldn't have children of his own, or even a lover.

But he was her child, and always would be. She knew she'd both save him *and* regret it.

She went in search of Rayat.

She found him in the old assembly chamber that the bezeri were now using as a storage facility for the maps. They were finding them in many places, and although the bezeri had been a small population clustered in a limited part of the ocean, they had certainly preserved a lot of history.

Rayat was sitting on a shell stool, staring at a shell map. He had a thin instrument in one hand like a stylus.

"Are you reading or writing?" she asked.

He preferred to talk the old-fashioned way and seemed afraid to become like her and surrender to the metamorphosis. The host's reaction to the changes their *c'naatat* brought about really did seem to influence it; it was almost as if it was listening to your wishes. Rayat seemed to think it was some sophisticated feedback system involving stress and pleasure hormones. Either way, *c'naatat* seemed uncomfortably like a genie, and equally hard to put back in its bottle.

Be careful what you wish for.

"I'm reading," he said. "I actually *understand* this now. Pictograms. It's not exactly *The Rise and Fall,* but they've catalogued millennia here. Extraordinary. They love keeping records."

"I guessed."

Rayat seemed totally caught up in it. Whatever had upset him when he went back to the ruins of the colony had been forgotten for the time being.

"Look," he said. He held up the map. "This isn't just a chart. It records what happened when the isenj arrived. They were here for years before they overran the place."

"That's what happens when you keep doubling numbers."

"This stuff goes back . . . oh, I reckon fifty thousand years. The isenj don't show up in the records until about five thousand years ago." He held up the map. "See that pictogram?" It looked like a black asterisk. "That's how they depict the *spiny ones*."

Lindsay's stomach could still churn, metamorphosed or not. She'd help wipe out a species that had been making records for longer than humankind. It made her feel even more of a monster. "Oh God."

"Want me to teach you to read this?"

"Okay."

"Yeah, I know. It doesn't make me feel any better either. But at least their culture can be preserved if we try to learn what we can."

Rayat was always up to something. Lindsay knew she would find out what it was the hard way, but he had a valid point. She could, if nothing else, ensure the bezeri weren't totally erased if the last one died out. She was determined that neither would happen. Rayat began pointing out the recurring pictograms indicating clans, life events, places and seasons. The pictogram for the annual spawning—which seemed to produce nothing like the numbers of offspring of terrestrial squid—reminded her of an air force roundel, blue and red with a pearlescent center.

"I think I'm going to start with the oldest ones and work forward," said Rayat.

Lindsay settled down with a pile of the shells to struggle through her maps like a kid, clutching a piece of weed for a snack, and the sheer bizarre irony of it made her want to weep although she didn't seem to have the glands for that any longer. They sat in watery silence for an hour or more. She was starting to get a feel for the time cycles now; her body knew something that her human mind couldn't detect.

"Oh," said Rayat.

"What?"

"Look."

He drifted across to her and held out a more intricate azin shell record whose symbols seemed to suggest that their recording styles changed over the years. It was like looking at a medieval manuscript against text on smartpaper. It was also exceptionally beautiful, a riot of color even now.

"What am I looking at?"

She'd played this guessing game with him before back on *Actaeon,* when he showed her the original telemetry from the *Christopher* mission and where the ship had originally landed: Ouzhari. It usually meant he was about to make a shocking point.

"This," he said. "What does it look like to you?"

She stared at the sand image, trying out her full range of perception from the visual spectrum to density changes. "A big lump."

"Not bad, not bad at all." He traced the outlines with his little finger as he read them out. "This symbol means *big,* but this means *food,* and this means *hunt.* And this is an animal or very large fish, for want of a more taxonomically correct term."

"Just cut to the chase. I don't mind being marked down as the dim kid at the back."

"I wondered what had happened to the big animals down here. No whale equivalent, no shark equivalent. Not that I've seen the whole ocean, but it's quite striking that there's nothing around here bigger than those killer whelks, as you call them."

"They died off too? The isenj pollution?"

"No," said Rayat. He had that look of detached fascination on his face. The lights in his hands shimmered and pulsed with each sound he made like some base line decoder at a high-school dance. "The bezeri hunted them. I think they hunted them to extinction."

F'nar, Wess'ej: January 2377

Shan stood by the window looking onto the city, chewing her thumbnail and seeming lost in thought.

"*Isan,* come back to bed," Aras whispered. He worried about her. She hadn't slept since they left for Bezer'ej and even with *c'naatat,* she could still look tired and drawn. "There's nothing you can do about Vijissi right now."

"You're a fine one to talk. You don't sleep through either."

"I'm wess'har. You know we don't sleep like that."

"I'm sorry. Did I disturb Ade?"

"He's asleep. He sleeps well whatever happens."

"Soldiers can sleep anywhere and eat anything. Good habit to have, I reckon." She stepped back from the window and opened the cupboard very carefully. "Might as well have a cup of tea. Solves anything, a cup of tea."

Aras took the jar of dried leaves from her hand and motioned her to sit down at the table. This was his job: a proper *jurej* provided food and kept house and raised children. He could do two out of three, and that made him happy. She folded her arms on the table and let her chin rest on them.

"Poor sod," she said quietly. "What's he going to do? He's the only one of his kind. I have you."

"I was the only one of *my* kind for quite some time."

"Sweetheart, I'm sorry. That was thoughtless of me. Well, you know better than anyone what he'll go through."

Aras knew all too well. It was no surprise that every other wess'har who had *c'naatat*—and who hadn't been killed outright by explosion during the war with the isenj—had taken their own life. It was agony to see everyone you cared for age and die, especially if your culture emphasized the natural cycle of life and death.

Five centuries in exile, most of them alone. No wonder I

was happy to see the human colonists and be accepted by them. They thought I was a miracle sent by their god at first.

"Did I tell you my first *isan* killed herself?"

"Mestin told me. I must have put you through hell when I spaced myself. I really am sorry."

"But you're back now. And you love me, and you love Ade, and we're happy as a family." He strained the liquid from the tea leaves and poured it into cups, then sat next to her on the bench. "The pain is forgotten."

"Which makes it even harder for me to imagine how Vijissi is going to cope. Ussissi are total pack animals."

"People."

"I count humans as animals. No offense meant."

"I agree that he'll probably find it very hard to bear." He eased her arms out of their folded position and wrapped her fingers around the cup. She always seemed to like a little extra fussing. "I'm not sure which is worse. Being unable to have *oursan,* or knowing everyone you care for will die before you do. An eternity of bereavement."

Shan sipped the tea. "So, they fired you as the resident stand-up comedian, then?"

"I can tell how distressed you are by the speed at which you descend into tasteless jokes."

"Sorry."

"I wasn't being critical. Just concerned for you. Feeling responsible for Vijissi's death, and then feeling responsible for his isolation must be hard."

"Hey, I'm the one who got all the breaks. Don't pity me." She leaned against him and kissed him. Her mouth was warm and fragrant from the tea. "And drifting in space minus a suit is pure unadulterated fucking hell. I still have nightmares."

"Anyone else would have gone insane."

"Who's to say I didn't? Maybe *he* has."

"We can help him adjust."

"I'm up for that. Are you? Don't take on my debts. I need to sort my own shit."

"There you go again. Please, don't shut us out. Part of the joy of being a family is to support one another."

She looked away for a moment. "Okay. I know I've got a nasty mouth on me and I lose my rag way too often, but I think the world of you. You know that, don't you?"

"Of course I do."

"And I know I spend a lot of time with Ade. I don't want you to feel I've pushed you aside."

"He's your new *jurej*. That's normal. And I don't feel neglected, because I have a brother, and that's a very precious thing too."

The more Aras basked in his newly stable marriage, the more he could taste the misery that Vijissi had to face in the years to come. The temptation would be to infect a mate to ease the loneliness.

But I did that. I saved Shan from death because I couldn't bear being alone any longer and I couldn't face losing her in particular. I didn't even give her a choice.

"Nobody should be forced to face an infinite life on their own," said Shan. "He could only have caught the bloody thing from me when he was injured. The least I can do is be there for him now."

"He still has to face having no mate."

"Don't remind me."

"I recall you were the one who said you needed nobody. You seem very positive about relationships now."

"I still don't *need* anybody." Shan inspected the contents of her cup. She didn't smell quite right. He knew she couldn't be ill, but it still concerned him that she was under stress. "I'd survive. I know exactly what I can survive now. But given the choice, I'd rather be with two blokes who I love. Even if do you drive me bloody mad sometimes."

"Ah, I'm a *bloke* now. The ultimate approval." He wrapped his arms around her. Wess'har didn't kiss but he had enjoyed learning the *gethes* habit and he felt he was competent at it. "Come on. Finish your tea, and sleep."

"Only if you come back to bed as well. No wandering around looking for jobs to do."

"Yes, *isan*."

"One day, someone's going to call me Shan." She stood up and grimaced. "Jesus, my stomach's playing up. I hate Eqbas food."

"It won't kill you."

"Exactly. Just feels that way."

Ade didn't wake up but he murmured in his sleep as Shan edged into bed and nestled against his back. Communal sleeping took some getting used to: Aras enjoyed the extra warmth, but wess'har only had single alcoves to doze in for brief periods. And neither *oursan* nor reproduction had anything to do with beds anyway. Humans seemed unable to separate beds and sex. They even used one word as a euphemism for the other.

Odd creatures, humans.

Aras was happy with them, though. He tried to curb his restlessness and laid his head against Shan's shoulder, contemplating the strangeness of being with two creatures who wanted him there beside them even though they were not conscious. Perhaps, one day, his *c'naatat* would take the hint and tinker with his sleep pattern to make it fit theirs.

Poor Vijissi. This will be beyond you now.

There was one positive aspect about the bittersweet discovery of the ussissi's survival, though. It appeared to have taken Shan's mind off Lindsay Neville and Mohan Rayat for the time being.

Aras wondered how Lindsay would react if she knew her son's gravestone had been smashed.

I worked hard on that glass. It mattered very much to her that it was perfect, even though David couldn't see it.

Like Shan and Ade, asleep and not really knowing I'm here. Things that can't be seen still matter to someone.

Who would want to smash the headstone?

The end for the isenj has started sooner than any of us imagined, and I feel no regret.

Should I?
Aras sank into a gradual, delicious, and very human sleep.

F'nar: Mestin's home

"Vijissi went out early this morning," said Mestin. "He thinks we haven't spotted him, but he spends the day up on the ridge overlooking the ussissi village."

Shan stood at Mestin's door and wished that all this had happened at tidy, separate times. Vijissi was one drama too many, and she'd done exactly what she did so many times in her past: she dropped the personal ball—the one that mattered most—to get the job done. Umeh would have burned with her or without her, and Esganikan really didn't need her help at all. But Vijissi did. And she hadn't been there for him when she'd promised to be.

"I've just got back from Bezer'ej," she said. *Feeble, pathetic excuse.* "I really should spend more time with him."

"He doesn't care for anyone's company at the moment, not even mine." Mestin stood back to invite her in but Shan shook her head. "Had you been here all day and every day, he still wouldn't have responded. None of us can reach him."

"I've got to at least see him."

"I understand. Bring him back if you can."

The ussissi village was full of temporary refugees from Umeh and Shan could hear the noise long before she caught sight of the eggshell domes of the part-buried houses. If she stuck to the long route, she could walk up to the ridge almost unseen from the top. She was halfway up the incline when she saw Vijissi skylined at the top of the ridge. He was lying flat exactly like a dog, chin lowered on his hands, and staring out over the village. You didn't have to be a ussissi psychiatrist to work that one out.

Shan wondered about the wisdom of interrupting him. But she had to. She took exaggeratedly noisy paces towards him and saw his ears twitch; but he didn't move.

"How you doing?" she said, and lay down beside him, propped on her elbows.

"I'm recovered."

"Anything I can do?"

"It's enough that you worry about me."

So worried that I neglected you, yeah. "I can guess why you come up here, but I might be wrong."

Vijissi said nothing for several minutes. Then his head jerked as if he'd seen something and he lifted himself a couple of inches into a crouch. Shan followed his line of sight as best she could and he was looking down at a knot of ussissi, male and female, doing that strange weaving motion almost like a dance, mirroring each other's movements for no apparent reason.

"Talissari," he said. "And her new mate."

She'd guessed right. One of them—Shan had no idea which—was once his love and now she was someone else's. She wouldn't wait for the dead: not unreasonable, but no less painful for the reality. And she'd brought her new male home with her, another turn of a painful screw.

But it was more than his female that he missed. He was cut off from his pack. And a stranger from Pajat had taken his place.

"I'm sorry," said Shan. "Does it give you comfort at least being able to see her and your clan?"

"No," he said. "But I don't know what else to do, because I see them wherever I go anyway."

Shan had burned out her rage at being infected in days, but the doubts and disorientation had taken months to settle. It was still early days for Vijissi. "Come on," she said. "Let's go back to Nevyan's and see Giyadas. Change of scene."

He settled down for a few moments as if he hadn't heard her and then he eased himself onto his hind legs. It was a start. They walked slowly back to F'nar and climbed the terraces to Nevyan's level in silence. If anyone should have known what small talk to make with a *c'naatat*, it was her, but silence seemed the best option. At least he was walking with her.

"Lisik's always got something ready to eat on the stove," she said as they walked the last hundred meters. "You can always get a meal at Nev's. In fact—"

Shan saw Eddie step out of the door of Nevyan's home and he saw her. There was nothing remotely odd about that because he lodged there, but she realized she hadn't told him Vijissi was alive. *Shit.* Maybe Nevyan had. She'd been so anxious to keep the news about Rayat and Lin quiet that she'd stopped telling Eddie anything.

Eddie paused and did a double-take.

No, Nevyan hadn't told him.

To Eddie's credit, his reaction was one of delight—feigned or otherwise—but he was obviously shocked and he speeded up his pace. "Oh my God it's *you!*" he said.

Vijissi froze for a few seconds, then spun around and bolted up the terrace in a flat run like a greyhound. Shan called after him but he vanished in the warren of alleys and tunnels, and she didn't feel up to chasing him.

"Shit," she hissed.

"What did I do?" Eddie floundered. "Christ, it *is* him, isn't it? Why didn't you tell me? He's got it too?"

"You're so used to us undead by now." It struck her that he wasn't as appalled as he had been about Lin and Rayat: maybe Vijissi was just a friend after all.

"Hey, I didn't know, okay? How was I to know he'd shoot off like that? What's wrong, anyway?"

"Let's just say he's not taking his new *c'naatat* status terribly well." She hoped he was heading for Mestin's home. He couldn't come to any harm now, but being out on a chilly damp day was the last demoralising thing he needed. "His pack can't have contact with him for the usual reasons, and his girl didn't wait for him, so that's pretty well pariah status for a ussissi."

"Oh fuck."

"A doctor writes."

"If I can do anything—"

"It's okay. He'll come back."

"Let me know, okay?"

Eddie hesitated as if waiting for orders, and then disappeared in the direction of the Exchange of Surplus Things, probably to drink with the marines. Nevyan came out onto the terrace to see what was happening; F'nar had superb acoustics, especially when you didn't want them. She beckoned to Shan to come in and they found a quiet corner in her library amid Eddie's editing equipment.

"I'd love a day when something goes right for a change," said Shan. "I should have told Eddie. And I have no idea what spooked Vijissi, other than it can't be fun being a novelty freak when you're that depressed."

"He's not making progress."

"What has he got to make progress for? Aras is probably best placed to understand the isolation, but who wants to hear that it's the first five hundred years that are the worst, and then maybe you meet the right girl?"

"Aras wouldn't put it that way."

"No. I know." Shan put her head in her hands and braced her elbows on her knees for a few moments. She felt irritable and restless. "I haven't heard from Esganikan, by the way. I thought we were—"

"Shan, you seem different."

"I'm not my usual perky optimistic self, I'll give you that."

"No, it's more than that." Nevyan inhaled audibly. Her pupils blossomed and she cocked her head, then *froze*.

Something had not only surprised her, but *stunned* her.

"Why did you not tell me?" she said.

"Tell you what?"

Shan felt ill. She'd been asphyxiated, and frozen dry, and drowned, and smashed, and torn by high-caliber rounds, but she hadn't felt *ill* in a very, very long time. It was a general feeling of discomfort and unease. It disoriented her. *C'naatat* didn't get sick. They didn't feel *unwell*. It didn't happen.

"You've conceived," Nevyan said.

"Don't be stupid. I had the plumbing removed a long time ago."

"What does that mean?"

"I had my reproductive organ removed. It's a long story."

It was impossible. She'd had a hysterectomy twenty years ago. Ade had been sterilized; and Aras had confined himself to *oursan*. Reproduction was a separate act for wess'har, a separate organ, a separate biology. "Just can't be."

"You have the scent. I can smell it." Nevyan sniffed again. "It's slightly different, but then you're not wholly wess'har. But you are carrying an embryo."

Shan's mouth filled with saliva. Nevyan's voice was coming from a distance, oddly muffled. "Just one problem there. No uterus, and Ade's been sterilized too. And I don't have to draw you a picture about Aras. Wrong *sanil*. *Ain't possible*."

Shan realized she was denying this rather too strenuously. The pulse pounded in her ears.

Something at the back of her mind said she'd ignored something far too obvious. *C'naatat* had kept her alive in space, and under water, and with a chunk of her skull blown away. It could do anything it pleased.

It could remodel anything it took a shine to. It could also remodel Ade.

And . . . it tended to respond to its host. Shan recalled her powerful maternal protectiveness towards Giyadas. It had been an almost overwhelming sensation.

"Shit," she said. It was the worst thing she could imagine. She was as close to panic as she'd been when she stepped out the airlock into colder-than-cold airless space. "*Shit*."

She was pregnant. And a *c'naatat* just couldn't allow that to happen.

16

*This is an unprecedented opportunity in human history to
adopt a sustainable and compassionate way of life. We
know the Eqbas vigorously promote sustainable systems
and don't exploit other species in any way. We should be
talking with them right now and making it clear there
are plenty of people on Earth who'd welcome the changes
they could make. All the arguments against a green vegan
lifestyle are rendered pretty well invalid if the Eqbas can do
what people say they can.*

Spokesman for Gaia's Guard, Australian branch,
interviewed on BBChan 557

Memorial cairn, F'nar plain

Shan sat next to her own grave and realized that Ade had
picked a perfect spot for it.

The view from the top of the butte was spectacular. Spring
was a few weeks away but there was already a carpet of fresh
growth—gold, red, sage green—in sheltered pockets. The sun
caught the polished pearl coating on the carefully constructed
pyramid of rocks beside her and made it instantly magical,
like giant almond dragées. She'd never liked them: they always looked more delicious than they tasted. Coated, hidden,
dishonest things like that always disappointed.

Am I wrong?

She had no right to be pregnant and she had to do something about it. Nevyan had promised to say nothing while she
worked out how she was going to break this to Ade and Aras.

Both of them had reasons for passing on their *c'naatat*
deliberately, and she was *sure* she wouldn't have taken the
same decisions. Shit, she *knew* she wouldn't. She'd spaced

herself to stop Rayat getting his hands on it. You never knew what you'd do in a tight spot until you were in it, but there was no spot tighter than that, and she'd *done* it.

But that certainty was illusory. She'd never been faced with the same choice involving someone she loved. It really was tougher than killing yourself.

Doesn't make any bloody difference. You've got to take an objective view.

If *c'naatat* was that much of a risk, then *why* hadn't she destroyed all of them? She was still alive because Aras had saved her by infecting her, and just by being alive now she had *accepted* that. That meant she only decided to kill the hosts she didn't have feelings for, plus herself of course, because that was all part of her bloody stupid look-how-noble-I-am approach.

And Ade wondered why she was so hard on herself. But it was the question that wouldn't go away.

Make your fucking mind up. Either this thing is so dangerous that you wipe it out, period, all of it, now—or it's not. Where's your principle?

And that was the thin end of the wedge. She knew the only logical answer was that they should *all* be eradicated. But she had no idea how she would bring herself to kill Ade—poor loyal Ade, whose only mistake had been to volunteer for the mission and meet her—and Aras, who had endured unimaginable isolation for centuries. They didn't deserve to die.

Outcomes, outcomes, outcomes. Motive doesn't matter. Motive doesn't change the consequences. Loving someone isn't a reason not to take the decision.

Taking a lover's life was more unimaginable than taking your own. She remembered having to arrest an elderly man who'd killed his terminally ill wife, and how she thought she was being the compassionate copper by making the charges disappear for him. She found out that he'd killed himself a few days later; she was first at the suicide scene, in fact. Tidy paperwork, and a tragedy topped and tailed.

She'd compromised over *c'naatat* already. That meant she could compromise over the child. It was hard to think of it in those terms, though. The trail of logic led her further into a monstrous flow chart that didn't appear to have an end, killing and guilt, until she finished herself off; or not killing, and a constant biohazard risk and more miserable lives—and guilt. Love made you do expedient things. She knew she mistrusted it for a reason.

And there were no moral absolutes. She just made up a few uncrossable lines to keep her sane, just as Giyadas— clever, wonderful, wise kid—said you had to.

Okay, so you don't have the balls to finish off Ade and Aras. So what if you do *have the kid?*

Shan got up and walked around the butte for a while, circling the flat section where the cairn stood. There was a smaller pile of rocks, just a handful of pearls, that marked the spot where Aras had buried Black, the rat. Shan stared at the two memorials in defocus and tried to apply the logic of species to it. Aras hadn't saved the rat, but he *had* saved her, and that made no sense in wess'har terms either, because all life was equal.

I'm a mistake, a lapse in Aras's judgment. I shouldn't be here.

She knew what was at the core of this. She was morally adrift after being so damned sure that a bracing spell in vacuum had sorted her priorities and cleared her mind, putting her beyond all pain and uncertainty because *nothing* could be worse than spacing yourself and not being able to die. She'd faced oblivion, called God a useless, incompetent fucker, and come through irrevocably changed. But she was *wrong*. She'd gone back to being a real person with the same set of dilemmas she'd always had. She was flesh and blood.

No, she *had* to be clear about motive before she acted. Motive did matter. Motive stopped you looking at the outcomes dispassionately. She needed to see clearly first.

Maybe *c'naatat* was influencing her, though. That was what Aras had said once: just like *toxoplasma gondii* affecting its host's behavior to make the most of its own chances of re-production. Shan hated the idea of a microorganism making her think it wasn't so bad to have a few more *c'naatat* around the place. Well, it hadn't been able to stop her stepping out that airlock. Her mind was her own, not the parasites'. She stared at her hands and the array of lights seemed no more than a party trick. The flashes didn't mean a thing; *c'naatat* scavenged the photophore genes because it *could.* It probably didn't have a plan in mind. It was no different to humans or amoebae in that respect.

So what's really pissing you off about being pregnant?

She didn't want a child at all, but Ade and Aras would have liked nothing better. She knew that. She also knew how she'd judged Lindsay's unplanned pregnancy: if you really couldn't face having a kid, then you didn't open your legs, and if you did, then you had to live with the consequences. Even Lindsay—knocked up when she was drunk, the irresponsible cow—had accepted that and turned down a termination.

Okay, so you have the kid. You don't have to do the maternal thing. Ade and Aras are just gagging to be dads.

Shan stared out across the plain and defocused again, reducing the complex landscape to a blurred gold tapestry. She tried to imagine growing up as a *c'naatat;* and now she knew why the parasite and the host were both given the same term by the wess'har, because it defined you.

The word meant *unending.*

How fast did a *c'naatat* fetus develop?

How did you tell a kid that they were never going to die?

And what happened when the kid realized there were no others like them, and that they'd never have a lover or children of their own?

They could never have a normal life unless more *c'naatat* hosts were created. *Here's your little friend, sweetheart. I've made you a new one to play with.* Jesus, it would be condemning them not only to a lonely existence, but a permanent one that locked them in a continual emotional childhood, where the only people like them would be their parents.

You couldn't stand by and not be tempted to make just a few more hosts so they had the chances of happiness that you had.

And then where did it stop?

There would be generations, each facing the same dilemma: *do we stop this here and now?* Shapakti said he might be able to remove *c'naatat* from humans, but she couldn't have a face doing that, knowing she'd watch her child die of old age—and that they would watch, normal and mortal and probably resentful—while she lived on.

Shan squatted by the cairn to see if her warrant card was still wedged between the stones and then took a brisk walk back down the slope and across the plain to the patch of fields where Ade and Aras were working.

Take a run at it, just like you did at the airlock. Just tell them. Maybe they'll see it more clearly than you.

She never used to agonize over decisions like this.

Aras straightened up at her approach. "*Isan,* we have a surprise for you." He never quite managed a human smile, but he beamed wonderfully, and it was disarming. "Ade, show her."

Not half the surprise I've got for you. "What is it?"

"Potatoes," Ade said. "They grew really fast."

He held out his hand, palm up, with a few soil-caked tubers about the size of eggs. There was something inexplicably exciting about crops.

It's your child, Ade. It can't be Aras's. This is between you and me. "No mint," she said. "But who needs mint with them anyway?"

"What's wrong?" asked Aras. "You've shut down your scent. You said you wouldn't do that with us."

"Sorry." They might as well have been telepathic after all. "Habit."

There was always a fraction of a second that was the right time to say something difficult, and when it passed it became impossible again. Shan had always cut to the chase. Now she struggled. She floundered between sorting out her own mistakes and debating what rights Aras and Ade had in this. They both looked at her, so transparently focused on her welfare that she hated herself with renewed vigor.

Yes, Aras too. His genes are as much a part of this thing as Ade's.

"I've had a few nasty surprises lately," she said. "I'll sort myself out in a few days. Look, give me those spuds and I'll take them back to the house."

"We've got enough for potato salad *and* a few chips," said Ade. "I know new potatoes make poor chips, but . . . well, *chips.*"

He grinned. He was artless and sincere, and she longed for the certain, old days when everyone she met was a bastard to be nicked and not to be trusted. She'd break his heart.

"I love you," she said. "Both of you. I don't say it enough."

That was all she could take right then. She turned and walked at race speed back to the city, where she couldn't get behind her own door fast enough to punch the wall in the washroom over and over again until she broke bones and her knuckles were raw and bleeding. She *wanted* to bleed because *c'naatat* always stopped the flow, and she was determined to beat the fucking thing just once, just *once.*

It hurt like hell and that was *fine.* She put her palms flat against the wall and let her head hang while she caught sobbing breaths. Her blood was vivid and ugly against the pale stone, far harder to clean off than she expected, but her hands were already whole again as if nothing had ever touched her.

She'd never be able to abort this fetus. *C'naatat* wouldn't let her.

It struck her that the last thing she had considered was what the child might have wanted if it could choose.

Bezer'ej: Bezeri settlement

Rayat was almost grateful for the revelation that there had once been other large aquatic species in the oceans of Bezer'ej.

It took his mind off the fact that he had no immediate way of getting off the planet. *Tough. The whole point is not to crack. This is about time. Time—you've got time, more than you can even count.* He'd come up with unexpected solutions in desperate situations so many times in the past that he had every confidence that he could do it again, and again, and again. He didn't have a deadline. And if his government had one, he neither knew it nor could he do anything about it. The trick of endurance was to concentrate on getting through the next moment and not look at the daunting length of the road ahead.

But the history of the bezeri wasn't just an artificial diversion to hang on to his sanity.

It mattered. For some reason, it *mattered.* If the bezeri had hunted another species to extinction, then what he'd done to them took on a whole new moral perspective. It also changed the context of what the isenj had done here. And that . . . *that* would put the wess'har in a very different position too. He was pretty sure he knew how they thought now.

"Hoist by your own petard," he said.

Lindsay, still and glassy, looked up from the azin shell map. "Me?"

"Them."

"Don't gloat. We don't know this for sure. Only that some species disappeared. Like that hasn't happened on Earth."

"Like *we* didn't make it happen on Earth."

"Does it make a difference?"

"Yes. It makes the bezeri far less blameless."

"Mohan, that's like saying Auschwitz or Rwanda or Nepal were justified because we killed the last tiger."

Nobody had called him Mohan for years. It startled him. He almost wondered who she was talking to. "I didn't say justified. Only less black and white." He looked at the long row of maps that he'd stacked like dishes on a draining board and decided to drill down. There were at least a

thousand now. "Help me out with this, will you? I want to
find the point at which these large animals disappeared.
These maps run from oldest to most recent. Start sampling
them at intervals from your end until you see this pictogram." He pointed to the symbol for the large animal, a
vivid blue oval striped with yellow lines. He wondered
what created the blue color: lapis deposits? The ovals
were on every one of the most ancient maps he'd seen so
far. "I'll do the same from the earliest end. Get cracking."

Rayat's spirits lifted. He liked tracking down information, hunting facts. Oh yes, he understood what drove Eddie
Michallat. There was a blind exhilaration in it and it almost
didn't matter what you found as long as you found it. Somehow the same mindset operated in him, and Eddie, and
Shan Frankland. Spies, journalists, detectives; all hunters,
all prone to feeding frenzies.

You could only truly hate others for showing you the
things you recognized in yourself.

They worked in silence except for the scrape and clack of
azin shell plates as they gradually moved towards each
other along the line of records. He forgot time. Eventually,
with his stomach growling for food, he pulled a sheet at a
ten-record interval and the blue ovals were nowhere to be
seen.

"Got it," he said. Lindsay stopped. "They're gone by this
period, I think."

She moved towards him and started pulling records at
shorter intervals, and then checked every one in a run of
twenty. She shook her head; that much of her was still very
human, Rayat thought.

"Nothing like that from this point on," she said. "I
haven't checked them all, but it doesn't look as if they reappeared. I mean, they might be—oh, extraplanetary for want
of a better word, like the wess'har."

"Either way," said Rayat, "they were here for a very long
time, and then they weren't, and their presence is linked
every time to the pictogram for *hunt*."

"Let's pin it down on the timeline, then."

They attacked the task with renewed vigor. Eventually, Rayat pulled a record with a blue oval, and Lindsay pulled the one ahead of it, and there were no more pictograms like it.

"Here's the end of the line," she said. "What's the date?"

Rayat was still tackling the detail of the timeline. The shell plates were marked with indentations that had probably been added afterwards at a point where the bezeri had adopted a kind of numerical dating system. But it was long before the wess'har arrived in the system, and long before the isenj colonized the planet; he took a guess at between 15,000 and 30,000 years ago.

"I'll ask Saib to check it for me," said Rayat, and put the shell record carefully inside his shirt. "And there are some pictograms I still can't understand. Time to ask a few questions."

Lindsay might have smiled at him. It was hard to tell with the increasing transparency of her face.

"Eddie would be proud of you," she said. "If he even knows you're alive."

F'nar, Wess'ej

Eddie leaned around the open door and knocked on it anyway. He always approached Shan with due caution.

"Hi," he said. "Holy shit. Why didn't you tell me Vijissi was alive? No, you're right. Stupid question. Like you wouldn't tell me if Lin or Rayat had a dose of *c'naatat* too."

Shan had never been a pretty woman but she usually appeared luminously fit, and her strong coloring and psychotic fixed gray gaze made her at least striking. But now she just looked ill. *No, stupid, she sucks vacuum for an encore. Ill doesn't happen to her.* He invited himself in and noted that she was scrubbing potatoes.

"So now you know he's alive, what are you going to do?" she asked.

She gave him a baleful look but something told him it was meant for someone else. He just happened to be in the line of fire.

"Same as I did when you survived. Say nothing. Don't you think I've learned my lesson?"

"You're forever polishing your conscience about what you should and shouldn't report, Eddie," she said. "How do I know when you're going to get all ethical about *c'naatat*?"

"At least tell me I'm not going mad and that I was right about the other two."

She paused. It looked as if she really wanted to concentrate on those potatoes and he was interrupting. "There was a good reason for it."

"You'd *never* have let that happen on your watch."

"I think you better stop right there."

Aras? Ade? They were the only two carriers who could have doled it out. Jesus, he was glad he wasn't in their shoes. But she'd seemed pretty affectionate with them; he couldn't begin to piece this together, and he shouldn't have tried, but old instinct made him yearn to pursue it.

It was a story. Stories made him tick. He fell into trying to coax it out of her without even thinking; and that wasn't the best approach with Shan. *She* asked the questions. Her police days might have been over, but she'd never left the interrogation room.

"It's Vijissi, isn't it?" He thought about offering to help her with the potatoes, but that wouldn't have worked either. "I know how badly you felt about him. But he did the big gesture of his own free will. Not your fault."

"You're not thick, Eddie. You know how serious the implications are of having another *c'naatat* on the books."

"The whole bloody ussissi colony is going to be in a tight spot."

"You always manage to make me feel better, you know that?" she said wearily. "Can you just fuck off for a while?"

"Who pissed in *your* corn flakes this morning?"

"Sorry. I decided I was getting too nice lately so I'm brushing up my bastard skills."

"You sure you're okay?"

"I'll live. Look, Vijissi is a pack animal who can't ever be part of a pack again. His clan won't go near him. They're upset, he's upset, the whole fucking ussissi mob is upset. I promised I'd be there for him and you know what? There's nothing a human female can do to help a ussissi kid who's a leper."

"Kid?"

"He's only just past the juvenile stage. I didn't realize that either."

"Oh shit."

"Yeah."

"Maybe he'll change like Aras did."

Shan turned very slowly. It was pure menace, and not for effect. He knew her well enough to see that savage violence when it was being tightly reined in: her face was a mask and her pupils set wide. Her eyes were such a pale gray that the sudden dilation to black changed her whole face.

"I don't like where that line of logic is heading," she said. The quieter her voice, the more scary she was. "So it stops. Now."

Good old Shan, good old honest and courageous Shan: but she could be the Shan you'd run and hide from, and hate too. Eddie felt his adrenaline start to pump. Maybe she'd had a fight with Aras. Ade wouldn't say a word out of line to her; he thought the sun shone out of her arse. So it *had* to be Aras. But they'd kiss, make up and be all over each other again in no time.

Eddie shifted tack. "Come on, let's go and find Vijissi."

Shan turned back to the sink and stared at the wet potatoes as if willing them to bake spontaneously. "Okay."

Eddie gave up trying to make small talk while they walked to Mestin's home on the opposite side of the caldera. Shan always knocked: wess'har found it hilarious for some reason. Sevaor opened the door and made an exaggerated come-in gesture.

"Vijissi?" he said.

"Is he okay?"

"No."

"Can we see him?"

"Ask him." It wasn't as abrupt as it sounded. Sevaor's English was limited, but it was polite of him to try to speak it in front of Eddie. "He does not talk to me."

Shan walked past Sevaor, and Eddie followed her down winding passages. Vijissi was curled up in a ball on the floor. There was no bed, just a typical alcove set in the wall: Eddie wondered how wess'har managed not to roll out of those holes when they fell asleep. Once their chambers reminded him of submarines lined with cramped bunks, but they seemed more like catacombs now.

"Hey, fella," Shan said. She squatted down and shook his shoulder. "It's okay. Want to talk? How'd you like to stay with us for a while?"

The ussissi opened his eyes. They really *did* look like roadkill now. *"Shan Chail."*

She leaned over and did something that only another *c'naatat* could risk with impunity. She nuzzled his sharp little meerkat face and even kissed his head. "I am so, so sorry. It must be hard seeing her like that. Whatever it takes to get you through this, I'll do it. *Whatever.*"

Eddie had never seen Shan display emotion quite that openly. He'd chipped the ice on the pond a few times and seen the angry bitch beneath, but sometimes he also caught a glimpse of a truly broken woman who'd seen too much and yet still kept going. Sometimes, though, she was actually affectionate in a way he found almost embarrassing, and he wasn't sure why.

"Let me die," said Vijissi. His voice was a whisper.

"No, mate, we're not going to let you die." Shan straightened up. "You're like us now. Now, I know that means—"

"You should have let me die." He was very clear. He uncoiled himself and sat back on his haunches. "Everything dies in time. Everything *should* die in time. They should have destroyed me. It's wrong. It's *wrong*."

"Vij, come on home with me. Nobody knows what you're going through better than Aras. He was on his own for centuries and he came through it."

"But he has you, and Ade."

"Yeah."

"Ussissi can't live alone. *Ever.* And I can have no children now. You think you're helping, but you're not." He didn't meet her eyes. "Please, leave me. We can talk later."

If Vijissi had spat at her, Shan couldn't have looked more crushed. Eddie wondered if she'd have felt so guilt-ridden about a human. Two legs was usually bad as far as Shan was concerned. He caught her sleeve and steered her away.

Shan paused and looked back at Vijissi as she left the room. "I won't pester you, but you know where I am. Anytime, okay?"

They ambled along the terrace back to her home. She thrust her hands deep in her pockets and said nothing.

"I thought they'd be more supportive of him," said Eddie.

"I don't understand them yet."

"They don't tolerate difference well."

"Funny how wess'har do."

"Just because they evolved together doesn't make them identical."

"Nah."

"Are you going to be okay, doll?"

"Funny thing to ask a *c'naatat*."

"You're not yourself."

"Shitty week all round. I'll survive."

She didn't ask Eddie to stay for lunch. He saw her safely inside—a weird thing, fretting over an immortal's welfare—and went back to the haven of his makeshift studio in Nevyan's tunnel-warren home.

Three more *c'naatat*, then. This was what Shan had dreaded: one, then three, then six, and where would it end?

And one of them was Mohan Rayat. That was something worth worrying about.

Bezer'ej: Bezeri settlement

Whatever mistakes the bezeri had made in their past didn't make Lindsay feel any less responsible for bringing them to the brink of extinction.

The last bezeri—forty-four now—were contemplating their slow decline and watching their species fade from the universe, a terminally ill patient forced to see the look on his doctor's face. *Should have used a bigger device and done a quick job.* She waited while Saib examined the azin shell record.

Rayat looked triumphant. She hoped it was simply that he enjoyed being a clever boy and finding things out. Somehow the idea that he thought it served the bezeri right was sickening.

"What does it mean, Saib?" he asked. His lights flashed and pulsed simultaneously with his speech like someone signing for a deaf person as they spoke. "Am I right about the dates?"

Saib's tentacles caressed the shell record, lifting it to the light and pulling it close to his eyes. *Eighteen thousand years ago. I could be more specific but I would need to consult another record to be certain.*

"And what does it mean?"

Explain.

"The blue ovals are another species, aren't they?"

Birzula.

"What happened to them?"

They were all killed, every last one of them.

Lindsay respected Saib's lack of euphemism. She waited for Rayat to frame his next question. So far, he was managing not to lead.

"Who killed them?"

We did.

"Ah . . . so if this pictogram means *hunt,* then I take it you hunted them to extinction." He paused and Lindsay felt it might be for effect, and the only person who could be affected by human speech tricks was her. *Bastard.* "They were your prey."

Saib suddenly became a rippling cascade of red and violet. *They were not our prey. They encroached on our hunting grounds and we found less to eat every year. They were too big, dirty and dishonest and stupid. We hunted them down and slaughtered them all so that they would never take our food again.*

Rayat actually leaned backwards a little as if he was taking a step away from the angry bezeri. Lindsay was stunned. She stepped in front of Saib, her lights pulsing.

You wiped them out deliberately, she said.

Yes.

Do you feel regret? She certainly did.

Never.

Is that because it was long before your time?

No. It was because they were inferior.

The answers were not what she expected. Rayat found his composure again.

"Saib, what happened to the other large animals in the ocean?" he asked. "We hunted a lot of ours. Whales, creatures like that. Did all yours become extinct?"

The food ran out.

Lindsay's image of the harmless bezeri struggling to survive against the carelessness of invading isenj and then the brutality of her own decision had taken a hell of a blow.

She needed to rethink things. Her tidy logic of cause and effect, crime and punishment, good and evil, had been shaken out of order. She needed to look at the pieces again. She swam back to the storage chamber and found herself cutting as cleanly through the water as a seal, without the slightest conscious effort. She settled down among the stacks of shell records and let the shock take her.

After a few minutes the entrance darkened and Rayat drifted slowly towards her. He came to rest against the intricately carved wall that she suddenly realized was an image glorifying the triumph of the bezeri over the rival birzula.

"Well done, Commander," he said. His expression had shifted a fraction from triumph—yes, he loved to nail down a story every bit as much as Eddie—to bitterness. "How does it feel to ride to the rescue of the Nazis?"

17

Unless we want to maintain a permanent garrison on Earth—and that will stretch us greatly, given the distance— we'll need to identify gethes *who can be taught to run their own affairs sustainably. From what you tell me of the Constantine colony, they seem very well suited for this. I think you should consider giving them governmental responsibilities when you reach Kamberra; Deborah Garrod strikes me as an ideal* isan *for the role.*

What are Christians, by the way? If they share this belief in an invisible guardian, they should work very well with the others who like this myth, like the Muslims.

CURAS TI,
senior matriarch of Surang,
in a message to Esganikan Gai

F'nar, Wess'ej

If you were pregnant, you couldn't get any more pregnant than you already were. But Shan didn't go to bed that night.

How do I tell them?

She couldn't face it. If she told Ade or Aras—especially Ade—then it would be not so much sharing a problem as dragging him into hers. She spent the night on the sofa, and hoped they thought she was fretting about Vijissi.

And it *was* a problem. Whatever she did would have an unhappy outcome sooner or later. There was no chance of her miscarrying: *c'naatat* didn't make that kind of mistake. It wanted its host to live. If it had learned to resist being removed from the host, then it wasn't going to give in easily.

She lay staring up at the ceiling and missing the days when a truly pitch-black night on Bezer'ej could summon up a light display from her optic nerve. That had been before she contracted *c'naatat*. The constant noise of wess'har in their warren homes reminded her of living too close to a bar with the constant nocturnal chorus of drunks. But eventually she dozed off.

Something touched her face and she sat bolt upright, smacking her forehead into something hard, heart pounding.

"Shit," Ade whispered. Her low-light vision and infrared picked him out: he had his hand to his nose. "Sorry—"

Poor bugger: he'd tried to kiss her. At least she hadn't pulled her gun, not that any damage would be lasting. "'S'okay. Did I break anything?"

"Nah." He knelt down next to the sofa and stroked her hair. "Is it me? What have I done?"

"Not you, love. Not Aras either. Go back to bed."

"Something's wrong. Come on. Tell Ade all about it."

"What's *not* wrong? War, invasion, Vijissi, genocide, the full Armageddon tour. If you see four blokes on horseback, tell them to fuck off."

"I don't even know where to start," he whispered. "But I'm here."

It just made it worse. Ade was a man who deserved to be a father; he'd be good at it. She had to tell him because this could only be his child, however impossible the whole thing looked. Aras, like all wess'har males, would see it as his too. The continual exchange of genes gave him a real stake in it. If they only hadn't all been *c'naatat*, she'd have accepted the situation without a second thought and made the best of it for Ade's sake. She was too old and too pissed off with the world and too far from good mother material to do it well, but she'd accept it.

If only. It wasn't a phrase she used often.

But it was the equivalent of three in the morning and her courage failed her. She'd work up to it, but not now.

"I'll never be angry with you again," she said. "You're a bloody saint. Don't let me forget it."

She noted that Aras hadn't attempted to coax her off the sofa. It wasn't that he didn't care. Wess'har males just knew when to leave *isan* to it.

Shan lay awake for another hour trying not to hear the sounds of wess'har leading lives denied to her. Given what she had that the rest of creation didn't—especially Vijissi— she felt petty and ungrateful. But her mind, which had once been uneasy at surrendering her body to the occupation of an unseen and unknown colony, was in turmoil at the presence of a real, definable, utterly unknown life in her. No primeval bond was there. No wondrous transformation or communion had taken place. She was just a woman who was pregnant despite her plans and precautions, and that brought her down to the level of Lindsay Neville.

She dozed off again. It was almost light when she opened her eyes and Aras's gardening tools were gone. He and Ade always made an early start on the crops; creatures of routine, just like her. She got up and prepared herself for a difficult day.

But difficult came in many forms, and she was far from the only person with problems.

Giyadas turned up at the door and remembered to knock, even though it was open.

"Shan, have you seen Vijissi?"

On Wess'ej, small children could wander cities safely on their own. The community was their parent, and they were miniature adults anyway. Shan felt a knot of proud affection form in her chest and then the realization that she was gestating one of *these,* an alien thing known as a child, crashed back down on her and killed the sensation.

"No, sweetheart," said Shan. "He didn't want to see me. I'm staying clear until he wants to talk."

"He's very unhappy."

"Perhaps he's gone to see his clan." *Some chance.*

"No, I checked."

"Ah." A note of concern had crept in. "Are you searching for him?"

"Yes. We all are. He got up this morning and left, and we haven't seen him since."

I did that kind of thing. Shan remembered being so fucked up by the idea of her condition that she'd sometimes withdraw to a deserted spot to mull it over for a few hours. It was on for months. Aras often pulled her out of it.

I did that kind of thing. She'd also dealt with a lot of *mispers,* missing persons, one of those bland little police terms that actually meant *abducted, murdered, drowned, had enough of the job, can't cope with the kids, sick of life.* So she knew how to organize a search.

"Tell you what, I'll come and help," said Shan.

It was what she needed. She found herself alone most mornings while Aras and Ade were tending the crops or whatever housebrothers did when she wasn't around. She usually liked her own company, but she didn't want it right now.

I'm pregnant. At my age. Minus a uterus, by a bloke who's been sterilized. Nobody can accuse me of being careless.

Giyadas sniffed as Shan pulled on her jacket and reached behind her back—pure muscle memory and old habit, nothing more—to check her gun was secure in the back of her belt.

"You're carrying an *isanket,*" said Giyadas. She sniffed again, head cocking left and right. "Why haven't you told us?"

After the stunned split-second had passed, Shan crashed into a trap of identification. *Isanket.* A little girl: Ade's daughter. The knowledge crushed her and for a few moments she wasn't sure how she would pull back her shoulders again and carry on as normal.

She suppressed her scent again. She always did when she went out. So wess'har females could smell a pregnant sister up close, and now she knew they could even spot the gender of the fetus: but then females were rare, outnumbered four or five to one by males, and it was probably useful for an *isan* to be able to spot a sister with that kind of cargo.

"Giyadas, this is important." Shan squatted down level with the kid and reminded herself that she had the subtlety and intellect of an adult. "I don't want anyone to know. Only Nevyan knows, and I haven't told Ade and Aras yet. Please don't mention this to anyone. You know what the implications are for people like me."

"Yes. I'll say nothing. I understand."

Yes, wess'har kids did. They even understood secretive, deceitful, inconsistent *gethes* like her.

"Thank you."

With the cocktail of genes she'd picked up from Aras and Ade via *c'naatat*—which seemed to be perfectly designed for transmission back and forth through *oursan*—she might have been carrying a little female that would be just like Giyadas.

As if I need this to be any harder than it already is.

"Off you go," said Shan ushering Giyadas ahead of her. "We'll find him. Don't worry."

Don't worry.

It was the kind of terrain that was a pain in the arse if you were doing a door-to-door search. F'nar was a maze of tunnels and alleys, but there were no woods or bodies of water to comb, so Shan took a section along the western edge of the broken caldera, Giyadas at her side.

It felt comfortable.

Don't get used to this.

It ambushed her. She'd always been repelled by human kids, not just unmoved. Alien infants—like animals, like *anything* that wasn't the self-obsessed, destructive, lying, violent apology for a monkey—slipped under her radar. They were clean. She could cope with a Giyadas Mark II. This wasn't the end of the world. She had no idea how she'd deal with it, or how any of them would handle the problems, *eternal* problems, that went with it, but if it had to happen then it could be *dealt with*.

It was tidy coppers' talk: *Who's dealing?* Whose case was this, who had the files, who did she have to liaise with about this incident? All were distilled down to *who's dealing*. Language, even in her thoughts, helped put some cool distance into the process.

She showed Giyadas the ropes. She taught her how to check in with the search team and how to look for things that might not be seen from certain angles, and how to be systematic so you didn't miss anything. It was probably obvious to a wess'har, but it felt natural and rewarding to do it anyway. It was *enjoyable*.

Her swiss chirped. Since the ITX had been fitted, she could link to wess'har networks, and she felt a lot more in control. It was Mestin.

"Shan Chail, we've found him."

Her stomach flipped. Her mind defaulted to securing the scene for forensics and informing next of kin. She assumed *dead*. "Alive?"

"But he's in the armory below and he has—"

Everything should die in time. You didn't need to be a detective to work that out. "He's holed up, hasn't he? He's going to do something stupid."

"I shall talk to him."

"You keep him talking, nice and calm, and I'll be right there."

Shan broke into a jog, Giyadas at her side, and she found now that she could even run down the steep steps that linked one level of terraces to those below. She'd fallen down steps a few times in her regular human days when she was in pursuit on foot. Come to that, some of her prisoners had a habit of falling down stairs, too. She missed the clean certainty of those days: guilty and not guilty, law-abiding and villain.

The less attractive industrial side of F'nar—the workshops, utility plant and warehousing—lay buried in tunnels that ran for kilometers beneath the caldera. Shan reached the chambers that housed F'nar's very old but thoroughly efficient defense hardware and saw there was a small group of *isan've* with Mestin and Sevaor.

Mestin was trilling very softly. Shan could hear her telling Vijissi on the other side of the blast-proof safety doors that he would be cared for and that he had nothing to fear.

The negotiation was taking place over her *virin*.

Shan could hear Vijissi's voice.

"I know I have nothing to fear. I am perfectly calm."

Giyadas went to her grandmother's side. Shan had a completely random thought; as all Nevyan's family was adopted when their *isan* died, then there were other grandmothers, genetic ones, *ten* of them out there somewhere. Then she snapped back to the present. She held out her hand for the *virin*.

"Mestin, can I talk to him?"

The matriarch cocked her head. "You understand better than I do how he feels at this moment."

"Probably," said Shan. "But apart from the fact that I got him into this mess, I'm also trained to deal with suicide attempts."

By six-legged alien meerkats? You stupid bitch. Listen to yourself. You're just trying to save the day again. You're addicted to it. Anything rather than face your own problem.

Mestin handed her the *virin* and she took it anyway. She could have used the swiss. But it paid to use one dedicated channel, without interruptions. People who were close to killing themselves could be spooked by multiple voices breaking in. It was receiving audio only.

One voice. One reassuring voice: one friend.

"It's Shan, mate." She listened for clues from the ambient sound. *Best voice, okay? All calm.* Suddenly her pregnancy seemed unimportant. "Want to talk?"

Pause. A click and a rustle. "If I talk, this will be harder for me."

"Nobody wants to make it harder, Vijissi. But if I say I know what you're going through, you know that's true. Don't you?"

"Yes."

"I know what you've *been* through, too. You and me. We're the only ones who know what it's like. And I'm fine now."

"I'm glad. I'm not fine." *Click, rustle.* "I know you want to help, but I've given this much thought and I know what Targassat would counsel."

Some ussissi were actively Targassati in outlook. They didn't just fit in with wess'har society, they embraced it. And Shan knew Targassat well enough—by reading her essays, anyway—to know that she wouldn't have welcomed *c'naatat*. It was anathema. It was imbalance and excess.

"Vijissi, you've got a weapon in there of some sort?"

"This is an armory."

"Yeah, but shooting yourself won't work. Ade emptied a clip into me. No permanent damage. So maybe it's time to have a talk about it out here. Trust me, it looks a lot better if you take a bit of time and get used to it."

"I have a *fragmentation* device. I learned what would kill and not kill us by seeing you shot, on more than one occasion, actually."

He'd been there when Shan had pulled the pin on a grenade and held the catch down to force Chayyas to release Aras. Shit, she'd taught him how to kill himself properly.

She switched tack. "Yeah, but you'll just injure yourself with that and get pissed off if you don't place it right. Look, it's not going to do the job. Put it down and let me tell you about Shapakti."

She could do this. It was a basic copper's task. *Talk them down. Get them of the roof. Put the gun down. There's nothing so bad that it can't be sorted out, son.*

"Who's Shapakti?"

Got him. "He's an Eqbas scientist I know. We can deal with that. The Eqbas can even remove *c'naatat* from some species. One day they'll find a way of doing that for you." *Liar, liar, liar.*

"And if they cannot?"

"We're your friends. We'll take care of you."

He was horribly calm. He'd worked this out. God knows he'd had enough time to think about it and nothing else: and it was one thing to calm a person on the knife edge where they still weren't sure if they were ready to die or not, but quite another to persuade someone who wasn't panicking.

"*Shan Chail,* this is the way *c'naatat* will spread—a concession here, a concession there. I will be one more potential vector. How many more? First there was only Aras. How many now?"

Oh God. I know he's right. Rayat and Lindsay. Who's next? My child. Vijissi was as good as miles from her. She couldn't even grab him, or blow the blast doors and take the decision out of his hands.

*Hands. Jesus holy shit I called them hands for once and
not paws and—*

"You never thought you were a kind person," Vijissi said
softly. "But you are. And you mustn't blame yourself for
what was an accident."

"Vijissi—"

He hadn't taken any notice when she stood at the airlock
and told him not to follow her.

He never did listen to her.

The line fell silent and she hoped it was just a pause before he carried on talking, but the light in the *virin* had gone
out. A muffled boom shook the doors and a little dust rained
down from the roof of the lobby.

Vijissi never spoke another word.

18

These people want an artificial world, not a natural one. Our people have always lived by hunting and managing our natural resources with restraint and respect. It's an insult for the animal welfare lobby to seek to impose a new world order of vegetarianism on indigenous peoples, especially as it's their host culture that seems to be the one that's had the most adverse impact on global ecology. Stuffing yourself with soybeans doesn't give you the moral high ground. This is a theme park mentality.

IRNIQ SATAA,
indigenous person and Canadian Peoples' spokesman,
in response to suggestions that animal welfare groups and
vegetarians would lobby Eqbas Vorhi to end the
use of food animals

Maritime Fringe/Northern Assembly border, Umeh: crossroads bomb site

"It's been years since I covered a tree-planting," said Eddie. "And never in a bomb crater."

Crater was overstating the case, but the patch of cleared land was definitely concave if you looked at it carefully. The bee cam made a sedate circling movement around the perimeter like a circus horse, pausing at the end of the lap to take static shots. The only thing missing was the great and the good of local society, jostling for their moment of screen time. The isenj who had gathered to watch were there to see, not to be seen. The fighting had died down: there were skirmishes on the border, but the uneasy cease-fire was holding.

Minister Rit had never planted a tree before. She fumbled with the spade, which was more like an apple corer, and eventually Eddie did it for her. He found the image unpleasant in a way he couldn't pin down; a subjugated people playing happy for the media, except the isenj weren't subjugated, and Rit wanted to do it, and there was no media opportunity in it for anyone except him.

"Minister Rit thanks you," said Ralassi. "She adds that Ual would have been amused by the spectacle."

"You should expand this into a park and name it after him."

When you've cleared a few more isenj out of the way, of course.

Esganikan insisted on being there. Eddie thought it was insensitive given how the land had been cleared, but she was fixed on her mission and she wanted isenj to see a tree in real soil, and focus on what their restored and remediated and Eqbas-approved planet could look like.

The explosion had ripped out paving and exposed dark chocolate soil. Somehow Eddie expected it to be light ochre, an unhealthy pallor befitting a natural world that hadn't seen sunlight in a long, long time. The isenj were fascinated by it, and some of them scraped it with their footpads or lowered themselves to reach down and crumble it between their hands. Food plants grew in nutrient-laden water; the thousand different fungi that isenj cultivated grew in vats and on barklike medium. Earth was a novelty and they seemed to relish getting their hands dirty.

They have hands. Sod zoological accuracy. I have hands, so they do too.

"They say they recall this," said Ralassi. The isenj were excited, chirping and almost squealing as they tottered around on bare soil. Whatever it meant to them, it was far more than any human dependent on word of mouth or memoirs could ever understand. If they could recall past military glories from their ancestors, then they could also remember what it felt like to cultivate soil; and this was more than human nostalgia. It was reliving the experiences of their ancestors, as vivid and personal as it had been for the long-dead.

Eddie saw their attachment to their colonies in a new light. This might have been how it felt to stand on Bezer'ej, and recall a time when it was called Asht, before the first wess'har had arrived in the Cavanagh system. If a familiar smell or song could catapult a human into the past, he wondered how much more intense genetic memory was for an isenj.

Shan said it was like being that person for a few moments. Eddie could see it was both blessing and curse.

"I've learned something," he said.

"They are resilient people."

"Damn, you'd have to be." The bee cam followed him like a beggar. "Now you've planted it, who's going to look after it?"

Isenj didn't have a good record on horticulture. Ralassi indicated an isenj festooned in dark pink beads who was taking a keen interest in the leaves. There seemed to be a queue forming.

Eddie wanted an aerial shot, a pull-out from the tree that gradually took in the wide shot and showed that the impromptu mini-arboretum was in the middle of a battle wasted neighborhood. It took two attempts but the bee cam returned with a rather poignant shot that made Eddie wonder if he was overdoing the symbolism.

He had no idea of the death toll. He could calculate the area devastated, and the population density, and come up with numbers—a hundred thousand, fifty million, a billion; but like all statistics, that told him far less than the shattered buildings or eerily untouched but empty streets scented with decaying bodies.

It really wasn't much of a tree at all. Botanists might have argued about its taxonomy, but it looked more like a cycad than anything, and as far as Eddie was concerned, any long-lived plant was a tree.

He thought of the dead. "Was it worth it for a tree?"

Esganikan's pupils were black flowers and her head was tilted to take in the scene in as much detail as possible.

"Ask the tree," she said.

F'nar Wess'ej: Nevyan's home

Eddie leaned back as far as he dared in his rickety square
box of a chair and watched the transmissions for a while:
Europe, Pacific Rim, Sinostates, Americas. There used to be
a cam feed from Mars Orbital, but it was gone now.

When he paged the data, it showed him a report—ten
years old—saying that the station had been shut down in a
cost-cutting exercise because the pharmacorps who were its
main users refused to pay the rental.

"Balls," he said. He'd never seen Mars Orbital, even though
he'd passed through there on *Thetis*. He'd been chilled down
at the time. It gave him a pang of regret.

But it was time to talk to Jan, duty news editor in Mick's
absence. He rolled the bee cam across the table like a
snooker ball and it righted itself to focus on him.

It must have been about two AM in the newsroom. Jan was
clearly a night person because she looked chirpily alert, and
that wasn't hard when you were a child—which was what
twenty-something seemed to Eddie right then. A few years
on 'Desk would knock that out of her.

"Hi, Eddie," she said. "Sorry we've not been running
your stuff, but it won't be wasted."

He still hated the few seconds of delay while the signal
crawled between the instantaneous ITX node and the final
light-speed relay to Earth. *Hey, you used to think delays
were normal, remember? Don't take ITX for granted.* "It's
not like I'm going anywhere."

"What have you got for us?"

"I'd run through my possibles but I don't think you're going to want them, are you?"

"Everyone's gone off the hurricanes now. Back on to the
new cold war."

"FEU and . . . ?"

". . . everyone. Except the Americas are staying silent.
We're waiting for the Sinostates to formally condemn FEU
pressure on Australia and the rest of the Australasian states

have put their reserve forces on standby. Statement expected soon."

"Agenda?"

"What, apart from objecting to aliens landing in the front garden?"

"Jan, there's nothing anyone can do about that. If they think they can, they're dangerously stupid. If they've worked that out, the leverage is about resources or trade territory or access to Antarctica. Sod all to do with aliens."

"I'm not sure their threat analysis ties in with yours."

"Didn't I send you some images down the line? You know, the Eqbas Vorhi boot-boys on tour? Coming to a star system near you?" He rubbed his forehead. Did they think he was making this up? He hadn't even sent her all the pictures. If she'd seen the recent stuff . . . but isenj getting killed wouldn't, bring it home. "And I sent you a big piece about the civil war on Umeh just to illustrate what's coming down the road. Jan, they *erase* cities. You have no idea. I showed you the pictures. What part of *blown off the map* does the government not understand?"

"Probably the bit that says it won't happen on their watch." She was tapping a screen to one side of her. "And maybe the bit that says surely something will turn up before then."

"They'll need fucking Captain Atlantis, then. With an upgrade to his superpowers."

"Okay, give me a doomsday piece."

"Oh yeah. Like that's going to help the situation."

"We're not about helping, we're about informing."

Silly little cow. I was doorstepping ministers before your mother was born. "Thank you for clarifying that."

"Tell you what I *would* be interested in, though, Eddie. We've got this row brewing between the Greens and the indigenous peoples about life after the Eqbas arrive. They both stand to gain from environmental restoration, but they're fighting over eating meat."

"Wow, the cookery slot." No, it was a pivotal point: because Earth didn't seem to realize how serious wess'har and their cousins were about not eating your neighbors. The attitude to species was at the core of the conflict. "Okay. Maybe an interview with Esganikan Gai, the mission commander."

"Didn't you have the undead eco-terrorist cop on your patch?"

"Frankland?"

"I'm assuming they don't come in multiples."

"Yes." *Shit, shit, shit. I can't tell them she's alive. I did the story saying she spaced herself and how fucking brave she was. I filed it before I knew she'd survived, or I'd never have mentioned her c'naatat at all. Shit.* "What did you have in mind?"

"Her name cropped up a few times in the last few weeks. Some Greens regard her as a martyr to the cause."

"She spaced herself." That was inarguable. "It doesn't get much more heroic than that."

"Well, it might make a nice piece. I mean, I looked at the archive. The Green legend is that she went native when she was a counterterrorism officer, helped some militant treehuggers evade arrest, and took the fall for it. Better to be busted for incompetence than criminal charges, I suppose."

Now, how many people knew that? Green Rage must have kept notes. And she'll kill me if I use that name.

"So I heard."

"Is it true?"

"It fits her M.O., but she would never confirm that on the record—or off it." He swallowed. "I got to know her pretty well and she struck me as the most competent copper I'd ever met."

"Real martyr, then."

"Very committed, our Shazza." *You have no idea.* "You want to step out an airlock and see what martyrdom feels like? And she . . . was very adept at not answering questions."

"What if I can get a Green to stand up the story?"

"It'll mean nothing without documentation. It happened more than eighty years ago."

"She's dead. She isn't going to sue you."

I swore I'd never say she helped out Green Rage. Does it matter now? Maybe not, except that I promised her.

Eddie rubbed his forehead. "I can do a piece on her. She . . . I liked her. For all the nasty violent side of her, she had a streak of really unshakeable decency. She became very committed to the wess'har too."

"How about the colonists, the Christians? Did she find God?"

"If she did, it's only because he never paid his parking fines." Where was Jan going with this? He hated news editors who tried to fit the story to the gap in the news agenda. She looked like a woman who wanted a god-bothering, god-fearing angle on a story that was actually about humans being on borrowed time. Yes, like Barencoin had said, the Second Coming: the religious crazies were cranking up on Earth, doing a bit of wailing about the Eqbas and Armageddon or Judgment Day or salvation, according to taste. *Fuck you, lady, I don't do infotainment.* "Tell you what. Let me get you an interview with Commander Gai, and maybe even Curas Ti, the . . . well, Eqbas defense minister for want of a better word. Tell you what—let me send you a nice little package, saying behold what the Eqbas did to other planets, and what they're doing now on Umeh, and what's heading your way in thirty years. You'd better break out the toilet tissue, because it's fucking scary. And you *had* that material and didn't run it."

Jan stared back at him, flipping her stylus over and over between her fingers as if she was twirling a baton. It simply reinforced his view of her—perhaps unfairly—as a perky, girlie little cheerleader. It was a shame he couldn't let Shan loose on her, because she'd have disemboweled the kid with her first sour word.

"It's going to have consequences."

Uh-oh. Chicken, chicken, chicken. Loss of bottle imminent. "You still being monitored by the ministry?"

"Not since the UN took over the ITX access from them."

"Wouldn't make any difference. You can't hide this for long."

"We had some serious riots after the last piece you filed on Eqbas Vorhi."

"Whoa, I'm responsible? Maybe I am, and I know it could happen again, but what do I do? Let everyone think it'll be like that old movie? The one with the robot where the alien stops the world?"

"The Day The Earth Stood Still."

"Whatever. I've seen this firsthand. I've been in an Eqbas warship when it took out a city. It's not a special effect. People need to know that."

Jan seemed to be losing her nerve. Eddie was suddenly aware that he was leaning forward, arms braced on the table as he stared at the bee cam's red focus light. *Why am I doing it? Nobody on Earth can do a bloody thing about this. It'll just cause panic. Why can't I get this straight in my head like I used to?* He had an urge to discuss it with Shan first.

He could still tell her. He had to. She needed to know he wasn't blabbing about Lindsay and Rayat. He could repair some of the damage he felt he'd done, or at least not make matters worse.

Jan stopped twirling her stylus. "Okay. Let's do it. We can package it with the Greens saying ecological judgment day is at hand, and that Inuit guy arguing with the meat-is-murder lobby."

"Lovely," said Eddie. "Would you like a bit on a tree planting too?"

Her face was set hard now; unamused, and with that look that said she was trying to work out how to assert her authority over an older and unimpressable seen-it-all hack. "Pardon?"

"Umeh got its first tree. They cut down the people and planted trees. You have to admit that's a change from chopping down forest to make room for people. First tree in an open space for centuries."

She looked wary. "Okay." Long pause. "Are you okay, Eddie?"

"I'm doing fine," he said. "Can you find out something

for me? Is Graham Wiley still alive? Used to have a big science 'cast when I left Earth. I'd love to know."

Jan nodded, looking relieved. She was expecting something harder. "Will do."

Eddie wondered if the Eqbas had a parallel with this kind of predigested, cartoonized, simplified schematic of political complexity. He knew they didn't. He had no idea how he would explain it to Esganikan, or Curas Ti if she'd spare him the time.

He rolled the bee cam in his hands like a worry ball and longed for clarity of purpose and ambition for the future.

But there was one lonely tree on Umeh now. That had to count for something.

F'nar plain, Wess'ej

Vijissi had known the right thing to do all along. He shamed her: and shame galvanized you if you set yourself a rigid, inevitable moral code.

Shan didn't head for the butte this time. Everyone knew that if she wasn't in the city, then she'd be there. She headed further out into the plain where there were more outcrops of rock honeycombed with caves and fissures. She was looking for somewhere to hide for a time.

C'naatat wouldn't surrender the fetus to drugs, and if it could keep her alive in cold space, it could do anything. Fragmentation was all she could count on.

Keeping the grenades had been a good idea.

Every girl needed a grenade. And she had her swiss, a sturdy metal box, and a backpack stuffed with fabric, dressings and a sharp blade.

You did this before, remember? You go to ground. You lay up somewhere and turn feral.

When she suspected Aras had infected her with *c'naatat* back on Bezer'ej, she'd found a hide out in the wilds and cut her hand to see if she would heal fast and clean. She did. She'd wanted to rip Aras apart for doing it to her without telling her.

She'd ended up raging at him and even yanking him across the room by his hair in her grief for a robbed existence.

Now he'd have every right to do the same to her, and so would Ade. She was going to abort the child she carried; Ade's daughter, laced with a good proportion of Aras's genes as well. And she hadn't told either of them.

Okay, who went off in a rage when they found out about Lin and Rayat? You did, you hypocritical bitch. If Ade or Aras forgives you after this, you have *to change.*

She made a conscious decision to stop thinking of the fetus as a daughter, there and then. She stripped it of identity to get the job done. If she didn't do that right now, she'd end up giving it a name and then it would all be so much, much harder.

Shan knew she split into two personas at times like this, and the one that had the upper hand was Detective Superintendent Frankland, unshockable and robotic, the kind of copper who relished using fist and baton, and who ate her sandwiches watching postmortems while other officers threw up or fainted. She was granite: nobody could even scratch her.

The persona that the Superintendent was hauling along by its collar for a nice little chat in a soundproofed cell was a woman called Shan who dreaded the pain awaiting her, was guilt-racked by the pain she would cause two good, kind men, and wasn't sure she could live with herself afterwards.

The really useful thing about paying attention at postmortems was that you got to know where organs were almost as well as a surgeon. And she knew what they looked like when the deceased were flat on their back. Soft organs spread and settled. Besides, if she pressed hard enough with her fingers, she could now feel the uterus, a brand new one that *c'naatat* decided she was missing.

I should have known. I should have seen it coming.

Speed mattered. If she dithered, she'd chicken out. She found a sheltered spot; the crevice in the rock went back about three meters and was big enough to hide in. And there were pieces of rock she could make use of.

There'll be a bit of blood, but you have to get a move on to stop the thing healing you up too fast.

She'd run through the sequence in her mind so many times in the last few hours that she'd reduced it to a few strokes, like being a surgeon in the old days.

No anesthesia. Speed, speed, speed. Don't lose your nerve. You can't die. You can't get it wrong and lose the patient.

She spread a piece of felted *efte* on the floor of the cave and stripped off her pants. *Speed. Don't even think. See in 3-D. Top of the uterus is near the navel. Don't think* my *navel,* my *uterus. Top of pubic bone: here.*

One, two, three.

It was true what they said about suicides: they made a few experimental cuts before the big one. She flinched at the first and then went all out. The truly odd thing was that the pain went from off the scale, enough to stop her breathing for a second, to a distant screaming there-but-not-there near-nothing. *What's it called? Latin for anesthesia by injury. Fuck you,* c'naatat, *you can't close this wound oh my God I never knew it was so hard to cut flesh and it's a mess and it's so so* so *bloody hard and I daren't let go now—*

Screaming had always been beyond her. She could hear herself going *ah-ah-ah* in panting shock and her hand held something far smaller than she imagined, an organ the size of a fist. She let it drop and instinct made her curl up in a tight ball with her arms folded tight to her belly.

"You bastard useless thing," she sobbed. "All because I looked at Giyadas, and you thought you were doing me a favor? Don't do it again, don't, don't, *don't* . . ."

C'naatat might have been listening. It was worth a try.

The pain flooded back like sound when you opened a window and the moment was pure animal madness. After a while—two minutes, two hours, who gave a shit anyway—she sat up afraid to look. She'd seen enough crime scenes. Superintendent Frankland told her to get a grip and get on with it. There was surprisingly little blood around for an abdominal incision by an amateur because *c'naatat* was very practiced at stopping blood loss.

I won't even have scars. Isn't that ironic?

She didn't look at the piece of meat that had once been her. She didn't want to think what might be in there, either. She set the delay on the grenade, put it in the box with her conscience and piled slabs of loose stone on top.

Directs the blast downwards, contains it, concentrates it. Makes certain. You've seen enough bomb injuries to know that you don't always end up with a pile of hamburger.

Shan walked out of the cave and got clear. Five, four, three, two . . .

If anyone heard, that was too bad. She waited for the dust and smoke to clear and checked the aftermath; a decent blaze was devouring the stained *efte* and the box was shrapnel. She waited for it to burn itself out and checked again.

Job done.

She walked home.

19

*You have clearance to land at the Temporary City. Da Sha-
pakti's survey team reports that the bezeri remnant has settled to the south of Ouzhari and will help you locate them if
you need assistance. Please return the* niluy-ghur *on com-
pletion of your task.*

Message from ESGANIKAN GAI, Temporary City,
to Shan Frankland

Bezer'ej: Bezeri settlement

"Funny how the moral high ground tends to flatten out at
times like this, isn't it?" said Rayat.

It was increasingly hard to spot the subtleties of expression on Lindsay's face now, but her light display seemed to
be taking its place. If *c'naatat* was stimulated by the brain
chemistry of its host to carry out its remodeling jobs, as he
suspected, then Lindsay had chosen an interesting species
with which to fit in.

He refused to believe *c'naatat* granted wishes. His ride
home hadn't arrived, anyway.

"Their views might be repellent, but that doesn't make
them guilty of a genocide that happened thousands of years
ago," she said.

"But they still approve of it."

"They know *nothing* about it except what they've read in
their records, and neither do we." She was suffused with a
fine shade of royal blue now: that meant she was sad rather
than angry, despite the noises she was making. "And it still
doesn't make them responsible for what their ancestors did,
and it certainly doesn't justify what *we* did here. If they met
a birzula now, they'd . . . anyway, you can educate people

out of those prejudices. Racial attitudes on Earth changed over centuries, so why not here?"

"Well, Professor, Earth history doesn't appear to be your subject, does it? What a load of crap. Humans are as bigoted as they've ever been. It's hard wired. It's part of the tribal bonding instinct."

"You're so arrogant."

"I've so been on the receiving end of bigotry. Remember my name?"

"I think this is called passive-aggressive behavior. Perhaps even martyrdom."

"You're going to really miss that mouth of yours when it evolves away completely."

The argument was pointless. Whatever motivated Lindsay to be here wasn't what motivated him. All he knew now was that he wanted to go home, that he felt liberated somehow, and that he was suddenly very anxious to find Aras Sar Iussan and tell him just how his precious bezeri had become the only sentient species on Bezer'ej.

Why?

He felt that wess'har would change as a result of what they knew. He didn't see denial as one of their failings. He supposed he didn't want the bezeri to get away with it, whatever *it* had been.

"Do you feel duped?" he asked.

"Let's say I don't feel comfortable," said Lindsay. "But I helped kill bezeri, so I still owe them. A whole species can't be evil."

"I wish people would talk in terms of *risk* instead of religious concepts."

"There are forty-four of them left. That's all. Their genocide doesn't excuse ours."

Rayat had forgotten how well sound traveled in water. Saib and Keet appeared at the entrance to the chamber, red and green and curious. Without the translation lamp, they didn't have a clue what the argument was about. All they knew was that Lindsay was blue and upset. There was a great deal to be said for being bilingual, Rayat decided.

Why have you stopped collating records?

"We're arguing about responsibility," said Rayat.

It is your job.

"Not that kind of responsibility."

I do not understand.

Rayat wondered if it was the scale of the trauma he was going through, but he felt he was abandoning all his professional control. An impulsive intelligence agent tended to have a short career.

"I'm trying to work out how you can play the victims of the isenj when you did the same thing to another species—except you did it deliberately, and recorded it as an event in your glorious past." Something welled up out of him from nowhere. Was it his emotion or someone else's? "I hope you rot in hell, actually. I *wasted* remorse on you. You're the very last of your kind, and you deserve oblivion."

Rot translated, but he wasn't sure that hell had any meaning. But survivors like these knew what wishing them decomposition meant.

Saib hung there for a moment. Keet edged backwards. From their unlit silent reaction, Rayat guessed that his outburst was beyond their experience. It certainly would have been if the only off-worlders who spoke to them were the wess'har.

"Did you ever tell Aras Sar Iussan about your track record in war crimes?" No, that was beyond them. He didn't actually have a light signal for *war crimes*. "Did you tell him your people killed off their neighbors?"

We never discussed our history beyond the time when the wess'har came to the system.

"Well, we Cro-Magnons don't usually have a public guiltfest about the Neanderthals, either," said Lindsay. But that was for him, not for them. "And we still killed the bezeri. We owe them. *I* owe them."

None of these concepts could possibly make sense to the bezeri. But Rayat felt better for venting.

"I'm going," he said suddenly.

The announcement surprised even him. His carefully planned, scrupulously rational self had taken a break. They couldn't kill him: and he didn't owe them anything. He was walking out of here, or at least going above water where he could stay human and sane until help came. It was astonishing how humans complied with their jailers and would stay put even when they could leave.

We all follow each other, and if we can't find anyone to fit in with we'll go looking for them. Monkey, monkey, monkey.

He pushed past Saib, and found that the bezeri patriarch was as solid and as heavy as a horse. He hadn't actually touched one of them before.

You will come back.

"Of course I will." Rayat swam slowly at first and then picked up speed.

"You've got nowhere to go, you bastard," Lindsay called after him. "Nobody's coming for you, and the Eqbas will frag you when they catch you."

She didn't chase him. Not even the bezeri attempted to stop him. There really was nowhere to go.

Rayat wasn't going to let that stop him.

After a while he touched bottom and straightened up. It was a relatively short walk to Ouzhari—not a swim, a *walk,* because he was a human being—and he knew the Eqbas were still working in the area. All he had to do was sit on the shore until they showed up again, and give them an interesting history lesson.

He was going to breathe air again.

And he didn't feel guilty any longer. It was only the absence of it now that made him realize how heavily it had weighed on him when he gave himself the time to wallow in it.

He finally felt the offshore current and began rising up the slope that ended in white sand that he had blackened with cobalt bombs, and reached inside his shirt to check that the azin shell records were still there.

F'nar, Wess'ej

"I'm happy to do it for you, Boss." Ade leaned on the doorframe, arms folded, and not entirely convinced that he *hadn't* done anything wrong. "Are you really going through with this?"

He slipped his arms around her waist and pressed his pelvis against her. He was still at the stage of the relationship where he found sex an irresistible novelty—and she'd been sleeping on the sofa for the last week.

She rubbed the back of his hand and eased herself away from him. A week ago she couldn't leave him alone. Something had happened. Aras thought she was taking Vijissi's suicide badly, but Ade knew he'd failed her somehow. She was being extra kind, not angry. But she wouldn't let either of them touch her.

"Just tell me what's wrong. Please?"

Shan took out a shirt and folded it again a slightly different way. She'd packed her grip three times and didn't seem to be aware she'd done it.

"Nothing you've done, Ade. Absolutely nothing." At last she fastened the bag and stood staring down through it, unseeing, with her fists on her hips. "Actually, sweetheart, would you come to Bezer'ej with me? Both of you. I really don't want to be on my own at the moment."

He brightened immediately. He was back in favor again. "Anything. Absolutely anything. Just say the word."

"I've got to finish the job. Rayat and Lin. If I don't . . . well, it makes a mockery of Vijissi. Not that it's the main motive, but he shamed me."

"Aras and I can do it. You don't have to."

"Oh, I do. I *do*."

"I'm not that stupid, you know."

Her head jerked up. *C'naatat* didn't do a thing to disguise that look in her eyes, her focus on a point of nothing a few meters behind him. He'd seen that on plenty of his mates after combat. "I need to talk to you and Aras. And I know that afterwards you're both going to question what the

hell you see in me." She nodded towards the door. "Go and
call him in, and make a pot of tea. Please."

Ade's mouth dried instantly and his throat, stomach and
thigh muscles filled with cold water. It was different to
physical danger: it was worse, because there was no way of
firing back at it or running. Aras, frozen in apprehension,
sat next to him on the sofa and Shan stood with her backside propped on the edge of the table, arms not so much
folded across her chest as hugging herself.

They waited.

"Shall I blurt this out?" she said. "Okay, you've spotted
that I haven't been very physical with you two the last week
or so. Thing is, I've—" She stopped and punctuated what
she seemed to be thinking with little emphatic stabs of her
clenched fist, gaze fixed on the wall. "I found I was pregnant but I'm not pregnant any longer. And I'm sorry, but I
couldn't see another solution."

It took a few seconds for Ade's brain to process the
words. *What do I say? How can that have happened? Is
it—was it—Aras's?*

Aras didn't move a muscle and he stared at Shan the way
he always did.

"Please, I know you're going to hate me for not talking to
you about it." Her voice switched suddenly into the Shan
she always used to be, briefing the payload, putting Rayat in
his place, taking no shit. "Hypocrite, after what I said about
you two not consulting me? Yes. Guilty as fuck, because I
know both of you would be willing dads? Yes. How do we
go on now? No idea. Your turn."

Aras found his voice first. "This child was Ade's, yes?"

"Can't be yours, Aras. Wrong dick." When she slipped
into total callous cop-speak, Ade knew she was struggling
to maintain control. "I should have known. Christ, if this
thing can keep me alive in vacuum, then rebuilding a uterus
is going to be a piece of piss for it. Or Ade's plumbing,
come to that."

Ade swallowed. It was far too early for him to begin to
take it in emotionally so he moved on to logistics. He had a

vague idea how terminations were carried out; but he couldn't imagine how Shan had managed it. *C'naatat* didn't yield to drugs.

It didn't yield to anesthetic, either.

If she had cried or asked for sympathy, he would have known the motions to go through. But she didn't. It was like dealing with a wounded oppo. He slipped into jollying her along, pretending things would be all right, just as he was praying they would be.

"I'm sorry, love," he said. "I'm so sorry. This is all my fault."

"Nah." She shook her head. She sounded as casual as if she was disagreeing about a soccer game. She put her hand to her mouth for a brief moment and then jerked herself back into the unshockable copper again. "It was the only option. Really. It was. Vijissi was right."

Her voice was coming from a long way away now. Ade fought to stay expressionless. "It's okay, Boss. I understand. Are you all right?" *Tell me. Tell me what you did to yourself.* "Oh God I wish you'd told me. Oh God."

"It's done," said Aras. "You don't have to explain why, because I know. And I would still have loved to have a child. And I can't hate you for that."

"Okay," she said. "And we need to avoid a recurrence. So I'm going to see if Shapakti has any ideas. He's the *c'naatat* biologist now. So until then, maybe it's better that we just hold hands. Okay? Do you understand what I mean?"

It was like listening to a wash-up after an exercise: things they did right, things they needed to do better next time, and what would definitely not be tolerated in the future. Ade preferred it that way because it enabled him to keep his professional head on, but the Ade beneath remembered longing for kids and killing the thought as soon as it formed. He felt he'd made this happen by *wishing*. He began wondering what was happening in his own body. *C'naatat* suddenly seemed like an alien.

"Why didn't you tell me? Or Aras?"

"Puts the burden on you. My problem."

"Don't you trust us? Don't you know me by now?" *Me*. No, he meant *me*. He wasn't Aras. Aras could deal with his own hurt. "You shut me out. You make me feel like I ran out on you without knowing it. I'd never do that, not again."

She didn't trust him. She didn't think he was up to the decision. He wanted a kid and he'd almost had one and now he didn't have one anymore. It was worse than accepting he never would. He hurt; Shan had hurt him. He knew it was impossible. He made a physical effort to think rationally.

"Okay, if things had been different, I'd have wanted nothing more," he said. "And while it was a kid it would have been wonderful, and then it would grow up and need someone to love but not have anyone, ever. I *know* that. I understand that."

"But that doesn't stop it hurting you."

"Or you."

"I didn't want a kid."

Aras had been quiet and still, his agitation scent no worse than if they'd had a minor tussle over dishes.

"Wess'har can't have unplanned conceptions," he said. "It's not how our bodies work. The idea of having a child you don't want is alien to me."

"God, I knew you'd never forgive me for this."

"Forgiveness isn't relevant. I gave you no choice about being *c'naatat*. This is a consequence of my decision."

"For Chrissakes, let's not start on some sodding interminable academic debate about guilt and causality, shall we?" Shan was suddenly very white-faced, pupils dilated. "I took a knife to myself. I used a grenade. I took a life that hadn't asked for it. I robbed you two of a child. And it's going to hang over this marriage like the stink of shit for a long time. I get it wrong and other people pay the price."

Ade couldn't bear it. "No. It was a bloody awful choice between something quick and painful and something *permanently* painful. I'd have done the same if I'd had the guts."

No, Ade knew he wouldn't. But he still knew why *she* did it, and he thought she was mindlessly brave to go through the pain, and he wanted to scream at her for shutting him out and not letting him do what a husband should. He couldn't pin down one fixed emotion now.

"Wasn't guts," she said. "It was shame. And fear. And now I have to tell Nevyan."

But it hurt. He hung on to the fact that he still had Shan. He had her back, back from death, and he was never going to let grief over a child that could never have been get in the way of that. He was determined not to give in to the screaming voice that said something had been taken away from him, and that he should rage at her.

The rest of the day was like a wake, with the topic never mentioned but the loss almost coloring the air around them. Shan tinkered with the grenade harpoon that the wess'har had rigged for her to use to hunt down Rayat and Lindsay: Ade managed to detach totally into his weapons instructor state of mind for an hour or two. It helped. Aras joined in. Somehow all their voices had changed, and they were getting to know strangers again.

Even the tea tasted unfamiliar.

Shan practiced reloading the chamber late into the night.

"I promise," she said, "that one day we're going to have a life so normal and boring and devoid of crisis that we'll have to take up knitting to stay sane."

She had an early night and slept in the cupboard of a room that was once his. Aras made flatbreads in distracted silence.

"I thought I knew her," said Ade. "I mean, we share memories, right? You can't know someone any better than having their memory. I thought she'd tell me everything."

Aras slapped the bread on the hot range. The disks of dough puffed into cushions. "I know her mind too, and she's done things without telling me. She donated her DNA to make a bioweapon, one that might even be used on Earth now, and yet she's strongly opposed to such unnatural science. She's an uncomplicated woman negotiating a complex world in which she finds fewer certainties every day."

"But she knows *us*. She should know we would have been there for her."

"She knows herself, and she knows that would have made

her decision harder. She also thinks we need protecting from unpleasantness. While motive is irrelevant in outcomes, it's certainly relevant in understanding someone."

"I don't want to be angry with her."

"Then don't be."

"What about you?"

"I grieve. And I would have done as she did. I'll find it hard to look at her sometimes because of what might have been, because she was ready to let me go if *c'naatat* could be removed from me, just so I might father a child."

"It's hard not to think of it as my kid."

"*Our* kid."

Ade had some way to go before he felt like a wess'har instead of just not being surprised by their attitudes and practices. But he would work at it. He tried to get to sleep that night wondering if he would have had a son or a daughter, and imagining the child growing up and facing a life in isolation; hunted or shunned, celibate, outliving everyone, and where the only people who were like them had a lover, and they never could.

Vijissi had reached the same conclusion. *My kid—our kid would have faced the same. Remember that if you start to resent Shan for this.*

She'd said it was time he saw her for what she was: not a goddess at all.

Maybe the kid could have had *c'naatat* removed. But nobody knew if Shapakti could really do it outside a flask in his lab.

Okay.

It didn't occur to him until he was close to nodding off that he had no idea whether the child would even have looked human.

20

Australia has confirmed it will go ahead with its pledge to provide facilities for a visiting alien fleet due in 2407. The FEU Foreign Minister said troops stationed along the Sino-states border would remain there until the unilateral hosting offer was referred to the UN for what he called "an inclusive global debate." The Sinostates says its mutual aid agreement with the FEU will remain suspended until troops are withdrawn.

Meanwhile, environmental groups meeting in Calgary have called for an indefinite moratorium on all leisure air travel in a bid to reduce further degradation of the atmosphere. The FEU and the Americas described the ban as "unworkable" and claimed it would threaten nearly a hundred million jobs in service industries worldwide. Canada has already banned nonessential flights from its airspace.

The Business Agenda news in brief, BBCHan 4622

Ouzhari, Bezer'ej

The Eqbas could have been any human biohaz team as they worked on the beach, features shrouded in loose pale gray suits.

Rayat burst gasping from the water and lay struggling for air as they laid aside their tools and clustered around him. They must have known who and what he was. They made no attempt to touch him, let alone help.

He counted up to thirty to keep himself from panicking. *It'll pass soon.* The pain in his chest wasn't as bad as he remembered; his body was learning. He coughed up mucus and water and lay flat on his back as they watched, heads tilting and bobbing as his gills closed and his lungs filled with air again.

Rayat rolled onto his side. The sand was fine and mostly white, and it was only when he realized that what he thought was black grass was the charred remains of organic material that what he'd done hit home.

I killed the island. But I still didn't kill off c'naatat.

He eased himself into a sitting position. The clean-up team seemed to be taking great interest in the bioluminescence in his hands.

"Any of you speak English?" he asked, not expecting a response. He wasn't sure if they could even hear him through the layers of protective fabric. *Keep it simple.* "I request asylum. I have something to show you."

Of course: they didn't understand a request for asylum. They had a much less complicated take on law and civil rights. And he was a criminal as far as they were concerned, one who wouldn't get a call to his lawyer.

"You can only be Doctor Rayat." The voice had that double tone like the wess'har. "I believe I saw you a few months ago."

Rayat hadn't expected that; but he was running out of things that could shock or amaze him now. "I am. So you know I carry *c'naatat.*"

"I may be able to help you," said the voice. The Eqbas flicked the filter back from his visor, revealing a rectangle of dull mid-brown skin and copper eyes. "I have done research. I am Da Shapakti."

"Sorry?"

Shapakti looked him up and down. "I am a scientist."

"I had no idea it was reversible."

"In humans, perhaps. Not so easy for wess'har."

Rayat suddenly had to rethink his universe. His whole mission had been about acquiring the parasite and denying it to other governments.

A superweapon with an antidote.

That changes everything.

His mind went through a leapfrog sequence: unique asset—unable to acquire—deny asset to others—acquire asset—seek to find route to deliver asset to command—identify countermeasure to asset.

So what did he struggle to get back to the FEU government, *c'naatat* or the means to neutralize it? Or both? His task had now doubled in complexity. It wasn't as if it had been an easy one to begin with.

Shapakti encased him in a plastic bag that really *did* make him feel like he was being digested by a *sheven*. It was a decontamination device: he'd walked on the surface of Ouzhari unprotected, and although the radiation couldn't kill him and the cobalt levels were already falling at extraordinary rates, he was a risk to others if they didn't clean him up.

The plastic bag clung to the side of the Eqbas ship, a dull blue torpedo-shaped vessel with red and blue chevrons pulsing along its sides and the occasional wash of something like a violet coronal discharge that swept the hull at regular intervals. Then he found himself sucked through the hull itself and he was standing on a deck in a confusing maze of flimsy half-visible bulkheads and lights, surrounded by a smell of chemicals and something not unlike yeast extract.

Rayat was completely disoriented. He tried to focus by reaching inside his shirt and taking out the azin shell maps that showed the bezeri's war crimes.

"You need to see this," said Rayat. "I have proof that the bezeri carried out the extermination of another intelligent species on this planet."

Shapakti—minus his hazmat suit now—took the maps and gazed at them as if they were works of art, which they were.

"We're returning to the Temporary City," he said. "Aras will be very interested to see these, having been closest to the bezeri."

"He's there now, is he?"

"He arrived yesterday with Ade and Shan Frankland."

Shapakti held the maps under a brighter light and looked lost in admiration. He might just have been trying to read the symbols, of course.

Rayat was suddenly uneasy. "Why are they here?"

"Shan said she was going to hunt you down and kill you," said Shapakti. "And now we have only to find Lindsay Neville for her. We have you already."

Temporary City, Bezer'ej

Shan was back to normal. Her face was pure hard-set murder and Ade made sure he kept the grenade launcher well out of her reach.

"If you were looking for a lift back to Earth, arsehole, you're out of luck," she said.

Rayat looked like a man rescued from a raft after weeks at sea, minus the cracked skin and exposure burns. He was ragged and exhausted: and he looked faintly translucent. Ade was reminded briefly of horror movies where characters dematerialized. Someone seemed to have interrupted Rayat halfway through the process.

"I'm just completing my mission," he said. "Like you completed yours. Although now I'm not entirely sure how to interpret it in the light of new data, and I'm not sure if I can safely ask for guidance on that from the Grid now."

They were waiting on Aras. It was a regular little *c'naatat* tea party: only Lindsay was missing. Aras was poring over the azin shell maps and his scent was getting stronger and more acidic by the minute.

"You okay, mate?"

Aras raised his head. "How did I never see these? Why did I not know these existed?"

"Are they genuine, then?" asked Shan.

"Yes." Aras sagged visibly. The poor sod had dedicated five centuries to protecting Bezer'ej and now he'd been told—by a spook—that the species he nursed back from the brink of their last extinction had a murky past on a par with any nation on Earth. "Why did I not know about this?"

"Same reason I don't know what's in the Bodleian Library," said Shan. "Never had reason to look, and I wouldn't know *where* to look without a good reason anyway."

Wess'har had a very clean, clear view of the universe. Humans might have shrugged off a genocidal past as just part of growing up as a nation, but wess'har never would. That made them more alien than their two voices and two dicks and weirdly pretty seahorse heads.

"They're no better than the isenj in their way," said Rayat. "And the isenj didn't set out to slaughter anyone, not that wess'har care about motive. The bezeri did, and they still seem to think it was okay." He gave Shan a little half-smile. "Not that I'm imposing my cultural morality on them, of course."

"We live in a galaxy of right bastards, then, don't we?" Shan said. "I'll never be out of work."

Rayat really looked as if he understood her for a second. "Nor me."

Ade watched the exchange between them and didn't like the brief comradeship. It vanished again as fast as it had sprung up. Shan didn't look quite as incensed as she had before, though. But she was smart enough to outmaneuver Rayat if he was playing one of his games again.

"Okay, what happens now?" he asked.

"I was going to execute you," Shan said calmly. "But now I'm going to let Shapakti play with you and see if he can extract *c'naatat* from your cells and leave you standing. You're the first human specimen I've been prepared to try that on."

"Ah, the anti-vivisectionist, aren't you?"

"I like to think of this as therapeutic intervention with a risk factor for the patient." Shan didn't blink but Ade could read her at a much more subtle level. "I'm getting better at negotiating the gray areas of life and death now."

"Well, let's get cracking, shall we?"

The bastard never showed fear, Ade had to give him that. He wondered if the spook ever crapped himself or threw up like he did. He doubted it.

"First, let's find Little Miss Perfect," said Shan. "I know your game and it's actually not that much different to mine. But she's a fucking wild card."

"We all throw in our lot with some tribe or other—even you, Superintendent. She just picked a group of Nazi squid because she felt guilty. A sort of Stockholm syndrome."

"Just take me to her." Shan stuck her head out the door and warbled in eqbas'u, then stepped back into the room and fastened her jacket. "You don't have a tribe. Except maybe spooks. Or do you?"

Rayat opened his mouth as if to say something and stopped dead, looking as if he'd heard someone say something, someone who wasn't there. Ade had never seen him do that before. He had no idea what went on in his head just then, but if he was acting, he was the best.

Spooks were, of course.

"What happens if I survive the extraction?" asked Rayat, all cool detachment again.

"I haven't made my mind up," said Shan, checking her 9mm like she'd missed slotting bad bastards, as she called them. "I'm such a girlie."

Ade let her have the grenade launcher back once they were settled in the Eqbas submersible and diving for the seabed. Ade wondered why Rayat wasn't more set on stealing Eqbas ship technology, because it was a lot more use than *c'naatat:* the bloody stuff they used could shape itself into spacecraft, rafts and submarines.

He leaned back, closed his eyes, and concentrated.

"*Nee-loor-ee-khoor.*" Yes, he could do it, both tones, two voices. "*Nee-loor-ee-khoor.*"

Shan grinned at him, lips parted in surprise. It was the first time he'd seen her look happy in a while.

"Clever boy," she said, almost in a whisper. "*Very* clever boy."

Bezeri settlement, south of Ouzhari

The submersible made a few passes over the bezeri village but there was nobody visible. Rayat knew there were usually twenty or more elderly bezeri who stayed there while the younger ones went out to gather food. Maybe something had driven them inside. Whatever it was, it certainly hadn't been a large predator.

"You're not going to piss me about over this, are you?" said Shan. She shouldered the launcher. Rayat wasn't sure if he was disturbed or impressed by the fact that whatever weapon she handled, she looked like it suited her. "Just get the bitch out in the open."

"So you shoot her, but I get to be the lab rat as a reward."

"I'm getting soft lately. Yes."

Rayat liked the idea of staying alive. What he didn't like now was not being sure what his mission was—or more to the point, how he should interpret it. Things changed, but you hung on to your objective to stay sane and focused; this kind of work was not for quitters.

His task had been to investigate rumors of "invulnerability," secure *c'naatat,* and prevent its falling into anyone's hands except the FEU government. That included European businesses, even the friendly helpful ones who supplied the government. The *c'naatat* mission was asset denial.

If I take this back home, I need to take the technology to remove it too.

If I succeed with that, then there's a source of the parasite and a means to remove it. And that makes it a viable tactical weapon, not a strategic one; it makes it more commercially viable for other uses, too.

Everyone would have wanted a dose, until the consequences hit home.

But everyone would definitely want it if it could be controlled.

Rayat had kicked the idea around in the last few hours and his logic had told him what his gut first thought: that this made *c'naatat* a bigger threat for Earth, not a lesser one. He was clear what his mission was now, and he took duty seriously. His duty was to keep the thing *here.*

Asset denial.

It had taken some time coming, but now Shan, Lindsay, Aras, Ade and himself all had a single objective—to stop *c'naatat* being exploited anywhere else.

If he could do that as a regular human, he wasn't sure. But at least he was now clear that the last thing he should do was to go home carrying the parasite.

The hatch opened and he swam out of the flooded airlock.

"Saib!" he called. "Lindsay! I'm back."

He swam from chamber to chamber, finding nobody, coming back to where the submersible was waiting on station so they could see that he hadn't made a run for it.

But the settlement was deserted. The records were gone. The only evidence that the last bezeri had ever been there was a pile of carefully broken shells that had once housed the things that Lindsay called killer whelks.

The hatch opened to readmit him and drained down, leaving him feeling suddenly heavy and hot.

"They've cleared out," he said. "And that's not like them. They're not exactly nomadic. And Lindsay's gone too."

"Maybe she'll be back later," said Shan. "Perhaps we should lay up and wait."

"No, she's done a runner with them." He had an idea what she might do, but he had no idea where she might have gone to do it. "I know. I know, because she's taken the bits of stained glass that she removed from her son's gravestone."

Rayat decided he hated standing around in wet clothing. If they wanted to turn him back into a normal man, he didn't mind at all now.

Temporary City, Bezer'ej: Eqbas commander's day cabin

Esganikan was waiting for Shan when she got back.

"The *bitch* has disappeared," said Shan. There was no eqbas'u for "bitch." "We're going to have to comb the entire planet for her now."

"It isn't urgent." Esganikan seemed more preoccupied with the Earth mission. Her day cabin was spread with images and *virin've* projecting numbers onto the walls. "I need to carry out more intensive liaison with the Australians now. Are you prepared to help?"

Shan couldn't get Lindsay out of her mind. That was good, because it didn't leave room for remorse about aborting the child. It just gave her an extra insight into how a woman like Lindsay—a woman who'd lost a kid—might think. It made her a better copper. She could always make good use of personal pain.

"I love to be helpful," she said. "And fabulously talented as I think I am, I'm not a diplomat, and I'm not a soldier. So, no. Sorry. Maybe you need Mohan Rayat, if he survives Shapakti's procedure."

Esganikan cocked her head. She didn't seem to take the slightest notice of the word *no.* "This is what I've learned over the years, Shan. Restoring balance with the cooperation of the existing dominant species is better than having to eradicate them totally."

"I'd never have thought of that," said Shan. "Silly me."

Esganikan ignored the jibe. She probably didn't understand. It didn't quite translate in eqbas'u. "Earth is a delicate operation because the ecology is still complex."

"Fry all the humans and you take out other species with them."

"Yes."

"You committed your forces to this mission. You should have thought through what resources that was going to take."

"I know my own trade, as you might say. I *know* what this takes."

"Okay, sorry. Out of order."

"There are many sympathetic humans in all nations. The ones you call Greens."

"Oh yeah."

"You can help me mobilize them."

For a moment Shan thought that Esganikan just wanted a

list of contacts and a few suggestions. *Yeah, here's the address for Troops of Gaia. I'm a bit out of touch, but they're okay. And give Earthwatch a call while you're at it.*

But the word was *mobilize.*

"How, exactly?"

Esganikan was either proof that Eqbas had fundamental behavioral differences with wess'har or else she had learned a few sharp monkey-boy moves. She wafted a little agitation. Her head dropped slightly. It was a placatory gesture, a junior matriarch to an alpha, and for a moment Shan checked herself with a discreet sniff to make sure she hadn't emitted *jask* and taken the lead role.

"They regard you as an icon," said Esganikan. "You can unite them."

"Nobody told me about being any fucking icon." Shan didn't like that one bit. It was the temptation and weakness she had always avoided. Once she gave in to wanting to be seen as the hero, she could no longer trust her own motives. And motives still mattered to her—her own did, anyway. "I've been gone for nigh on a century, not that many knew what I got up to even back then. Who gives a toss about me now?"

"Eddie Michallat's reports on your sacrifice and endeavors proved inspirational."

"Remind me to punch the bastard sometime." She liked Eddie. But sometimes he was a complication she didn't need. "I don't want a PR man. Anyway, I'm dead. He never told them I survived."

"It isn't Eddie who has told the current generation of Greens about your actions."

Esganikan made the bulkhead of her cabin dissolve into transparency and stared into the blue and amber haze of short grasses that covered much of Constantine island. It was just as Shan had seen it more than three years before when she was an amazed visitor who had been plucked from her daily existence at a moment's notice and sent twenty-five light-years from home. But there was no biobarrier now, and the Bezer'ej wilderness has reclaimed the territory the humans had carved out. Except for the deep caverns still in the ground, there was little sign that the *gethes* had ever been there.

"I hate mythology," said Shan. "And I don't trust history."

Esganikan seemed hesitant, as if she knew whatever she said next would irritate Shan. Maybe she was scared of pushing her into unleashing *jask* too, not because she wanted to keep her status but because she knew Shan couldn't do her job. Shan knew that too. Perhaps that was the cause of the deferential gestures.

"Somebody you know has asked to speak to you," Esganikan said slowly. She held out the *virin* and squeezed it to activate the controls. "She left this message and would like you to contact her."

"I'm dead. Nobody knows I'm alive." *Oh shit. Eddie, I'm going to kill you, you mouthy little bastard. You promised.* "So nobody's leaving any messages. What's this really about?"

"*I* told someone you were alive," Esganikan said. "I didn't explain how. I just said technology made it possible. Lying is quite hard, I find. I told someone in the Australian liaison team, an *environmentalist.* Isn't it interesting that you have a separate word to describe someone who cares about balance? That means anyone who isn't an *environmentalist* is probably a despoiler, yes?"

The implications of that logic were filed instantly while Shan wrestled with a more urgent and a more personal problem. *And who the hell knows me now, anyway?* Shan ran through her short and superficial list of names at the UN, the FEU and the Australian government that might want to talk to her. She knew of them, but she'd never spoken to them. Dead women didn't.

"Okay," she said. *Shit, when will I ever learn?* "Give it here."

Esganikan's *virin* was slightly warm, like a living thing. Shan clasped it as Nevyan had taught her, lining up human fingers that weren't designed to operate a *virin* like a wess'har's could. As she looked down at it, its transparency became an image, a face she didn't recognize at all, a woman with gray hair and a gaunt face. The message spooled.

"Shan Frankland. Good Lord, Shan, it's been a long time, hasn't it? I never expected to see you again. I can't tell you how pleased we all are that you recovered the gene bank. You're an inspiration to the movement. This is quite extraordinary."

The voice. Shan knew the voice. She *knew* it, and she wasn't sure how. She shut her eyes to concentrate.

"It's time you came home, Shan. You've earned it. Whatever Eugenie's motives, you never lost sight of what you had to do. You saved an ecosystem. You're saving the planet."

Eugenie Perault.

Oh shit.

Shan knew the voice now. Her scalp tightened and her mouth filled with saliva as Bezer'ej and its vivid grassland and the day cabin simply disappeared from her vision like a superfast zoom and she was left listening to the pounding pulse in her own head.

It was Helen Marchant. And she should have been long dead by now.

But so should I.

She looked about sixty; Helen Marchant, eco-terrorist and sister of Foreign Minister Eugenie Perault, the politician who shanghaied Shan out here.

Helen bloody Marchant. Helen, who she'd kept out of the line of fire when Op Green rage went pear-shaped; Helen, the only person who had ever really manipulated her, the woman who recruited her to the Green cause.

Even if Eugenie Perault hadn't marooned Shan to keep the scandalous family link quiet, Helen was still the individual who had set her life on an unimaginable course, and Shan wasn't sure how she felt about that.

Right now, she was too shocked to work that out.

"You fucking bitch," Shan said aloud, even though Helen Marchant couldn't hear her. "Don't you play the messiah card with *me*."

21

*Shan Frankland went apeshit about Esganikan revealing
that she'd survived. I got the feeling at the time that there
was a lot more than just having her cover blown that pissed
her off, though. There was the shock that Helen Marchant
had been cryo'ed down with a terminal condition and then
revived when they had a treatment. That would, I suppose,
freak even a tough bitch like Shan. But if I'd known at the
time what she'd had to do to herself, I'd have been a lot
gentler with her. The trouble with keeping up the appearance of being a psychopathic ice maiden is that nobody al-
lows for the fact that one day you might want to sit down
and grieve for a child.*

EDDIE MICHALLAT,
private Constantine journals

F'nar, Wess'ej

Aras decided the crops could do without him for one day
and Ade had foregone his morning run. Neither of them
wanted to let Shan out of their sight. She disappeared into
the washroom with her swiss and shut the door.

"Oh shit," said Ade. "I hate it when she does that."

She could come to no harm. But they waited anyway, listening for worrying noises, trying to concentrate on breakfast. She emerged fastening her pants.

"What?" She looked at both of them and shoved the
swiss in her pocket. "Can't I have a pee now? Look, I check
my abdomen daily now with the ultrasound probe in case
parts of me start growing back again."

"Boss, it's no big deal."

"Bloody well is for me." She sat down and began shovel-
ing food mechanically. "I'm checking everything in future."

"Let me have a chat with Shapakti. He'll think of something."

Aras felt invisible again but it was inevitable that Shan would still be focused on Ade for a while. It was a new bond, a fascinating novelty for them. And then it had been snatched from them in the most painful way.

"I'm fine," she said abruptly, not looking up from the plate in front of her. "I'm just pissed off. I'm not suicidal. I'm not scarred for life. I'm going to be fine. So stop hovering."

Ade exchanged glances with Aras and rubbed Shan's spine idly with one hand while she ate. There was no point asking her what was troubling her because she had, as she put it so elegantly, a fucking big list to pick from.

But Aras knew what was uppermost in her mind, or at least the new complication that was jostling for attention: the woman from her past called Helen Marchant.

"Your sense of duty will always drive you," said Aras.

"No, I won't be set up by Marchant's little dynasty again." Ah, he was right, then. Shan pinched the tip of her nose, a gesture he had only seen her use when she was under extreme stress. For some reason that tiny gesture was more conspicuous than any of her cursing. "Been there, done that, bought the one-way ticket."

"I've never known you be reluctant to make a hard decision. But I'm afraid this will wear down your resolve."

"Bollocks. I am *not* the El-fucking-Cid of the Green movement. No bastard's going to strap my corpse to my horse and send me out front."

Aras didn't understand that. But Ade managed a humorless laugh.

"I mean it," she said. "All bets are off. I've had a gutful."

She sounded as if she was talking herself out of something. Nobody could make Shan do anything she didn't want to, but the slightest hint that she might be slacking always provoked an odd blend of anger and self-doubt that catapulted her in extreme action. It bewildered him that a woman of such immense discipline and reckless courage could be manipulated by *pressing one button,* as Eddie called it. Esganikan knew where that button was, and so did Marchant. Aras felt immediate and defensive hatred, a truly primeval urge to protect her. She was his *isan,* but she still sometimes triggered the reactions in him that a child would, and he reacted paternally.

"I think you should leave Esganikan to deal with her own mission," said Aras. "Her influence on you has not been positive."

"That's what Nevyan says."

"It's true," said Ade.

Shan stopped chewing. For a moment Aras braced for a lecture on how she could choose her own associates, but instead she looked suddenly crushed.

"How can I walk away now? I've seen what's happened to Umeh and I'm scared for Earth. But I shouldn't be. The Eqbas are supposed to be what I think Earth needs."

"And you think Esganikan's going to listen to you? Boss, you think *you're* extreme, but the Eqbas are off the scale. Listen to Nevyan." Since the abortion, Ade had trodden a fine line between thinly disguised hurt and a desperate need to make things right with Shan. The sudden halt to their sexual relationship only made matters worse, and it seemed to be Shan who was most upset by it. "You're a different person with the wess'har. You felt *safe* with them. Jesus, I do too. For fuck's sake walk away from them and concentrate on *us.*"

It was what Aras wanted to say but felt was too selfish and narrow in the light of events. But they'd started seeing things on too broad a canvas.

Shan had not yet simply learned to *be.* She had to *do.* She now had the chance of settling old scores, though, and turning the tables on those who thought they had exiled her on a spurious mission. She could also pay the debt she owed a long-dead gorilla whose sign language she had failed to understand, and whose plea for help she had not heard. It was a seductive package of lures that would keep her focused until they were expended, and then she would be hunting for purpose again.

"You have more than four years to think about it," said

Aras. "And things will become clearer. You don't need to do anything now."

"Don't, mate." Ade's voice had an edge and he emitted a little aggressive musk to make his point. "If she doesn't tell Esganikan to shove her mission, then I will."

It was the kind of presumption that usually drew a reaction from Shan, but she looked at Ade with sad longing.

"I'm going to do that," she said. "Before I do anything else I regret."

It was hard to tell which event she meant. As she'd said, it was a very long list.

"Come on, eat up." She swung her legs over the bench and stood up. "Lots to do today. Time to get the hemp planted and then we can have plenty of oil for frying and making soap."

She still had her pistol tucked into the back of her belt while she attacked the soil with a spade.

Superintendent Frankland had not yet retired. Esganikan could probably see that as clearly as Aras and Ade did.

Bezer'ej

Bezeri were fanatically attached to place. Lindsay should have realized it.

It should have screamed at her; they had a whole planet to spawn in but they stuck doggedly to the shallows around the Ouzhari coast. And it meant they were sitting targets for the cobalt fallout.

Their history was recorded on azin shell maps and their maps were recorded in azin shell records. They were one in the same; their maps *were* their history, indivisible in every sense. And *transparent*.

And they had a planet full of hunting grounds to choose. But they embarked on a genocidal war with another species because territory was sacrosanct. For creatures that could squeeze through any gap like an octopus, they were extraordinarily inflexible.

But this small band of bezeri—the last of their kind—hadn't committed any of the crimes of their ancestors, if those were crimes at all. Lindsay was finding moral judgment hard these days. There were just forty-four left, and most were old and frail, and their population could never recover. They would be gone forever soon.

And *that* was her fault. *That* was a judgment she *could* make.

She hadn't been sure what she could do for them that would even begin to atone for genocide, whether accidental or rigorously planned. Now she wondered why it had taken her so long to see the obvious.

The sea darkened as she swam closer to land with Saib and Keet behind her in a convoy of bioluminescence, and she didn't have to look back to know that Keet was grumbling violet and gold about the unfamiliarity of it all. It was a new territory, and his ancient bezeri fixations said that he didn't like change one bit, especially change of place.

But change was necessary. She'd persuaded Saib. They had to make a truly massive change—of place, of culture, of everything—if they were to have a chance of surviving as a species.

Beaching herself was easy now. The first time she had surfaced after developing gills had been agony. It got easier after that; *c'naatat* learned fast and now when she moved from air to water and back again, it was no more to her than adjusting to bright light after a darkened room.

Lindsay was amphibious.

She touched bottom with her foot to wade up the gently sloping shore and stand on a new landmass a long way from the chain of islands that had dominated bezeri history for millennia. The land animal in her admired the rounded hills, backlit in the distance by the recent sunset. She turned around to the sea and called to Saib and Keet in lights.

Come on. You've come this far.

This is madness, said Keet.

Leenz has proven it can be done. Saib still thought he was the boss fella, the old fascist. *We must trust her.*

She nearly wiped us out once and now she tries to complete the task.

Lindsay had never thought it would be easy to change their minds as easily as she could change their bodies.

Do it. Please, just do it.

The two bezeri floated motionless in the shallows for a few minutes. Then the dome of Saib's mantle broke the surface of the water just as the first bezeri had beached themselves to get a better look at the Dry Above. They were stepping into space, just as Shan did, but for the opposite reason. They were taking the biggest risk of all to *survive.*

Come on. It's scary, I know. Lindsay beckoned yellow. *Come on. Trust me.*

Saib lashed three tentacles forward like an angler casting a line and dug the tips into the beach. He hauled himself clear of the water and began crying in green-lit pain and panic.

Bezeri could survive out of water for a brief period. But Saib and Keet had all the time in the world now.

All they had to do was accept change. *C'naatat* could do the rest. It went with the new territory.

"Leeenzzz . . ." Saib said, breathing air for the first time.

Clever boy, said Lindsay, fluent in light. *Clever boy.*